Legendary:
The Genesis

By: Kourtney Cooper

I would first like to thank God for allowing all of this to happen. I would also love to thank Mattie Boone who was so excited in getting my work published. A huge thank you to Bridgette Holt whose consistent enthusiasm for more kept me writing. And to Lester Martinez Jr. whose friendship helped inspire this epic tale.

Now faith is the substance of things hoped
for, the evidence of things not seen.

Hebrews 11:1

Order this book online at www.trafford.com
or email orders@trafford.com

Most Trafford titles are also available at major online book retailers.

Printed in Victoria, BC, Canada.

ISBN: 978-1-4269-2190-2

*Our mission is to efficiently provide the world's finest, most comprehensive book publishing
service, enabling every author to experience success. To find out how to publish your book, your
way, and have it available worldwide, visit us online at www.trafford.com*

Trafford rev. 12/14/2009

 www.trafford.com

North America & international
toll-free: 1 888 232 4444 (USA & Canada)
phone: 250 383 6864 ♦ fax: 812 355 4082

Acknowledgements:

I would first like to thank God for allowing all of this to happen. I would also love to thank Mattie Boone who was so excited in getting my work published. A huge thank you to Bridgette Holt whose consistent enthusiasm for more kept me writing. And to Lester Martinez Jr. whose friendship helped inspire this epic tale.

Now faith is the substance of things hoped
for, the evidence of things not seen.

Hebrews 11:1

Contents

Chapter 1: Substitute

I ALLOW MYSELF TO DRIFT INTO THE SILENT SEAS OF thoughts, rushed by intense and raging waves of emotion. I try and grasp a hold of reality yet it seems there is no way to escape such thoughts — such emotions. I have tried and tried to run from the past that hunts my present life. It's not so much as the past that hunts me just the unanswered question that seem to affect the everyday life in which I try and live. Who am I, really? Who are my real parents, where are they now, and why did they do this to me? Didn't they love me? Didn't they want me?

Dawn was going to be peeking its way through my window at any moment. I stare at the night stand beside my bed. The alarm clock sitting on the metal spiraling furniture holding up a circular glass piece reads five forty-five. I realize that if I want to make it to my eight o'clock class on time I have to get up now.

I strain to pull myself up to an upright position and examine the room in front of me. The room is so familiar but it's also a stranger to me. In the far left corner of my room was my computer desk. Along with my computer sat my unfinished Sociology homework, empty Red Bull cans and a half eaten cold slice of pizza that I couldn't bring myself to finishing the night before. On the opposite side of the room was my closet that was half open, displaying my poorly organized collection of tennis shoes and dirty laundry that was almost a week old. And straight ahead of me was the entrance to my room. My room reminded me much of myself. Full of nothing. Nothing that brings it to life or makes it bewildering to a stranger who enters it. And everything in it is unorganized, waiting for someone to come along and bring some life and neatness to it.

I can now feel the icy waves of depression beginning to engulf me. My eyes are quickly filling up with tears and I can't seem to fight the knot that is forming in my throat. But even being as close as I am now, I have never cried. And today will be no different. How I envy the people who can give in to their emotions, allow the waves to pull them deep beneath the surfaces of the water and drown them quietly. But my waves only seem to thrash me on the surface, never pulling me down even though they were strong enough.

I didn't deserve the life I had. My best friend, Brycin, was more than just a best friend. He was more like my older brother. And Rachel, my foster mom, cared for me as if I were her own. Yet, it felt like it wasn't enough.

Rachel taking me into her home out here in Corvallis, Oregon was the best thing that could have ever happened to me. If it wasn't for Rachel, who knows where I would be now. Upon her return from her parent's house in Eureka, California with her late husband, Michael, she found me wandering a dirt road in the midst of a storm wearing nothing but a pair of ripped jeans and a bloody t- shirt.

All I remember of that day is walking endlessly into a vast of nothingness. I hadn't seen any cars on the road pass me by. Then, a voice of an angel called for me, unfamiliar to me. I turned to the angelic voice. She was just as beautiful as her voice. She was precious. She was kind and gentle. I could tell by the pain resting in her eyes that she genuinely cared for me. I could see a mother burning bright in them.

That rainy afternoon, she rushed me to the Providence Medford Medical Center in Medford, Oregon. I can still remember the rain drops shooting themselves against the windshield like bullets and how profane Rachel would get whenever someone would cut her off or drive slowly. She kept looking back at me as we drove telling me that everything would be okay and that I was going to be just fine. But I never acknowledged her. I just laid on her back seat, motionless, staring blankly out the windshield thinking of absolutely nothing.

The doctors immediately began examining me, fearing that I had lost a lot of blood evidently due to my shirt. But they found nothing wrong with me. All of my vital signs were normal, my breathing was normal, temperature was average, in fact, the blood on my shirt wasn't even mine. I was healthier than normal. Not even so much as a cold had escaped into my body.

Rachel was ecstatic. She wanted to take me home as soon as the doctors stated that I was fine. But Michael was afraid that someone was going to come looking for me. Rachel, as much as she wanted to, couldn't disagree with him. So, they placed me in a foster home in Corvallis near their home and Rachel visited me almost every day for six months.

One day, she had come to see me and I threw myself into her arms. She greeted me with the same enthusiasm.

"He only is like that when you are around." the head mistress pointed out.

Rachel released me and shoved me off to play. I obeyed but was well aware of them speaking. "What do you mean?"

"That enthusiastic. That sociable. He is never like that when he is here amongst the other kids or myself for that matter."

"Well then maybe it's time I take him home with me now. I mean it's been six months already, no one has claimed him and no one has declared that they have a child missing."

"But your husband? Kayden shows much restraint when it comes to him."

"That won't be a problem. I am sure spending time with him will change all that." The head mistress pursed her lips, smiled halfheartedly and then shrugged her shoulders.

That was the day she brought me home.

I was too afraid at the time to appreciate the majesty of the house. Almond brown, eggshell white and gray triangular tiles decorated the floor as soon as you walked in, circling until all the colors met up at one point in the center. The white tiles trailed off toward the right and into the dining area and kitchen. To the left, the stairs began along with the caramel toned carpet. But what made this area of the house all the more breathtaking was the crystal chandelier that hung above the point at which the colors met on the floor, sparkling and glittering the walls with rays of rainbows that transmitted through all of the fragments of glass.

She guided me into the living room where Michael stood staring at an empty wall. Again, I was too fearful because of what Michael would think when he saw me that I didn't soak in the beauty of the room. The white, suede sofa and its matching recliner livened up the room along with the white, silky curtains. The colossal entertainment center sat furthest from the entryway to the family room. It was overstocked with soft rock from the 60's and 70's and classic contemporary. In the center sat a 34" television which made the entertainment center look that much more crowded.

She called to him and he began to turn toward me. He'd only turned a quarter of the way, his lower jaw mostly visible, when I began imagining his face when turned and saw me standing beside the love of his life. I was positive it was going to be threatening, full of hate and disgust. He didn't seem enthusiastic at all about me previously so why would he be now?

His side profile didn't give me much to go on. It was hard to distinguish between what he was feeling from it.

Three quarters of his face was visible and then…

His eyes didn't search at all. They were locked on mine as soon as he'd turned around. But what shocked me more than the thought of his anger was the reality of his kindness. His face was soft, pure, porcelain-like. As if he were molded delicately by the hands of a god. His lips pulled over his teeth into a wide smile. He walked to me and knelt down and suffocated me in a hug. I searched for air and a reason for his kindness. Was it genuine or was he trying to impress Rachel? When he released me I looked back at Rachel but she just smiled.

She walked over to Michael and kissed him on his cheek. He returned the favor, kissing her lightly on her lips, almost as if he was afraid that the strength in his lips and the passion behind them could easily fracture her. That day I studied them carefully, more than I ever had. It was amazing they were only human. They could easily be mistaken for as models—or better than that—angels.

Her long, velvety, brunette hair swayed elegantly down her back. Her copper brown eyes glistened with health and happiness. She dressed very classy. Business suits, pearl necklaces and earrings and high heels.

The magnificent warmth and comfort one would receive whenever she smiled was epic.

Michael was just as beautiful. His eyes sparkled a deep blue. Always cleanly shaved and well built. Best way to describe him would be godlike. In both beauty and body. His rusty brown hair could have survived on its own without any product but the smell radiating from his hair gave that away. They were too perfect. How could they not have everything? They deserved a child of their own. Not some freebie they found on the side of a road. But I couldn't deny the happiness I placed in their eyes. It was a glow, a completion. I completed them that day.

Growing up was a bit overwhelming. I never wanted anything yet they ambushed me with gifts and love. It took me longer to get used to it from Michael but he grew on me and I soon loved him just as much as I did Rachel.

Every year around this time, we would take our annual trip to Crater Lake. I hated it now that we didn't do it.

Ever since the accident with Michael, Rachel couldn't visit the site where her husband fought to protect us and lost his life. I remember that day like it was just yesterday.

It was my thirteenth birthday and Michael wanted to take our trip early. He knew I would love that more than any toy or video game. There were multiple reports of bear sighting but Michael figured we'd gone there every year without a problem; this time wasn't going to be any different. Plus, he really wanted to make me happy on my birthday. He was finally going to teach me to fish.

We traveled into the forest to another area beside the lake as we usually did where the fish overpopulated the riverbed. Rachel and I found our favorite rock. The rock was a deep burnt umber, almost a dark violet shade. She loved its uniqueness in color. We sat and watched as Michael prepped his carbon fiber fishing pole, tying the lure to the hook at the end of the fishing line and casting it into the waters.

Michael was overly joyous by all the fish he had caught in just a matter of minutes. Michael caught fish after fish after fish. It was the best he'd ever fished.

I was then distracted by a low growl. I looked all around me, searching for something dangerous lurking behind a rock or something preparing itself to pounce within the thicket but I saw nothing but emptiness throughout the forest. I turned back around at Michael and laid back against Rachel.

After another few minutes, the growl returned. But this time it sounded closer and it was different from the first growl. It was slightly higher in pitch. Then another one. This one deeper than the first.

I searched for the source of the growls but there was nothing there. The low growls were getting deeper and closer and I couldn't see them. Rachel hadn't heard anything. Whenever I looked up at her on our rock, she just sat there smiling her angelic smile, watching Michael have so much fun.

"Ha! Kayden," he began, grunting as he tugged onto both the fishing line and my attention. Amazing how such a godlike man was capable of showing such childlike qualities. He was excited and his smile gleamed brighter as the sun reflected off his teeth. "You watching?! One day you'll be just as good as me!"

"Ha, no one is better than you, Dad!" I shouted back at him as he still tugged on the rod.

I looked up at Rachel. Her lips pulled over her teeth, displaying her brilliant and luminous smile. She kissed me on the forehead. "Happy Birthday."

I smiled up at her and laid back down against her, her arms wrapped around me, and we continued to watch Michael fish.

It wasn't a surprise that as soon as I blocked out the sounds of something vicious approaching through the edge of the forest, that something would come bursting out of the woods.

The rawness of the flesh had attracted three black bears, their footsteps thundered against the forest floor as they charged toward us. I listened as the growls turned into roars and the oversized beasts rushed in our direction. Michael's head snapped in our direction at the sound of the roars. He pulled out a long blade from his boot that he used to gut fish. Rachel grabbed me forcefully, giving me whiplash as she did and ran toward Michael. I looked back as I ran with Rachel, holding tightly to her hand, processing the intense rage and hunger in all three of their eyes.

Michael ran toward us, then past us, and slid under one of the bears—the one with the higher pitch I concluded—shoving the blade of his knife through the bear's chin. The blade cut through the fat and the flesh of the beast with ease and exited through the crown of its head.

With much force, he pushed and kicked the bear off of him, tugging at the blade stuck in its skull. The bear fell to the side but the blade snapped from its base. He was defenseless.

A second bear tackled him. The bear snapped at him as its enormous weight crushed him. Michael grabbed it by its throat as the bear launched its jaws at his face, making a loud snap as they came together after every failed attempt. The third bear was feeding on the pile of fish Michael had caught effortlessly.

I couldn't imagine what Rachel was feeling. Let alone the terror in her eyes as she sat helplessly and watched. I could feel her tremble as she held me close to her bosom.

I couldn't just sit back and watch. I was on the verge of becoming a man. I had to help. I shrugged Rachel off my shoulders and ran toward the hungry bear that was on top of my father.

"KAYDEN!" Rachel screamed and Michael turned to the cry of her beatific voice. He let go of the bear's throat with one of his hands, gesturing me to stop.

"Stay, Kayd-" Before he could finish, the bear had his throat. Tears pulled up under my eye lids as I saw his blood stain Rachel and my rock.

I was frozen, my face turned white. Rachel cried out in a horrific sob, pleading for help as she watched the bear gnaw away at her husband's throat.

She pulled me to her, holding me closely in her bosom. She wept and cried Michael's name. Both of us watched horridly as a huge part of our life slipped away into a forever sleep.

Luckily, her screams alerted a nearby hunter. He shot the bear with his rifle and the other bear fled into the forest with its raw cuisine.

Rachel strode to the side of her husband. I couldn't move. I was stuck, glued in that spot by fright.

What did I do? I remember thinking. Someone as beautiful, kindhearted, and loving as Michael did not and *should not* have deserved such a gruesome and cold death.

There was something she said that cut me, cut me deep within my chest and gave birth to my assaulting seas. "How will my heart go on without you?"

I couldn't react. My limbs and nerves were paralyzed. Though the bear carried out the deed, I was the true killer here. I'd caused Michael to lose focus, killing him and by killing him, I killed Rachel internally.

Rachel cried for years. The warmth in her smile and the healthiness and happiness in her eyes slowly began to fade away. I wanted to grieve with her. I wanted to cry but...I couldn't. Though I could feel the excruciating pain ripping at me from the inside, I couldn't cry. I began to hate myself and it was the first time I thought of *them*.

Had they not abandoned me, Michael would never have wanted to fulfill making me happy to the fullest extent, the bears would never have came searching for food, Michael would *not* have had to risk his life to save ours, and I wouldn't be responsible for killing an angel internally.

I recalled my thoughts. I let out a deep sigh. Most would kill for the life I have. It may not be *that* luxurious but it's better than most. Rachel was a district attorney. Not to mention Michael owned his own boating industry that manufactured motor boats, yachts and other water crafts. After his death, she was left with a little over half a million dollars.

She spent thousands of dollars on me to keep *me* happy. But didn't need it as much as she did. But I knew it was wholly based on the fact that I was the last thing she had and she wanted to spend every moment with me.

She bought me the latest toys and video games, clothes of all brands, more shoes than necessary...and I hated it. But she loved every minute of it. So I submitted for her. She deserved all the happiness she could get. It was the only time that same healthiness returned into her eyes. She even bought me a silver, 2003 Dodge Charger that I would have to wait two years to drive because I was too young at the time to drive it.

Yet, I wasn't happy. How could I be so ungrateful? So selfish to her? So sad and miserable?

Two thoughts entered my mind as I ask myself these questions. My real were still a mystery to me. I was more than grateful for Rachel stepping in and filling in the shoes of my real mother but it wasn't fair to her. In all honesty, it really wasn't her responsibility. I wanted truth and understanding. I wanted to know what did *I* do as a child that was so horrible that made me deserve this life of uncertainty. It wasn't fair to hurt and not know the origins of the pain.

The other thing was that I have always felt like I didn't fit anywhere in this world. I couldn't help but feel like something was pulling at me from the inside, luring me into a place and into a world where I truly belonged. I even felt at times, most of times actually, that I wasn't even human. I grimaced at the thought. Though I knew I was human, I couldn't prevent my feelings from being so strongly attached to the idea.

I look back at the clock and see that its now six o'clock. I pull the comforter lying on top of me to the side and slide my half asleep body out of the bed. I drag my feet across the floor and slowly open my room door. I search for the scent of lavender, the sound of rushing water, or a glimpse of light, something that tells me that Rachel was up. Nothing.

I continued to drag my almost lifeless body across the caramel carpet and into the bathroom that was no more than four feet away from my room. I flipped the switch, the bright, luminous light stinging my eyes like venom. I slowly close the door and force all my weight onto my hands as they pressed against the counter.

I looked up at my reflection. I stared at myself, examining carefully, trying to find some abnormality in the person staring back at me. The auburn brown hair that was thrashing in every direction was completely normal. My skin color was a bit paler than usual this morning but the house *was* freezing. Normal. No extreme discoloration in my skin or anything. 5'9" and athletically built (though I'd never entered a sport a day in my life).

Everything was normal. Everything except for one thing. The brightness in my sea blue eyes was fading. It seemed to get worse day by day. As if something was draining the life from them.

I shrugged. I guess, in a way, you could say that that, too, was normal.

I let out my second deep sigh of the morning. I took in another breath this time, a deeper breath, bringing my lungs to life. I turned on the cold water, splashed it in my face to wake myself up, and began with my morning routine. It was obvious I was going to be late for school after all.

After taking a fifteen minute shower, brushing my teeth and putting my hair together in a much neater arrangement, I headed down the stairs. As soon as I hit the base of the stairs, the scent of lavenders invaded my nostrils, almost suffocating me. Rachel was up. "Rachel?" I called out.

"In here." she responded. She was in the kitchen but even without her voice's assurance of where she was, I could have easily followed the scent's trail to find her.

I walked around the stairs and into the kitchen. She stood next to the stove where the toaster sat. Her fingers moved one after another upon the counter continuously. She was waiting for whatever was in the toaster to spring itself out.

Ding. Out popped two toasted wheat bagels that she placed on a saucer one after another, shaking off the imprint of heat they left. She then turned to me with a warm expression and even warmer smile.

"Good morning, Kayden." Her voice was nothing far from angelic. She was so feminine and classy. She was beautiful. Her hair curled itself down her back and over her shoulders. Her eyes had a little more life in them today. I wish it was that easy for me. How could two people of opposite worlds live in one house?

"Good morning, Rache." She never really pressured me to call her mom now. When I was younger I did but now I had questions, uncertainties. I couldn't put any deep attachments on her until I was clear on everything about myself. Not at this point. "Sorry I can't stay for breakfast. I'm already late."

She shook her head. "No need to feel sorry. Nothing big anyways. Just a bagel." her lips lifted into a smile, baring her warm smile, the same one that she used to possess when Michael was alive. She took another bite out of her bagel and chewed it rhythmically. After swallowing the contents in her mouth, what was left of her uneaten bagel, she threw it in the garbage. She pulled her wrist up chest high and looked at her watch.

She moved gracefully across the floor as she gathered her things. She pulled her suit jacket off of the chair nearest her and walked toward me with a smile. She placed her hand on my shoulder, pulled her lips up to my cheek and kissed me. Her lips were still warm from the bagels she consumed. "Bye, Kayden." She hugged me, holding the back of my head like I was still the child she had taken in fourteen years ago. "I love you, Kayden." she whispered in my ear. She stared into my eyes for a long moment.

It was odd. Her eyes. They possessed…life. Hope. I remember seeing that glow in her eyes whenever Michael was in the room. Indeed odd.

She broke the connection and brushed passed me and I could hear her keys being removed from her purse. "Be sure to lock up honey." The sound of the door closing echoed throughout the solitary house.

"Yeah." I replied long after she was gone. I didn't deserve her at all. But I was what kept her smiling, kept her blood running warm in her body. I was all she held dear. I couldn't fix myself to even think of suicide or anything of that nature. She deserved happiness and I became her happiness after Michael's death.

I pulled my keys off the hook on the wall, ran upstairs, pulled my unfinished homework off the desk and the cold slice of pizza and rush out the door, locking up being the last thing I did. I entered my car, placed my keys in the ignition and listened as my car purred to life.

I drove silently with only the faint whistle of the wind rushing over my car. I couldn't help but be sucked into my vortex of thoughts once more. My hands trembled and my face twitched every now and then. Why? It irritated me how complex I seemed to be. Why am I feeling like I am so alone when clearly I'm not?

I set aside my thoughts as I entered one of the many parking lots to Oregon State University. All the closer parks were gone and I had to park in one of the furthest parking spots from campus. I shut the care off and soaked in the silence. It was ironically soothing. But I couldn't allow myself to dwell much longer on the sensation. The dashboard clock read eight eleven. I was already late.

I pulled my bag from the backseat, took the incomplete Sociology homework sitting on the passenger seat and placed it in my bag. I pulled myself out of the car, permitting the warm rays of sunlight that reached over the horizon to touch my skin. It was the most peaceful I had felt all morning.

But again, I couldn't give into the sensation that seemed to sweep over me and change my mood so abruptly. I had to get to class.

I entered the sociology class that had started fifteen minutes ago. Professor Yates glared at me with persecuting eyes as I walked into class late…again.

"Mister Pruitt, late yet again I see." It was a ritual. The same thing every morning but now it had gotten so predictable on my tardiness and his reaction that the uproar of *oohs* and laughter had seem to die out completely over time. That made coming to class a little less stressful and relieved my already unstable emotions from embarrassment.

I ignored him and his attempts to embarrass me and trailed over to my seat next to Brycin. Brycin was really my only good friend. I had known him for only four years but it felt like I had known him longer than that. His light caramel skin tone and almond shaped eyes complimented by the soft shade of brown his eyes were and his full body features made him easily one of the most attractive guys on campus. He'd received several scholarships for athleticism. He was a passionate swimmer, high school star receiver, and an exceptional tennis player. But they weren't his true passion. He wanted to be a psychologist. Another natural gift of his.

I released a huge huff of air as soon as I took my seat.

"You seem to be in a livelier mood today." His voice soaked in sarcasm.

I glared with resenting eyes. "Very funny."

Brycin always hated this mood I seemed to bring to school every day. He was one of the two who tolerated me and it. Clearly I didn't deserve either of them. They cared so much about me. It wasn't fair to put myself on them like this. "What is it this time?"

I hesitated. "I feel like," I began in a faint whisper, trying desperately not to lure any attention to us from Professor Yates. "I'm losing it. It just feels like I am just living day to day. As if I have nothing to live for. But I know it's not true." I hurried and corrected myself. "I have Rachel and you as my best friend. That should be enough. It *should.*"

"You want too much." He said with a laugh, teeth beaming white. "You can't have everything. You want the land, the sea, the stars, and the moon, the sun, the universe and everything in it. But it just doesn't work that way. I think Forrest Gump put it the best." We both snickered at his comparison and Yates caught us laughing. He gave us a look of disproval and continued with his lecture. We both let out another faint laugh once he turned away. "Life is unpredictable. And you continue to beat yourself up for something you had no control over." It's amazing how he knew the roots of my problems without me saying anything. I guess when it's like this on a day-to-day basis, it becomes rather predictable. "Your mom and father abandoned you. Rachel doesn't deserve for you to take it out on her."

"You don't think I know that!" I whispered harshly. I didn't mean for it to come out that way, especially not toward the only person willing to help me. "Sorry." My whisper now calmer. "But what do you do? When you can't cry from the pain? When you can't deal with it? I tried running away but it seems to catch up with me every time. I just want to know what they were thinking."

He shrugged. "Their loss."

I knew he was right but my stubbornness wouldn't let that sit. "Well I still want to know why. It's not fair living life everyday without answers."

"Kayden, everyone lives every moment of everyday not knowing if the earth is even going to be there when they wake up. That's a part of life that we must accept. It's reality. You are hoping for something unattainable. Hope is a blinding tool. It covers up reality so we can fantasize about the way things should be and not how they really are. Your parents abandoned you. Rachel is your parent now. Why is it so hard for *you* to accept?"

I do. I do accept her. I just want to know.

I looked up at Brycin and saw the pain in his eyes. Clearly he suffered when I did. We were indeed best friends. Better than best friends. We were brothers.

Everyone was lifting from their seats and exiting the room. Class had flown by and I hadn't even noticed. Brycin and I both had the same classes today and we walked to Theology together but Mrs. Hay wasn't in there. She was a rather large woman with ruby red hair, freckles, pale skin, and glasses with small round circles that sat on the edge of her nose. She was very old fashioned and too much of a disciplinary. Students joked all the time that she should be a parole officer or something of that nature.

I could over hear a few of the students speaking across from me as Brycin and I took our seat. I could hear them saying that Mrs. Hay had some viral infection and called in sick.

"I heard he's cute." one of the girls commented with a snicker. I came to the conclusion they were speaking of a substitute. That was rather odd. A substitute? In college?

Before they could finish, a tall dark man entered the room in black slacks and a black button up shirt with a small brief case in his left hand.

"Sorry for my tardiness, class. I tell you teachers are stupid." His voice was silky, almost harmonic. It was deep, yet lively. He was taller than any of the students in the classroom. He was dark skinned and his eyes were a deep brown.

"But *aren't* you a teacher yourself, *sir*." one of the students pointed out in a tone that was somewhat mocking.

His laughter possessed the same melodic quality as his voice. "No, I hate teachers. They piss me off just as much as you. They are like the flies around the rear end of a horse. No matter how much you try and swat them away, they still come back." The students laughed at the analogy he used to describe teachers, everyone loved him immediately. "Well, without further ado, let's get class started. My name is Professor Portman and Mrs. Hay personally asked if I could take over her class today. I am not going to go over any of the material in your text book today. Instead, I am going to poke around and see what it is you guys know about the word 'religion.'

"Who hear can give me a direct definition on what it is?" The room went grimly silent. It was as if he never asked a question. He poked around trying to see if anyone would try and answer but no one did. "Religion is the belief in a system set up to guide our everyday life. It is the foundation of our morality for the most part. And it is composed of members who are defined as gods or goddesses who lay out specific rules to guide us through that everyday life."

Everyone seemed to nod agreement.

"But clearly that's boring." The class was overpowered with laughter and the substitute was obviously pleased with the reaction. "I want to speak of a legend that was long lost. It was a story the Romans never thought to be true but just because they ignored it, does that mean it's false?

"It spoke of God destroying the Earth thousands of years ago. Too much evil dwelled here. Murdering, thievery, persecution toward the righteousness, world domination had become the lifestyle for mankind. Survival no matter the cost.

"Because all this evil was so potent on Earth, the earth itself began to wither and die. Weather patterns were unpredictably strange, the animals of Earth were incapable of reproducing normally, thus making food scarce, vegetation was dying worldwide and the seas refused to give life to creatures or allow anything to dwell in them. This was a way of God punishing man, a way to get them to realize the degree of harm their actions were forcing upon the world but it seemed that not even this would force man to acknowledge the wrong and the evil lifestyle they'd inherited. Man refused to give up their evil ways. There was only one thing left to do to the world. Destroy it.

"God sent armies of angels down to destroy everything; the people, the evil, the earth itself. He planned to create a new world, an Earth II. A world of only holy beings. The first Earth would no longer flourish with life. It would rot away dark and abandoned forever.

"But when Lucifer, said to be the most beautiful angel to ever exist, grew aware of these plans, he wasn't just going to sit around and let this happen. So, he opposed God, opened the Eye to Hell and unleashed his legions upon the angels. His interference only angered God further. God took his eyes off of Earth, and focused it all on Lucifer. A new plan was thought up. If Lucifer was destroyed, there would be no need for this Earth II. Evil would no longer exist, thus the corruption over mankind would falter."

I looked around, breaking the attention I had on this legend he was speaking of. The class was never this attentive during Mrs. Hay's lectures.

"The war between angels and demons, good and evil, God and Lucifer was underway and it lasted a very long time. Months. But with warfare comes fear. Followers tend to separate from their leader. And that's exactly what the human race did. Some separated themselves from God and the entire divine world.

"The legend states that some humans had supposedly found a gateway to heaven which granted man access to heaven, a holy asylum, a sinless place. God would never allow that. As an immediate reaction, the gates to heaven were closed and he cast those who found their way into heaven out in bolts of fire. By default, the Eye to Hell had to close for everything must remain in balance.

"But God did not leave with promising something first. He forewarned the world of his return. That Earth II *will* come into existence. That everything will come to an end soon.

"When it was all over, the world *was* nearly destroyed. Nations had fallen, empires that had taken centuries to establish had crumbled in months and all hope seemed lost. It appeared impossible for man to overcome such devastations.

"These had become desperate times and man needed to bring life back to their world. Yes, man took heed to the war and the near loss of their kind and Earth slowly began its way toward being reborn. But there was a slight complication.

"The angels and demons that fought endlessly were trapped here on Earth. They had no way in returning to their rightful domains because only their rightful leader could open the gateways. They had no choice but to make Earth their new home.

"Humans were not ignorant of their existence alongside them and it spiked a new evil in the human hearts. They channeled their hate for God and Lucifer toward the angels and the demons. People became very violent towards angels and demons but without a command from their leaders, they couldn't fight back. It even got to the point where they figured out how to kill the angels and the demons. So to prevent further divine blood from being spilled, they hid their wings and blended in with the human race and they would live as humans 'til the returning of the war.

"But this only made more room for *more* complications. Forced to live on Earth for so long would come with a price. You see God can only track the minds of humans, sinners I guess you could say. Not those of holiness. So he knew nothing of what his angels were thinking or feeling though he could easily see them. These beings began to feel a human emotion known as attraction. They became attracted to humans. As did some demons. And when the bloods mixed, new creatures were born."

He turned to the board and began to write two names on the board. In an unbelievably elegant handwriting were the words *Neatholytes* and *Demilytes.*

"Have you guys ever heard of the terminology Neatholyte or Demilyte?" Silence shrouded the class yet again. It was a subtle sound and without Portman's silky voice traveling throughout the room, it was somewhat noticeable. I turned and looked at Brycin, awestruck by his behavior. His posture was tense, his jaw was tight and he scolded Portman with hateful eyes. It wasn't so much he looked angry. More like…worried. Why?

Even as I sat there studying him, wondering why he was behaving so…oddly, he didn't notice me.

"It's okay." My head snapped to the front of the room when he began talking again. It was going to be hard to pay as close attention to Portman's lecture sidetracked by Brycin's behavior. "I didn't really expect you to. Neatholytes are human/angel half-breeds. They share a human and angel blood line. With that being said, you can put definition to Demilytes. Because these half-breeds were born and have the ability of shifting balance tremendously, the entire Revelation prophecy was thrown out the window. With the existence of these two beings, the battle at Revelation could go either way. Because what factor determines who wins a war?"

A girl with blonde hair curling down to her shoulders raised her hand. She had porcelain skin and beautiful warm cheeks. And her dark and intense eyes demanded attention. "Those with the bigger guns?"

The class snickered quietly at her response. It didn't sound like she was trying to sound unintelligent but it came off that way. Professor Portman raised his hand to shush to class and its faint snickers. "She is actually right. He who has the largest army and better weapons is most likely to rise victorious so with the chance of losing in mind, God needed to collect as many of these half-breeds as possible."

"But that defies everything God is perceived to be." a boy with dark curly hair from the top of the class chided. He had squared glasses and was very slim. "The all knowing and fearless. I mean it sounds absurd to me. Too farfetched."

Portman laughed melodically. "And that is a brilliant observation. I am trying to get your brains to work and I am impressed. That is exactly why the Romans threw the story out. Because it made God appear to be not all that he was said to be. It was a contradiction. It made God appear nearly human.

"So here is the question for you to ponder. Is this legend true? Do we walk among these so called half-breeds? And if we do, would we react as fanatical as some of our ancestors had done so long ago to the angels and the demons? If we ran into one outside, how would we treat them? Like humans or like aliens?"

Portman seemed quite impressed with himself when the class spread into a many whispers. I analyzed every question and answered them to myself. I didn't know why but a part of me believed it to be true. I would love to live side by side with something amazingly fascinating as a half-breed. Life would be all the more interesting. And of course *I* would never act with such a barbaric behavior against something of much splendor.

It was amazing how perceptions were capable of erasing an entire story from the web of history.

But as I thought more on the legend I began to think to myself and ask question rather than answer the ones I hadn't yet. Before I knew it, the words flowed out of my mouth. "So what is an angel/demon half-breed?" I regretted the question as soon as it came out because the whispers halted immediately and everyone's gaze was upon my face. "I mean I figure that if they've discovered this gift of attraction, then couldn't they have found the enemy attracted, too?"

Professor Portman looked intrigued and caught off guard by my question. "What is your name?"

I bit my teeth together, eyeing the room as all the students stared at me, waiting for me to answer. I could feel anger sneak its way into my body, pulling my hand into a tight fist, forcing my stomach to twist and ache, coating my eyes with rage. My anger intensified when I noticed Brycin on the side of me laughing. There was nothing to laugh about! Couldn't he have just answered the question like any old regular teacher?

I shoved my pride aside and calmed myself, taking two breaths before answering. "Pruitt. Kayden Pruitt."

"Well, Mister Pruitt, that is a myth within a legend. They are known as the Nexusytes. More powerful than their brethrens, the Neatholytes and Demilytes. They are said to be an evil like none other. That the evil they possess makes Lucifer appear human. They could bring more wrath and destruction to Earth than God or Lucifer could ever imagine. Their existence throws the entire cosmos off balance. If one was to ever rise, hypothetically speaking, then the world would suffer a relapse and the evil days that once haunted to the earth before would return."

I wasn't so fond of living side by side them as I was the Neatholytes and Demilytes. What they were capable of frightened me in the most terrifying way.

"It may be caused by the overwhelming events that seem to take us by surprise day after day after day but many are starting to take notice in these forgotten writings and believe that these signs are pointing to an uprising, a war between the divine."

It was hard to believe class was over now. It felt like we'd just taken our seats and he began his lecture. For some odd reason, I wasn't fully satisfied. I was still…curious. There was so much more I still wanted to know. *Was* it true? There was no denying it that Portman easily believed in these tales. And if it is true, then when will all these *things* begin to happen?

I shook my head, realizing that I really shouldn't be caring, hoping that I could shake the thoughts from my mind. But, they remained attached to the forefront of my mind. It almost seemed as though the curiosity was amplifying itself, becoming unbearable, becoming lethal.

Brycin was rising from his seat. I grabbed his forearm. I hadn't realized the amount of power I put into my grip until I saw his face grimace from the pressure. My arm suddenly tingled. I put so much pressure into the grip that I practically felt it myself. "Sorry." his face relaxed. "Can you stay behind with me? I want to ask him a few questions." It was easy to read the frustration on his face but I needed his presence to give me a dose of courage. He noticed my genuine interest and conceded.

I rose from my seat, a burning sensation beginning in the pit of my stomach. The apprehensive flame scorched my nerves and my blood, traveling through my entire body, making me more anxious about approaching Portman.

I couldn't believe how afraid I was. Why? My legs were shaking, I fumbled for words over and over again in my mind, I felt my forehead grow moist. Why was I so terrified?

He was erasing the words off the board when I approached him. The flame was hotter now than ever before.

"Uhmm, Professor Portman?"

He turned with a smile very inviting yet it didn't ease my fear. Why was I so afraid? What could I possibly get out of asking him what was hammering my brain so intensely? "Ahh, Mister Pruitt. What can I do for you?"

I took my third deep sigh of the morning, organized my fumbled words mentally, and began. "Uhmm, I don't want to sound… persecuting," I shoved my hands into my pockets. "But I can't help but question your exceptional knowledge on something that was said to have been lost in the past centuries."

There was that melodic laughter again. It *almost* eliminated the flame broiling through my blood. "My family, you can sort of say, has passed the story down from generation to generation. I had…" I immediately caught his hesitation. "*Ancestors* who were alive when these events were occurring." I did believe him, but I was very watchful for the words he chose and wondered why when he used the word 'ancestors' that it was not the word his mind pushed for. "You can pretty much conclude that my family heavily believes in this phenomenon."

"So these *myths* are accurate?"

"Well, that all depends on who you are telling the story to and how much you tell them."

"So there is more to this…legend?"

"Ha ha ha," There was that laugh again and its effect. "Are you really that intrigued with this?" he laughed again. "Why?"

I was hoping that he wasn't going to question my reasons of interest. "Well…I don't really know, actually. Just…well…"

"It's okay. *You* don't need a reason." Why was there emphasis to that? What does he know that he isn't saying? He threw a glance to Brycin whose presence I had forgotten about. Brycin was acting unusually weird toward Portman. He glared at Portman with intense eyes. His breathing was somewhat heavy but it was steady nonetheless. I turned back to Portman and his attitude to Brycin's behavior was rather accepting. It was as if Brycin wasn't looking at him in a threatening way at all.

"Kayden, we have to go." He spit. The atmosphere took on an unsettling and distasteful quality. I didn't like it. Even though there was so much more I wanted to know, I could tell that Brycin hated every second spent in front of Portman.

I turned to Portman with apologetic eyes. "Sorry, we have to go. Thanks for your time, again."

Brycin was more than ready to leave, pushing me ahead of him and keeping his eyes locked on Portman. We were almost out the door when Professor Portman called my name. I turned and he was close enough to me that I could feel the air fly against my face as he breathed. I stumbled backward slightly. He handed me a paper that was no bigger than a business card. There was an address written in an old English cursive. "If you still want to talk, come there. You aren't the only one who wants to know more about the subject. I hold private lectures for individuals who are more *inspired* by the legend." he then turned his attention to Brycin. "You should come, too." he suggested.

Brycin grimaced. "Thanks for the invitation but no thanks."

He nodded casually. "Your decision but *you* could make a valuable member to—" He insisted.

"Again, thanks but we really need to be going." he cut Portman off. Strange. I'd never seen him act like this toward anyone. He was always genuinely nice and accepting. I felt immensely remorseful for Brycin's behavior toward Portman. He then pulled me with his eyes and I was right behind him.

As we walked to our cars, the atmosphere was still somewhat tense. I wanted to question him about his behavior toward Portman. Was it really necessary? "What was that all about? Back there?"

"What are you talking about?" he asked.

"I mean between you and the substitute. Do you two know each other?"

"Kayden, let it go."

I stepped in front of him, stopping him with my hand. "No."

He glared at me, his jaw was tight. He looked away for a fraction of a second and back at me. "I've heard the legend before; I think it's stupid." He brushed passed me.

My eyes went narrow with disbelief. I ran and caught up with him. "So you must've sensed that he was covering something? Like he wanted to say something but he didn't…or couldn't? But why? It's not like there is any concrete evidence to the legend being true. I mean, really angels and demons? Walking the earth? Sounds a bit absurd but it seems as though he was implying some type of truth to the legend—" I hadn't noticed all of the questions I wanted to ask Portman had vomited from my mouth until Brycin cut me off.

"Kayden, let it go!" the volume in his voice startled me and stopped me dead in my tracks. His eyebrows pulled together. I didn't realize it had gotten to him so extremely. "It was just a crazy sub with a crazy story. Nothing to go risking you neck over." It was puzzling. His attitude was extremely off today. I didn't like this new, aggressive nature of his. He sighed apologetically and dropped his head. "Promise me you will stop thinking about it and let it go?"

"It's only a story, Brycin." I defended. "An intriguing one at that."

"You know what, forget I said anything. I don't blame *you*, actually." he turned, leaving me with raging thoughts and questions that aroused from that last statement.

"What does that mean?"

He stopped about two meters ahead of me. He slowly turned and met my gaze. Remorse clouded his past expression of frustration. "Well…you…never developed properly. In the sense socially, I mean. Not that there is anything wrong with your social skills. But…" He was defending himself, realizing that what he said had, in fact, offended me. "You didn't get to grow up the way a child is supposed to. You grew up with questions and doubt. And I have sympathy for you. It must be alarming to finally find something out there that makes a lot less sense than you. But you shouldn't be prying into things that can be life threatening just because you have unanswered questions."

"And what can be so *life threatening* about wanting to know more about a legend?"

"Nothing…you know, forget I even said anything. My apologies." He turned and walked to his car.

How could I forget?

I couldn't help but think maybe he was right though. There was no reason in prying for answers that had nothing to do with me. It was just a strong surge of curiosity.

He was probably right. Maybe it was just so intriguing to find something more insanely absurd than my enigmatic life. Something with such extreme lunacy had to be so appealing to me because it gave me a since of normalcy. That there are people out there who needed help more than me.

I pulled the slice of paper from my pocket and stared at it. Henkle Way. I knew where this was but that was a bit of a drive. It was one of the side roads off the Alsea Highway. I guess I wouldn't be making any trips here. I dropped it to the ground and finally walked after Brycin who was almost ten cars away from me.

After catching up with him, I ignored the intensity of the atmosphere and pondered on the idea of what made him repel against the substitute and his legend. "Can I ask you something?" He looked at me with annoyance so I knew not to linger on the subject. He nodded and pulled out the keys to his car. "Well, I just want to know, what is it exactly that you don't like about the legend?"

He waited a while looking for the words, not moving an inch as he rested his arm on the top of the black Toyota Camry. He pressed his head against the arm that was on the car only for a second. He looked up at me and he knew that I wasn't going anywhere until I got an answer. "Do you really believe that God is that reckless? That he would just throw angels out into the world without knowing that the devil will find some way to interrupt his goals? I mean I am not much of a 'church-goer' but still I know when something sounds completely preposterous."

It was understandable and with that, came my previous state of being, feeling like I was the only one with no clear understanding to existence.

Brycin immediately picked up the vibe. "Look, I am meeting up with everyone. You want to come?"

Our other friends. Emma, James, Claire, Jakob, Frankie, Amber and Jennifer. I really didn't feel like I was part of their social circle. I always felt…uncomfortable for some odd reason. "No, I was just going to go home and tidy up a bit. I haven't done laundry in a week and Rachel keeps riding me about it."

"All right. Well you have my number if you change your mind."

I nodded and walked back toward my car that I previously passed. I entered my car, and threw myself into my sea of torment. The waves weren't as aggressive as they had been earlier, but they still did damage.

I drove home silently and when I got there, the lavender scent was long gone. The house was so empty.

I rushed up the stairs. I put all of my dirty clothes into a laundry bin, walked them downstairs, and began washing them. I loved the distraction. I was engulfed with my duties that the thoughts of depression never trapped me into the waves I was so used to. I wasn't ready for the depression to return. After placing the first load into the washer, I started my Sociology homework. I didn't think it was really going to take two hours to finish but it did. I had four Red Bulls within that time. After my homework was done, I finished my laundry and during folding, I fell asleep in the warmth and spring scent of my clean clothes. That night, I dreamed I was an angel flying into the sun, high above the seas. It was nothing I've ever felt. It was…peaceful.

Chapter 2: Nonsense

TODAY I MADE IT TO SCHOOL ON TIME AND SOMETHING felt different, I didn't know what it was. I wasn't sure if it was how peaceful the night had gone with everything I'd occupied my time with or if it was due to the fact that I wasn't so obsessed with thoughts of who I really was and who my real parents were.

Or maybe that dream had something to do with it. The dream I had of me flying into the horizon above my raging seas which tried their best to reach up at me — never even coming close to grabbing me. I teased the seas, showing off my wings and doing tricks, letting them know, without the usage of words, that it was nearly impossible to get me. I just flew. I flew over the waters until they became completely motionless and turned dry and brown. I loved it up there. Flying with the birds until I was flying toward the sun; even though I never made it to the sun. But who cares? I wasn't sad at all today.

And Brycin, as observant as he was, immediately picked up on it. "Your happy today? What happened?"

We didn't share a single class today so when I met him and the others by Jakob's Range Rover, my mood was the talk of the circle. "Nothing. I just feel light today. Probably something you said yesterday. It may have clicked on a dull light."

"Or maybe you got some!" Jakob said smiling, throwing his arm over my shoulders and rubbing his knuckles into my head. I pushed him away with no sign of seriousness. I couldn't help but laugh. Not because it was a completely idiotic assumption but because he couldn't be further from the truth.

Jakob always wore his dirty blonde hair messy. Water was the only thing he believed should be in anyone's hair. He called it the 'natural hair product.' His eyes were a dark chocolate brown and his complexion was a shade or two darker than mine. He was small but he wasn't without muscles.

"You are such a pig, Jake." Claire interrupted the laughs. Claire was beautiful and kind. She reminded me a lot of Rachel in her early years, before the attack. The only difference was she was a lot more petite, her hair was a deep sangria red, and her eyes were a soft, velvety kind of green. She was also a little more modern in the way she dressed. Her beauty was very natural and Jakob tried his hardest to become hers but she considered herself too mature for him, too good for him.

She was right. Jakob was very outspoken and rambunctious and sometimes his personality got him in loads of trouble.

"Awww, Claire when are you going to admit that you dig me?"

"When hell freezes over."

"You're so hot."

"Ugh! Shut up! Can't you see that there are more important things than you right now? Like where all this happiness is coming from." She smiled looking back at me.

"Well?" Brycin pressed.

"Well, I sort of had a dream last night."

"Sex, huh?" Jakob asked eagerly, wanting to know the details.

"You're impossible." Claire rolled her eyes.

"No, I…" I thought out the words before I spoke. *I dreamt that I was an angel, flying high above the clouds and into the blazing warmth of the sun, letting all of my depression and problems drown in the seas below me.* Brycin would blame yesterday's events on that and I knew he would immediately shoot down my happiness.

I could imagine the thoughts in both Claire and Jakob's head as they registered what I was saying. *Weirdo. He needs professional help.* I couldn't help but take in consideration their prejudging thoughts even though they may show more understanding than Brycin, I knew they would listen to Brycin and agree with him mentally.

"I dreamt of me, as a baby." I lied. "At least I think so. Probably some mental image stored away in mind when I was a kid. I think I saw my parents." Wow. I was impressed with that lie. I didn't even think that I could be so convincing even to myself. My tone was calm and even. Though I paused, that could be a natural response from someone who never seen their real parents.

There was so much sympathy in Claire's eyes. She loved men who didn't fear their emotions. Who embraced them. A quality Jakob lacked. "That's so cute, Kay." her smile was wide and forced me to smile and flush red in the cheeks.

"So you feel like your questions about your parents are answered?" Brycin questioned. It surprised me that *he* believed me. But then again, he really didn't have a reason *not* to.

No. Of course I didn't feel like my questions had been answered. That's why it was a lie. But only I knew that. I still didn't know who my real parents were or why they did this to me. But I had to keep to this lie. "Not really. It just made it easier to accept the days I am living now." When did I become such a good liar? It must have been some overnight thing.

He nodded thoughtfully and folded his arms. I noticed his face shifted, tensed as he looked down at the floor unseeingly — he was apprehensive about something. He suddenly turned and looked over his shoulder. I hadn't noticed all the many flickering eyes flashing in our direction. Everyone seemed a bit uneasy.

Brycin turned back to me, the same uneasy expression residing in the audience behind him, his face adopted.

"What?"

"Well—" he hesitated. "We're going to go to Crater Lake today. Did you want to go?"

A wave of absence swept over me as the last words rolled off his lips. The place that haunted Rachel's very existence. It was like for an instant I was completely empty. My mind was black and I stared blankly pass Brycin. I hadn't been to Crater Lake since Michael's death.

What would Rachel say if I came home and told her I had been to Crater Lake? I can't tell her. It would send her into a frenzy of pain, consisting of wheezing and horrific sobs. She hated that lake. The lake that claimed her husband's life.

I could see it all in my head, replaying like a movie without sound. I saw the bears charge from out of the forest and straight at me and Rachel. Michael running pass us and tackling the bears head on. I can see the hate in the bear's eyes as he snapped his jaws at Michael's face. Michael, a godly sculpted specimen, lay there with this giant on him, struggling to keep the beast's jaws at a distance. He is trying so desperately to shove the big ball of fur off of him. I could see him fight harder and harder with every second…and lose because of me. I distracted him. I was the reason he died.

My sea had returned and was thrashing me. This time I didn't want to wait for them to pull me under. I was going to swim beneath them. I was going to give into its icy touch and let the pressure of my depression crush me until there was nothing left of me.

The knot in my throat was expanding. Any minute, my throat was going to explode.

Brycin was waving his hand in my face and I watched as the bear which had his jaws tight around Michael's throat and the puddle of blood surrounding them disappear. "You cool with that? I told them that you might be objective to it. Everyone understood but Frankie. He threw a bitch fit telling us to leave you."

"No, its fine." I rushed the words out. "Really. I wanna go."

"You sure?" Brycin pressed.

It *was* Friday and I didn't see why not. "Yeah, sure. I'm down."

Brycin and Frankie's car, along with mine, we left at the university. We carpooled in Jakob's Range Rover. The girls were meeting us at the lake. The sun was perched high in the sky and it was hotter than normal this time of the year. Spring had arrived over three weeks ago and the heat was smoldering today. Jakob drove bare chest and Frankie, feeling like the Alpha male as always, felt the need to ride bare chest as well.

Frankie was your typical football jock. Big and muscular. His eyes were a lighter brown than his hair and his skin was a light russet color. He wasn't that much taller than any of the rest of us but his large and defined physique made him look so.

Both he and Jakob mostly talked about the girls the entire ride and who would look sexier in their swim suit. Frankie had money on Emma but Jakob, always obsessed with Claire, betted on her. It was funny how they made them seem like a football team or horses at a derby. A completely normal day.

We arrived at the lake. The sun was most breathtaking here than before. The shimmering sunlight dancing across the majestic waves proved to be an unjustifiable beauty. Trees towered over us, luxuriant in rich shades of green. Branches reached in every direction, sharing their touch with one another and giving refuge to other wildlife. Amazing how something as stunning as Mother Nature's impeccably and undeniably exhilarating beauty could be so easily overlooked.

Everyone was already here. Claire was dumping ice into a cooler, each ice cube sparkling prismatically with the assistance of the sun's rays. She looked ever so beautiful. Her long, dark red hair swayed over her shoulders as she leant over the cooler. Her eyes looked a softer shade of green beside the dazzling lake. She had on denim short shorts with a salmon pink and tan polka dotted swim top. I was more than positive Jakob's attention was drawn towards her assets.

Emma was helping Claire load up the cooler, following behind her more gracefully than a human should be able to with beverages and food. Emma possessed a superficial, yet natural beauty. I would never admit it aloud, but Emma *was* easily the most gorgeous girl in the bunch which was the exact reason to why she didn't appeal to me. She was *too* beautiful.

She had icy blonde hair with hypnotizing sapphire eyes. Her skin was smooth like porcelain, flawless, high cheekbones and a stunning body which was, just like the rest of her traits and attributes, flawless.

But there was one trait that stunned me more than her jaw-dropping beauty. It was her level of intelligence. She graduated top of her class, her schedules consisted of honor and A.P. courses, and she was always involved in some club or committee. She was capable of holding a conversation on just about any topic and know exactly what she is talking about.

A boy, whose looks were parallel to Emma's walked beside her, helping her fill the cooler. James was Emma's younger brother. He was a senior in high school and was just as superficial looking as his sister. I once thought that their parents may have been Barbie and Ken. He shared the same icy blonde hair which was always perfectly cropped, his skin was as flawless as hers, and his body was something straight off of a runway. The only difference they *did* have was his eyes were a deep blue, almost violet.

Also here with them were Jennifer and Amber.

Jennifer's dark hair and almond brown eyes were here most complimentary features. She was very athletic out of all the girls here. Head cheerleader in her high school days and swim captain of the girls swim team. She was nowhere near as beautiful as Emma but she was still well over average.

At one point, she had an obsessive crush on me. And it boiled her blood when I turned her down. But she grew to like me again when she realized that I didn't have my eyes on anyone else.

What she resented more than guys turning her down, was the typical stereotype people held over the thought of what a cheer captain should look like. The preppy, dumb, perky blonde. She moved to Corvallis three years ago with her father after her step-dad attacked her during one of his drunken episodes.

Amber was very opposite in attitude but attractive nevertheless. She had black hair as well with a milky chocolate skin tone. Her eyes were just as beautiful as her personality and she was very respectable. She was just as intelligent as Emma, maybe smarter, and loved playing music above all else.

Of course she tried her hardest, though not very conspicuous with the way she did it, to get Brycin to notice her. But sometimes I felt like he was too obsessed with being there for me as a brother that he took the lime light away from her. If she hated me, I would completely understand.

I seemed to be his only concern these days. I wasn't absolute if this was the average behavior of a best friend or some evidence of some sort of lack of trust in me — due to a previous, unforgettably distressing occurrence.

I grew tiresome of the unanswered questions and forever mysteries that seem to consume my life; I had decided to go looking for my parents, leaving the state and not returning until I found them.

Brycin immediately disagreed, ripping that thought to shreds. I argued back, trying to convince him that this was best for me, something I needed. He left me with a comment I would never forget. *Well maybe you belong dead, then! That's all your real parents really wanted for you anyways! That's what they thought was best for you! I only want to look out for you but if you don't want my help then go! Go on! Do what you want! See if I care!* Even he knows that those words still remain as fresh in my mind as the day he spoke them.

The words stung. It felt like there was a creature present in my chest, ripping and eating the contents within it until there was nothing left.

With the pain in my chest and the sense of nothingness and worthlessness cooling my blood to a deadly temperature, I drove out of Corvallis with no sense to where I was going. I just drove blindly down the rainy highways. It was then, at that very moment, I felt a pressure rising, pushing against my heart and plummeting the temperature of my blood to irreversible degrees. It was that day that my tormenting and destructive seas manifested, growing stronger and stronger off of my sorrow until it was strong enough to attack me and force my foot relentlessly down on the accelerator and rocket the car off a cliff.

All I could remember was that I was out for sixteen days with no recollection of what happened within them days. All I know is that when I came to, I was at home, my car was fully intact, and I was without any scars of the incident or bruises.

Rachel was worried for me the entire sixteen days I was gone. She thought I had just up and disappeared and blamed herself for it, that maybe it was something that *she'd* done that forced me to leave.

The experience showed me whose life I would truly have been throwing away. It wasn't mine. But it was hers. It ripped a hole in her chest which I doubt had even healed completely. I hurt her more than what was allowed. That's why I have to live for her.

As for Brycin, the experience only seemed to worsen him. It flooded him with guilt to know that he almost killed his friend, thus amplifying his protective nature. But for Rachel's sake, I would never allow it to get to me like it had before.

We were slowly approaching the edge of the lake. I immediately notice that of the one tree was hunched over. It looked like it was sad or tired. Michael called it the 'hunchback tree of Crater Lake.' I knew exactly where we were. I knew that if I walked a little over a mile, beyond the trees, passed the pastures, I would come face to face with the murderer of Rachel's hopes and dreams. The place that claimed her dear husband's life.

All the girls were laying their blankets on the burning rocks, then laying on them beneath the scorching ball of fire perched high in the sky with their oversized sunglasses.

We parked beside Emma's fourth generation, flaming red Camaro. She loved that car because it was rare. Hardly anyone owned one. Matched her perfectly because, just like it, hardly anyone possessed her kind of beauty.

As soon as Frankie and Jakob exited the car, they started fighting over who looked better. They trailed over toward the others but I had a more personal agenda with the lake today. I had to revisit this asylum of disaster. I jumped out of the car and headed into the trees.

"Kay!" I turned to see Jakob jogging over in my direction. I really wasn't up to discussing or explaining why I was heading in *this* direction. "Where are you going?" He said nearly out of breath. "Everyone's over there. It'll mean a lot if you were a part. We don't really get to spend that much time with you."

That was completely unexpected. Jakob was showing…compassion. And he was sincere. His voice was calming and at peace. His body language was relaxed and he wasn't overly touchy or obnoxious. It was a characteristic that caught me off guard — almost made me want to stay with the group. But I had to satisfy this craving of curiosity. I wanted to see it again. The place that brought me happiness as a child and that will remain forever the story of Rachel's misery. "Uhmm…I just wanted to see something. I haven't been here in little over six years and…well it's a long story."

"Well then you promise to tell me it when you come back?"

I tilted my head, my eyes narrowed, carefully analyzing him. This was nothing like him. *Nothing.* The only thing Jakob ever cared about were girls and who looked better in what? "Yeah. Sure?" I answered skeptically.

I turned and scoffed after witnessing the old Jakob spring to life. He jumped on Frankie's neck who then threw him into the lake. Laughter sung into the air and I listened as Mother Nature drowned it out with her symphony of bird calls and chirps and rustling of leaves as the light wind played in them. Every step I took contributed to the orchestra. She made Beethoven look like an amateur.

After about fifteen minutes of walking I saw the opening of the woods. I can see the waters swaying from side to side, almost dancing. The blue looked so refreshing and the trees and mountains behind them panted a silhouette irresistible to man.

Then, I saw *it*. *It* was the rock. The boulder Rachel and I made ours. It wasn't as purplish anymore but I knew it was ours because it was still pretty unique in color for a rock. Not to mention the dark spots on the rock. I could only think of one thing that that could be. Blood from six years ago.

I could feel the tears swell up. I pushed them back behind my skull even though I knew that to be unnecessary. Just because this place held so much heartache, it wasn't enough to force me into a plummeting cry that I so longed to have.

I knelt beside the rock that was my source of happiness six years ago. I sat down beside it and lightly pressed my ear against it and closed my eyes smiling. It was warm, almost life like. Even though we had been absent for so long, the life in the rock never went away. I was more relaxed than I had been in quite some time.

The feeling immediately washed away when I heard a low growl erupt from behind me. My eyelids flew open, relaxation complete depleting itself from my body. I stared at the surface of the lake. Déjà vu? This was how it all began. I knew what was next. I would look behind me and see absolutely nothing.

I lifted my head from the stone and stood to my feet, never breaking eye contact with the water. I peered over my shoulder, afraid that maybe something lurked in the forest behind me, stalking me.

Michael. He died here. Rachel would live in a forever pain knowing that I died in the same place as he. She would curse this lake forever—until she was dead herself.

My peripheral vision was empty. Nothing was out of the ordinary. Nothing big and black or life threatening. But I already knew that.

So I turned my head back to the lake and closed my eyes. I concentrated, waited for more growls to come and interrupt the wind's whistle. I waited and waited and waited…

Nothing. No growls, no sign of the mafia of black bears with angry-coated eyes. Just my imagination picturing everything so vividly I suppose.

After convincing myself that everything was fine, I figured it wasn't worth the risk to see had anything actually been skulking in the forest behind me. I turned away from this haven of joyous memories, this curse to Rachel's and my life and walked back to the rambunctious crowd that awaited me.

The walk back was a lot faster. When I reached the break in the trees and saw everyone frolicking in the lake's water, I noticed that one person wasn't with them. I looked up at the sky and saw that the sun wasn't as high in the sky as it was before I left.

How long had Brycin been in the car?

I opened the door of the car and Brycin never flinched. The music was playing on the radio and the cool air rushed through the vents of the car. He simply stared out his window. Something lingering over the lake had his attention. If only I knew what it was. I saw nothing but he stared out at the lake. He was trapped in a deep thought and I wondered what captivated him in such thoughts. It wasn't like him to get so caught up in daydreams. "Bryce?"

He looked at me, almost startled. I realized that he wasn't in the car, mentally anyways. "Yeah?"

"Are you all right?"

He let out a deep sigh. "Yeah, I'm fine. Just wondering—" he broke off mid sentence, hesitating for some odd reason. "Why did you lie, back at the school?"

My eyes were forced wide with astonishment because of the unexpectedness of his accurate assumption. I almost forgot how to speak within that small fraction of a second. *How could he have possibly known?* I questioned myself mentally. I thought I was rather convincing. "Uhmm…I wasn't." I lied.

"You're lying to me again. I know I don't have a perfect history as your friend, but—"

I cut him off before he could drown us both in guilt. "You really need to stop beating yourself up over that. I'm fine now. Everyone's fine now."

"Well then why are you lying? What are you hiding?'

I couldn't lie now. It was almost as if he was in my head as I thought up the lie. I pulled myself into the car and exhaled deeply. "Well, I was afraid that you would hate what I really dreamt about"

"Try me." he demanded.

Oh great. Just what I needed. For him to pass judgment and rip me apart on such nonsense. "Well, I *did* have a dream. But it wasn't about my parents or me being a child. It was about me…being an angel." In my head it didn't sound at all weird but when I expressed the dream verbally, it made me question my own sanity.

Brycin burst into laughter.

My eyebrows pulled together tight and I glared at him and his reaction. "See, you're casting judgment!"

"Ha, no! I'm not. I just can't see how *that* made you so happy." he said, laughing harder after every word. "Plus, why is that worth lying about?"

"Did you not hear how crazy it sounds?"

"Some dreams aren't supposed to be rational."

"Yeah but the *irrational* ones aren't supposed to make your depressive thoughts invisible."

"Was the dream irrational to you?" He inquired.

My expression softened. "No. Not really."

It annoyed me. This new and understanding persona he was displaying. I should be relieved that he is being so reasonable and understanding but I wasn't. Oddly, I wanted him to fight me on this because that was the reaction I was expecting.

"Aren't *brothers* supposed to be understanding?" he asked, placing his hand on my shoulder.

"Yesterday you weren't."

"And I apologize. I was just…" he trailed off, something outside grabbing his attention.

"What?" I asked following his eyes.

It appeared as though Frankie and Jakob were fist fighting. I rushed out of the car. When I reached them, I was just as surprised as everyone else. Nature would have deemed Frankie victorious based on size but it was Jakob who hovered Frankie.

"What happened?" I asked watching Frankie slowly rise to his feet,

"I was trying to tell him that Jakob bumped into me on accident. But he pushed Jakob and before we knew it, Frankie was on the ground." Emma explained, her scowl targeted toward Jakob.

Brycin walked up beside me. He glowered at Jakob also. "You know."

"But he—"Jakob lashed out.

They exchanged looks, communicating in a language all their own with their eyes. Jakob pushed past us, ramming his shoulder into Brycin and walked toward his car.

Just as fast as we got here, everyone was packing to leave. I watched as my last visit to Crater Lake rushed to an end. I was never going to get the chance to come here again. I would never be able to soak in the refreshing aroma from the lake. I would never hear the soothing sounds of the wind swaying through the trees, ringing the bristles on the branches and contributing to the natural symphony Mother Nature conducted. I would only get the suburban chirp life from birds which would never fully connect to the scenery around them.

"Kay, if you don't come on, I swear, I will leave you! I swear it!"

The rage in Jakob's voice was peculiar. Jakob was never the type to take anything serious. I wasn't absolutely positive if it was Frankie he was pissed at or Brycin.

The drive back to the campus was an awkward one. It was a silent one. Frankie sat where I previously sat, holding a rag with ice in it to his lip. Brycin looked overwhelmed with frustration and annoyance. Though everyone appeared annoyed and angry with each other, that was only the here and now emotions they felt. As soon as tomorrow dawned, everyone was going to be happy with each other like nothing ever happened and the subject would never come up. It was a very Hollywood relationship. Something you saw on television and dreamt about.

When we arrived to the university, Frankie and Jakob made up and were again laughing. It happened sooner than I expected but still, I knew it would. Claire rolled her eyes when she saw them laughing and playing and I heard her say "boys" underneath her breath.

Brycin and James, who was for the most part in the background, were talking. Claire and Jennifer were trapped in a deep conversation.

Emma and Amber were discussing beauty topics. Everything seemed as it should be.

I was leaning up against my car, staring into the space above that was painted in beautiful colors. It appeared as if there was a war between the colors, a great divide, a fight for dominance. The dark and cool colors of space pushed the bright and warm colors further and further behind the horizon. Symbolically, I assigned the Neatholytes to the warmth of the sky and the Demilytes to the coolness of the space. In that instant, I wanted the warm colors to rise over the dark colors and claim the sky.

I watched as the stars slowly started to sparkle up the night sky one by one, interrupting the train my thoughts seemed to be on. My thoughts suddenly took aboard a different train. I couldn't help but picture thousands of half-breeds flying across the sky. Complete freedom. A carefree lifestyle. Able to go anywhere whenever you want. No rules to live with.

A depression-free life.

Maybe that was the message behind my dream. No matter how much it tries, my seas of despair would never get the chance to destroy me ever again. And the only way it could was if I dove into the waters and submitted. I would never submit.

"What are you thinking about?" Brycin asked walking up to me.

"Hmmm…what it must be like to be a half-breed." I answered still looking up in the sky.

I heard him let out a deep sigh. I looked down at him and his face was toward the ground. "You really need to let go of what that guy said. Your dream, too." He then looked back up at me. "I'm not so sure if it's healthy anymore."

It was as if the entire life essence of my body had been drained. The veins in my body ran dry and for a split second, I hated Brycin. "What was all that this afternoon? All that talking about it was completely rational?"

"It was nonsense. You thinking like *this* is *nonsense*. It's not healthy to dwell on this fantasy of yours."

"Fantasy?" I hissed. "Since when did questioning become a fantasy? Are you really persecuting me for a spike in interest?"

He stepped forward, inches away from my face. "I'm trying to protect—" he suddenly stopped. "Nothing." He relaxed himself and back off a little. "You'll never understand."

"Humor me."

He shook his head. "You'll *never* understand." he hissed the word never at me and turned back toward the others.

"And you call yourself a best friend? A brother?" I questioned him, scowling him as he marched back toward me.

"I have been there for you more than necessary." He stated pressing his index finger against my chest.

"I never asked you to, did I?" Before I realized the words, I saw how deep they cut. But I didn't feel the guilt that I should have felt. He cut just as deep.

It was stupid to fight with him on stuff like this. It wasn't worth the friendship we built.

"What's the matter with you?"

His jaw tightened and his posture stiffened. I saw over his shoulder that Claire was coming over.

"Kayden? Brycin? Is everything okay?" She asked empathetically.

"Everything's fine." He barked, leaving me and Claire with his lie.

She watched him as he left. My eyebrows were pulled tight together. "You do know he cares?"

She looked back at me and examined my stance and expression. My hands were clenched tight into fists, now angry at her for siding with him. I couldn't be mad at her though. She didn't do anything wrong.

Just concerned.

I let out a deep sigh and loosened my fists. "Yeah I know. It just irritates me how he treats me. He doesn't treat me like his friend or his brother. He doesn't treat me like an equal. He isn't that older than me. Just one year. Wow!" I stated facetiously. She laughed but it was before I said wow. Did I say something funny before that? I shoved the question from my head. "But anyways, he treats me more like…like a…"

"Child?"

"Yeah!" I shouted, not intending to sound enthused about it. "Sorry. But that's how I feel."

"He's very protective over people he comes across. I have gotten used to it over the years."

I never questioned how long they knew each other prior to just now. "How long have you guys known each other?"

"For awhile." She answered.

I was beginning to feel serene again. The softness of her mellow pitched voice was soothing. I knew she was right and I hated it. I hated his overprotective traits. I felt more trapped by my own friend than my unexplainable life.

She looked over her shoulder at Brycin as he slid into his black Toyota Camry. "Just a matter of time." I heard her say under her breath.

"Before what?"

She looked at me as if I wasn't supposed to hear her. "Before he will let his guard down over you. There are just some things that are happening in his life that he doesn't want to get you involved in. He loves you a lot. More than you see. He's protecting you from himself more than anything else."

I couldn't help but think the worst. What was he going through? Drugs? Could he have some deadly disease and not tell me? There was that wave of guilt washing over me. I wanted to run and tell him sorry but he was long gone. "I'm sorry. I will try and behave. I promise."

"Just no more of this thinking. Brycin finds it discomforting." I couldn't believe how much she knew. I tried not to let the feeling of betrayal express through my eyes.

"But why? It's…nonsense. Why is it so appalling to him? Why does he feel like ripping my head off whenever I talk about it?"

"I'm sure he has his reason. I would rather he tell you. In fact, he would rather he tell you, whatever it is. Just be patient. He *will* tell you. He has no choice."

Before I could even ask her what was that supposed to mean, she was half way across the lot. I pressed my back against the trunk of my car and inhaled deeply, taking in the oncoming night air, then, exhaled deeper.

Everyone was leaving now. I watched as they departed, waving to each other as they did so.

They had all left the lot. All except Frankie. He was just pulling out of his parking spot. As he passed by, he came to a stop and rolled his passenger window down. "You okay?" He sort of yelled from the driver's side.

Another shocker for the day. Frankie I never saw as the type who cared about the feelings of others either. With the way he talked about girls and especially after the little episode both him and Jakob pulled today. But there was complete sincerity in his eyes. Had I not been around them for that long that they've all developed new personalities — tolerable personalities? "Yeah I am fine. I am about to leave now."

He nodded and drove off.

The truth was, I wasn't okay. I just hurt my best friend unintentionally. There was something going on that rested deeper than what everyone was telling me. I felt so trapped. Kept in the dark like a child.

I tilted my head back and stared into the sky's abyss. The moon was beginning to shine against the darkening blues. Surrounding it where smaller freckles of light. The night air was cool and refreshing. I let the small breeze molest my skin, causing the small hairs on my arm to rise up and the emptiness of the lot added to the serene effect. No voices, no laughter. Silence.

I closed my eyes and allowed the calming sensation to invade my body and cool my blood. My heart was slowing and the veins in my body pulsated with warm blood again.

I brought my head back down and I moved to the driver's side of my car, opened the door and slid in. The air escaped inside with me and I was thankful for that because its calming powers were still in effect.

I twisted my keys in the ignition and listened as the car purred softly. It was as though my car was just as calmed by the night's air as I was. I pulled out the parking lot and drove home, with the night air keeping my mind and thoughts in control.

When I got home, Rachel was cooking chicken parmesan. The smell was inviting as soon as I set foot in the house. The overpowering garlic, fresh basil leaves, and ripe tomatoes from Rachel's homemade pasta sauce lingered in every area of the house. I walked in on her as she was topping two fully loaded plates of food with cheese. It wasn't until Rachel looked up at me that I realized I was salivating heavily.

Rachel laughed her goddess like laugh. "Hungry I see."

"Maybe just a little." I laughed. I never realized that I hadn't gotten the chance to eat anything at all. My stomach was pounding against everything inside of me, demanding food. I sat at the table and purged the contents sitting on my plate. Rachel made small jokes about how I was eating but I wasn't really paying attention.

I had eaten everything so fast, that my stomach was aching now. I grabbed the small glass of grape juice that I never seen Rachel sit in front of me and consumed everything in it.

"I have never seen you eat so much. And so fast." She stated smiling.

It always made her happy whenever I appreciated her cooking. It gave her purpose to be the mom she was always destined to be. "Yeah, we really didn't get a chance to eat anything. Frank and Jake got into a small altercation and it ended the day early."

"I bet they were all fun and games later on, huh?"

She knew them better than I thought. "Yep." I smiled at her and she smiled back.

"So Brycin called twice before you arrived." She was pushing for something. I searched her eyes for some intimation of what she was talking about. "You two at each other's throat again?"

I shook my head slowly. "He just thinks I'm being stupid because I am looking too much into some legend a substitute had shared with our Theology class on Thursday."

"Well I don't think that there is anything wrong with believing in legends. Unless you join a cult that's going around killing people who don't believe in it." I hinted a smile but it wasn't as funny as she meant for it to sound. "Believe in whatever you want. I know he's your best friend and all but there comes a point when he needs to back off and-"

"Mom, he means no harm." It wasn't me defending him that caught her off guard, but because I called her 'mom.' It shocked me as well. I haven't called her mom in almost three years.

She nodded and shoved herself away from the table. "As long as it's not making you feel uneasy."

I could see under her expressionless face that she was smiling. I rose from the table, shoved my dish into the sink with the dishes she was washing and I kissed her cheek. "Good night." I whispered.

"Good night, Kayden."

I pulled my bag from the base of the stairs and ran to my room, closing the door behind me. I sat on the edge of my bed for a moment. I then threw myself back on the bed, letting out a deep sigh. I stared at my ceiling and wished for just one night I could sleep with the moon and the stars. Having the night air there to keep me calm as I slept soundlessly. I didn't want any angels tonight. No demons. Just peace.

I kicked off my shoes and pulled myself back up to a sitting. I reached down to pick my shoes up, my eyes flickering to my desk, immediately catching a glimpse of something resting on it.

I left my shoes where they were and walked over to the desk. It was a slice of paper...no bigger than a business card.

It was flipped over so that whatever was written on it was facing down. I slowly picked it up and turned it over. It was the address that I threw to the ground yesterday.

How did it get in here? Instantaneously, the powerful curiosity I felt for knowing more about the legend yesterday had returned.

I had forgotten about how much I wanted to know more about the legend. Who all knew about this legend? Just because no one I knew heard of it, was it that less of a popular legend? I was sure that wherever Portman was from, it had to be famous there. Did the human's who knew before, now know? Was the legend passed down from those individuals?

What I really wanted to know was what did some of his statements mean. Regarding me and knowing about the legend.

Tomorrow is Saturday. Maybe I will go and visit this address.

Chapter 3: The Visit

UPON AWAKEING, I REALIZED THAT THE DAY POSSESSED a very unusual and disturbing sensation. There were numerous reasons to why I *could* have felt like this today. It could have been due to the storm that was brewing outside my window. Trees thrashed from side to side and back and forth. Leaves and debris flew faster than a bullet shot out of a Hawk 7. The sky wasn't a light gray or a middle gray. It was nearly black. The clouds were a very dark gray and its eerie presence would force Rachel to shield me inside. Knowing her, and I did, she was going to come up with some creative way to take advantage of the situation. Probably a movie day or a festival of board games.

I watched the storm outside my window, waiting for the first droplet of water to stain the pavement in a dark gray or black. I waited for the deafening thunder and ferocious lightning to accompany the harsh winds but the storm teased. It was showing the city of Corvallis that if this is the amount of power it has with just its winds, *imagine* what it can do with everything else. The dark clouds didn't even seem to be moving — as if the storm had made its permanent residence here in Corvallis.

Or this uneasy feeling could have been because of the crushing secret that rested in my chest. A secret that could rip the walls of Rachel's heart to shreds. If she ever found out that I had gone back to Crater Lake, who knew what the ramifications would be, the degree of hurt Rachel would fell after she found out that I sat on our rock?

But I knew the real reasons behind my anxiety. One: how did the note Professor Portman presented to me days ago mysteriously end up in my room on my desk. Rachel was the only person other than me who had a key to the house. Even if someone was to come in here, placing a note at my desk would be the last thing on their mind. In fact, it would never cross their mind. Only two people could have placed it there. One of them I had already ruled out because he hated the idea of me going. Why would he lead me to the person who would overstuff me with something he felt was ridiculous? That left only one person. Portman. But how? He didn't even know where I lived. So who was left?

I let out a long sigh after my mind had slowed to a stop from all of the attempts of figuring out.

The second source of my anxious mood came from knowing that I was going to pay Portman a visit today. No matter what the weather was like outside, I wasn't going to rest until Portman and I discussed the causes of my fanatic thoughts. Something he said had stuck with me ever since that day. It's the real reason why I can't let any of this go. *You don't need a reason.* I replayed the words in my head. What did he mean exactly by that? There was something deeper behind his meaning and today, I was going to find out.

There was only one thing that stood in my way of that happening. Rachel. I was sure that she would lunge herself in between me and the door as soon as I grabbed hold of the doorknob. I can hear her asking me have I seen the outside. But I wasn't going to let up until I was on the other side of the entrance door, finding shelter in my car from the callous winds. And I knew she wasn't going to give in until I refused to fight any longer and find refuge in my room where I would be warm and in bed.

I had to try.

As I was coming down the stairs, Rachel was rushing. She gracefully sped walk like a gazelle to the coat rack and grabbed her coat. She threw the jacket over her shoulders and forced her arms through the sleeves. Her face was hardly relaxed and something was annoying her.

"Where are you going?" I asked, trying to sound as needful of her presence as possible.

"I have to go down to the office. One of my client's is being harassed by her husband again. I swear I won't rest until his ass is behind bars." This side of Rachel was very aggressive, a side I was unaccustomed to when I'd first met her. She was recently working on a case involving a woman trapped in a violent relationship. The number one thing she hated. She hated men who treated women like property and felt that there were no validations for hitting a woman. After Michael's death, she was forced to be more independent and this aggressive side of her emerged more dominant than ever.

"Oh." I didn't try to sound sad but I did. I just wasn't expecting to confront her without a fight.

"Oh, sweetie, I promise I will be back as soon as possible."

"No, it's fine." I spit the words out. "Brycin was going to come over and we were going to go chill with Claire and the others. It's fine. I promise."

"Okay." She pulled me down by my neck, pulling herself up the rest of the way, and kissed my forehead.

Rachel left and the house echoed with silence. It'd been a while since I was in this house on my own. Everything was so different than my first visit here. Michael's absence affected her in more ways than one. The entertainment center that sat against the wall six years ago, Rachel had gotten rid of. Most of Michael's CD collection she sold along with the oversized television. There was now a more up to date television. It lay flat on the wall with the surround system stretching around the house. The white suede coach and recliner were now almond and included a loveseat. Beige and white and cream pillows were neatly arranged in patterns on the large sofa. Just two white pillows rested on the love seat. The curtains were a dark brown now. The room was too homey, almost sickening. The only thing that separated the common looking family room from normalcy was the silver objects scattered around the room. Round balls, vases, artificial plants and portraits with silvers and black covering the canvases made it seem more personal.

Rachel loved the color silver. It was a simple beauty. It didn't need to be as conspicuous as gold to be beautiful. She loved that quality silver possessed.

After comparing the family room I knew today to the one I missed, I ran back up stairs and grabbed the note. I threw my red sweater over my head and shoved my feet into the black Converses. I was moving faster than necessary. I had nothing to hide. Rachel wasn't here and she wasn't going to be back for a while.

I hurried out my room and down the stairs. Midway down the stairs, a figure brought me to an immediate stop. Brycin.

"What are you doing here?" I asked, almost annoyed because now he became the obstacle in between me and Portman. I had forgotten about the note in my right hand and slowly slid it in my back pocket, shoving my other hand in to the other pocket. I was trying my best not to look so suspicious.

"I bumped into Rachel on my way in. She said it was okay to just walk in."

"Oh, well, I was on my way out."

"Yeah? Where were you going?"

My mind was empty. I had nothing to come up with. He knew that he was the only one I would really hang out with outside the college. Being around the others only came when Brycin invited me. If I said I was going to hang out with any of them, it was very possible that he would ask to go with. And even if he didn't go, he'd ask whoever I brought into this lie what did we do. I had to tell him the truth…

"I was going to go to the college. I have a test for LaBurn due this Wednesday. I figured with nothing to do, I could use the free time I have wisely."

I couldn't tell if he believed me or not. His eyes were vacant. He looked more saddened by the rejection. "Okay. See you at school." He said nodding.

He turned and walked out the front door. Guilt washed over me but it wasn't enough to keep from going to see Portman.

I grabbed my keys from the hook hanging on the wall alongside the staircase and ran out into the wind storm.

The wind was vicious. Debris shot at my face, feeling like little bites from unseen insects. If it wasn't for me forcing my weight to the ground, the wind could have easily swept me off my feet and into the air. My clothes and hair whipped in the direction of the wind violently.

It was a challenge getting the key into the door but once I had it in and the door was locked, getting inside my car was the only thing on my mind.

When I turned, Brycin was walking across the street. I froze, my clothes and hair the only thing moving evidently due to the harsh wind. He walked across the street without any struggling, fluidly. Effortlessly. It was only his clothes which submitted to the fierce winds.

I felt the wind push harder. I ran to my car, flipping through the keys and searching for the right one. The hairs on the top of my head felt like there were going to be removed from the roots in any second.

I hurried into my car and closed the door, using it as a shield so that I was protected by the wind and its ammunition of debris. The little taps hitting against my window were becoming annoying. I hurried my keys into the ignition, brought the car to life, and pressed the power button on my radio, drowning out the annoying little taps.

It'd been a long time since I played the radio in my car. Led Zeppelin was the last thing I was listening to. *Led Zeppelin IV* had been Michael's favorite CD when he was alive. I remember getting into a fight with Rachel when she wanted to sell it.

She was erasing Michael from the entire house. All his fishing equipment, his 1967, black Chevy Impala, the entertainment center, some of his clothes, his CD collection, almost everything. At least with this CD, I could say she never completely erased him.

It wasn't much of a coincidence that his favorite song was playing. *Stairway to Heaven.* It was the perfect song to listen to as I pulled out of the driveway and drove toward the highway that was going to lead me to some answers.

I couldn't help but think to myself as the music played in the background. At first, I actually thought that driving to go see Portman about something completely irrelevant to my life was silly. It was just some legend his "ancestors" passed down through the generations.

But it wasn't the story that I had questions to really. Why did it seem like he felt that he knew me? I sensed that he wanted to tell me more but couldn't because of the public atmosphere. I needed to find out what he knew. He told me that I didn't need a reason to want to know these things. In some way, it sounded like he was telling me that I *needed* to know. But why? How could some myth involving angels and demons have any significance to my life?

Could this myth actually be true? I didn't see how. Angels and demons? Half-breeds? I had better luck believing in Santa Claus.

The drive to the highway was a quick one considering the streets were nearly empty due to the ferocious winds. Light poles were torn from sidewalks, dangling from the power lines they were attached to. But it was far too dangerous for anyone to do anything about them now. Fixing them would have to wait until the storm passed.

I watched as the city slowly shrunk in my rearview and side view mirrors. I drove down the I-20 until I reached the point where it split into the Corvallis Newport Highway and Alsea Highway. The Corvallis I knew was no longer in my mirrors at this point.

I drove several more miles. There were nothing but trees here and there and open fields and an occasional house every so often on the side of the road. Most of the houses were behind these fields or trees. The storm made it somewhat difficult to see anything around me.

The storm seemed to get a lot heavier the more I drove. Rain gradually began to build itself over my windshield. The thunder started booming over the mountains and the lightning peeked brightly through the clouds once in a while. It was building itself up into the perfect thunderstorm. I then began to wonder if I was ever going to see *my* Corvallis again.

Michael's CD continued to give me company even though it was now starting all over again. I removed the slice of paper from out my pocket and stared at the directions in its perfect cursive.

Henkle Way

R. Off Alsea Hwy.

R. On Silverhead Peek.

Only house.

I remembered seeing only Henkle Way on the paper before but never the additional directions that the paper now possessed in the exact same hand writing. They weren't there before.

I shoved the thought out of my head as soon as I noticed Henkle Way was coming up. I did as the slice of paper directed, making a right at Henkle Way. I followed the road about a quarter mile in when I saw the street Silverhead Peek. Again, following the paper's direction, I made another right. I followed the road, waiting to come across the only house on the street. But it seemed to never come. Just acre upon acre upon acre of green pastures. The further I drove, the heavier the storm became. I could barely see the road but my curiosity was overpowering the fear within me. I wasn't going to turn back. Not now.

Finally after fifteen minutes of driving I reached the house. I shut the car off, giving the windshield wipers one last swipe. After clearing my view, the rain wasn't so heavy anymore. They were just little specs that now fell from the dark clouds. I opened the door to my car and the icy winds invaded. *That* made me want to turn back and go home but I had already made the journey. Might as well finish it.

I hopped out of the car and closed the door. I turned toward the house and wondered how a substitute teacher could afford something so regal. It sat on top of the hill, seeming so stationed and secure. It was painted with elegance. The sheer white looked as if rain had never touched it. Pure gold strips outlined the windows and the door frame. It seemed as if all of it didn't even fit into my vision. It was a very wide, two story mansion. He couldn't have been the only one to live in this behemoth of a house.

I walked the pathway to the double doors of the house. I knocked softly on the door but it wasn't soft enough. I can hear my knocks echo through the house. In a matter of seconds, Professor Portman greeted me at the door. "Kayden!" He seemed surprised enough. I waved and he pulled me in. "Come in, come in. Don't want you catching any colds."

I wanted to laugh. I had never caught a cold a day in my life. "Sure."

The inside was nothing compared to the outside. This place was of pure royalty. White marble tiles ran throughout the house. Sculpted lions sat on top of the white wooden poles of the staircase. There was a gold strip that ran up the stair rail and ended with another sculpted lion. Portraits hung all over the place. I had never seen or heard of them before. There were two openings in the front of the house excluding the staircase in front of me. There was one on the right side of the staircase and one to the left. It was so bright in the house compared to outside. I couldn't take my eyes off of any of it.

"Do you want coffee?" He said walking toward the hole in the wall to the right.

I was focused again. I couldn't waste time. I had to get this over with. "Actually," he turned as soon as the word was out. "I'm on a bit of a time frame."

He nodded and walked towards me. He went through the hole on the left instead. I followed. The living room put the entrance of the house to shame. The white marble tile continued through here. Sculptures of Greek legends were everywhere. There was a divine fireplace made out of the same marble tile that Rachel would have killed to have in our home. Paintings covered the walls. The furniture was breathtaking. The sofa was a beautiful magnolia white. It had a matching chaise with golden pillows scattered on it in a non-particular way. There were two side tables painted the same white. They were round in shape with a clear glass resting within the inner rim of the table. In front of the sofa was a large coffee table. It had two square pieces of glass separated by a white line and they rested within the rim of the table. It sat on top of a black bear rug that made me shiver because of the memories it awakened. It looked like the home for a true king.

"I take it you want to talk about the subject I presented to your class the other day."

His voice broke the hypnotic trans the masterpiece of the living room had me under and my attention was now focused on him and what I needed to know. "Uhh, yeah. Who lives here?" I couldn't help myself as I blurted the question out.

The question seemed rude and inappropriate at the time but he seemed to take no offense to it. "Just myself."

"But you're a teacher."

He chuckled at the obvious observation. "Are we here to talk about legends or my estate?" he said with a smile. He wasn't angry with me at all. Had that been anyone else, I probably would have been thrown out by guards. No. Royal knights. That was more fitting for this place.

"Sorry."

I swiftly recognized that I was the only one here. "Didn't you say you hold a class or something like that?"

His jaw tightened slightly. "Yes, but I canceled on everyone else just for you today. You seemed a lot more interested than anyone else I've ever introduced the subject to."

"Yeah." I replied, my eyes trailing to the floor.

He walked over to the sofa and sat. I stood, still baffled by what I was in. "Well, what do you want to know?"

I crossed my arms around my chest and took a deep breath. "Everything."

"And exactly what is everything?"

I didn't like the beating around the bush. I just wanted to know everything now. "Everything you know. There seemed to be some things you wanted to say when we first met but didn't or…couldn't. Why? What more is there to that story?"

"Nothing to *that* story." There was that emphasis on words again. "*That* story is completely false."

My eyes burned with disbelief. I came all the way here for nothing. For him to tell me that the legend was a false legend. My blood seemed to be getting hotter, overflowing with rage.

"It was just a story people made up to justify everything that was happening at the time. They blamed God for the infiltration of half-breeds. They thought he had disowned them all. That he wanted them all dead because the world was so corrupted. But God had nothing to do with the outburst of half-breeds."

"So there is a legend?"

He was about to speak but he froze with his mouth half open. I watched as his facial expression change dramatically. It wasn't inviting anymore. His eyebrows lowered and his lips took on the form of a smirk. He laughed. It was a devious laugh. His entire aura of goodness had undergone complete depletion. He was a new person now. "Your angel will tell you soon."

"What?" I couldn't even begin to decode the meaning of that statement. Now it was obvious. He *was* hiding something. I wanted to know and he wasn't telling me fast enough. I was becoming annoyed.

His face was tense and serious, stone-like. He shook his head and folded his arms. "You shouldn't be here."

What? How could he go from being so content to malevolent in less than a few seconds? "Did you forget that you invited me here?" I questioned him. His lips twitched a little but that's the only reaction I received.

He stood and walked toward the entrance of the living room. I followed him, wanting to know what was the matter with him. *Had I* succeeded in offending him? When I reached the entrance way to the living room, he was holding one of the doors to the house open. He was kicking me out.

"Out."

What else could I to do? I exited the manor, leaving my dignity on the other side of those doors.

I jumped into the Charger, bringing it to life with the turn of my key. I could feel each individual wrinkle in my forehead emerge as my eyebrows pulled together. I was far beyond annoyed. No word could describe the magnitude of loath I felt toward Portman as of right now. I wanted to beat the legend out of him.

No. I wanted to create enough distance between myself and the house and push this car to full gear. I wanted to see the gauges on my dash board break due to a speed beyond the limit of which this car was allowed. I wanted to crash *this* car into the walls of *that* house. But someone with this grand of a house could afford the best lawyer money could buy.

I put the car in reverse, turned it around, and headed back down Silverhead Peek Road.

Michael's favorite song was on again. Not even that could cool the fire that ran heavy in my veins.

The storm seemed to pick back up as I drove toward home. Everything the storm was capable of now had emerged. The vociferous thunder cracked with a loud boom strong enough to crumble a mountain. The fierce lightning licked the ground like venom and destructive winds snapped the trunks of thin trees effortlessly. I drove fearful of the storm, afraid that the wind would become strong enough to tip my car over.

Even though these mighty forces of nature struck fear in me, I knew I was safe. I knew that the thunder's roars couldn't do much harm to my ears as long as I was inside my car. I knew that the lightning would never get the chance to taste my skin and I knew that the winds could not carry me off into the skies.

But the rain I couldn't succumb to. The windshield wipers were no match against the ocean forming on top of my windshield. I thought many times to just pull over and allow the monsoon to let up just a fraction but I was still too angry to just sit and wait. I needed to be at home. I need to be in my bed so I can dream hateful dreams that were of me destroying Portman.

The visit hadn't gone the way I had planned. I *expected* to arrive to some nice apartment or a not-so-bad house. He would welcome me in and dish me out everything I wanted and needed to know about these legends. But clearly that was nowhere near the case at all.

I took a deep breath and gathered my thoughts.

So the legend Portman presented prior to this visit was a false one, a manifestation of the humans hate for the infiltration of half-breeds. Which conclusively meant that another, if any, legend existed.

Okay, that made sense. But what did *your angel will tell you soon* entail? Was he admitting that they *were* in fact real? If so, why is it so hard to say so? And what could *my* angel mean?

I grunted. It was all so mind-boggling, head-aching and frustrating.

It must've come from attempting to unveil everything I was presented with, but in that instant, I realized where this fascination for these creatures came from. I hadn't thought of it in the longest time but it had to be.

After Michael's death, every night for almost seven months, I dreamt of people relatively similar to this, now, false legend. Some had wings of a bird and others had bat-like wings. They fought endlessly in my dreams, battling for dominance over the skies.

Whenever they fought, a storm would emerge. The clouds would become a deep, dark gray and shadow everything it touched…Similar to the one outside my window…

It had to be only a coincidence.

Every dream ended the same way. In complete silence. All of them lay on the ground lifeless. Some, wings broken and others scorched. Death became all of their fate. All of them except for one. The shadows shrouded his wings and blackened his figure. So I never knew if he was a bird or a bat. The shadows made him a shadow. All I could make out of this mysterious creature were his eyes. One glowed white and the other shimmered a crimson red.

That was why I needed to know so badly. I dreamt of these creatures without anyone ever telling me of their existence as a kid. Now that I know who they were, I now needed to know why I knew them before three days ago.

I was relieved, happy even when I hit the corner of my street but that happiness instantaneously vanished when I noticed two cars in front of my house instead of one. Rachel's car was parked in the driveway but alongside the curb in front of our house sat a black Toyota Camry. Brycin was here. He must've gone to the school and saw that I wasn't there, called Rachel and asked her of my whereabouts. She must've gone frantic, consumed by worry because I told her I was going to be with him today. She hurried home, frightened, the possibility of the loss of something precious to her now questionable. I would never forgive him for this.

I pulled into the driveway, perturbed to what waited for me beyond those doors. Would she be worried and crying as I enter? It would be like seeing a ghost.

I opened the door and heard the opposite of crying, the opposite of a frantic mother. Laughter? I walked into the kitchen and Brycin and Rachel were…laughing. There was no sign of worrying. She saw me and came to hug me. "Hey, sweetie. You aren't cold are you?"

Why didn't she question me on why Brycin was here without me? Instead of blurting out something that could possibly get me in trouble, I decided to let it all play out. "No. I'm fine." I said plainly.

"I told Rachel that I had gone to the University with you and helped you study for LaBurn's test and that you wanted to look something up before you left and that you would meet me here."

I stared blankly into Brycin's eyes. He knew. But didn't scold me on it. He was rather calm about it all, not a glimpse of hate or disappointment in his eyes. "Oh."

"So," Rachel began, walking back to the seat she came from at the center bar. My gaze was still stuck on Brycin. I waited for just a flicker of hate to flash in his eyes. I know he was angered to some sort of degree. I know he was. But…I could not tell. "Bryce was just telling me of your trip to Crater Lake yesterday."

My head snapped in her direction now. My eyes were full of worry. My heart was hammering savagely.

"Why didn't you tell me? I would love to know what it looks like now. I haven't been there in a while because," she paused and I could see it pained her as the images replayed in her mind. "Well you know why and *I* don't plan to go back. But I think that it's nice that you went. You really loved that place when you were young. I shouldn't stop you from going just because of me."

What was going on with everyone today? Was there a bug going around that I was immune to? Brycin seemed rather mellow, Rachel was understanding and Portman was a complete jerk to me today. It had to be a bug. A bug that inverted the innate reactions of someone.

I continued to stare at Rachel now, nervous and on the verge of a nervous breakdown. She pulled her wrist to her face and read her watch. "Well I will leave you boys. I need to wind down for a bit." She kissed me on my cheek and headed upstairs. The warmth behind her kiss kind of washed away the heavy apprehensiveness that seemed to overpower my body.

I watched her as she walked up the stairs. I listened for the room door to close. Once I heard it, I turned back to Brycin. If looks could kill, his now scolding eyes would have given me a repetitive death, painful and blistering. His jaw was tight and his eyes barely narrowed but the hate in his eyes burned brighter than the lightning flashing outside. "I knew you were lying to me as soon as you told me where you were going."

"Bryce, look, I am completely capable of taking care of myself. I *am* an adult."

"You have no idea what that world is like out there."

"And I suppose you do?"

"I know enough."

"Yeah I forgot that. I forgot that you seem to know everything. What's best for me, what the world is like. Just how you know that me believing in some useless legend is somehow harmful." I stated sarcastically, all of it almost in a single breath.

"Well forgive me for looking out for a friend." he murmured.

"Looking out for me? You're practically smothering me. Back off some, dude."

"This world is vicious and will destroy you the chance you let it."

"The only thing destroying me now is your paranoia!" I hissed, aware of Rachel who was upstairs. The last thing I needed was for her to play judge, jury and attorney. "Do you want history to repeat itself? You practically pushed me off the last cliff…wanna do it again?"

I left him speechless. I had finally won a fight against him. I hated that I had to use that incident but I had to cut as deep as possible in order for him to understand me.

His eyes possessed a deathly quality to them. As if he *were* dead, a corpse who died with open eyes, the terror of the death still portrayed through them.

"This overprotective nature you have has got to stop. Or I can't be your friend anymore."

That seemed to hurt. But it was the truth. He was too overprotective and I hated it. I felt like I couldn't eat, couldn't sleep, couldn't drink without him feeling like I would choke on something, or never wake up, or drown from the beverage. He was rubbing his fingers against his forehead. If it wasn't for me feeling so strong about this, his saddened expression would have flooded my body with guilt.

"Have you ever noticed that even though we are so close of friends, you know nothing about me? My family? Where I came from?"

I pondered on the thought. I couldn't believe it. He was right. The only thing I knew about him personally was little things like his passion for swimming, that he wanted to be a psychologist and that his birthday was March eighth.

I nodded after realizing this. For some reason I felt like the walls that were holding the flood of guilt at bay were about to burst.

"I had a brother once. A mother and father, too. We were the perfect family you could say. My father was in the army and my mom looked after us. Most of our wealth came from inheritance.

"My brother and I were very close. He was the most important person to me." I felt the guilt seeping through, the pressure of the flood growing, creating cracks. I could feel the walls put up a good fight against the flood but…my barriers were failing. "But one day, when he wanted to go hang out with some friends, who I didn't like; he fought me on it. He said that I was being too paranoid and too protective, that I should stop being his father and start being his brother. I turned my back on him that day and let him do whatever it was he wanted.

"Days had gone by and not only hadn't my brother been seen but neither of his friends either. When we noticed him and his friends' consistent absence from home, we went looking for them. Several miles away from our home, we found him and his friends. All of them lay lifeless on the ground. Breathless. My brother died that day. All because I didn't protect him as I good as I could have." And there it was. The gates keeping the guilt from invading my body seized and guilt washed through me like a raging river.

"You have become my brother in more ways than one." I watched with sympathetic and guilt filled eyes as he talked using his hands to help his story flow. "I never told you because it hurts to bring it up. Knowing that I could have done something to prevent his death. So there are times when I know that the things you are getting yourself into are going to lead to something you may not get out of. I lost one brother once. I can't lose another one. If I lose you, I won't make it." I never seen him so close to tears before.

I took a deep breath and closed my eyes. I didn't know where to begin or even *how* to begin. He'd just explained his reasons for overprotecting me. And I somewhat understood. But was it still necessary? I'm here now. I'm safe. There is no need for protecting something that is, for the most part, always going to be all right. But I couldn't let him know that that's how I felt.

"So...what happened to your parents?" I asked, hating that I wanted to know more but couldn't help the need to know more.

"Well, let's just say that they knew exactly who murdered my brother and his adolescent friends. They went after them. Revenge was all they wanted. Justice. They never returned." The last sentence he let out with a sigh. It was almost as if the air was the only way to get the words out. "And it didn't take me long before I was able to piece it all together and figure out who was behind all of this. So, I had gone after them.

"They'd left me all alone and with nobody. Everything I held dear was gone. They were going to pay.

"I barely escaped with my life. I *wish* I had died that day. It was harder to *live* without them, especially my brother. A fate, to me, far worse than death."

If there was enough room in my blood stream, more guilt would have invaded it. My veins pulsed with pain and remorse and betrayal. I wanted to end my life for forcing him to go back in time and reanimate the events that haunted him. I only lost one important person. He had lost three. My eyes wandered toward the ceiling, as if I could see through it and see Rachel; lying in bed, peaceful and warm. I couldn't even imagine losing her too.

"Who were they? The ones who—" It pained me to even think the word. It was going sting much harder when I said it. "*Killed* your family." I winced after the word was out.

"A ruthless and heartless gang." he said through his teeth. "There were too many of them to take on. Twenty. I counted their faces when I confronted them. They terrorized everything wherever they went. Everyone thought them to be just some made up urban myth. Some even used them as bedtime stories to scare their kids into going to sleep."

I soaked in everything he was telling me. From now on, I was going to try my best to put less of a grievance on him.

Few more hours had past and we had talked about everything I didn't know about him. Where did he live when all of this happened? I noticed that he stalled before answering *that* question. I figured it was just so hard to remember everything. He told me he was born outside the states but never clarified where.

His brother was three years younger than him when he died. With all of the inheritance left over from his grandparents and parents, he used it to move to Corvallis, buy a home and car, and register in Oregon State University.

It was almost midnight and the storm, after pounding Corvallis with its power, had softened. The rain drizzled and the thunder was softer than a kitten's purr.

Brycin pulled himself away from the bar. He removed his keys from his pockets, the chiming of the keys disrupting the silence that shrouded the room awkwardly for more than five minutes. It wasn't that we didn't have anything to say, it was just that the conversation had reached a point of discomfort. I asked him how did the gang kill his family. I didn't mean to ask *that* question. It was just one of the questions that manifested when he opened his life up for discussion. But when I ran out of questions, it shoved its way out my mind and projected off my lips.

He told me that he didn't know. That when he saw his brother and his friends, bones were broken and blood was everywhere. No bullet wounds, no stab wounds. Nothing. I couldn't imagine how this gang could have killed ten kids without any use of a weapon. How could not one escape? He also said that he found his mom and dad the same way.

There were two things worse than imagining these corpses lying dismembered on the ground with ruby red fluid gushing from them. The first thing was the way Brycin's voice broke whenever he described them. Hearing the pain in his voice as he described it to me was unbearable, a pain I never wanted him to experience again.

The second thing was imagining this young Brycin seeing his family, looking down at them and their gruesome death. How he couldn't tear his eyes off of their bodies. Not because of the repugnant death his family portrayed, but because it was *his* family. The disbelief that washed over him like a tsunami.

My face was apologetic as he lifted from his stool and headed toward the door. "I'll, uhmm...I'll see you later." The door opened and the icy wind invaded the house. The hairs on the back of my neck stretched from their roots but it wasn't enough to stretch my thoughts away from the stupidity I felt trapped in.

I catapulted from my seat with rage. I wanted to throw myself from the tallest building the world had to offer. I spoke profane words as I stomped my way up the stairs but I was cautious not to slam the door because Rachel would have stormed into my room, asking me things like what's the matter and what can she do to help. I didn't have time to tell her that I was the antagonist of *this* story.

I took off my black jeans and tossed them into the closet over my shoes. I pulled myself into the bed and wrapped the comforter over my head. The icy howl of the wind that had picked up power and the rain that tapped against my window was my lullaby. I drifted into a deep slumber. I didn't even find peace there tonight.

Chapter 4: The Nightmare

SHADOWS WERE EVERYWHERE, CASTING THEMSELVES on everything in front of me. They touched and communicated in a language only known to them. I looked up and the clouds were dark and spine-chilling. I was standing in a wasteland. The soil was dry and hard with cracks scattering in every direction. Nothing green took residence here.

The wind blew my clothes and hair in every direction. The sand traveling on the winds grazed against my skin. But the sand wasn't the reason I couldn't see. It was the eerie shadows the black clouds created over this land.

I looked all around me but there was nothing. Emptiness and shadows and dirt in every direction. I questioned if I was even turning around.

The earth and sky began to rumble and everything began to quake. But as quick as the rumble came, it left. Afraid that the ground would crumble beneath me, I slowly step with one foot at a time. After feeling that the ground was secure enough, I started walking the forever plain, hoping to come across some evidence of life. I knew the chances of that were slim.

The earth and sky rumbled in unison again, and again it faded. It was as if the earth was breathing. But the fear the earth planted within me wasn't enough to keep me from moving on.

I hadn't noticed that my walk had quickened. I was soon running and my panting was my only company. The sound of my feet colliding with the ground with every step was all I wanted to hear. The sound of my heavy breathing and footsteps disrupted the conversation of the shadows and I didn't care. This land was of little importance to me. I wanted to go home.

I was running faster than I had ever imagined possible. The dryness of my throat, the short breaths, the sweat in palms and even the warm, painful sensation that ached my muscles satisfied me. I didn't care about the wind throwing sand at me, trying to slow me down. I kept running and I kept my pace. I ran to my escape. I wasn't going to stop. I refused.

I was suddenly forced to a halt. Something flew over me, an isolated shadow. I looked up in to the black blanket of cloud that shrouded this world. I didn't see anything up there. Even if there was something up there, I wouldn't see it against the clouds. I didn't feel any type of hope in escaping this haunting, inhospitable wasteland.

A surge of fear suddenly infected my body. I heard…breathing… coming from in front of me. I felt frozen, afraid to even bring my head down to see what was it that presented itself to me.

The sweat on my brow turned icy. Fear had undergone complete saturation, infecting every vessel in my body. I dropped my attention from the sky and ahead of me.

I didn't know what this *thing* was. It looked like a man with his head down but it appeared as though the shadows around him…created him. The figures body wasn't still. Though *it* didn't move, the shadowy, black flames swirling and dancing off his body gave him motion.

Its head twitched and I flinched. Running was no option. If I did run from this monster, where would I hide? There was nothing to hide behind, nothing to hide under. There was nowhere to go.

When it finally started to move, I could taste the fear resting on my tongue. It was bitter and I wanted to spit it out.

Its head lifted and I stared at the white and red glowing objects on his face. They were his eyes. There was such purity in his white eye. Peace and hope. It suppressed the fear in me a little.

But when I transferred my attention from his glowing white eye to his crimson glowing red eye, it augmented the fear already lingering in my blood.

My palms were sweatier than before. I was soaking in my sweat. I could feel the dirt sticking to the sweat on my face. I could only imagine how dirty it looked.

There was a knot forming in my throat. If this entity didn't kill me, my throat bursting into little pieces surely would be suffice. I couldn't control the shakes my body seemed to undergo. I was trembling in fear, afraid of the blackness that shape shifted into a man.

This was the demon from my dreams long ago. The demon I would dream about every night after Michael's death. I hadn't had this nightmare in years. But *this* wasn't the same nightmare. Just the same demon. There were no birds or bats fighting in the air. But with as black as the clouds were, they probably were up in the sky, fighting for dominance; I just couldn't see them.

"Kayden!"

I couldn't identify if it was the wind calling my name or if it was this demon. My name was spoken deeply and low, perfectly annunciated.

I was frozen again. My mind ran away but my body wouldn't follow. Everything in my head was black. The only things that seem to function were my five key senses. I saw the terror in his red eye stalk me like prey. The saliva in my mouth turned to powder, leaving my mouth icky and dry. The smell of my sweat was tremendous. All of my senses were extra sensitive, yet I couldn't get my body to move at all. I could feel the wind grow icy. I might have mistaken it for the icy touch that came with death. The wind continued to snarl at me, pushing against me cold and fierce. I wondered if the wind was trying to tell me to flee from the fiend.

In an instant, I was forced down to my knees, pressing my sweaty and dirty palms against my ears. The pain was excruciating. The inside of my ears burned and ached as the ringing traveled through the canal, beating against my ear drum mercilessly. I tightened my jaw, trying to fight the sound out of my head. The figure had burst into a raging high pitched scream. The wind blew violently, wiping my clothes and tearing them. The ground was rumbling and I wanted to get away. But the strength of the screams was too intense, preventing my body from moving. It rattled my entire skeleton. I could feel all the blood rush to the back of my body, leaving the front of my body dry and colorless.

The ground continued to rumble. Surges of lightning flashed from the dark clouds and the thunder boomed like a mighty drum. The lightning ripped holes into the wasteland floor. I would have tried to dodge them, considering how close they got to striking me, but I was under the spell of the banshee. My body submitted to the screams. What could I do?

I looked up and the figures mouth was wide. Black winds rushed from his mouth and the anger was intense in both his eyes. Though the demon had no facial properties, where his eyebrows would have come down into a piercing look was easily readable. What struck fear in me more than his eyes, was the event happening behind him. The ground was lifting into the air. All the dirt, all of the rocks, vanished into the abyss above me. The sky was sucking the world into a permanent nonexistence. It was getting closer to me and my demon. The demon kept me trapped by its scream and its gaze. I was helpless. My eyes burned from the wind throwing debris in them but I couldn't close them, afraid that my demon would kill me before the sky would.

It was getting closer.

It was almost here.

My demon vanished in an instant, sucked away into the black vortex that hovered above me. I knew there was no escaping the pull even though I was free from the banshee's scream.

The irresistible force sucked me into the air with the dirt and rocks of my world. I was pulled up by this vortex with my demon, with my shadows. The air in my lungs was gone and I feared it was never returning.

An intense surge of air rushed through my mouth and slammed inside my lungs, catapulting me into a sitting position. It was like the breath of air you would see in movies whenever someone was revived from death. I could see my chest inflating and deflating from the fear I was consumed in by my nightmare. My hands were shaking beneath the blanket. I couldn't ignore my breathing. It was the only thing I could hear in the solitude of my room. I was happy to see my pitiful excuse for a room. My computer, the plain walls, my overly crowded closet of shoes comforted me.

I turned and looked at my clock. Eight minutes after three. It was still dark outside and the trees tapped my window. The wind still lingered. I pulled myself out of bed. I rushed to my door and flung it open letting it bang into the wall. I made it to the bathroom in one stride. I flicked on the light still out of breath. I looked at myself in the mirror. My hair appeared as if the hair in my nightmare traveled into reality. It was messy and all over the place. My eyes were a pale blue, lifeless. More so than ever before. It looked as if I had dipped my head into a pool of water. My neck felt sticky when I ran my hand from the back of my neck to the front and back to the back again.

I turned the knob on the sink marked with a 'C' so that the pipe was gushing out cool water. I pulled my face into the puddle of water that rested in my hands and fiercely scrubbed my face. When I brought my head back up to look at myself in the mirror, I was thrown into the wall behind me, bringing the rack of blue and green patterned towels on the side of me down. I fell to the floor looking for the air that I knew was there but couldn't find. I couldn't breathe. I hadn't seen my reflection at all. At least it didn't look like me. It was my demon. Its blazing white eye and demonic crimson eye stared piercingly back at me.

I sat there on the ground bringing breath into my body. If I was able to measure the amount of air in my body, I probably would have been diagnosed as an asthmatic.

Rachel rushed into the bathroom. Her sudden presence knocked the breath that I had just found back out of me. Cardiac arrest, asthma attack, stroke. I read the possibilities of death I was going to experience at any moment in my head.

Her eyebrows pulled down with sadness. She said my name and I crawled to her, wrapping my arms around her neck.

"My God, you're burning up. And why are you shaking?" She asked me, her voice shaky and full of pain. She rocked with me back and forth. I didn't answer. It's not because I didn't want to. I couldn't. I didn't have enough air in me to speak. "Kayden, talk to me." She demanded, still rocking me in her arms. "Your heart is pounding against my chest." She pointed out, pain possessing her tone.

I had found comfort from her touch. She was restoring rhythm of my breathing. The scent of lavender infiltrated my nose, uniting with the fresh air I was capable of storing in my lungs.

She pulled my face away to look at me. I was literally on the verge of tears. Could today be the day I give into the emotion and the ramifications that came with the emotion? She held my face in between both her hands. There was so much worry in her eyes. "What happened?" She said gazing over my shoulders, looking at the towel rack that lay behind me.

"I...had...a...bad dream." I answered in the form of breaths. It sounded so childlike. But it was the truth. I just couldn't tell her what it was and what happened, how the nightmare invaded my reality.

She pulled me back to her chest, allowing the warmness of her body and the serenity of her touch to revitalize me. There was nothing more I needed. There was no one I could think of to be with right now other than Rachel. I cherished her. She rocked with me all night, until I had fallen asleep in her arms. I never even thought twice about my nightmares returning as I drifted into a slumber within her arms.

I woke up in the strangest place. The bathroom. My ear was pressing against something soft and warm. There was a light thud coming from this object. I turned my head up to see that this wasn't an object. It was Rachel, staring down at me with peace in her eyes. I also found worry in them.

"You scared me last night." the sound of her voice was angelic, harmonic. The light smell of lavender invaded my nostrils as she spoke the words.

"I'm sorry." I replied. I was sorry. I didn't know that my demon was going to follow me into the bathroom. I turned my head back down and pressed my ear lightly on her chest. She laid her head on mine and ran her hands through my messy hair.

"You really scared me." I had already apologized and I would have done it again if my lungs didn't feel so absent of air. "You told me you had a bad dream last night. What was it about?"

Tell her the truth and look crazy in more ways than one? Tell her how I was haunted by shadows and dark clouds? Share the experience of being sucked into nothingness with a nonexistent world? As if she could even begin to fathom with thoughts of me dreaming of demons and them following me into the bathroom, into my reflection. Lying seemed to make everyone happy around me. Well, everyone except for Brycin. But it would be a talent I would soon master.

I took in a deep breath and let it all back out. "I don't remember." I lied, immediately feeling guilty. "Something was after me." I half lied. Now I felt a little better.

"Well you're okay now." She kissed the top of my head.

I embraced her warm kiss and the touch of her fingers running through my shaggy hair. "Thanks. For staying with me." I felt her grip grow tighter around me.

She kissed the top of my head again and I felt her pull away. "I'm going to go get breakfast started. Wash up and I'll meet you downstairs, okay?" She was just as beautiful waking up as she was dressed up. Her dark hair was pulled up into a pony tail. She was wrapped in a white bathrobe and was completely without make-up. Beautiful. My mother. No love could replace her.

She lifted from the ground but not before kissing my head one last time. She walked out the bathroom and I remained motionless on the floor, my back against the wall.

I felt the tears building to a crescendo, wanting to spill over. Again, disappointment washed over me because the sobbing satisfaction I needed teased as usual. Why was this natural ability so hard for me to do? It would make coping with things like this easy.

I wiped the sleep from my eyes and looked up, seeing only the top portion of my bathroom mirror. Anxiety entered my body. What would I do if I saw him again? I couldn't sit here all day. Rachel was cooking for me. She would be expecting me in a few minutes.

I pulled in as much air as my lungs could hold. I mustered up all of the courage that my demon hadn't drained from me and pulled myself up. My reflection was what it was supposed to be. Messy auburn hair, blue eyes and my skin tone looked healthier and brighter. It was what I wanted to see. I sighed in relief and closed the door, leaving myself to get ready for the morning. But as I did this, I couldn't help but feel like someone was watching me; something.

When I emerged from the bathroom, I felt refreshed externally and internally. I nearly forgot about my demon and it was refreshing. My breathing was normal, the shakes were gone and my body temperature felt normal again. My eyes were brighter than ever. Everything was normal. I embraced the smell of hotcakes and bacon and eggs as the scent fluttered throughout the house. I ran down the stairs and greeted

Rachel with a kiss as she was placing the last of my food on a white and gold plate. She smiled and greeted me with a hello.

I sat at the table and wasted no time beginning my feast. That nightmare must have drained everything out my body. I had no energy and my stomach was empty. She sat across from me after filling her plate with food. I grabbed the maple syrup from the center of the table and oozed it over my hotcakes. It wasn't so much as purging, but I was eating a lot faster than Rachel deemed necessary.

My posture froze with the fork half entering my mouth when I saw that she was watching me eat. "What?"

She smiled and braided her fingers above her plate, resting her chin on top of them. "You remind me so much of him." I slowly brought my fork down and slowly wiped the side of my mouth with a napkin. "You are just as sincere. So warm and noble. Kind. Selfless. Handsome."

Was she serious? I didn't consider myself any of those. In fact, I thought I was self-centered, only worried about fixing my problems, never analyzing the dangers it may cause myself or the pain it may inflict on someone else.

Before I could speak, a ring at the doorbell saved me from the awkwardness. I rose from the table slowly replaying the words she just spoke in my head. She described me with words that only Michael could be. I wasn't him. Sincere. Noble. Selfless. Warm. I was selfish and cold. Maybe one day I would live up to those words but today was not that day.

I opened the door and Brycin, Claire and Jakob were at my door.

"What's up?" I said trying not to sound so surprised by their presence at my door.

"We were wondering if you wanted to go to Willamette Park today." Brycin began.

"We figured since the wind isn't all that bad and the storm passed, that we could go hike one of the trails." Claire suggested.

I never noticed the weather. The winds died down a fraction and the clouds were a light gray. There were small patches of blue scattered throughout the sky. It was a perfect day to hang with my friends. It was probably what I needed at the moment.

"Yeah sure. Be back." I said putting up one finger.

I walked back into the dining area and explained the plans to Rachel. Always so understanding. I may not deserve her but I need her. I gave her a kiss on the cheek, took another bite from my plate, grabbed my coat off the rack behind the door and jumped out into the icy air.

The car was full of over talkative teenagers and laughter but I didn't engage in any part of it. I looked up into the sky as we drove, waiting for the sky to turn black like it did in my nightmare. I didn't know when or how I flew into thoughts of my nightmare. I had been trying my hardest all morning not to think of it. Maybe it was when I strangely noticed that everyone was wearing the color black, almost imitating shadows. Shirts, coats, pants, umbrellas, even hair ties; they were all black. How ironic was it that the day I dream of shadows sending a sprite to haunt me in my dreams, that everyone wanted to wear black?

There was no use in fighting the thoughts. The darkness was all round me, communicating in a language that I tried to understand. Every now and then, the conversation was broken by a white umbrella or a tan trench coat but that would only last for a second. I let myself be swallowed up by thoughts of my nightmare.

I remembered everything so vividly. My sweaty palms increasing in moisture as I stood in fear, my breathing irregular from all of the fright disseminating through my veins and my eyes glued on the shadow replicating the identity of a man with his white eye making me feel secure and his scarlet eye piercing through me soul, killing me internally; it was all so easy to remember. Everything in my dream was in place except for two things. The landscape around me was scattered with life and edifice. And the sky never went darker than a light gray.

After realizing I had been away for a while, my mind returned to the car. There was one thing that changed within the car besides the journey my mind had taken me on. Brycin. He seemed kidnapped by his thoughts too. Or he was kidnapped by my thoughts. He didn't seem like he was himself. He was portraying everything I was feeling. His face was expressionless. The warm brown in his eyes was dull. His chin rested on his knuckles as he stared blankly out the window.

"Brycin?" I waited. I waited for the soft brown to lighten in his eyes. I waited for him to turn and answer me. But he never did. He never acknowledged me. I called out his name one more time but still, no response. He was hypnotized, trapped in a trans that not even the voice of his best friend could break. The car had stopped and it wasn't because Jakob and Claire overheard me calling Brycin's name. We reached a red light after all the constant driving.

This hurt me in a way that I didn't expect. I never thought that the power of Brycin's silence could strike overwhelming pain in me. He was my best friend and I didn't see my friend in the car beside me.

I slowly turned my head back around, taking my attention back out the window. My heart's pulse accelerated, crashing into my ribs almost breaking them. My body was erect and I was leaning forward. I stared out my window. I was panicking and completely without breath.

There it was. The entity that haunted me in my sleep and moved into my mirrors last night. It was my demon. My breathing was getting more and more out of control and my heart was beating a million times per second. It was across the street, staring at me with its white and ruby red eyes. The moving cars distracted my focus from the demon. I almost believed it was moving toward me.

I had my hand on my belt buckle ready to unfasten myself and run back home. Sure I would have to explain it to everyone in the car later but this was my reaper I was up against. I waited for it to make a move. I couldn't control the tremors of my hands. I could feel the sweat building on my face. My heart was about to erupt out of my chest. Fear had completely consumed me.

A large eighteen wheeler passed in front of my demon and it broke my focus. I watched as the truck passed and left. I scanned every bit of the area for my demon. It could have easily been hiding in the ocean of black clothing that scattered the streets. But it wasn't there or anywhere for that matter.

I can feel my heart slow to a steady and normal pace. The severe shakes my hands were hypnotized by slowly disappeared and I could feel the sweat under my skin diminish.

I let out all the air my lungs seemed to have held in. I wasn't aware that I had stopped breathing. I leaned back against the seat and swallowed all the fear that I still had in me. I closed my eyes for a second and let the normalcy wash over me.

As my breathing slowed and the car began to drive again, I noticed that there was heavy breathing coming from inside the car. I was normal again so it wasn't me. The two in the front never stopped to even take a breath from their talking. I turned. Brycin and his posture were extremely tense. His left hand sat on his lap balled up into a tight fist and his right elbow rested on the door, his right hand just as tight into a fist and pressing against his lips. He was almost shaking. His eyes continued to stare out the window. Fear inhabited them. No one in the car seemed to notice the heavy breathing but me. Not even Brycin.

I had watched him the rest of the way. Several minutes after I detected his heavy breathing and fearful state, he calmed. His eyes closed for a fraction and he was okay again. He was under the same apprehensive hex that I had seemed to be under when my demon was across the street.

Could he be something other than human? Portman did say that my *angel* would tell me soon. Is that why he was so protective over me and knew exactly when I was lying? Because he was my angel?

I shook the thought from head. Brycin was just as human as I. It was absurd. But I couldn't help but begin to wonder about that comment Portman made. *Your angel will tell you soon.* That itself forced me to believe that these beings do exist. Plus with my demon following me, how could I not believe in this hidden world of beings.

We reached the park. Emma, James, and Frankie were all waiting and chatting amongst themselves. Claire and Jakob were already out and walking toward the others. I opened my door and allowed the wintry air to swim on the surface of my skin. It was somewhat refreshing. There was a sense of mellowness that came from the touch. I hopped out and shut the door behind me. I never saw Brycin get out of the car or heard his door open. But it closed and he was standing in front of the car. His arms were folded and he looked irritated.

"Last night I told you everything. Now it's time you start answering some of my questions." I had never seen him so serious. I had hoped he forgot about my disappearing act I pulled yesterday.

But that wasn't important right now. I had to ask while it was still fresh in both of our minds. "Not before you answer one of my own." His posture shifted on to his right leg and he seemed more annoyed by me than usual. "Why were you so scared in the car?"

He walked up to me with repugnance lingering in his eyes. His arms were still folded as he approached. I can feel the air he released from his nostrils blast against my cheeks. He imitated a bull and its natural reaction whenever it sees the color red. "Why were you?" the words were coated in resentment as they bolted from him mouth.

He turned around abruptly and shoved his hands into his pockets, leaving me there in the cold wondering when had he noticed. There was no yelp or heavy breathing or anything conspicuous. The normal things that would lead an individual to believing someone was afraid. How did he know?

I was surprised at the reaction I had adopted now. It wasn't disbelief that he knew I was afraid nor was it guilt because it seemed to hurt his feelings. I was angry. I was annoyed by the fact that nothing was hidden from him. It wasn't healthy for me. This was a lot deeper than overprotection. This was obsession. He always watched me, waiting for me to screw up and then tell me how wrong I was and how to prevent it from happening again. The things I should avoid and the people I shouldn't talk to. I felt like his brother. His *real* brother. He wasn't being my *brother,* he was being my father. I had none now so the role wasn't his.

After comparing myself to his brother, I couldn't help but think that something bad was going to happen to me soon. It was a pacified feeling. I wanted it to happen. To let him see that this is the results when you cross boundaries, when you smother people with how they should act and what they should do. But what could I do that could be so life threatening? Corvallis didn't offer much creativity.

This day hadn't gone the way I intended it to. I didn't want to stay at home fearing that my demon was lurking around in some reflective object. I expected to go out with Brycin, Jakob and Claire to get my mind off of my demon. Instead, it followed me out. There was no escaping this demonic entity. I wanted to be surrounded by laughter and enjoy the presence of all of my friends. I wanted to watch Jakob and Frankie fight over who would look better in a raincoat, Emma or Claire. I intended on having an anger-free day. No thoughts of Portman or Brycin's overprotective nature or demons and angels. I didn't want any of it. Yet, my day didn't seem to like that thought very much.

Everyone had already trailed off onto the pathway. I lingered behind thinking to myself and wondering about recent events. It was appealing to me how everything that seemed so normal to me before,

I now was questioning. For instance, Brycin and this domineering quality he possessed never bothered me as much before. So why now all of I sudden I feel like ripping him to shreds whenever he feels obligated to know of my whereabouts. Why am I so obsessed with this new phenomenon of half-breeds and angels and demons? I know I had dreamed about them for a long time long ago but was this coincidence in subject worth the obsession?

I walked with my hands connected behind my neck. I looked up and soaked in the park's natural attributes. The large cedars stretching high into the air, the shrubs and ferns and the sound of the Willamette River I found very relaxing. I breathed in all of the parks essences. The smell of the moist soil from the rain and the refreshing aroma of every plant around coming together and forming one natural, overpowering fragrance was inviting. The chirps of birds and squirrels and the light breeze whisking through the trees and onto the path was appealing to me. It was the perfect recipe of collectivity.

"I want to apologize about earlier."

I heard Brycin's voice but I was under the spell of the park that his voice startled me. I didn't even see him come into my focus.

"I know I come off strong as far as wanting to know things-"

"Strong is a bit of an understatement." I interrupted, my hands still behind my neck and my attention up toward the blue-gray sky.

"Things are not easy right now."

I waited for the explanation but it never came. Did he expect me to just accept that as his fighting argument? Was I supposed to accept that this was the reason for all of the unjustifiable behavior I had seen him undergo in the last four days.

"What's so uneasy about letting me wonder about things the world has to offer? People and their belief?"

He paused, looking for the right way to answer. "Do you think that we are meant to know everything?" I wasn't looking at him but I could tell he was looking at me with wonderment. "That everything we hear we should instantly analyze? Dissect it apart until we fully understand what it is, who it involves and where did it come from? Especially stories about angels and demons and half-breeds?"

"What's wrong with wondering?" My hands were down and my attention was in the conversation. "If it wasn't for great people wanting to know how things are, we wouldn't be living in the world that we live in today. Sometimes wondering can kill you but ignorance can be just as lethal."

"But on the things that matter nothing to you?"

"It does matter to me."

"How?"

The day I resented. Telling someone about the dreams I used to have and the demon that was haunting me. It was the only way he was going to fully grasp why I needed to know. "Have you ever dreamed of something that no one ever exposed you to?"

I can read his expression and he knew nothing of what I was talking about.

"Well, when I was younger, after Michael passed," I took in a deep breath of air preparing myself for my confession. The perfume of the park made it easier to assert. I looked down as I began. "I used to dream about these things. People with bird wings and bat wings fighting for dominance. The dream would come every night for seven months. I never told Rachel because it would just turn into one pity fest over Michael's death. She had enough on her plate already." I looked back up at the sky, restraining from making any eye contact. It would make the situation all the more awkward.

"And that's the source of your obsession? This dream?"

I shrugged and brought my head down, finally looking at him. "Well yeah. And the way it ends."

"And?"

Of course I was stalling. I didn't want to sound anymore psychotic than I already had. I mean, dreaming the same dream for over half a year had to be classified as abnormal. "It ended with all of the beings dead on the ground. Some of them now wingless and others burned to ashes. All of them except for one." The part of my dream I dreaded. I couldn't even bare to speak its existence aloud. "I couldn't tell what he was. Angel or demon. It has one red eye and one white and is completely covered in shadows. And lately I've been seeing it. In my reflection and outside of my subconscious."

Brycin was being perceptive and not casting any judgment. He was being a friend. "And all of this happened the day Portman came to our class?"

It felt somewhat nice to confess all this stuff to him. If only he had made the journey easier in the beginning I wouldn't have been so secretive about it. "Yes and no. I hadn't dreamed the dream in a while. But when he was explaining it, it was all so familiar in my head. I knew I had seen it somewhere before." I couldn't bring myself to admitting my visit to Portman's yesterday. He would chastise me for it surely. He would shower me with "I told you so" and "you should have listened to me." I withheld the information and continued. "But last night the dream came again, only different. No fighting and no creatures. Just that shadow. And I saw it last night for the first time outside of my dreams and again today. In the car."

I didn't know what was going through his head and I wasn't sure if I wanted to know.

I could see everyone walking toward us.

"What's wrong?" Brycin asked as they came back.

"Someone was killed." Claire began. "They are shutting the park down for investigation." I couldn't imagine them searching the two hundred and ninety acre park for someone or something. There was something more to the way Claire presented. Something hidden in the way she said it. It was almost as if she knew. It could have been due to how she didn't present it to the both of us. Just Brycin. Or maybe it was the passage of more words through their eye contact.

We left the park and Jakob dropped me off at home. It was night now and the moon was hidden by the audience of clouds. I entered the house where it was warm and completely silence. I assumed Rachel was asleep.

I dragged my body up the stairs and into bed without removing any of my clothes. The day's events replayed in my head as I slipped into unconsciousness. How it went from worse to good to worse to bad to good again. It gave me a headache thinking about it. Sleep was a lot more powerful tonight than before.

It had been a while since I'd seen my ocean of despair. Flying over the waters held so many obstacles. Things that were too hard to deal with. Things that challenged my friendship and my sanity. I allowed the wings that I subconsciously inherited to wither away and plunged into my icy sea of torment. For once, they comforted me.

Chapter 5: Silverhead Peek

THE ENDING OF MY WEEK SEEMED IMAGINARY. THE friendship Brycin and I shared seemed to be tested to all degrees. The lack of trust we had towards one another all began with the telling of some false legend which coincidently emerged the remembrance of an old childhood subconscious obsession.

As a child, I would dream about angels and demons fighting each other for dominance high above the earth. Recently I'd had a recurring dream about it but not so much identical. The only similarities between the two dreams were the barren wasteland and a specific character.

It was a person, a man. Neither demon nor angel — as far as I could tell. He was created from the shadows around him. He possessed a white eye full of beauty and purity and goodness while his red eye scorched my soul, leaving me numb and full of fright.

It followed me out of the world of dream and into my world. The world of reality. Somehow it slipped through the planes of consciousness and unconsciousness, haunting me in the form of my reflection and out in the real world.

If *that* wasn't enough to handle, the fact that it seemed as if everyone around me was hiding something added to my uneasiness. Their facial expressions, the way they communicated through their eyes with one another, it all pointed to something I didn't know, something deeper. Something *I* was going to find out.

Mystery after mystery lurked behind every corner. It's time I started unveiling some of these secrets. But I would be smarter this time around. This time, I would work at a much steady, retard pace.

This morning broke the cycle of heart chilling nightmares and heavy thoughts forcing me to act in reckless ways. The night had passed by smoothly, dreamless. I didn't see my demon at all in my unconscious state of being. Everything was black and I preferred it that way. The darkness didn't give me anything to obsess over. Just comfort.

I rolled over to see my alarm clock. It was almost five fifty.

I lifted from my bed and walked to my door. The absence of lavender and the shadows stretching from downstairs and reaching to my room stated that Rachel wasn't up yet. Had everything gone back to normal over night? Or had I been dreaming the entire thing?

I walked into the bathroom and I immediately tossed that last thought out of my mind. I stared at the towel rack that still lay on the ground after my demon had infiltrated my mirror and took the form of my reflection. I forgot I never picked it up. I grabbed the cold metallic pipe and placed it back on the wall. I folded the towels back to the way they were before my weight pulled them down.

My pace started to slow as I placed the last towel over the other towels. My pulse accelerated a fraction. The heat of my skin I could fill begin to blaze. I had forgotten about the very object that gave my demon access to haunt me. The mirror. Just because I didn't dream of it didn't eliminate the fact that it did exist. I slowly turned. To my relief it was just me. Blue eyes blazing bright, bushy hair and sleep still lingering in my eyes. I sighed with relief and closed the door, leaving myself to my morning ritual of getting ready.

After twenty minutes, I emerged from the bathroom. Something was missing. The very fragrance I was always so welcomed to wasn't in the air. Lavenders. I shut the lights to the bathroom off. No lights were on downstairs. Just when I thought that my morning was off to a normal start.

I walked down the stairs and the shadows glued themselves to every wall. They were my only company this morning. I expected the scent of lavenders and toasted bagels to raid my nose. To see her in the kitchen placing her hot bagels on a small plate and greeting me with a wide smile that would force me to grin. None of that was here. Just me and the shadows.

My hand searched for the light switch in the shroud of shadows. The light only brightened the kitchen. It was Rachel's presence that brought it to life.

A white paper caught my attention hanging on the refrigerator door. I walked over to it and ripped it off. A note from Rachel:

> *Kayden,*
>
> *I have gone to Salem and I won't be back until tomorrow night. My client's husband has finally been put on trial. I left money for you on the counter. $100 for food and $350 for you to do whatever with. There is a list of groceries next to the money as well. Please pick up everything for me.*
>
> *I love you,*
> *Rachel*

The note slowly fell to my side as I registered the fact that she wasn't going to be here until Wednesday. I didn't want to stay in this house all by myself for two days. The whereabouts of my demon was still unknown. And what if I have another dream? How would I be able to soothe myself back to normalcy?

Then again, I did have a dreamless night. Maybe I could get lucky again and have another. I could probably use this as an opportunity to find out more about Brycin. Stay over his house. I would use the time as an opportunity to unravel the hidden truths kept in his head.

I grabbed the four hundred and fifty dollars off of the black marble counter and headed for the front door, evaluating the morning I was having so far.

Besides Rachel's immediate absence, everything was normal. No nightmares, no demons, nothing. The morning was as normal as any other morning I'd had before last Thursday. Maybe I should just drop it all. Let go of all of my thoughts and all the questions. Continue to live in mystery as I did the first eighteen years of my life.

I was outside and the sun was just peeking over the horizon. I slipped into the car and slid the key into the ignition and brought the car to life. Led Zeppelin was playing and I left it on. Another thing not so normal about the morning but it was comforting.

I drove to school and made it to Professor Yates' Sociology class. Late. A morning wasn't a morning without him stating the obvious of my tardiness. I wondered if me being late and him telling me how late I was, was the only thing he was good at. His teaching sucked. I never understood anything he was saying half the time. He spoke with such proper dialect and words that required you to have a dictionary beside you to get the complete gist of what he was saying. He was tall and slender. A well dressed man but an ill dressed personality.

Yes. A normal day indeed.

Or so I thought.

Brycin's seat was empty. He never missed a day's class. Even with Professor Yates' horrible teaching tactics, he was always here. I've even heard that sometimes, he would be the first one in here. Books ready, notepad and pencil out. He exceeded in academics, sports and attendance. This was *not* so much a normal day anymore.

I sat down and stared at the vacant seat. I couldn't help questioning his absence. It wasn't like him to skip class. Maybe I was the reason he wasn't here. I have been a bit of a nuisance lately. I have been lying more than necessary and getting into things that clearly had nothing to do with me. I wondered that if the next time I saw him, would he tell me? Or would he lie about it? Ugh! Just another mystery to throw on the fully loaded plate I already have. Would I ever figure out at least one of these mysteries?

"Mister Pruitt! What classifies as deviance?!" He yelled, scolding me with piercing brown eyes.

I was so drowned in the absence of my friend that I never realized that Yates had been asking me a question.

"Oh, uhmm…I'm sorry repeat the question."

"I said, what classifies as deviance?"

I hesitated a moment, letting my mind enter back in to the classroom. "The society in which the deviance is being defined."

"Good." he spat the word out, obviously disgusted by my wandering mind.

Lucky guess if you ask me. In Sociology that seemed to be the answer to every question.

Class was over and I walked to Theology alone, something I had never done before. It was different. I always had Brycin there to keep my mind off of the people around me. But as I walked, I couldn't help but watch people as I passed them. I wondered what they thought of me. Did I look like your everyday crazed person? Or did I look normal enough to blend in with them? But no one ever looked at me directly. They simply proceeded to their next class, listening to their I-pods or on their cell phones texting or chatting with their friends. *Not* a normal day.

I entered my Theology class and was immediately drowned in awkwardness. Last time I'd seen him, he threw me out of his grand estate after promising me facts about an ancient legend.

Portman. Standing in front of the classroom watching everyone walk in. I couldn't believe he was here again. I could feel his eyes burn through me as I entered into the room. I tried my best not to look directly at him. This was going to be even more of a challenge without Brycin.

I took my seat, looking down at my table. I didn't want to look up, afraid that if I did, Portman would be grimacing at me with a deadly expression.

I pulled my sight slowly off the black table and up to Portman. As I thought, he was looking dead in my direction. I took a deep swallow and exhaled. The anxiety was overpowering.

I was now wishing *I* had skipped school. Brycin should have warned me. Or invited me. He invited me everywhere else. Why all of sudden things seemed to change around me?

Portman never took his eyes off of me, even when he began to speak. "Mrs. Hay is still out sick." His voice was far from inviting. The man that kicked me out that stormy afternoon was here in my classroom. He finally pulled his attention away from me, breaking the long contact our eyes seemed to be engaged in, and announced his reasons for being here. "She is still out sick. She has given me direct orders that there will be no talk of legends today." Cover up. He knew that his presence would reemerge unanswered questions I still may have had. He knew that here, he couldn't kick me out. He could, but for asking a question?

I bet Mrs. Hay knew nothing about his speech. If she was as sick as he made her seem, speaking would be the last thing she could do.

"Instead, she wants you guys to write a two page summary on the complications of a one world religion. How would this one world religion effect mankind? Will wars manifest over this, how would governments come together as one to flourish a one world religion, and if it is ever succeeded, would things be easier or become more complicated?" he gave the directions with an edginess to his voice. His tone was sharp and quite often, as he gave out the assignment, he looked at me. The side of me that wanted to annihilate him was completely repressed. Instead, I wanted to run from all of this.

The uncontrollable shakes my legs were overpowered by started to irritate me. It all annoyed me. Everything. Portman, my shaky legs, the way my posture seemed to shift in my seat every minute, the speed of time, Brycin's absence. All of it annoyed me. I wanted to scream but I used every ounce of power within me to suppress the yell.

My eyes transferred back and forth between Portman and the clock, my posture tense in my seat. I wanted the hands to hurry and meet at the top of the clock at the twelve but the long hand took its time as it just past over the ten. My hands were clutched into tight fists. Moisture was forming within them the tighter they became. My breathing quickened. Everything in the class seemed to blur in and out. I felt dizzy as the anxiety trickled throughout my body. But I refused to show any signs of weakness, especially to Portman.

It was almost as if he heard my thought. His head lifted and his eyes were on me. His jaw was tight and his eyes narrowed, burning through me. His gaze amplified the dizzy spell I was already under and I fought harder to resist the temptation of fainting. Fear barricaded my throat, preventing me from swallowing or letting any air enter my lungs.

Why wouldn't Portman tell me? Or why couldn't he? It was the only reason either of us felt how we felt.

As the event of me going to his home slowly replayed in my mind, a different emotion overtook me. I was suddenly looking at Portman just as threateningly. My anxiety had dissipated. Hate was all that fueled me. Not just toward him. Brycin knew something as well. My morning thoughts of tip-toeing my way to finding out the truth had completely been annihilated by Portman's immediate presence and

Brycin's absence. I was as keen about finding out everything now as I was before.

Everyone was now packing. Finally. Class was over. I joined in on the ritual, putting my things into my bag and throwing it over my back. Everyone was headed to the front of the room where Portman stood, handing in their assignment. I followed. Portman watched me as approached.

Our gaze was never broken, never interrupted. It was as if we were the only two in the classroom. Both our eyes burned with a hateful passion for the other. I had my reasons of hating him. I wondered what was his.

I set my paper on top of the pile already in his hand, never breaking the connection our piercing gazes seemed to be locked in. So much rage and intensity in our eyes. Neither one of us liked the presence of the other and this circumstance of forcing us into the same environment only contributed to that hate. When I passed him, the connection was broken and I headed for the exit at a normal pace.

"Very disappointed in your work Mr. Pruitt."

I almost wanted to stop, run back and punch him. But I didn't. My walk quickened and I sped to my car, almost stomping. I gritted my teeth together, spitting out profane words beneath my breath as I headed for my car. I was fuming and there was no way to repress the feeling. I entered the silver Charger and slammed my door. I pulled out of the parking lot and sped off of the school grounds.

Michael's CD wasn't enough to calm me. The anger was far too strong for something as precious as Michael's favorite CD to eliminate it. I shut the radio off. There was no way it was going to dissipate on its own.

I sped home consumed by evil thoughts. I wished I could see Portman walking in front of my car and deliberately hit him. Of course I'd lie about it but who would know. Only the two of us. I was always presumed to be the 'good-kid.' No one would believe him if he forced the accusations on me.

Or I could meet him at his home with some vicious weapon. A knife…or a gun? Something subtle I guess. The less conspicuous the better. Something I could blame as an accident. But I didn't want to become a murderer. I just wanted to see him hurt.

I *could* go to his house again. I could force myself to apologize to him. He might accept it. And if he does, then I will attack. I could ask what was at the top of his stairs. After being so forgiving, hopefully, he would show me. After the tour I would make sure he was in front of me and I'd push him down the stairs and make a run for it. No one would ever come for him.

It was brilliant.

I made it home faster than I imagined. The evil thoughts didn't seem to make everything go away but it helped a tad. Rachel wasn't here and I had the entire house to myself. This was not good. I didn't have anyone to talk to. Rachel was in Salem and Brycin was missing. Maybe I'd hit him with my car, too the next time I see him.

The house was already clean for the most part. I needed something to do. To keep my mind off of driving back to the school and burning Portman alive. I found cleaning supplies underneath the sink and started cleaning up already clean stuff. Rachel never left the house a mess. I was going to scrub every bit of this place until the colors came off.

After thirty minutes of cleaning, I headed to my closest. There was only the red sweater I had worn the last time I went to Portman's and the black jeans. I started pulling clothes from the hangers and shoving them all into a laundry bin. I sorted the clothes out and began washing them.

I went back to my room, threw my backpack on the computer desk and emptied it. Nothing. No homework or anything. I shuffled through the papers hoping that I may have overlooked something. But there was nothing.

This wasn't healthy clearly. I was washing clothes that were already clean and the house burned my eyes from the mixture of bleach and hot water.

After taking a moment to breathe, I went downstairs, made myself comfortable on the recliner and turned the television on.

This was pathetic. I flicked through channel after channel after channel finding nothing to take the anger out of me. "How could we have over five hundred channels and nothing be on?" I questioned aloud.

I let out a deep sigh and closed my eyes. I didn't realize that I had fallen asleep. The feeling of complete submission to sleep was invigorating. My eyes burned for a moment from all of the hot bleach in the atmosphere but the darkness my eyelids created soothed the heat almost immediately. I could slowly feel the anger drain from me and relaxation completely take over me. A place I would want to live in forever.

I woke up still on the recliner. The air was cleaner and fresh. The burning sensation that lingered in the atmosphere before my nap was completely absent. I pulled myself out of the chair and walked into the kitchen. It was two fifteen. I wasn't even sleep for a whole two hours. What the hell could I possibly do with all this spare time?

I ran upstairs remembering the load of laundry that I left in the washer before my nap. I pulled the damp clothes from the washer and shoved them into the dryer. After throwing the fabric softener into the dryer and starting it, I began the second load of clothes. I tossed everything into the washer, checking the pockets as I did. Even though I knew they were clean, it was a habit Rachel rubbed off on me.

I picked up the black jeans and checked the pockets. There was something in them. A slice of paper. It was the note with Portman's address. I looked at it and was shocked with what I saw. One line. Only one line of information. There wasn't four lines worth of directions anymore. Just one. The street's name. The one I had seen before the other three had appeared.

Henkle Way.

I knew I didn't imagine any of it. The other set of directions. Silverhead Peek *was* on this slice of paper. Wasn't it? I remember the drive as if I had done it yesterday. I drove to the I-20, drove the Alsea Highway to Henkle Way. I made the right, drove almost a quarter of a mile until I reached Silverhead Peek. I drove passed field after field of green pastures until I reached his house. The only house on the street.

None of this made any sense. I shoved the pants into the washer with the other clothes, poured washing powder on top of them and started the machine. I ran back down the stairs and head to the phone in the living room. I dialed Brycin's phone hoping he would come over and take my mind off of what I was now thinking of doing. My minds itinerary had shifted after reading the note. I was going to go up to Portman's house and talk to him. He was going to tell me what I needed to know. Voluntarily or involuntarily.

No one picked up.

I didn't know what to do. Brycin wanted me to drop the subject but how could I when abnormal things such as these were happening. I wasn't crazy…I don't think. There had to be some rational explanation to all of this. There was only one person I knew who knew the answers to the questions floating in my head.

I sat on the edge of the sofa. My eyes closed and I rocked back and forth, my forehead resting on the palm of one of my hands and the other folded across my lap. *I'm not going to go. I'm not going to go. I am going to stay here. I am going to stay here.* The thoughts were nowhere near convincing. My eyes flew open and I jumped off the couch. I sped toward the hook where my keys hung and stormed out of the door.

I locked the door and headed to my car. The air was moist and there was slight cloud coverage. The breeze was light and it brushed against my skin in a seductive way. The weather was beautiful. But its beauty wasn't that much of a distraction. I was going to follow through with my minds plans. Portman was going to answer my questions. I was going back to his house. I was going to go back to Silverhead Peek.

I hopped into my car and pulled out of the drive way. I drove in silence. I sped to the I-20. The police was the last thing on my mind and if I did get trapped in pursuit, I wouldn't stop until I was at Portman's mansion.

I reached the Corvallis Newport Highway and Alsea Highway junction. I drove onto the Alsea Highway and sped to my destination. I couldn't help but think of the last time I drove down this road. Everything was being pounded by rain droplets and the air became very vicious. The surges of lightning were violent and struck wherever they pleased. The thunder exploded within the clouds, echoing over the fields. The wind swept rain off the roads and pushed more onto them. Neither the lights from my car nor my windshield wipers were enough to make the road visible. Just line after line running beneath my car was all I could mostly see.

Today was by far opposite. I could easily see the houses sitting on top of hills and the fields as I passed. The trees flourished with green and the wind lightly swayed the branches. The sun began its decent over the land. It was all so beautiful.

Still, it wasn't enough to take my mind off of Silverhead Peek.

Henkle Way wasn't that far from me now. I immediately recognized the red house sitting on top of the hill before you turned onto Henkle Way. I made the turn. The butterflies in my stomach were fluttering out of control. I didn't know if it was how close I was to the road that led me to Portman's home that made me so anxious or the fact that I was revisiting him.

I drove and drove. I stopped the car when I noticed that I had gone over a quarter of a mile. I hadn't seen the turn. It was brighter than before and I was able to spot it last time. I made a u-turn and drove back the way I came. There was still no Silverhead Peek. There were nothing but fields and scattered homes. I made another u-turn and drove a little while more and stop the car alongside the road.

I opened the door, walked around my car and stood where the vast ocean of grass began. I gazed at the field as it stretched into the distance. There wasn't a street or anything. Just a large field of green.

I walked into the green ocean and headed toward Portman's mansion. I mean, at least that's where I thought I was headed.

I walked the field and the wind seemed to pick up. I wasn't sure how much walking I had just invested in. I wasn't really getting anywhere. The further I walked, the greener it became, the further away my car was appearing. *Where was his home?* Had I really dreamt everything up? Had Portman hated me today for no apparent reason? My head ached from all of the confusion.

I stopped after walking almost thirty minutes. I wish I had turned around a long time ago because I couldn't even see my car anymore. This turn of events reemerged the anger that my sleep had gotten rid of. But I realized it wasn't so much as anger. It was disappointment. I was hoping to end everything today. I was hoping that all my questions were going to be answered today. Everything was supposed to end *today*.

How could an entire street disappear? Better yet, how could a mansion as huge as the one I was in vanish?

The walk back to my car was going to be long. The car was smaller than a bug to me at this point. I walked, still bewildered by the absence of an entire street and a house as huge as Portman's.

The wind suddenly became intense in less than a second. It whipped my clothes in every which direction. Good thing I gelled my hair this morning or else it would be slapping relentlessly against my forehead right now. The green was getting darker and the darkness headed toward my car. I had never seen clouds so thick before. Nor had

I seen clouds move so fast. Within seconds, the entire sky was black. The shadows had swallowed my entire world. The bright and beautiful green field I was once standing in was completely replaced by an eerie black ocean of darkness. Shadows now inhabited the field, speaking in that language that I hated so much.

My dream?

No. The earth didn't roar. Nor did the sky. But it was close enough. Home was the only thing on my mind now. The stupid legends... forget them. They weren't worth my life.

I walked forward and a lightning bolt struck a foot away from me. "WHOA!" The bright flash of light and its close strike threw me to the ground. My lungs were overflowing with fear. I tried to fight against the fear and bring some air into my lungs. I was beginning to sweat and I couldn't bring myself to blinking. Where did this storm surge come from? It was so bright just a minute ago. Now it was darker than night.

The first lightning bolt from the sky clashed in front of my face. The odds of that had to be slim. The sky was roaring at me now. The sound was far more deafening than my dream. The vicious winds whipped leaves and grass at me, replacing the sands of my horrid dream. It was overpowering.

My ears were suddenly alert as I sat motionless on the ground. I heard something hitting against the earth. Thud. Snap. THUD! SNAP! *THUD!* I turned to the right — ducked — praying that the tree the wind had just thrown at me would fly over me.

This was far worse than my dream. The earth attacked me in this world. At least the only pain I had to deal with in my dream was the scream of my demon and its piercing stare.

I shoved myself to my feet and ran through the blackness. The lightning struck the earth all around me, shooting the dirt and grass upward as it struck the ground.

I dodged and I ran. My adrenaline was high from all the fright that swam through my bloodstream. The thunder began with a low grumble and gradually grew into a booming crack. It silenced but only for a fraction. It was then followed by a shattering roar.

The ground beneath me suddenly lifted due to the vibration of the thunder, throwing me onto my face. I wasted no time lingering on the floor. I flung myself back up to my feet and headed back toward my car.

I could feel my feet blistering in my shoes; the pain in my legs almost brought me back down to the floor but I wasn't going to let them crumble beneath me. My heart had never raced so fast before. I knew my ribs were going to be bruised once this was all over. If I made it out alive that is. It hurt to breath. It felt like glass was scratching against the inside of my throat with every breath of air I took in. The adrenaline mixed with the fear gave me more energy than necessary. I was sure that once I stopped, my body was going to want to keep going.

Instantly, something flung me around and my face was in the soil again. A loud whoosh came from the force that turned me and knocked me to the ground. I looked up and I could *see* the wind. It was black. Swirling and dancing and whooshing around me. Every chance I got to escape, the black winds knocked me back to the ground. I stood back up to my feet and looked all around me. The winds swirled up and up until they were touching the black clouds. My chest pushed out and pulled itself back into my body. The fear was already hard to deal with. My breathing made everything more difficult.

The black winds never stopped swirling around me. I was trapped in this tornado of dark winds and I couldn't see anything. My legs buckled beneath me. I fell to my knees and shoved my left hand into the ground. I was grabbing the left side of my chest with my right hand.

My heart. It hurts.

I felt myself slipping away. Into unconsciousness. I was scared. Rachel. Brycin. Everyone I ever cared about invaded my mind. My loving thoughts of them and the memories I shared with them made slipping into death much easier but remorse lingered in me as well. I would be leaving them and no one would ever know what happened to me. I wish I never came. I had come here once before. The last time I came here, I was rejected from the information I wanted and thrown out of a majestic manor. Now, this place was going to become my grave.

A waste of life. I never even got any of my questions answered. They were the reason I was dying now anyways. I don't care anymore. I hated that I even pried. I should have listened to Brycin and left it alone.

A stupid…irrelevant…myth. My body crashed into the floor. I felt my breath slowly slipping away and my heart slowing.

Maybe these were the first sounds you heard before you die. Lots of banging. They were abnormal bangs. They were followed by yells and cries and grunting. It sounded more like a fight but I didn't know. In fact, I didn't want to know. My eyes fell and waited for the icy touch of death to come.

I felt my body fly through the air and slam back into the ground. I could feel a warmness flow down my face. It was thick and slow as it traveled over the terrain of my face. Death was being cruel to me. I never felt the icy touch that came with death. I just felt pain. My head hurt and so did my body.

My eyes remained closed. I suddenly realized my breathing was being restored…

It was easy to breath and my heart was slowing, adopting a regular, lively tempo. Was I coming back to life? NO! Why not let me die now? I was a burden to those around me.

I *was* alive.

I could hear and feel ferociousness of the wind fade. I could hear the thunder soften and I assumed that the lightning was absent along with it.

Something landed near my head. A tree? The wind had thrown one at me earlier. It was a possibility.

My body lifted from the ground. Something was holding me…or someone. This thing was soft and warm, a lot like Rachel. There was a soft, fluttering thud coming from this thing. I pressed my ear against the fluttering as it soothed me into a deeper unconsciousness.

The whooshing returned and my body lifted and fell. It continued to do this.

I fought against my eyelids and peeked through my lashes. It was bright here; it burned my eyes. The sky was blue and the sun was a bright orange. It seemed closer than ever before.

There was one thing wrong with this scene. The clouds. They were beneath me. My eyelids wouldn't let me register everything I had just witnessed. I slipped away completely, submitting myself to death.

I had to have been dead, for I had just received a glimpse of heaven.

Chapter 6: Attack or Accident

THE LIGHT WAS BLINDENING AND IT JUST SEEMED TO get brighter and brighter. I had gotten used to seeing nothing but blackness that it was almost unbearable to proceed into the light.

This must be it. Finally, I must've been moving on. Moving on into my everlasting paradise, the place where I would be of some use. Michael and I would do our best to keep Rachel happy here on Earth. I wouldn't be so much of a burden to her. She'd learn to live without me. Eventually, she would be happy.

I had no thoughts about anything. My mind had been congested with thoughts of mysteries, nightmares, legends and confusion because everyone around me seemed to be covering up so many things. It was unnecessary and nerve-racking. But at this moment, as I floated to my destinies fulfillments, the day where I was actually going to be needed for something great, none of that mattered to me. Soon I will have wings of my own. There would be no need to obsess about other beings with them.

I didn't know heaven came with a constant beeping sound. It was annoying. It was high in pitch and made my soundless trip to paradise uneasy.

Ouch! Why was I in so much pain? The left side of my head was pounding and my breathing was hoarse and painful. My left shoulder burned in pain. As for the rest of my body, I couldn't feel anything. I couldn't feel any of it. Just my shoulder and my head.

My eyelids slowly pulled up and an angel was staring in my eyes. The angel's eyebrows pulled down in worriment, eyes full of pain and sadness. The angel's hair surrounded her face, flowing down and straight, her face looking slimmer, but still beautiful.

Rachel.

Her forehead met my chest and her body shook. She broke into a horrific sob as soon as she saw my eyes open. I felt the pain she was in. I instantly regretted thinking that being with Michael was the best place for me. She needed me here. I knew this but for some reason I constantly needed reminding.

"Oh, Kayden!" she muffled into my chest. I brought my right hand up to place on her head. There was an odd device sitting on my index finger. I looked around and found myself in an unfamiliar room. The ceilings and walls were white, I was surrounded by vertical blinds and I found the source of the annoying beeping. It was the EKG machine I was attached to.

I was in the hospital.

Guilt plagued my body. I was sick of putting Rachel in these kinds of situations. She deserved a painless life.

Before I could think any more negative thoughts, the angel's face reappeared. "Oh, Kayden, I am *so* sorry!" she broke off into a sob on the word 'so.' "I promise I will never leave you again. I *promise!* I am only thirty-eight. I could retire. I mean, we have enough money saved up in the bank. It won't be a—"

"No, Rache. That's stupid." I objected. My voice was harsh and raspy. It felt like I had swallowed shards of steel and they scratched my throat as they went down. It was more painful to talk than it was to breathe. I pulled myself up into a more comfortable position on the uneven hospital bed. "You're great at what you do. Don't quit over my recklessness." All this *was* my fault. Not hers. There was no need in punishing herself for me. "I'm sorry."

She pulled my forehead and kissed it. It hurt and I flinched. She sat back with apologetic eyes. "I'm sorry."

I shook the pain away but that seemed to make it worse. "It's fine."

"Kayden, I nearly lost you. I breathe only for you now. Not for that job. It's more like a hobby for me now! If you stop breathing, so will I!" She was becoming a tad bit hysteric. She almost hissed the words through her teeth. I couldn't be mad at her for it.

My eyes trailed off behind her. Everyone was behind her. Sitting in chairs, talking amongst themselves. Brycin, Claire, Jakob and Emma. The other three, I would have expected them to come and see me. But not Emma. I sort of smiled a light smile. I never gave her enough credit. She was a brilliant girl. Very beautiful, very brilliant.

The smile slowly left my face and my eyes squinted, my head tilted. A storm of questions invaded my mind. Here we all were in the hospital but did anyone really *know* why? "What happened to me?" I asked gazing into Rachel's eyes.

Rachel rubbed her face with one of her hands. She ran her hand through her hair. She was finding a way to say it. Not for my sake, but for her own. I could see how much it pained her to think of it. But what was it she thought happened to me? "An accident. There was a pursuit. You had the right-a-way during the intersection. The driver being chased slammed directly into the side of your car. Your car flipped four times before coming to a stop."

"Lucky for you, you didn't lose that much blood." Brycin said with a smirk, walking and standing next to Rachel. "How you holding up?"

Lies! They're all lies! I thought to myself. I knew exactly what happened to me. I remember. I can remember the lightning almost splitting my skull. I can remember how the whooshing black winds and the earth attacked me.

But what I really remembered, more than anything else, was flying over the clouds, feeling the warmth of the sun and flying straight to it. "I'm fine for now." I stated with a taste of resentment.

But I couldn't tell them that. They would quickly transfer me from the hospital to a mental institution. I couldn't tell them how an entire street and a majestic, white mansion mysteriously disappeared. I couldn't tell them how the earth brought my dream, somewhat, to reality. How the shadows from the clouds blackened everything. How the earth and sky bellowed and unison and how they both seemed to attack me. They would think I was crazy for sure.

"If Brycin hadn't noticed your car, I probably wouldn't be here right now."

Oh really? I thought to myself. *What a coincidence?* The thought was sarcastic and I was sure that my facial expressions projected it. "Brycin saw my car?"

"Yeah."

More lies! There was no crash! My car was perfectly safe at…on Henkle way! "Thank you." I lied. I wasn't thankful at all. He was lying.

"Hi, Kay." Claire almost danced to my left side. She was so beautiful. Her cheeks reddened. She was blushing as if she heard what I thought.

"Hi."

"I'm sorry we weren't here on Monday. Something sort of came up."

"Well why didn't you guys invite me? It would have saved me from the insults of Portman's eyes."

"Who's Portman?" Rachel asked.

"Just some guy." I answered shaking my head.

"Brycin thought it would be better if you stayed. You know how Rachel is when it comes to your education." I turned to Rachel and she looked at me nodding in agreement.

I closed my eyes and let out a deep sigh as I fell back against my pillow. They were right but I still wished they had invited me. I wouldn't be here if they had.

I pressed my left hand up against the left side of head. It was like someone pounding a piece of steal against an anvil with a hammer. I was that flimsy piece of steal. I tried to push the pain out of my head but it wasn't very effective.

"You okay?" Rachel asked. Even with my eyes closed and all the different voices in the room, hers was the most angelic to me.

"Yeah, just a small headache." After a moment of trying to force the pain out of my head, I opened my eyes. Jakob stood where Brycin once was, speaking with Rachel about getting my car fixed and Emma now stood next to Claire, telling her something but I couldn't make it out. There were too many whispers to decipher all of them. Brycin was far in the corner. He was pressing his left hand against the left side of his head, exactly where my pain manifested. That's the second time he mimicked my pains and feelings. I looked at him with wonderment.

The doctor entered before I could finish figuring out why Brycin always imitated me. Emma and Claire moved out of the way to make room for the doctor. He had a clipboard in his hand, wearing his long, white lab coat, and smiled at me. He was almost godlike. Almost as much as Michael. Their features were almost identical except his eyes were a deep brown and he was slightly slender. "Looks like there was no serious damage." He stated lifting one of the papers on his clipboard, reanalyzing everything on them. "You will make a full recovery. But there was a very, very minor concussion. So I will need for you to bring him back next Thursday. Just a safety precaution, okay?"

"Okay." Rachel nodded and smiled. She then looked back at me and ran her hand down my face.

"Other than that, you guys are permitted to go."

"Thank you again."

"So remember, a week from today, bring him back."

A week from today? Thursday? Next Thursday? Today was Thursday?! THREE DAYS?! I WAS OUT FOR THREE DAYS?! It must've been worse than I thought.

After checking me out, Rachel rolled me out of the hospital in a wheelchair. The sun was bright today. My eyes had been without it for so long that it burned them.

I noticed Emma pulling up in front of us in Rachel's black Dodge Caliber. Emma floated from the driver's side of the vehicle to the passenger's side, opening the door for me. The both of them helped me and my dysfunctional body into the car. Being out for three days had left me nearly paralyzed.

I was most shocked at Emma and this newfound fascination I had for her. She was gentle with me as she helped me into the passenger seat, careful with me, as if one wrong move could crumble my skeletal system — telling me to watch my head and even went to the lengths of putting my seatbelt on.

My heart suddenly seized at her closeness. I had never been this close to her before. Close enough to feel her touch, close enough to smell the invigorating, irresistibly glorious scents she possessed, close enough to hear her breath, even and slow. It was…nice.

"How's that? Comfortable?" she asked in her alluring voice.

I gulped and she chuckled, our faces inches away from each other. "Yeah. It's fine." I gulped harder.

She pulled herself out and held my door open for another second. "Get well soon, 'kay?"

My heart hadn't started beating again yet. I smiled and nodded. She closed the door.

"Bye, Emma." Rachel said after folding and placing my wheelchair into the back seat.

Emma nodded and waved to us as we left.

Brycin and the others took off after I had checked out. I would have expected him to be the one who went to get the car for Rachel and me. But it was Emma.

As we drove, my heart found its way back to beating again after being mesmerized by Emma's unbelievable presence. The radio was off and I laid my head against the window, watching everything blur from the speed. I knew there were four white dots when I looked down at the street but they fused together as we drove. Everything sped past me in a blur, never truly examining anything thoroughly.

We came to a stop and I heard her let out a deep sigh. When I looked at her, her head was pressed against the steering wheel. "What's the matter?"

She flipped her hair up and ran her fingers through it. She was crying. How insensitive of me.

"What's wrong?"

Her sniffles were making my heart feel heavy. "Him." she answered, lifting her head off the steering wheel. She never spoke his name though I knew exactly who she was talking about. "I thought I was going to have to repeat everything all over again." She trailed off, looking down and she was messing with her French manicured nails. "I know...that I'm *not* your real mother but—"

"Rache. Stop. You are. You are my mother. And I love you every day. Sometimes it's me who feels like I don't deserve you. You have been nothing but kind to me and yet I feel like I don't appreciate you enough!" I felt my eyes water. I didn't think twice about crying because the chances were slim. I was just really hurt.

"You don't know how much you mean to me." She brought her attention to my face as she said it. "My heart won't take it this time."

"Mom," the word that always brought her such comfort. I meant it when I used but I also used it as a weapon. "I love you. My life wouldn't be this way if it wasn't for you. Your kindness should have rewarded you with a child of your own. But I am still privileged to be your son." I hugged her and I could feel her come to. Her breathing was returning to normal and her wet cheek against mine never became wetter than it was.

The light was green and the honking horn behind us signaling us to go startled us. We laughed and drove home.

We pulled up into the driveway and the absence of my car took my head back to Henkle Way. But for Rachel, I repressed the thought.

She hopped out the car and I heard her pulling the folded wheelchair from the back. She opened my door and helped me out. I felt so handicap, incapable of doing things on my own. I instantly felt sorry for those who have to endure this treatment on a day-to-day basis.

She rolled me into the house, closed the door and was headed for the kitchen. But I stopped her. "No!" I said grabbing the wall. She looked down at me and I could feel her hair on my shoulders. "I wanna just got to sleep, please?"

She reversed me and stopped me at the base of the stairs. "Need me to help you?"

I laughed. "No, I need to try and get the blood flowing back into my legs." I held the wall and slowly walked up the stairs.

Felt like an hour had passed and I had only made it half way up the stairs. My legs were numb. I didn't think being off of them for so long would hurt so much. My jaw tightened at the pain and my face grimaced. I took air in through my teeth from the pain but I finally made it to the top. I used the wall for support as I walked to my room.

I closed the door to my room and slowly paced myself to my bed. I sat on my bed with ease and looked at everything around me. The only thing that had changed was that all the clothes I washed three days ago were folded and in a basket. I shuddered at the thought of being out for three days.

I pulled myself under the comforter, submitting to the comfort of my bed and falling into a deep, deep sleep.

Sleep had given me everything I wanted. I was relaxed and the feeling throughout my body was restored for the most part. I had no dream again; just darkness. After three days of seeing nothing but darkness, I somewhat wished I had a dream or a recurring nightmare of my demon.

Eight thirty two. I gazed out my window. Night's arrived. The moon must have been covered by clouds because hardly any light escaped through the window. I was tired of shadows and darkness and the sense of nothingness.

I pulled my body out of my bed. I staggered a bit but my legs were fully capable of mobility. The blood ran warm through my legs and I was relieved that I was no longer a liability or completely dependent on the help of someone else.

I shuffled my way into the bathroom never thinking twice that my demon may have been lingering in the mirrors again, waiting to take the form of my reflection.

My reflection seemed to be getting more and more unfamiliar to me. Before, my eyes would hardly light up. Now, almost every day, they seemed to possess a foreign brightness to them. My skin complexion was always normal, never pale (except for after my nightmares). My hair never seemed to change though. It was always messy whenever I studied myself in the mirror.

I turned the knob on the sink. The water flooded the sink as it rushed from the facet. I placed my hands beneath the water, cradling the small puddle in both of my hands. I washed the drowsiness from my eyes and face.

I looked up, studying the figure in the mirror. Still my reflection. I finished up in the bathroom by brushing my teeth.

As I walked back into the hall, two things were different. I must not have noticed them because sleep had still possessed my body. The first thing I noticed was the scent of my favorite cake gassing the house, ruling the air with its aroma. Chocolate Meringue. My mouth instantaneously began to salivate and I felt my feet almost pull me toward the scent, wanting to satisfy my body's craving. The second thing was all the commotion that seemed to come from downstairs. It was apparent that Rachel was not the only person downstairs.

I slyly walked down the stairs, desperately trying not to step on any of the steps the wrong way. Half way down the stairs, one of the stairs creaked. I pulled my leg up as an immediate reaction. I listened to the chattering. It gradually softened. I can hear shushing. I continued back down the steps, skipping the one that had squeaked before.

I reached the base of the stairs and turned into the family room. Empty. I turned around and saw a shadow race across the floor. I walked toward the kitchen. Who could Rachel possibly have had in here?

As soon as I was under the archway of the kitchen, I was showered by the word surprise. The pulse of my heart quickened and my breath left my body temporarily.

Everyone was here. Brycin, Jakob, James, Claire, Emma, Frankie, Amber and Jennifer. As soon as my breath returned and I was able to register everyone and why they were here, a wide grin raced across my face. "What are you guys doing?" I asked, incapable of getting rid of the huge smile that possessed my face.

"I'm the guilty one." Rachel raised her right hand which had a pink, burgundy and white polka dot oven mitten on it. She wore an apron displaying the same colors and dots. Her hair was pulled up and she had a dot of flour on her cheek. It made me grin a little wider. "I invited everyone here; I wanted to give you a welcome home party. Or a get well party. You pick." She stated, her lips pulling up into a smile.

The kitchen was the largest thing in the house. Every woman's dream kitchen. Black marble counters, white walls, a large center counter where Rachel did most of her cooking which was surrounded by six stools and a large dining room table furthest from the archway.

I chuckled and threw one finger up. I raced up the stairs, ignoring any lingering numbness or pain in my legs, to my room and flicked on the light. I dashed to my closet and found my favorite white, skull-designed thermal. I found a pair of nice black jeans. I shoved my legs into them one at a time, threw a belt around my waist and threw my black shoes on. I rushed into the bathroom and ran some water through my hair. It was descent.

I sped back down the stairs and was now in the kitchen, presenting myself to my audience. Everyone hooted and shouted upon my return. It just made me blush even harder. If I smiled any harder, this grin was going to become permanently glued to my face. It was the first time I felt genuinely happy in a while. Seeing everyone happy around me, I couldn't ask for anything better.

Rachel and the girls were mixing and chopping up ingredients. They all did as Rachel told them exactly. For the most part they talked about cosmetic and men. When Amber stated that men should be more submissive to women and their feelings, everyone seemed to throw their own opinions in.

Frankie argued by stating that women were needy naturally. Emma countered inquiring, "Who are the ones who clean up after you men?" Even when she was serious, she was a goddess. Still beautiful. She wore an elegant, deep green blouse exposing her perfect shoulders. Her hair was pinned and flipped over her left shoulder. She wore blue, denim jeans and black, leather boots. Her sapphire eyes were beautiful and demanded the room's attention. "Us. We provide for you by cooking and cleaning and doing most of the parental work when it comes to kids. Therefore, if we are willing to give to you *men* so willingly and freely, we need the same portion of love and attention back." She finished with a smirk.

"That's so juvenile." Frankie's voice filtered the room, sounding disgusted. Frankie wore a plain, short-sleeved t-shirt, sculpting and fitting his muscle perfectly. Of course everyone knew he wore it to impress Emma. His black jeans were fitted and he wore his favorite white tennis shoes and white baseball cap. *"You scratch my back; I scratch yours!"* He stated with mockery. "That's so middle school."

"The day you go through everything a girl has to go through," Jennifer spoke. "Then you can come back and pass judgments."

"That's so stupid. We do just as much as women." Jakob interjected.

"Like what?" Jennifer inquired.

"Lots." Jakob spat back.

"You guys are only good for one thing." Amber countered.

"I could say the same about women." Frankie stated with a snicker. All the guys seemed to laugh at his remark.

"Oh, is that how you feel? Ladies?" Rachel looked around at the girls. "How about we leave the men to finish dinner?" She suggested. All the guys seemed to stop laughing simultaneously. The girls laughed and our immediate silence amplified their laughter.

Everyone went back to working and laughing and talking. Amber and Jennifer seemed to be dressed as opposites. Amber's top was white and tight and she wore black pants. Jennifer wore a black blouse that draped over her body and wore white bottoms. Both were fit enough to be models.

Jakob always was the simple dresser. He wore a white v-neck and black shorts. Brycin was dressed the more formal of the boys. He wore a black dress shirt with a white vest over it. He had on a pair of black jeans with white tennis shoes.

But Claire was the one who stood out to me the most. Her hair draped over her shoulders. Her lips looked a lot fuller with the soft red lipstick she wore. She wore a black, fitted sheath dress. Her eyes were more beautiful tonight than any other day I'd stared into them. Her eyes were bright underneath the lights and against the black mascara she wore. I watched her and Rachel as they laughed and prepped the food in front of us. They were almost identical yet completely opposite. I smiled to myself and continued helping out.

Jakob had been hinting to Frankie how beautiful Claire looked tonight compared to Emma. For once, Frankie agreed and didn't fight back.

After all the food was prepped and shoved into the oven to cook, Rachel shoved everyone into the living room. She ran up the stairs and seconds later, she was back in front of us with two games. Twister and the Monopoly board game. I grunted a little. I hadn't played either in so long.

I could see that she loved every minute of this. Having a house full of kids, everyone getting along and laughing. It was her dream come true. She would want to do this again definitely.

It must've been longer than I thought since I played Twister. I was completely inflexible. This game consisted of me, Jakob, Claire, Emma, and Amber. Frankie wanted to play with Emma just to have an excuse to be close to her, but he was too large and maneuvering ourselves around him was going to be a mission along with finding the right color and placing the designated body part there.

Arms and hands and legs were everywhere. We looked like a human tarantula. I was in pain, but it was a joyous pain. Sleep had just restored feeling back into my legs and Twister had brought back that pain.

Rachel laughed at us most of the time. She was hardly breathing as her and the others laughed at us and our entanglement. She laughed harder when we moaned or complained or rushed her to hurry up and spin the arrow.

"Okay, okay." she laughed and took a deep breath, regulating her breathing and trying to show much control. It was the happiest I had ever seen her. The health and beauty that was in her eyes when Michael was alive repossessed them like never before. "Okay, Kayden." She spun the arrow. "Right foot; blue."

I searched the mat. Impossible. My right foot was on the yellow way at the bottom of the mat and the only available blue was up near my head, by my left hand. Pillars of arms and legs were planted everywhere on the mat. I stealthily maneuvered my leg through the pillars. I didn't know how, but somehow I hit someone's arm or leg and brought the human tarantula down. Rachel laughed hysterically as did everyone on the ground. This was quickly turning into a remarkable night, an event soon to be repeated.

We never made it to Monopoly. The food's scent was overpowering. Everyone raced to the table in the dining room. This was the exact reason Rachel had bought a table that seated ten people. For occasions such as these. Dinner seemed to be the best part. Everyone laughed and talked as they stuffed their face. It was like we hadn't seen each other in a long time. Clearly that wasn't the case. We had just separated from the hospital several hours ago.

Somehow we started discussing our trip to Crater Lake.

"He got *soooo* mad!" Emma stated.

"She tried telling him that it was an accident," Claire pointed out. "But, Frankie being Frankie wanted to show himself noble for *Emma*." Claire teased Frankie childishly the way she said Emma's name.

"Whatever, man!" Everyone laughed on his behalf. He couldn't help but laugh himself.

"Did you have fun, Kayden?"

I actually didn't want to mention it but I didn't want to ruin the night. "Yeah, it was fun. I was glad I went. In fact," I braced myself. I couldn't turn back. I had already started the sentence. I had to finish it. "I saw our rock. It's still there. Nothing's different about it." Except for the dark stains on it but I couldn't tell her that.

"Awww!" She placed one of her hands over her mouth and her eyes watered a little. She put her other hand on my shoulder. "You should have taken pictures." She stated.

The night carried on with laughter and chit-chat. Midnight had approached. Though no one wanted to leave, the feeling of fullness brought the feeling of drowsiness along with it. After desert, everyone left.

Rachel had gone up to bed after everyone was gone. She had work in the morning and needed as much sleep as possible. Brycin was the only one who remained.

We sat across from each other at the black marble counter in the center of the kitchen. The counter was completely clean now. It was as though there was never any food preparation taking place here. We were finishing off the rest of the grape cider. "This was fun." Brycin pointed out.

I swallowed the cider that was in my mouth. It bubbled and tickled my throat as it flowed down and cooled my inside. "Yeah. I'm glad she did this." I stated, nodding my head. "I've never seen Rachel so happy. She really loved everyone and their company. She always wanted a house full of kids."

"Yeah, I could tell." He chuckled.

I let out a deep sigh, running my index finger around the rim of the glass of grape cider. My mind had eliminated everything that just happened. All of the fun and all of the laughs. The thoughts of how I ended up in the hospital and what everyone believed happened was all I could think about now. Everyone was just a distraction from what I really needed to think about. My mind wasn't here anymore. It was in the past. Three days ago.

Everyone believed me to be in an accident but I knew the truth. I was attacked. By something. The earth attacked me and the black winds thrashed me around like a rag doll. They tossed me into the air and my head slammed against the ground.

I had forgotten about the wound I had received on the left side of my head. The warm liquid flowing down my face was blood. I felt around the left side of my head for the scar. Nothing.

Brycin seemed to notice that I was deep in thought. "What are you thinking about?" He asked and lifting his glass of cider back up to his lips.

I hesitated a bit. My face twitched and I felt my stomach drop into my stomach. "Where did you see my car?" I asked with bitterness in my tone.

He wasn't expecting me to ask the question. He choked off of his cider. "Oh, uhmm, I saw it near the university. It was concaved and completely totaled."

I nodded, my face grimacing to what he was saying.

"You're lucky. That accident could have-"

"Oh, cut the crap, Bryce!" I cut him off, leaning across the bar and hissing the words out. I tried to yell as loud as I could with a whisper. "My car is perfectly intact! I wasn't in any crash! I was attacked!"

"Yeah, by a man running from the police."

"Oh, bullshit!" The words became harsher as they came out and I could feel my tone rise. I lowered my tone back down to a hissing whisper. "There was no accident! I was attacked!"

"It was an accident, Kay." I can feel him grow irritated at me but I didn't care. His eyes burned lightly with rage and annoyance.

"I…was…attacked!" There was venom in each word as I said the words individually, stabbing my finger into the top of the counter on each word. My eyes never left Brycin's.

"If you were attacked then who attacked you?"

I was too mad to tell him the truth. Quite honestly, I didn't know who. All I knew was *what* attacked me. "I don't know!"

"So how do you know you were attacked?"

"Are you serious?! I know because it happened to me! How are you or anybody else for that matter going to tell me what I know?! What I know happened to me?!"

"Clearly, the doctor misdiagnosed the severity of your concussion. I think you should go back and see the doctor in the morning."

I threw my hands up and let out an irritated grunt.

"Look, your fine and everyone's happy. Why are you ruining this moment?"

"Because it's a lie! Everything! It's all a *lie!*" I spat the last word out.

"So all of the happiness and laughter you witnessed today, all the people who took the time out to come see you because they cared about you and your well being was all a lie?"

"You know what I mean, Brycin. Stop twisting my words."

"You have been out for three days. You may have dreamt everything you *think* happened."

My face relaxed as he spoke the words. *Had* I'd been in an accident? I mean my car *wasn't* here. And I *am* in *my* Corvallis. But the description of the crash. Clearly my injuries did not match the severity of the accident. I should've been paralyzed, incapacitated to the fullest extent. A minor concussion did not do the description of that crash justice.

But I didn't have any marks on me leading to what I *"dreamt"* happened to me in the field either. The scar that I knew should have been on my head wasn't there. I remembered feeling the blood trickle down my face, think and warm.

One of them was a lie and the other was the truth...but which one. The left side of my head hurt from all of the confusion.

"You are the source of your own unhappiness! You don't wanna accept reality! You wish to follow behind some idiot and his idiotic legend which I begged you to let go! Why can't you just be happy? If not for you, then for her." He pointed toward the ceiling, speaking about Rachel. "Only you could bring a night like this down in flames." He coated the words with a poison that burned me. He abruptly stood up and placed on his coat. "I'll see you later."

The door slammed lightly and it caused me to flinch. It was unfair. Not knowing. Lately, I didn't live my life. People tell me what I have done and I accept it. If I let this go, then I will never know anything for certain.

My fist slammed into the counter. If I wasn't so angry, the stinging sensation spreading throughout my hand would have made me cringe and cater to it.

I pulled away from the counter and locked the door. I headed up the stairs. I entered my room and slowly shut the door. I leaned against the door, my head looking up toward the ceiling. My mind was irresolute of everything. I really didn't know. Everything was walking a thin line. Brycin *could* have been telling the truth. No one around me really had to lie. But...what if they *were* lying. I needed to find out. Tomorrow I will know for sure.

I shut the lights off, allowing the shadows to coat my room and I headed to the bed. My clothes were still on as I called the night to another unsettled end.

When I woke, my mind was on warp speed. All of the events that occurred yesterday plagued my mind. Everyone assumed me to be in the hospital due to a car accident. I was out for three days with a minor concussion. Rachel had thrown me a party, a welcome home gesture. At the end of the night when everyone was gone, I interrogated Brycin about my accident. He fought me when I accused him of lying about seeing my car. He wasn't convincing enough for me to buy into his false truth. I wasn't going to be so submissive to anymore of his inadequate arguments.

My night consisted of tossing and turning. It left me restless but not even sleep deprivation was enough to come in between me and the agenda I had mapped out. I was going to see for myself that my car was perfectly intact. I wondered what would they think when I came back with my car. It would be my weapon against Brycin. Clearly, everything revolved around him.

I had to work fast. Brycin and I didn't have any classes today. When he realizes that I wasn't in school all day, he would be here knocking on my door, demanding an explanation.

Friday. It was almost noon. Frankie was out of school now and probably heading home. I needed to catch him before he reached home.

I searched for his number in my cellular. After coming across it, I pressed the talk button and held the cold object to my ear. The phone rang twice before a deep voice invaded my ear. "Hello?"

"Hey, Frankie?" I replied, trying not to sound like I was up to something secretive. I had to act this out perfectly so he had no suspicions. "It's Kay." I muttered.

"Hey, what's up, man? You doing well?" he asked.

"Yeah, I'm fine." I calmly answered. "I was wondering if you could take me somewhere. I need to pick up something important from a friend and I don't have a car to go get it myself." I paced the living room as I waited for his response.

I noticed that he lingered on the phone without saying anything, hesitating and deliberating over it in his head. "Uhh, yeah, sure why not? I'm not doing anything today anyways."

My face fell, less tense now and my body was soothed by relief. "Thanks, Frankie."

"No prob. I'll be there in a minute."

I closed the phone and dashed up the stairs. I threw a white hoody over my head and shoved my arms through the sleeves. I still had on the black jeans I had slept in last night and slid my feet into the black shoes alongside my bed.

It wasn't until I was back downstairs that I realized that I was hungry. I turned toward the kitchen and walked to the refrigerator. I opened the door and I winced at the cold air. I dug through the leftovers Rachel had stored away last night. I couldn't choose between the five cheese pasta and the chicken casserole so I grabbed them both. I was eating so fast that it was becoming hard to breathe. I let whatever was in my throat fall to my stomach and I washed it down with some leftover grape cider.

Frankie honked the horn to his Ford truck seconds after I had completed my morning meal. I threw the dirty dishes into the sink and rushed to the entrance of the house. I locked up and rushed to the truck.

The day was a middle gray. No blue interrupted the gray clouds up above. The wind blew somewhat vigorously and the smell of rain gassed the atmosphere. I hopped into his truck. My breathing was heavy and fast.

Frankie immediately questioned my hastiness. "This thing must be really important."

"Yeah."

He put the car in drive and left my house. I led him to the I-20 and we were off to Henkle Way.

"Your friend lives pretty far. Who is it?"

It took a minute for his words to actually take my attention away from the road. I had been staring at it ever since he started driving. I had wasted too much time already to make up some lie. Every bone in my body seemed to ache at the idea of telling Frankie the truth but a side of me didn't care. I turned to him and he prompted me with his eyes and expression.

"Well—" I stopped, shrugging my shoulders. There was a lump in my throat and my stomach ached. I was positive that it wasn't the meal I had forced down my throat. "What if I told you that we weren't going to go pick up something important? That I wanted to see if Brycin and the others were telling me the truth?"

He looked at me with bewildered eyes.

"They told me that I was in a car crash, that everything was an accident and that my car was completely totaled. But the thing is I don't believe that I was in an accident at all." I had his attention. It almost scared me because he had more of his attention on me than the road. "I think I was attacked. And if my car is where I left it when I got attacked, then I need to figure out why Brycin is lying."

"I'm sure you might have just dreamt it all. I mean, Brycin speaks very highly of you. You're like his little brother."

Ha! He had no idea.

"I think you would be the last one he would lie to. Or any of them. I am kind of jealous the way Claire and Emma seem to talk about you."

That took me by surprise. "Emma and Claire?"

"Well, yeah. They always talk of you. Especially when Brycin's around. They are always asking *how's Kay?* or *is Kay doing okay?*" he imitated in a high pitched voice, coated with mockery.

Wow. I had no idea.

"It gets annoying after a while.

"I had no idea, honestly."

"I believe you but Emma, she's—" he looked for the right word. "Different. I mean, girls have been no problem for me in the past. I'm one of the most fit most handsome guys at the school," No argument there. He was large and had a face that appeared as if a god sculpted it by hand. "But she shows no interest."

"Why don't you just ask her out?"

"Well, I get nervous around her." I used to think Frankie to be shallow. Just as shallow as I used to think Emma to be, possibly more so. "Keep this between us, but I think I'm…" he stopped, grinned shyly and peered vacantly out the windshield. He shrugged. "I think I'm experiencing…that *one* word. For Emma." He laughed.

Now I was uncomfortable. I didn't want this to turn into some type bonding time with Frankie. I just to get to Henkle Way and find my car in one piece. But it kept his mind off of me so I submitted. We mostly talked about Emma the rest of the drive.

We made it to Henkle Way. "Park here." I demanded after driving almost a quarter of a mile. I hopped out of the car. The wind was vicious and icy here. The sky was grayer than before but the scent of rain was absent here.

Disbelief swept through my body like a mighty plague. I couldn't believe it. My car…wasn't here. Who'd come and get it? Better question, who knew it was here?

"I don't see your car." Frankie pointed out.

"I know." I responded in an icy voice and began walking the pastures where Silverhead Peek used to be for the second time.

"Dude!" Frankie shouted out. "What are you doing?"

I looked at him with possessed eyes. I didn't even feel like myself. It was if I was under some kind of spell. "I was attacked here. I need to see something."

I walked for about twenty minutes and Frankie chased after me, complaining about how cold it was and threatening to leave me. "Seriously, Kayden this is crazy! Let's go back to the truck where it's *LESS* windy and warmer!" I tuned out his attempts to convince me to turn back and continued to march forward. "For goodness sake man! This is ridiculous! There is nothing out here, dude! Ugh, I'm turning around!"

A laughter echoed through the air and Frankie stopped. I didn't know where he came from but Portman was standing directly in front of me.

"You are a lot stupider than I thought." Portman stated pacing back and forth. Frankie was on side me at this point. "You *are* reckless." he snickered. "Bringing a human into the mix. More fun for me I guess." His voice was venomous. He was not the nice and gentle man I had met a week ago.

"What are you talking about?"

"You just made everything a lot easier." He stopped. "Your angel can't possibly get to you in time. By the time he finds you, it'll be too late."

"What the hell are you talking about?!" The wind made it hard to yell. I wondered if he even heard my question.

"You are just one less Neatholyte we have to worry about." He lifted one of his hands with his palm facing me. Was he calling me a Neatholyte?

Before I could even decipher the meaning of his statement, an orange and yellow ball of fire shot from his hand.

Frankie shoved me aside, throwing me to the ground and forcing me to land on my left shoulder which hadn't completely healed yet, intercepting the attack Portman intended for me.

On the ground, I turned to witness the gap between Frankie's flimsy body and the earth's floor close. He plummeted into the ground about fifty yards away from me. "FRANKIE!" I stared with wide, horrid eyes. He laid face down, his body was utterly motionless.

What had I done? I never meant for this. I never meant to bring Frankie to his death.

I winced, grabbing my left shoulder. It burned feverishly, as if someone was melting it away with a blow torch.

I pulled myself up to my feet — my right hand still pressed to my shoulder and faced the monster who'd just claimed Frankie's life.

He smiled a malevolent grin. "You wanted to know answers last time I remembered." He pointed out, dropping his head and taking a step forward. I stumbled back an inch.

I was surprised I was able to hear him. Even with the rushing winds, even with his head down, even with the twenty foot gap separating us, I was still capable of hearing him. I came to the conclusion that the potency of fear running through my veins must've intensified my natural sense of hearing.

My chest became achingly sore due to the combination of my sprinting heart and the constant expansion and compression of my lungs. My eyes were wider than before, unable to comprehend what I was witnessing.

Portman's head lifted and his arms were stretched wide. His eyes possessed an emptiness that I'd never seen in eyes. There was nothing in them — no white, no iris, pupil, nothing. Completely…black.

I couldn't control my body at all. The tremors my legs and hands seemed to be engulfed in, the instability of my breathing and the racing of my heart all left me immobilized.

My eyes were fixed on the monster as two large, black-feathered wings stretched from out of his back. His eyes stared back at me but they weren't brown anymore. They were a deep and empty black. No white resided in them. "Does this answer your question?" His canine teeth seemed to grow a fraction as he spoke the words and his voice was much more malevolent. He was worse than my demon. My demon couldn't kill me. He could.

I stood wide eyed with fright. My jaw hung low in disbelief. Here it was…the reason for the hiding and the secrets. Here was the truth, standing yards away with a fearsome glare. His head tilted with haunting eyes. "What's the matter? Expecting a red body, horns and pointy tail?" he joked.

He lifted his hand again the same way he had when he first launched an attack at me. I knew what was coming. Soon, I would be where Frankie was. How would I even begin to apologize to him on the other side?

Before I could even consider my apology for Frankie, another dazzling yet destructive ball of fire hurtled straight for me. There was no use in dodging it. This one was faster than the last. I threw my hands up in front of my face.

I was hit hard and the pain hurt tremendously. But the pain… didn't come from the front where I expected. It was my ribs but only my right side. The wind was knocked right out of me and when I opened my eyes, the world was spinning around me, the colors blurred together disgustingly. The spinning stopped abruptly and I rolled across the ground.

I lay flat on the floor, inhaling the scent of the earth, the soil, the grass, and the oncoming rain, mind boggled and trying to figure out what had just happened. But the world, even though I was still at this point, continued to swirl and move around, making me nauseous.

I pressed my hands against the soft soil, still under the dizzy spell, and forced myself up onto my knees. I tried to shake the dizziness away but it worsened somewhat. I rolled over, facing the direction of Portman, still aware of his plan to be my executioner.

There was something else in front of me other than Portman. I could make out a second pair of wings. They were a brilliant white. The spiraling was slowing and my focus was becoming clearer and accurate.

I couldn't register it fast enough. I wasn't prepared for *this!* I was able to identify this 'angel.' The angel…was Brycin.

Chapter 7: Angels and Demons

I REMAINED MOTIONLESS ON THE GROUND, PARALYZED by my own fear and consumed by shock. I felt vacant, unable to hear the whistling of the wind or feel its icy touch. All I could feel and hear was my heart pounding against my chest.

My eyes were glued on the two people standing in front of me, staring each other down with an intense gaze. No — people was the wrong choice of word. People made them seem human, made them seem like me. They were creatures. That was a more fitting word for them.

To anyone else, there couldn't be anything more shocking than seeing two men baring a characteristic that belonged to birds. Wings. But for me, there was one thing more astonishing to me than seeing a real angel and a real demon. The angel was undeniably without a doubt my best friend. Two enormous, white-feathered wings projected from his back, shining against the silhouette of the dark gray sky.

I couldn't even begin to fathom with anything I was witnessing. Once a kind and inviting substitute who seemed so eager to introduce me to a world of unimaginable beings was now standing yards away from me with a malevolent and demented agenda. My best friend had been trying to rip the obsessive thoughts from my mind when the entire time he was telling me to forget, he was, in fact, part of the legend. He was one of them.

Was this the reason why he hated Portman so much? Because he didn't want me to have anything to do with this kind of world? He knew that humans couldn't handle the idea of living on Earth with creatures of such majesty and power. Or could it have been that in a way, Portman had revealed Brycin's true identity to me? Revealed their world to me and that I was going to come and ask questions? Or maybe it just came down to the both of them being mortal enemies.

Brycin looked at me over his shoulder. His body remained unmoved, facing Portman. I didn't recognize my friend. His entire appearance had changed. He was a stranger to me. His body seemed larger, more muscular. Not to mention two large wings grew out of his back. But there was one feature on his face that made him more of a stranger to me. More so than his physique or his wings.

His eyes. They weren't a honey brown anymore. In fact, there was no color in them at all. They were colorless, completely white. "You alright?" he asked. Even his voice had changed. It was softer, silkier, angelic. I was still consumed by my own bewilderment. I couldn't answer; I was tongue tied.

I was still adjusting to the fact that he wasn't human. I wasn't sure if my silence had damaged his feelings because his pale eyes left no room for emotions so I tried to gesture it to him that I was okay.

Even the muscles in my neck seemed to be locked in place by fright. His head dropped slightly and he turned back around and faced Portman.

I regained my ability to hear to wind's grizzly roar and I winced at the arctic touch it possessed. It was overwhelmingly powerful. It felt like in any minute I was going to be scooped off the ground and catapulted through the air. I looked around to make sure that no trees had been pulled from their roots and hurled in my direction.

But neither the biting of the wind's cold touch nor its strength and ability to hurl trees through the air seem to affect these two.

My eyes transferred back and forth between the angel and the demon. They were opposites completely. Enemies no doubt. Brycin's eyes were without color. They looked almost haunting. His wings were large, white and beautiful. I couldn't think of any bird whose wings could compare.

As for Portman, his eyes were dark and deceitful, empty, full of hatred and malevolence. It was like looking into a deep space where no stars or planets or moons existed. Just darkness. His wings were just a black as his eyes. They were large and the tips of his feathers were a very dark shade of violet. His wings reminded me much of a crow's wing. Even though his wings looked just as evil as he did, they were still beautiful.

The wind's rage was suddenly intensified, whipping my shirt against the bare skin beneath it and tossing debris into my eyes. I threw my hand up in front of me, shielding my eyes from anymore debris that may escape into them. The wind continued with this behavior for several more seconds…

It stopped. I dropped my arm and opened my eyes, little pieces of dirt still lingering in them. I rubbed them fiercely, trying to remove the little particles that I hadn't succeeded in shielding from my eyes.

I regained my sight again but as I did, I wished I hadn't. My fear returned more potent, more overpowering than before, possessing me and leaving me paralyzed…again. The fear was building and building and building to a point where it was going to be impossible to remove from my body. It felt like there was something caught in my throat, stopping me from swallowing and inflating my lungs with air. My eyes burned from the blank stare I was engulfed in and my arms were shaking due to the combination of fear and them preventing my body from falling backwards.

I watched in horror as they approached.

There were three. Three large birds were flying out of the deep gray sky and straight toward us. Their wings were black and enormous. The sound of their gigantic wings flapping sent a booming vibration through the air that nearly made the inside of my ears bleed. They swooped down and landed next to Portman.

They weren't birds at all. Three more black-winged creatures, all possessing the same demented, dark eyes landed beside Portman. All of them seemed to induce me with a heavy dosage of fear, turning an emotion into a drug, a drug that I was forced to take.

But one of them struck more fear in me than the others, turning the drug lethal. The amount of fear swimming through my body had enough power to stop my heart dead in its tracks, enough strength to compress my lungs and prevent them from pulling oxygen into my body, enough strength to kill me yet it didn't. It forced my heart to race faster, my lungs to beat against my chest, my eyes to soak in everything — it kept me alive.

He stood in the middle. His wings were almost twice the size of the others and his hair flowed down his back like a black river. He wore all black as did the others. His skin was pale and his eyes, even though it may be difficult for another human in my position to tell, were casting themselves on me.

Brycin seemed to noticed that too because he jumped in front of me, shielding me from his eyes and took on a defensive stance. He was half-crouched with open wings.

"Avin, it's a pleasure to see you." Someone spoke. I assumed it was the one who stared hauntingly into my eyes before Brycin disrupted the connection. His voice was deep and dark yet hypnotizing at the same time.

But who was he talking to? With Brycin in the way, I wasn't sure if he was talking to me. Maybe they had me mixed up with this Avin kid.

Brycin's stance relaxed. He stood up straight and his wings folded. "My name is no longer Avin. It's Brycin." he corrected.

Avin? Brycin must have known I questioned the name in my head because his head lightly turned over his shoulder.

"That's quite a change over the centuries."

Centuries?

"Enough small talk Balavon." Brycin hissed through his teeth. "Why are you attacking us? There hasn't been any divine blood spilled for centuries."

Centuries? I couldn't get the word out of my head. The more they used it, the more it attached itself to my thoughts.

Balavon's dark and demented laugh vibrated the air. "You must have your facts wrong."

"Our facts are right! We know you killed that Neatholyte down at Willamette Park!" Brycin's voice was acidic, filled with rage and hate toward Balavon. They seemed to know each other very well.

"Of course I did." He started to pace the field. "It was the only way I was going to be able to get your attention. Your family consists of powerful beings as do mine. Why must we live in the shadows of something weak? The human race?"

"Because it's the law and every half-breed, even Demilytes as demented as you, must abide by them. It's what's kept us alive all these years and it will continue to keep us alive."

"Well maybe it's time for new leadership."

"You're crazy." Brycin spat venomously. "You'll start a war. I know that's what you want. It's what you always wanted. You failed in your attempts centuries ago but with as many of us as there are now, you just might succeed this time." I never heard his tone so offensive before. It was unsettling to me. "You're crazy if you think we will stand by and watch that happen."

"You still don't get it do you? What I want is to come together as brothers and eliminate this pathetic race that dwells here. And if a war begins out of it, so be it. I will annihilate anything, any*one* who stands in my way." The venom in Balavon's tone made Brycin's tone look like purified water, no threats or harm in it at all.

Balavon stopped pacing and took in a deep breath, his eyes closed and his chin lifted up. The silence seemed to bother me more than them talking. I felt like everyone's attention was on the human.

Balavon suddenly brought his head back down and looked over his left shoulder. "I see there is no reasoning with you angels. Ester." He called out and the black-feathered demon behind him on the left stepped forward. He was small and frail looking. His wings were a tad bit smaller than the others but his look was just as frightening. His hair was pitch black and his skin was a bit darker than Balavon's. He wore a crescent moon earring on his left ear that dangled over his shoulder. His black shirt was short sleeved and tight, gluing itself to every detail of muscles on his body.

Balavon's head then turned to the right. "Seth." Seth stepped forward. His hair was a light gray, almost white but his face was too young to go with the grayness of his hair. He was bigger than all of the others but not so much. His black shirt covered every inch of his arms and molded flawlessly against his semi-bulky muscles. If I made it out of here alive, working out would definitely be on the top of my list of things-to-do.

"Portman." after calling the last name, he veered his attention back to us. "Kill the boy. Once he dies, my plans will be set in motion."

Portman, Seth, and Ester all smirked deviously and then one after another, their wings opened, displaying their feathers.

My eyes were wide. It *was* me they were after. I heard a soft growl stir in Brycin's throat.

In an instant, I watched as the three demons charged toward me and Brycin — Brycin on the defense — their feet lifting off the ground and their wings catapulting them forward. The fear swelled up in my throat again. My hands were sweaty and my eyes were frozen wide open with fright. My first instincts were to run but I was overpowered by my own fear; it glued me to the ground. Though Brycin was larger as an angel, the other three were just as large. They would make it pass him eventually. They would come after me.

Without realizing it, I had become something barbaric and atrocious. I had become a murderer. I had brought two of my closest friends to their death. And me...I was destined to die here. It was inevitable. With the odds three to one, I would not make it out of here alive. If I die...Rachel. She said she live for me. If I die...what happens to her?

Brycin's wings shot out and he sped through the air gracefully, like a knife slicing through butter — straight for the other three half-breeds.

Feathers danced all over the field. Their speed was unheard of. My eyes were incapable of processing such speeds. To my eyes, they seemed to vanish and reappear but in different spots each time, thrashing out several series of attacks. I wasn't even sure if any of their attacks connected. Grunts, yells, and snarls penetrated the air. The fight was epic.

Brycin launched into the air and the fight followed him there, making it easier for my eyes to dissect the fight. Brycin had his hands full with Portman and Ester, dodging every single attack, flying over them or under them and around them, never getting hit. But they dodged his attacks just the same.

Seth was at a distance, observing, learning the way Brycin fought and how he dodged their attacks. His eyes seemed to get darker, vicious. Even from here I could see that.

He used his wings to launch himself into the fight. His hand was clutched into a tight fist. He was using his wings to add extra power to the punch he intended for Brycin. His armed pulled back as far as it would go and when he was in reach of Brycin, he snapped his arm forward.

I held my breath.

Somehow Brycin ended up behind Seth, not a single bruise. He dodged it. I let the air that my lungs refused to release during the little event out.

Brycin launched his fist to the back of Seth's head. But Seth, being just as fast as Brycin and the others, dodged it too.

It was a pointless fight. Their fists and kicks went into blurs again, making it hard for me to make out anything. Even with the odds three-to-one, Brycin still wasn't taking any damage.

For a second, I had forgotten about Balavon. I was sure he'd be looking at me but he was just as in to the fight taking place in the air as I was. But as soon as my head dropped, so did his.

I looked back up immediately, pretending I'd never brought my gaze to him.

When I looked back up the fighting stopped. Brycin was yards away from the other three. Their wings were majestic as they moved up and down gracefully in their own unique rhythm.

Brycin brought his right hand up in front of his face. I could see that it was shaking. Had he been hurt or attacked? I only took my eyes off of the fight for a fraction of a second. His hand was now holding something. It looked like a white ball with white lines shooting from it. Electricity?

That's what it was. And the white lines shooting from it were sparks. In one swift motion, Brycin flung his hand at the others and bolt of lightning shot from it. It was almost blinding as bright as it was but I still managed to keep my eyes from losing any detail at this point.

The other three dodged the ray of lightning effortlessly and Seth charged after Brycin. A punch to the face sent Brycin plunging to the earth.

I hadn't seen Balavon move at all, but there was a burning sensation spreading through my mouth. The pain was overwhelming. The intensity of the pain caused me to roll over onto my hands and knees. It felt like I was hit in the face by a fifty pound bowling ball, if bowling balls went that high in weight.

I could feel something forming in my mouth. It was a warm and thick substance. I spat into my hand and the ruby red fluid was my own blood. But I hadn't seen anyone approach me or heard anyone. I guess with creatures like these who would.

"Ester." I rolled back over to see all of them staring at me. Three hovered in the air and Balavon remained unmoved on the Earth's floor. The gray sky and the dark green ocean of grass both seemed to be staring at me too. Hatred was all I could see. "Kill the boy." Balavon ordered.

I looked back up and saw that only two of the three remained unmoved. Ester was flying straight at me. My breathing was so fast, it hurt. Me hyperventilating only made the hold fear had me in more impossible to break. My heart was motionless. No blood pulsed through my veins and my body went cold. My eyes were frozen and I couldn't blink. All of me was frozen except for my chest, inflating and deflating swift and sharp. I was sure that I was going to become more acquainted with death this time. My only source of protection was hurt, motionless after Seth's attack.

What could I do? Run? As if I could get anywhere with the speed advantage Ester had against me. He was only several feet away from me and I was trapped in his stare.

I wondered how he would go about killing me. Breaking my neck? Strangling? Or something more vicious like snapping every bone in my body, grinding them into a powdery dust and then burning the remains to ashes.

The flapping of his wings was close. I could feel the gust of wind they created. He let out a growl and both his hands were pulled back. The color in my face vanished.

I flinched away, my left arm guarding my face and my eyes tightly shut. I felt an immense gust of wind fly over my head and a bone-crushing sound invaded the air. There was a grunt after the loud bang.

Where was the pain that I had expected? The sound of my bones cracking and breaking and the horrific yells that would echo from my mouth and plague the air? Why was I…untouched?

I dropped my arm, relaxed my eyes and slowly opened them. I turned my body so that I was looking forward again.

I was left without words, searching for ways to explain this implausible phenomenon. Though it was a new half-breed to enter this epic match, I, too, knew this half-breed. "Claire?"

I was wide eyed, analyzing this new beauty Claire possessed. Her wings were enormous and stunning. Her eyes shared the same emptiness as Brycin's. Her long dark, red hair flowed down her back and in between her wings. She wore a white, long-sleeved shirt with ruffles running down the sleeves with long black pants and all black shoes.

I couldn't believe it. Claire was…an angel too. But how? How was the two of them angels? Was this some kind of dream? Some weird nightmare that I would soon be waking up from? I touched the side of my face. The pain and the evidence of blood trickling from the side of my mouth reminded me that was no dream.

Instantly remembering my life in grave danger seconds before Claire's arrival, I searched the field for Ester. He was on the ground several yards away from Claire and I. She had kicked him away from me before he could even lay a finger on me.

He was trapped in her stare as he slowly recovered from her attack.

More whooshing sounds invaded the air, surrounding me. I closed my eyes, protecting my eyes from flying debris.

The direction the wind blew in…it was odd. It didn't travel in one direction, but two. From my left and from my right.

I slowly lifted my eyelids and the field was suddenly crowded with half-breeds.

Speechless. Awestruck. Captivated by the beauty of the angel standing on the right of me and flabbergasted, for I knew this angel too. Emma, wearing all white which complemented her soft blonde hair, had two pure white wings of her own. Her beauty seemed amplified as an angel but one thing took away from her beauty. The breathtaking blueness her eyes possessed had faded away, leaving them empty and white.

I was afraid to even look to the left of me. When I did, I flinched away. I'd mistaken Jakob for one of the others standing across from us. He didn't share the same characteristics as Brycin, Emma, and Claire. His eyes were dark but didn't possess the malicious quality of the others who shared similar characteristics. There was also something different between his wings and theirs. *Their* wings were pitch black but *his* weren't so much. They were a dark gray and the feathers got lighter towards the tips.

I couldn't believe it. All of my friends were half-breeds. I seemed more paralyzed now than before. Air was trapped in my lungs as I registered what my *friends* were.

I released it and waited to see what would happen next.

Brycin floated to the ground and landed in front of me and the others, eyes fixed on the demons in front of us.

"Emma." he said her name soft and angelic but still with commandment in his voice. "Get Frankie out of here before it's too late."

I'd forgotten about Frankie after the fight started, forgotten that my pride and stubbornness had gotten him hurt. But Brycin said *before it's too late.* He must be still alive. I felt slight lightness to my conscience.

Emma, whose beauty seemed amplified as an angel, flew out of my sight.

Ester was back on his feet and next to Balavon. The other two still lingering in the sky descended to the floor. I couldn't tear my eyes away from these marvelous creatures. These angels and demons.

"A Demilyte?" Balavon asked with surprise and a hint of enthusiasm in voice. Even though the three familiar half-breeds blocked him out of my vision, his voice left a scar in my memory. I could never forget his voice. "On your side? Indeed things are getting interesting. But there is no time for play. I have matters to attend to. This will have to wait."

I heard the flapping of wings. The sound grew softer and softer, further and further away until there was nothing but silence. Jakob was about to fly off into the air after them when Brycin hurried and caught his ankle. "What are you doing? We should go after them!"

Jakob protested, wings flapping ferociously and dragging Brycin's feet through the soil.

"No! Not yet." Jakob's wings were less vigorous in movement and his feet slowly met with the ground again.

They all then turned and looked at me. I was hyperventilating again. I wasn't sure if I was more afraid of them or Balavon and his gang. My heart pounded faster and faster against my chest. Brycin was walking toward me but he wasn't my friend anymore. Before I knew it, I was on my feet and running faster and harder than ever before.

The wind rushed through my hair and burned my eyes but my feet had a mind of their own. My lungs felt like they were going to burst out of my chest at any moment. I couldn't even tell if my feet were moving fast enough but I wasn't going to stop. The smell of my sweat was immense and the adrenaline flowing through every vein in my body was heavy. My mouth was on fire and my legs burned from the intense running. I stumbled a few times but I continued with haste in escaping this field.

I saw it. Frankie's truck. It was getting closer. Just a few more feet. I looked behind me and nothing was following me. I continued to my destination. I was here. I opened the door and the keys were still in the ignition. *Thank you, Frankie.* I thought.

I brought the roaring truck to life and the tires screeched as I sped away from Henkle Way.

I checked my mirrors every so often, making sure none of them were following. I couldn't get a grip of reality. My hands shook on the steering wheel and the anxiety was overwhelming. My jaw was tight and I felt that at any given moment, I was going to burst into tears. Everything lately seemed to push me closer and closer to the emotional cliff I wished to leap from and become swallowed up by the waves below.

I couldn't describe my emotion at this moment. Disbelief? Anger? Fear? Betrayal? It was a mixture.

I passed by the university and I knew I was only minutes away from home.

As I pulled around the corner of my neighborhood, a sense of relief washed over me. I was alive and that was all that mattered. I saw

Rachel's car and hoped that she wasn't downstairs when I entered the house.

I parked in front of the house and silenced the roaring truck. I hopped out of it and slammed the door unintentionally. Hastily, I walked to the door, looking around and up, making sure I hadn't been followed.

I stuck the key inside, unlocked the door, and launched myself inside.

Home.

I never wanted to be inside so much in my life. I leaned my back up against the door; my breathing was still heavy and my hands were still shaky. Petrifaction still had me under its spell. My head was tilted up as I fought to restore my breathing and slow my speeding heart.

The house was bright and the TV was loud. Rachel was here. I had to get upstairs before she saw me.

So much for that plan. Rachel came around the corner with a tub of rocky road ice cream. "Kayden?" She'd immediately taken notice to my apprehension. If that wasn't enough to emerge her motherly side, seeing the little blood I hadn't wiped off the corner of my mouth would surely complicate explaining myself. "Kayden what's the matter?"

"Nothing." I spat the word out at a million miles per hour and shook my head. "I'm fine. I just need to lie down, please." I said icily. My shoulder bumped her lightly as I passed her. She interrogated me as she followed me up the stairs.

I knew she was only worried but my mind wasn't here. I didn't care about her feelings right now. I knew that the guilt would have me later for this. I entered my room and closed the door behind me. I paced the hollow box, beleaguered by thoughts.

"All of them?!" I questioned aloud, venom in voice. "All of them?! This entire time?!" My latent anger didn't help my breathing. "Who else? Amber? Jennifer? Frankie?" No. Not Frankie. I watched Brycin take a thunderous punch to the face and still managed to remain conscious. Frankie would have survived that blast if he was one of them.

It was all too much to take in.

"Kayden?" I heard Rachel's muffled voice right after the knocks. "Can you talk to me please?" I knew I was hurting her but I didn't know what to say.

I remained silent.

"Kayden?" the muffle was soft and hurt.

Sorry, Mom. I wish I would have said it aloud. But I couldn't. I plopped onto my bed and washed the day away with sleep.

Morning. Sleep hadn't done me any justice. In fact, it made a more mess of things. Last night, my childhood nightmare returned. It was exactly how I would dream of it years ago. The angels and demons fought for dominance against a blood red sky. But there was a slight difference in the dream this time. Faces. The faces of people I knew were in my nightmare. Balavon and Ester and the others, Portman and Seth. They were all fighting against other familiar faces I knew. Brycin, Claire, Emma, and Jakob, they were all in my nightmare. And all they did was fight.

But as always, my nightmare ended the same way. Everyone dies. *Everyone.* And the last thing I would see is my demon hovering above them with his white and red eyes burning bright. And like always, I wake up right after seeing his sharp gaze.

I pushed myself up and rolled over onto my back. I gazed out the window. I felt how the day looked. Clouded and unsure. Clearly the clouds were irresolute to whether or not they wanted to turn into a storm or remain calm.

I was just as irresolute about everything. I couldn't distinguish between what was real and what wasn't. Realities and fantasies. Did I live in a world where such things existed? If angels and demons existed then does that mean God is real? And the devil? What about things such as dragons and witches and vampires? I wasn't big on religion but after witnessing everything I had seen yesterday, I will begin to reevaluate my belief system.

Yesterday. A day I will dread for the rest of my existence. I wish that none of it had happened. I wished that I had never seen any of it, experienced none of it. Everything forced me to question things. My friendships between people and more importantly, what role did I play in all of this? I remember Portman referring to me as a Neatholyte.

There had to have been some kind of mistake, some variable overlooked that made them suspect me as a Neatholyte. Clearly I was not or else I would have fought alongside my friends. I never would have gone to him for answers if I already knew of them. Nothing made sense. I was tired of the mysteries.

I turned my head and glanced at the clock. It was going on eight o'clock. School was out of the question today. I couldn't face Brycin after seeing what he really was or any of them for that matter. They all lied to me. They were all angels. Even if I did confront them, I wouldn't know what to say.

I needed some clarity. I tried to make sense of everything on my own but nothing seemed to fit anywhere. I no longer wanted to know if these *things* existed. That question had been answered. One mystery down, several to go.

I lifted from my bed and immediately stretched out the stiffness in my body. I headed to my room door and opened it. No lavenders. That was expected. It was far too late in the morning for the scent to still be lingering in the house.

I walked down the stair, rubbing my eyes. I was restless but I couldn't go back to sleep. The odds of me having that nightmare again were likely. I headed into the kitchen and I saw Rachel sitting at the center counter with a handkerchief in her right hand. She had been crying. There was nothing more painful to me, more unbearable than to see Rachel in a state of distraught.

She looked up when she saw me enter into the kitchen. "What's matter?" I asked.

She sniffled a bit, ran her free hand through her hair and answered, "Frankie."

After she said his name, my chest ached. "What about him?" I asked, pretending to be oblivious to the matter.

"You don't know?" I hinted sarcasm but I wasn't completely positive. "I mean his truck is outside our home and you don't know?"

My head dropped shamefully.

"Kevin and Barbara called me." She started crying. "He is in the hospital! Intensive care and he almost didn't make it, Kayden!"

My head snapped up. My eyebrows furrowed and my lips were tightly pursed together. I was without words. Frankie had almost... died. How could he even bring himself to forgiving me once he recovers? He will always look at me with disgust for I was the reason he almost lost his life.

"Kayden?" I stared blankly at Rachel as she approached me. She took my hands in hers. "What happened? You storm in here without giving me any explanations! Your lip was bleeding and Frankie is in the hospital! Were you with Frankie yesterday?!" I rubbed the side of my mouth, flaking off the small amount of dried up left over blood.

Yes. I was with Frankie. I couldn't get my mouth to speak the words. I was still too lost in thought of Frankie almost dying to speak. This was just something else to worry about.

"KAYDEN?!" Her yell startled me. "For goodness sake, his truck is outside our home! You came here *in* it last night! What happened?! Answer me!" I had never seen this motherly side of her.

"Yes." I answered flatly. "Yes. We were together yesterday." How was I going to make up a lie yet keep it truthful? I hated my life right now. "We were attacked yesterday. I managed to get away. I used his truck." How did *that* make me look? Like a coward, someone who is willing to abandon the life of a friend whose grip on life is slipping?

I sighed.

She wrapped her arms around me tight. "I'm glad both of you are ok." I wish I could agree. Here I was still breathing and reminiscing and Frankie was in the hospital, fighting to breathe, fighting to live... fighting to survive. I should be where he is right now.

I pulled away from Rachel. "I think I will go see him today. Make sure he is okay."

"He is." It was clear that she didn't want me going outside.

"But I need to see it for myself. Please?"

She hesitated a moment, then nodded and brushed passed me, wiping the tip of her nose with the back of her hand. "Please call me when you get the chance okay?" I turned and she was under the archway. One tear had fallen from her eye. That single tear delivered a devastating blow inside my chest. I fought against wanting to react to the pain. I nodded with a tense and painful expression. "I love you."

"I love you too, Rache." She walked up the stairs and I waited to hear her door close. The door closed and I let out all the breath I seemed to be holding in unknowingly. My eyes fell to the floor and the thoughts seemed to invade me like an army on a small country. It was hard to even depict which thought to linger on because they kept rushing through my head. I slowly pulled my body up the stairs and into the bathroom and got ready to go see Frankie.

I looked like crap. I still had some dried blood lingering on the side of my mouth and my eyes were bloodshot red. There was a dark ring under my eyes and my skin was paler than usual. I looked like a ghost. No, my appearance was more related to that of a vampire.

I turned away from the mirror and began with my morning routine of getting ready.

I emerged from the bathroom, my skin brighter, the dark circles beneath my eyes were nearly gone and my eyes weren't so red anymore. The outside of me was clean but I still felt corrupted in the inside, still heavyhearted. Now all that seemed to be on my mind was what Frankie would think when he saw me. Did he even remember anything? For my sake, I hoped not.

I drove to the hospital in his truck. My stomach turned. I walked into the hospital and asked the nurse sitting behind the counter in front of the computer where could I find Frankie Hendricks. She was a very petite nurse with large, round, dark eyes that seemed a little too big for her face and black hair that was shoulder length. She led me to his room.

Frankie seemed more irritated by the fact that he was in the hospital rather than that he was in pain.

"Hey, Frankie." I caught him messing with cords and clear tubes attached to him. If I wasn't mistaken, I would have guessed he was trying to escape.

It wasn't how I imagined him at all. I hoped to come in and he'd be sleeping — I'd see the readings on the EKG machine and he'd be completely fine and on his road to recovery. But his left leg was hoisted up, in a cast and his right arm had a cast on it also. He had several, tiny scars on his face and neck. They would completely disappear once they've healed. But I couldn't prevent myself from forcing blame on me.

"Kayden?!" My stomach fluttered relentlessly. I was tense. I wasn't sure if his tone was full of anger or surprised. "Can you believe this?" He said pointing to everything around him. He sat back against his pillow looking up at the ceiling. "I am really hating my life right now."

I was relieved that he didn't want to kill me. I assumed that he didn't remember anything. "So what happened to you?"

"Damn it, can you believe I got jumped?! I want to see these kids that so called "*jumped*" me!" he stated, gesturing quotations as he said the word jumped. "They must have been really big or had weapons out of this world."

Could I ever bring myself to telling him the truth? Could I ever *tell* him that I was the reason he was in here? Me and my overbearing curiosity? Looking at his condition continued to chisel away at my heart, branding it so I would never forget what I'd caused.

"Oh, you just missed the others."

That stopped my train of thoughts. "Really?" I asked. My eyes narrowed as I tiptoed further into the room. "They didn't go to school?"

"I guess not. They mentioned you." I walked around his bed. There was a chair stationed in front of his bed. I sat there. "Were you with me when I got attacked?"

I sighed, remembering vividly what happened. It was distasting. "Yeah." I answered flatly. "I escaped. Barely. But I ran to get help." I rushed the words out. I needed an opening to look as brave as possible. I didn't want him to believe I would abandon him in such a state.

"That's what they told me. I couldn't imagine you lifting me by yourself." He chuckled. "And you have my truck, right?"

I nodded.

"Good. To be honest, I don't trust the others like I trust you." Oddly, I knew exactly what he meant. "I mean, yeah, Emma's gorgeous but they all seem so, so programmed. I dunno maybe it's just me."

"No. I feel the same." I objected. "Brycin was…" I didn't try to use past-tense but it just came out that way and Frankie immediately caught on. "*Is* my best friend but lately I have been noticing that he has been lying to me. A lot." I looked down as I said this, afraid that my eyes would give away any signs of softness. "If we are as close as he says we are, shouldn't I know just about everything about him?"

"A friendship is a relationship. It is between two people of similar interest and you can always know them and never *know* them. There is always something that he will never know about you and there is something that you will never know about him. It's just the way things are." I looked back up as he said this. I couldn't believe how insightful he seemed to become. I wasn't sure if it was finally knowing that Emma would never give him a chance or what but he was…maturing. Maybe he was hit too hard. Giving him a new personality, a wiser one. "Could you honestly say that he knows everything about you?"

My mind processed the question, storming for something that I hadn't told Brycin. In all actuality, I think Brycin did know everything about me. "I'm not sure actually."

"You're a better person than most. You're not like everyone else."

I nodded.

I started to stare at everything he was attached to. "So, what did the doctors say?"

"They said I am going to need an arm brace for a while. My tibia was fractured so this brace is going stay on my leg too and I am going to need crutches. I have a huge ass bruise in the center of my chest…" I had stopped listening after that. My memory of yesterday was reignited. Portman hurled a ball of flame at me and Frankie threw me out of the way and the ball colliding into his chest, soaring him through the air. "-and I have to stay away from intensely physical activities for a while."

I wanted to tell him the truth. I wanted to tell him that he saved my life and that I wish I was where he was. I deserved it. Not him.

"You don't look too good." Frankie acknowledged.

"I didn't get much sleep." I murmured, looking down with a confused expression. "Uhmm, I think I am going to head to school. Try and make it to my Theology class." I stated, lifting from the chair.

"Ok. Hey, keep my truck safe, dude!" he said, pointing at me with his right hand which was attached to the IV cord. He almost ripped it out and we both laughed.

"All right, I will."

"See ya, dude."

Frankie was the last person who I thought would ever grow on me but in all actuality, he was the only person I could really trust right now.

I drove the truck to school. There was such a hardness to the way I walked now. I wasn't afraid anymore. I was determined to see Brycin. The way I felt this morning was completely gone. I was going on a limb, but something told me that Brycin would be at the school, knowing that I would be there, knowing that I would want to talk.

Mrs. Hay had returned and she wasn't pleased at all with my tardiness. But her small comments did nothing to me.

As I guessed, Brycin was here, awaiting my arrival I concluded. My eyes were fixed on Brycin. I immediately took notice to the edge in his posture and the stiffness in his expression as I entered. I ignored Mrs. Hay and walked my way to my seat beside Brycin. I slithered myself through the students and to my seat.

I tried not to look at him directly. Instead, I study him out of my peripheral. His posture had not relaxed a fraction. His eyes stared deeply past the front of the room into nothingness. They were inattentive and blank. His fist closest to me was balled into a tight fist. I think it took us both by surprised, even though we hoped for the other's presence, how ill-prepared *he* was to see me.

I wanted him to say something first. But after realizing that that wasn't going to happen, I took the initiative. "So are you just going to sit there as if I am not here?" I began in a low whisper.

He seemed surprise by me. I turned and looked at him with my head ducked down, almost touching the table. "I thought you wouldn't want to talk to me again." He answered, never looking directly at me.

"I didn't and I am not sure if I still do but we have to talk. Now."

"This isn't the time or the place."

"Well then make it the time and place!" I whispered harshly, swiftly glancing to the front of the room to make sure Mrs. Hay hadn't heard me. Her lecture hadn't been interrupted at all. I turned back to Brycin and ducked my head. "Four years of knowing each other? And you never felt the need to tell me? Why?"

"Oh, yeah, Kayden because that's exactly what you want to hear when you first meet someone." His eyes left the front of the room, narrowed and sarcasm coated his voice. "'Hi, my name is Brycin. My favorite color is green, I like to swim, oh, and by the way, I am an angel.'" he protested.

I took in everything he was saying. He was right but it still didn't ease the way I felt. "Point taken but it's better than this! It's better than being so uninformed about you and who you are!"

"I did what I had to do, to keep you safe and out of danger."

"I was never in any danger." I protested, my eyes narrow as I looked at him

"As far as you know." He responded, eyes returning back to Mrs. Hay.

"What is that suppose to mean?"

"Not now Kayden!" his voice was a bit harsher.

"Well why did you bring the rest of them into this? Why not just keep them away? At a distance? Because of you, I have built relationships with all these people and for what? To end the friendships I've made with them?"

"Trust me, you won't breaking any of the friendships you've made with us." He laughed the sentence. "I have my reasons for why I pulled everyone else into this. But, again, this is not the time or the place."

"Then when? And where?"

He seemed to linger and hesitate, thinking thoroughly about how to answer me. He sighed in defeat. He dropped his head. "I didn't want you to find out this way. But," he looked up at me. "It's only a matter of time 'til *it* happens to you?"

"What is *it?*" I asked.

He sighed again and hung his head. "Everything you want to know will be waiting for you at Willamette Park. Meet me there. Tonight." He packed his belonging in the midst of Mrs. Hay's lecture and stormed out of the room.

I was empty. I thought after confronting Brycin about yesterday that I would feel better, feel some sort of accomplishment. But I didn't. I felt hollow, vacant. I was now suddenly afraid. Afraid of what tonight would hold and how I was going to change after this.

Chapter 8: Legends vs. Legends

I WASN'T SURE WHAT TO EXPECT. I ADMIT, A PART OF ME was afraid, fearful that maybe knowing everything about Brycin and the others would create an irremovable, unbearable void between us. I didn't want to be alone again. I didn't want this night to be the end of all of the friendships I had made. I didn't want to take the risk.

But there was a stronger side, a more dominant side. A side that was tired of the lies and secrets. The side that was relieved that everything everyone covered up was going to be revealed to me tonight. I would no longer be kept in the dark, hidden from the truth.

I tried to remain as calm as possible as I drove Frankie's roaring truck to Willamette Park. But I couldn't control my fingers on the steering wheel that seem to rise and fall in sequential order from pinky to thumb. I tried to keep my breathing stable, reminding myself to inhale and exhale. But the anxiety was overwhelming and its scent radiated from the sweat on my palms and off my breath. The fear pulsating through my veins was hot, making the surface of my skin break out into a sweat. Even with the night air rushing through the window that was rolled down, nothing seemed to calm my sweat.

The more I thought of things, the harder it became to ease anxiety's spell. Ever since he stormed out of the class earlier today, my mind was being overflowed and ravaged by thoughts. The thoughts of knowing that my best friend Brycin and some of my other friends were all half-breeds, the thoughts of how a substitute teacher and his psychotic leader wanted to see me dead along with the angels who protected me and how that tonight was the night that all my questions were going to be answered.

But there was one thought that overpowered the rest, making them less significant and shoving them to the back of my skull. It was the reason why Balavon and the others wanted to see me dead. They called me a Neatholyte. Clearly that accusation was a false one. First of all, I had no wings to prove it. Hell, I didn't even have an ability. Frankie and I were the only humans in all of this. The only difference, I knew a lot more than him.

I looked at the clock on the dash board. It was five minutes 'til nine. The moon was high above the earth's floor and no clouds shared the skies with it. It had been a while since I had seen the moon for its true beauty. It was full tonight. It reminded me of a movie where someone or a group of friends would go out into the still of the night, full moon high above the earth, unaware that something waited for them in the darkness — something that was going to claim their lives.

I pulled in to the park's parking lot and I couldn't rip my eyes off of the second and only car here other than Frankie's truck. Brycin was standing right next to it. It was *my* car, *my* Charger. I shut the beast off and opened the door, allowing the arctic air to brush against my skin. I rushed to my car and knelt beside it, running the tips of my fingers along the icy exterior searching for dents or scratches. My behavior immediately irritated me. I knew I hadn't been in an accident so why was I checking my car as if I had? Maybe I was just glad to see it.

"Where was it?" I asked, still running my fingers across the cold, metallic surface.

It was quiet for a while and the thoughts of dents and scratches left my mind and the old thoughts returned. I slowly stood and turned to face Brycin. His face was vacant, expressionless. I could tell that he didn't want me here. *He* didn't even want to be here. "I had Jakob keep it safe for you." He answered, voice sharper than knives. Our eyes were locked on each other for a while. His head then fell and he took a deep sigh, breaking the gaze our eyes were trapped in.

I walked to the front of my car wondering what he was thinking. When his head lifted and his eyes opened, it was as if they had been open the entire time. He didn't even have to look for me. He knew exactly where I had moved without even seeing me. One of the many abilities of a half-breed I guess. "You sure about this?" His voice was deep and antagonizing.

I knew that he was trying to get me to change my mind by planting some fear in me. It was too late for that. I was already afraid. I wasn't going to change my mind. Not now. "Yeah." I answered flatly.

He started to walk toward me. For the first time since I've known Brycin, I was afraid of him. My entire body was tense, frozen in place like a sculpted statue. He brushed passed me, his shoulder slightly nudging mine.

I released the air sealed up in my lungs and turned around, watching him as he disappeared into the boundless labyrinth of trees. That's where the true darkness resided. Everything was black and eerie but if I wanted to know I had to follow. I slowly followed behind him into the dark forest.

I was deep in the forest at this point, leaving the moonlit Earth behind me. I trailed deeper into more darkness, the air more piney here and the soil more moist than before, feeling more and more disturbed by the eeriness this labyrinth possessed. The choir of chirping critters and the scurrying of creatures across the forest floor only amplified my fear for the darkness.

The fusion of the damp soil and darkness made walking and keeping up with Brycin impossible. Risen tree roots and shrouded ferns and shrubs intensified the difficulty of getting through this forest. I was forced to use the rough tree barks to guide me through the rest of the darkness.

I saw a light coming up ahead. It was a large field and it was lit by the moon.

We'd reached the forest's edge, entering into a large field surrounded by more mazes of trees and shadows. The size of the open field was equivalent to two football fields fused together. I never knew such a place existed deep within the park.

The earth's floor was a bit harder here but still moist. The air was refreshing, invaded by the scents of all the forests surrounding us and the nearby river. The moonlight was more stunning here than before.

I looked up. The clouds that had haunted me yesterday were gone, revealing the night's true splendor. The forever abyss was scattered with small specs of light and the large, luminous ball perched high above filled the dark void with beauty. I almost felt that the relief I was seeking, this meadow had give it to me.

The fluttering of feathers startled me. Brycin's wings were visible and behind him now stood Emma, Claire and Jakob. Three had white wings and white eyes and one had black eyes and dark gray wings but in the night, they reminded me much of Balavon's wings.

"Let me start by apologizing." Brycin ended the silence. "I only did what I did to protect you. I was keeping you safe."

I nodded, accepting his apology.

"Well," he began letting out a deep gust of air. "I guess I should start with what you *think* you know." He turned and he walked deeper into the field. The others followed and I obeyed too.

I watched them as we trailed deeper into the midst of the field, further examining them and their undeniable and illogical beauty. All of their beauties were amplified. They all looked stronger, appeared more beautiful and walked with such gracefulness that it would be impossible for a human to imitate.

Their feathers coated each of their wings uniquely, each formatted in their own pattern. It was almost hypnotizing staring at them for so long.

They stopped. I stopped as well. They all turned, almost in unison. Brycin took a deep breath and his eyes closed. After a minute or so, his eyelids lifted and his eyes returned to normal and his wings left his back. They didn't retract into his back or anything. They just vanished. The others followed his lead and their wings disappeared and their eye colors returned.

"Portman told you that we came into existence thousands of years ago. That God and the devil had a war and through circumstances, angels and demons were left here, to dwell on Earth and that after a while, they developed an attraction towards humans, creating us half-breeds." I nodded in agreement, recalling the legend as if Portman had told it to me yesterday. Yesterday. I winced at the thought, considering the *true* events which took place. "Well forget all of that. It's all a lie. That is a false legend. We came from one angel."

I was trapped in confusion. I recalled Portman speaking to me of an army of angels and demons. "One?"

"Yes. His name was Sapharius. He was one of the most beautiful angels to ever exist. He was an archangel of six, beautiful white-feathered wings. He had three on each side and his eyes were more brilliant than sapphires. His hair was long and silver, almost glistening whenever the sun touched it. He was a mighty and noble angel, heart of pure gold.

"But he would commit a deed that would banish him from Heaven and he would become a fallen angel."

I allowed my legs to bend beneath me, bring me down so that I was sitting on the damp soil with both my knees up against my chest, my arms hugging them. The clear sky, high moon, and dark forests around me created the perfect scenery for the story. The only thing missing was a camp fire.

"You see, Sapharius was a guardian, an angel of guidance and protection." He started to pace, gesturing with his hands to help him with the flow of the story. "He was the guardian angel of many *but* he favored one more than the others.

"Ishta. She was very beautiful but she was a very vulnerable girl and she required much of his attention. Because she required so much attention, he began to watch her more than others.

"She was the most beautiful thing in his eyes. She had long, elegant copper hair and light skin. She lived in a small village off the banks of a river.

"The village, you could say, didn't live prosperous and struggled to survive. They were a weak and small people. Their rivers were without fish, their herds were sick and feeble and it hardly rained, leaving them without any crop.

"Ishta and her family were not very essential assets to the villagers. They were capable of surviving with or without them. But it was because of their father and his faithfulness to the villagers that they kept them around.

"One day, Ishta's father had become terribly ill and with his illness came great grief. She needed to keep her father alive as long as possible for her and her brother were fairly young and she knew that without their father, the villagers would most certainly turn their backs on them.

"She'd gone into the nearby forest, searching for essential herbs to create a specific remedy to calm her father's scorching fever. But with the long search, came exhaustion, day turned into night and she still hadn't acquired every herb needed. So she rested beneath an oak, awaiting daybreak so she could find the remaining herbs.

"Upon awakening, she was greeted by a hunting party consisting of four large men from a nearby village hovering above her as she slept. Of course their presence frightened her but it was the objective resting in their eyes for her that made her nervous.

"She slipped passed them but it was only because they allowed her to. They were playing with her, making her *feel* as if she could outrun them, as if she had a chance to escape but in reality, she was a lot slower than them, a lot weaker them. After a while of playing chase with her, they cornered her with such morbid and cruel intentions.

"Sapharius broke rules that day, appearing in front of her and the four men, noble and proud as her protector. He was immediately disturbed by their loitering thoughts. It was the first time Sapharius killed a human being and it would become the moment that would reject him from ever entering Heaven again.

"Though he'd just saved her from the vicious men and their revolting thoughts, in his mind, he expected Ishta to be afraid of him and run back to her village. It was the human thing to do. But when the realization sat in that she wasn't, it amazed him.

"She stared at him and his wings and he had mistaken her stare for fright. But she wasn't afraid of him. She was in love with him."

"Awww, I love this part." I turned and faced Claire as she spoke.

I was completely lost in the story. I had forgotten that Claire, Emma, and Jakob were even present. I was imagining everything so vividly, Sapharius and Ishta and the men who wanted her for her beauty and body and how Sapharius came to saved her.

She was smiling hard and everyone seemed to scold her for disturbing the flow of the story. "Sorry. Continue."

"Anyways," Brycin muttered, rolling his eyes. "She asked him to come back with her that day, back to her village. She told him how sick her father was and how she required his assistance to save him. No longer did he have a place in Heaven and alongside Ishta, no place was more important.

"She delivered him to her father and he laid one of his hands on the old man. In seconds, the sickness evaporated from the man's bloodstream and he was healed.

"Ishta's love for him magnified and became boundless. She would love him, he would do whatever she wanted and her life would be irrevocably his and he would forever protect it.

"Word traveled fast throughout the village about this mysterious man capable of fulfilling miracles and the villagers immediately came knocking at Ishta's home. They requested permission to see him.

"Many expected Ishta to disregard their requests due to the treatment her and her family received by the villagers but she was ever so willing to grant permission. She asked Sapharius if they were permitted to see him. He asked her did she approve of them seeing him. She said yes.

"It was the first time anyone other than Ishta and her family had seen Sapharius. In their eyes, he was a savior, a god, a reason to hope for a better future. She told the tale of how she stumbled upon him and how he saved her from four, ruthless nearby villagers.

"As a confession for their disloyalties to Ishta and her family and the arrival of Sapharius, they wished to celebrate that night, giving their god and newfound goddess a proper welcome. Of course, Ishta was the one deemed as decision maker on whether or not they should go. It was a chance for her to feed her family and so she did.

"That night, Sapharius and Ishta sat high and watched the celebration unravel. He was painted on stones and statues were built of him but he didn't want any statues built of him. His request was that if he be built into a statue, so must his bride.

"Ishta couldn't believe any of it. She was finally important and it was all because of her angel, her lover. She couldn't understand his love for her but she never questioned it either.

"Days had passed. The villagers demanded that blessings be brought to their land. They used everything they could to convince him that they were in dire need. But Sapharius refused. He had everything he wanted. The love of his life was all he desired.

"It didn't take long before they came to the realization that his miracles were only followed through upon Ishta's request. They would beg Ishta to convince Sapharius to bless their land though there wasn't much convincing to be done on her part. Immediately, for her, he granted the wish.

"Weeks passed," Emma's voice chimed as she picked up the story. "And the villagers were shocked to find that their rivers were overflowing with fish, their herds were healthy and strong and they were reproducing, and they saw life beginning to form in their crop fields. Even the men of the village were stronger now, able to hunt and bring home more food. Everything seemed perfect.

"Later, Sapharius and Ishta would marry and her family would become leaders of the village."

"But something unfortunate would happen that would leave Sapharius brokenhearted." Brycin stated. "Ishta had become pregnant and was carrying three. Ishta was truly a goddess to the villagers now. There was no such thing as a woman having three kids at one time. Sapharius was thrilled about having a family with Ishta. It made everything perfect and Ishta wanted nothing more than him and her children. But with no medical system and the fact that she was carrying three, nonhuman babies, she died from the pregnancy.

"Defeated, Sapharius remained by Ishta's side 'til she took her last breaths. Sapharius' heart hardened a little that day. Sapharius left with her body and buried her deep beneath the earth under a mountain.

"The villagers became frightful, feared that he would never return and with only baby angles, it would take years before they could do anything. But he indeed returned.

"Stories say that upon his return to the village, his eyes were no longer the dazzling sapphire blue anymore. They were white and empty.

"The villagers noticed his heartache and found his distress and sadness most unsettling. The villagers immediately proceeded in trying to mend his heart. There were thirteen village leaders, two including Ishta's father and brother, and they tried their best to keep him happy. Feasts and festivals in his honor but how could he have been happy at such a time?

"It was that night he truly gazed into the eyes of his three sons. All of them possessed a piece of Ishta. They would become his reason for living now. He named them Simon, Ishra, and Kasi and with the help of Ishta's father and brother, the half-breeds would grow up to be healthy and strong.

"Years had passed and Sapharius remained their god. He didn't find love again, but he found comfort in six other village girls.

"They all became pregnant and bared one child each. All of them except for one. She had twins and survived the pregnancy. Her strength attracted Sapharius, a quality he once saw in his past love Ishta. She would remain by his side forever and eventually, he would fall in love with this girl.

"The village was more prosperous and larger than they'd ever imagined. The village grew exponentially, expeditiously and everything seemed to be perfect."

"But when there is too much good in one place," Jakob now picked up the story with majesty and power coating his words as he started. "The cosmos is thrown out of balance. Because so much good inhabited one place, it drained the rest of the world of its good and the rise of these half-breed children added to the imbalance.

"Evil began to corrupt everything except for this village. The world was literally dying and the people saw it. Killing and thievery, conquering and world domination became the ways of life. People didn't care anymore. Death, in their eyes, was all that awaited them.

"You see, Sapharius didn't know that upon the day of his arrival, the day of his first miracle, he started to drain the earth of its life. Around the world, crops stopped growing, rain seized, herds died, the oceans and rivers gave no life to creatures and the fittest were not fit to survive in such a world.

"There was too much evil, and nowhere to store it. Stories state that the corruption and maliciousness of the world converted into a flow, a pure energy source, and that the flow of pure evil gave birth to *him*. That upon the day of his conception, all of the flow inhabited the child's body, leaving him inhuman. That it was the only way to keep the world from dying so fast. That day, evil gave birth to the demon, Azer.

"The child grew faster than any human child. After six years, his age was equivalent to twenty human years. He was big and strong and on that year, he would receive his wings. Two large, black, bat-like wings each stretching twenty feet in length.

"With evil objections, Azer circled the world for strong men, corrupting them and their blood with demonic blood. The men underwent a rapid transformation and in minutes, they had wings of their own. But because of the human blood in them, they did not have bat-like wings. They were feathered, black wings.

"Years later, angel/human half-breeds were abundant and so were demon/human half-breeds. The demon/human half-breeds inhabited just about every area of the world, terrorizing cities and destroying everything in sight. They were killing the earth.

"Sapharius sought out to destroy Azer, realizing what his presence on Earth had done. He gathered all of his children together except for the ones who he favored most. Ishta's children. The world was dying and required his help.

"That day, a war none like any human had ever witnessed began. Skies were plagued with these angels and demons. The war destroyed more cities than imaginable. Nation's fell and empires crumbled. They fought endlessly. They say upon that day, the skies turned red and would remain that way as long as these beings inhabited the air. No place was safe from the wrath of these beings.

"The skies were never without a battle and the humans were smacked in the middle. The death toll was skyrocketing. Millions of humans died at the hands of the half-breeds. Rather it was intentional or accidental; there was no way for the humans to escape death. More humans were dying than anyone because they were the weaker species. Even the strongest of nations stood no chance against the divine. This would give birth to the humans' hatred toward Heaven, Hell, and all the divine.

"No one knows exactly how, but, after what seemed like an eternity of battle, both Azer and Sapharius vanished. When the fires settled, Simon, the oldest son of Sapharius, saw the results of the war and the panic it created. The world was in total darkness. They were going to be the cause of Earth's extinction. He made a truce with the demons. He declared that if they left the angels alone, than they would be free to live however they pleased but with restrictions. They would not be allowed to kill anyone. Humans or angels. The demons agreed."

"But the demons would no longer be their problem." Brycin started again. "It was the humans.

"The half-breeds expanded their living so that everything would remain in balance. We were used to living with our wings exposed and many nations accepted us into their cities. We helped rebuild empires and we learned to coexist with the humans and demons.

"But, some humans started to gather and a cult had risen. Established with the thought that humans were supposed to be the most superior beings. They believed that God had betrayed them. It was the only thing capable of justifying what was going on. They feared God and the Devil and felt betrayed by them. They were going to fight back, attack God and the Devil head on.

"They were the creators of the false legend and they led many into believing these lies.

"They then searched for ways to kill us and eventually, they succeeded. They found our weakness. Our wings. They give us our power and immortality...sort of. Chop off our wings, we become mortal.

"It was too risky for our ancestors to walk around with their wings bare, so, the hid them and disguised themselves as humans and they would remain that way forever."

The images continued to flicker in my mind. I imagined it all so well. So well, I almost felt like I was there.

It was silent for a while and I hadn't realized it before, but I was shaking. Claire came to my side me, her wings fluttered open and the color in her eyes faded. She sat beside me and wrapped one of her wings around me. They were unimaginably soft, more precious than velvet. They were warm and the comfort immediately put a sleep spell on me but I refused to give in to the spell.

"So, are humans still aware of your existence?" I asked, my body warm and with less vigorous shakes.

"No." Claire answered beside me. "When the cult died out, so did the knowledge of our existence."

I nodded thoughtfully.

"But now we are afraid that the Demilytes will expose us again," Emma muttered. "And everything is going to repeat itself."

"Because of the Neatholyte who was killed?"

Brycin nodded. "They killed that kid. Then they came after you. It's obvious what Balavon's intentions are. He is trying to start a war again.

"Portman was in your head the entire time. I tried my best to talk you out of it but his powers were too strong for me to break through."

My eyes narrowed into slits. "What are you talking about?"

"Portman sowed those over obsessive thoughts in you. You never *really* wanted to know as much as you did. When he sparked a fragment of curiosity in you, he was able to magnify it. Ability of emotional amplification. When you were asking questions and wondering more than necessary, there wasn't much I could do. All I *could* do was watch you as carefully as possible." The hurt in his voice was shameful, dishonoring. As if he had failed at protecting me. "It was hard for me. I couldn't really give you a reason to why you needed to let these thoughts go. I didn't want you to be a part of this world. I still don't especially when there is a war brewing in the atmosphere."

There was an indescribable feeling in me. My face was expressionless but I felt more than emptiness and vacuous, I felt soulless. I felt disgusted, sickened that such a creature had such control over me.

"As soon as he walked into our classroom," Brycin started again, his voice harsher now. "I knew who and what he was and what his agenda was. There wasn't much I could do. There are rules set in place. Rules that we must abide by or risk plunging into a world of disaster yet again.

"It was the perfect plan. Present to you the legend in front of humans, a place where I couldn't act in anyway, especially in a supernatural way, implant just a tiny essence of curiosity in you, and you would come looking for answers." My head fell shamefully. I had given Portman everything he wanted and he almost succeeded if it wasn't for all of the angels around me.

"I didn't know how to convince you to leave it alone. I was scared. I didn't want to push you too far over the edge again."

That wasn't his best choice of words. I cringed at them, remembering my near death experience I had had.

"Sorry." His head dropped. He took in a lungful of air and released it.

Silence washed over the field and all that was audible was the whistling of the wind and its light touch as it played with the branches and leaves of the many forests around us. With the wind, it brought with it nature's scent, relaxing my body along with Claire's wing that was still around me.

She rested her head on my shoulder and her fragrance nearly destroyed me. It was more heavenly, more invigorating than the scent of nature. Her scent immediately comforted me and I was awakened again. "They are trying to kill you to taunt us," her angelic voice rang in my ear. "You are the ultimate reason for us retaliating. And if we retaliate, others will come and we cannot afford to expose ourselves again." As she explained this to me, it was hard to concentrate on her words with the sweat building up in my palms and the sound of her voice singing to me like an orchestra of harps.

Brycin chuckled but for what? No one had said anything funny. "I think he is warmed up now." He protested with a light chuckle still in his voice.

She chuckled as well and her head rose off of my shoulder.

"Anyways," Jakob intruded, rolling his eyes. "The reason we must keep this from happening is because it would send us back into a period of chaos. Humans would be afraid of both angels and demons and with strongly developed religions, the ramifications will be deadly. The weapons the human race has access to isn't enough to kill or destroy us as long as our wings are intact, but it could be the beginning of mankind's road to extinction. Wars would manifest over religion mainly but also because of the death toll that will come with our fight. All three sides will suffer.

"Many In-Betweens have foreseen it. We have to stop this now before it gets too out of hand."

"In-Betweens?" I asked thoughtfully, horror in my eyes as I tried not to imagine what they must have foreseen.

"They are half-breeds who have not acquired wings." Brycin informed. "They aren't human but they aren't fully a half-breed. They are in between."

I nodded again thoughtfully.

World disaster. Global wars. Half-breeds bringing about the apocalypse. Last week, my most strenuous challenge was doing the laundry. Now, I was the key to Earth's Armageddon.

"And Balavon is calling the shots." Brycin spoke. "He wants this all to happen. He's seen it for himself. Claire caught a good read on his mind in the field. Our deaths lead to these days." I turned to her and she nodded with closed eyes.

So many questions surfaced with that explanation but I asked the one poking at my mind the most. "Our death?" I asked. "All of us?"

"No," Brycin corrected. "Just the two of us." He closed his eyes and his wings fluttered from out of his back, elegant and white, full of purity and strength. I watched them carefully as they move, looking at how the bones in his wings bent and formed, wrapped in strong muscles, flesh and feathers, gracefully and intricately stretching out. They were enormous and beautiful. I was getting used to the white eyed Brycin with wings.

"You see I am a type of guardian angel. A protector angel. The difference between a protector and a guardian is a protector's relationship with the one they are meant to protect is more complex. It's more personal, more intimate.

"When one is born and a half-breed is meant to protect him or her, their souls are fused together and they become one. Nineteen years ago, I felt that fusion and I searched for you but I couldn't find you. Something kept me from getting to you and even to this day I don't know what. But I wasn't going to give up. I searched everywhere and when I finally came across you that thunderous afternoon, your shirt was bloody and it looked as though you were attacked. I had to work fast and make sure you were okay.

"That day, I led Rachel to you."

My eyes were fixed in a stare. But not at Brycin, passed him. Disbelief overshadowed my mind and everything seemed so imaginary now. He took in another lungful of air as I stared vacantly passed him. "I brought Rachel into your life because I knew she would be the best thing for you. I was the one who turned Michael's feelings about you around and in the end he acted on his own feelings. They were without a child, you were without parents. Seemed perfect to me."

He walked up to me but my expression was still vacant. He knelt in front of me, Claire's arms and wings still around me and Emma and Jakob in the background with their arms folded. He knelt in front of me, eyes white and wings erect. "I know this is hard for you to take in at once. But you must understand that I have to protect you. I have to keep you alive. So we both can live."

The spell of disbelief I was engulfed in was becoming harder and harder to escape out of. I couldn't believe any of it. Brycin had known me my entire life whereas for me, I had only known him for four years. The more they seemed to explain things to me, the more bizarre things got.

"Whatever it is you feel, I feel it as well. Like your confusion and disbelief at this very moment, I feel it. Ha, it's kinda weird. Sometimes I don't even know if it is my emotions I am feeling or yours but I am getting better at differentiating between the two.

"But with that being said, *you* can never feel what *I* feel. In terms of emotion. That's also how I knew exactly when you were lying. You would become very anxious and nervous and I would feel that exact same nervousness and anxiety.

"On the other hand, when one of us is injured and endures physical pain, the other one will feel the exact same pain at the exact same magnitude."

Things were coming together. My mind was becoming less foggy with disbelief. Brycin was in my focus and he seemed happy to see that all the puzzle pieces to my intricate life were finally coming together.

"Was that why when Seth attacked you, I started to bleed?"

"Yes, and I truly apologize for that. I slipped up.

"You see, Kayden, that's the true reason why I am so protective of you. Like I told you, upon your birth, our souls were fused together. Our hearts beat at the exact same rate so I know when you are scared and I know when you are nervous. With that, if yours stops..." he broke off and it wasn't hard for me to fill in where he left off. "If you die Kayden, so do I. And the same goes for me; if I die, then you will suffer the same fate."

I had forgot how to feel, how to think, how to blink, how to speak. Everything he had just told me numbed me completely. I had accepted everything easily up until that point. Recurring thoughts started to rampage my head. I always made him feel like what he was doing was a nuisance (in a way it was) but he was only protecting me…I mean *us*.

"Again, I know this is a bit hard to take in all at once but rest assure, we are going to do all we can to protect you."

Claire rubbed my back with one of her hands comforting me. I wasn't sure if it was my expression or Brycin's expression that gave away how I was feeling but her methods of comfort along with the warmth emanating from her wings was defrosting my numbness. I swallowed, took a deep breath and accepted it. "So does every human get a protector?"

Emma chuckled underneath her breath and pressed her full lips together. Jakob seemed to laugh a little and so did Claire and Brycin. "You're so cute, Kayden." Emma indulged.

"What?"

"You still haven't figured it out?" Emma asked. "Ha ha, you are a half-breed, Kayden. You're a Neatholyte. The blood of an angel rages through your veins."

You are just one less Neatholyte we have to worry about…then they came for you…you are the ultimate reason for us retaliating. All of the clues led up to it. Portman said that I was one and now they were. "No." I spoke in a faint whisper but there was suddenly edge and volume in my voice. "NO!" I threw Claire's wing off of me and jumped to my feet. "There has to be some mistake! I…I…I don't even have wings or an ability! How could you be so sure?! Are you sure?!" I was breathing heavy and loud, disturbing the cool wind's whistle as it swept across the field.

"We're certain." Brycin calmed me, both hands on my shoulders. "You are one of us; you are a Neatholyte."

I fell back to the ground, stunned. My brain swarmed with inconceivable thoughts, pounding and aching from these thoughts.

"So you guys were angels all along, surrounding me? Just to protect me?"

"Yep." Jakob stated. "Nice human disguises, huh?"

"What do you mean?" I looked up at him.

"He means that the personalities you saw, for the most part, aren't really our own." Brycin explained. "It was our way of blending in with the present. Jakob isn't *really* that obnoxious. It's just that when he was told he would be going undercover with us to protect you, he mastered this obnoxious, overly pompous personality."

"Which I don't understand why?" Claire retorted.

Jakob chuckled.

"And Emma is nowhere near being self-absorbed, that she has reasons to." I looked at Emma who was smiling gloriously, almost triumphantly. "But we do it only to blend in, how our personalities were to be if we *were* human. But some of us need to be reminded that we *aren't* human." Brycin barked softly, looking at Jakob.

It took me a while to figure out why he said that. "Oh, that's why you all scolded him when he hit Frankie? Because Frankie's human and he's not?"

Jakob winced at the memory.

"Yeah. Not only that, it is against our laws to hurt humans in any type of way. Jakob knows not to stoop to human levels."

"But Frankie can get so annoying. He thinks that just because he is bigger it makes him stronger but, ha, if only he knew."

"So you really hate Frankie?" I asked, hoping that I wouldn't have to feel awkward in front of them when they were in each other's presence.

"Ha, of course not. It's just pure amusement to see how easily fired up I can get the brute."

I chuckled softly beneath my breath. That was a relief.

Claire's warm wing was back around me, sending a wave of calmness though my body, slowing my breathing and seizing my rampaging thoughts.

As the warmth her wings emitted merged with the coolness of the nighttime air, I was beginning to lose the battle against my eyelids, rapidly drifting into unconsciousness.

"It's been a long night." Brycin indicated with a light chuckle. "Let's call it night."

"Wait!" I objected, my arm extended before me. I wasn't ready to leave. Who cares what my body wanted? I wanted to know more. "Please just a few more minutes?"

Brycin chuckled lightly again. "What's the rush?" he asked, his bright teeth beaming in the moonlight. "You're a part of this family now."

Family. Something I always felt I didn't have. But now, I had what I always longed for. A family and a newfound understanding of who I am and what I am.

In so many words, knowing that I was a Neatholyte answered questions I've spent a lifetime wanting to know, questions I never thought would ever be answered. I was a half-breed which meant that one or both of my biological parents had to be one as well. It was rather relaxing, comforting to come to terms on where I came from.

After walking me back through the forest's maze and everyone saying goodnight to me, I was in my car and on my way home.

I never realized how much I missed my car. It was silent compared to Frankie's raging truck.

Once I reached home, I paused. It possessed an eerie, frightening quality. It looked vacant, abandoned. All the lights were off. Not even the porch light on.

I edged forward toward the house, looking for any signs of paint fading away or webs, anything that actualized the uncomfortable thought filtering through my head.

Nothing.

I entered the house and every inch of it was engulfed in shadows. The shadows amplified the emptiness and I felt alone in the silence of this abandon-like fortress.

Though everything was where it should be, I knew where this new growing pain emerged from.

Soon, I would become a Neatholyte, a being that ages gracefully, beautifully, slowly. I am close to immortality. That meant, eventually, Rachel would…I couldn't even think it. How will I live without her? Would I manage? *Could* I manage? Would I grow used to her absence? She's been there with me almost since my birth. She *was* my mom. How do I just say goodbye to that?

Do I even tell her what I am? I wasn't even sure if some humans were exempt of knowing. Besides, I'm certain that she would notice my ageless face and body.

Well when the time comes, I will think of something.

I walked up the stairs to my room, threw off all of my clothes and laid with the shadows until sleep came for me.

Chapter 9: Not Normal

MY EYES SLOWLY PULLED OPEN, GREETING THE MANY dark shadows that decorated my room in strange shapes and designs. I soaked in the silence, lathering in the newfound peace I had awakened to.

For once, I didn't wake to the violence of my seas tormenting me, thrashing me around on the surface of its waters, pounding my emotions with its fierce waves of depression and sorrow, but never giving me the full satisfaction I longed for. To be pulled down to the arctic depths where I would drown silently in my tears.

For once, I didn't wake consumed by deviant and obsessive thoughts.

In one night, almost nineteen years worth of questions had been answered…well sort of.

Only one thing remained a mystery to me. I didn't know who my real parents were or even why they abandoned me fourteen years ago with a bloodstained t-shirt and ripped pants off the roads of nowhere. But I knew what they were.

One of them had to have the bloodline of a Neatholyte running through their veins. I would one day, soon I hope, become one myself. A Neatholyte, the angel/human half-breed.

The thought was implausibly soothing to me. I felt like I had a purpose, a reason for my existence. Once I received my wings, I would help my family of half-breeds protect the world from plunging into a complete nonexistent state.

A family. The thought forced me to smile.

All of them, all of my close friends were half-breeds, Neatholytes. All of them except for two.

Frankie, even though he was the biggest of us all, was in fact the weakest of us all. He was a human.

And Jakob *is* a half-breed but not like the rest of us. He is opposite of us. He is a Demilyte, the demon/human half-breed. His eyes are darker than the depths of the deepest ocean and his wings are a very dark gray which get lighter towards the tips.

It was bewildering to me. Why would a Demilyte associate with Neatholytes if we were natural born enemies?

Neatholyte.

Every time I thought the word, a wave of calmness would rush over me.

My mind began to drift elsewhere. I was suddenly curious to what abilities I would acquire once I had my wings. Maybe electrical abilities like Brycin or maybe superhuman strength. Or possibly x-ray vision and invisibility. I chuckled softly in the darkness at the thought. Those powers seemed *too* comic bookish.

What if one day I became what Brycin is? A protector. God, I hope not. I could not bear to go through what Brycin has to go through with me on a daily basis. To never be safe from the-one-who-I-would-be-meant-to-protect's emotions, never safe from the severity of their depression or deep obsessions, forever a slave to each other's physical pain. It was an unimaginable, unfathomable thought.

But none of that, emotionally linked or fused to each other's physical pain, compared to the ultimate price that came with being a protector. Once an individual is born and a Neatholyte is deemed "protector," your souls immediately become one. If I became one, I would have to intensively monitor the-one-I-am-meant-to-protect. Not to mention, I would have to be extremely cautious with what I do as well for if I die, so do they and vice versa.

I winced at the thought.

I removed the blanket off of me and jumped out of bed, fully awake and full of energy. I was thrilled to get to school today, to be around all of my extraordinary friends. I rushed to the bathroom and immediately began getting ready.

The morning seemed to be on fast forward, almost a blur. I rushed down the stairs invited the by the sweet, sweet scent of lavenders. Rachel was spreading cream cheese over a bagel, beautiful as ever, when I rammed her, trapping her into an inescapable hug. I twirled with her in the center of the kitchen and she screamed with laughter, pleading with me to place her back on her feet. After placing her lightly back on her feet, she straightened up her white skirt with black pinstripes and matching jacket. She was still laughing as she did this and questioned my joyous behavior. I answered just because and rushed out the door after placing a kiss on her cheek.

Now, I wished my English class would go by just as fast. The anxiety was immense, unbearable, building and building, overpowering my nerves. My breathing was hard and I couldn't control myself from constantly tapping my pencil against the top of the table. I heard the girl beside me sigh heavily. I sensed she was annoyed and seized the tapping.

I eyed the clock, mentally rushing it but my efforts were futile. The hands didn't oblige, in fact, they appeared to slow down, trapping me in this point in time.

I let out a low growl. From the corner of my eye, I could see the short, frumpy dark haired girl shift in her seat, now sitting on the edge of her seat furthest away from me, eyeing me with irritation.

Oddly, it didn't bother me the slightest bit. Anxiety left no room for anger or irritation. Besides, she was only human.

"Okay class," Professor LaBurn began. My head shot in his direction at the sound of his voice and off of the girl and her ridiculous behavior. "I want you guys to finish up the text of *Pride and Prejudice.* I would like a two page, typed summary of the story. You have your review sheets and finals are only but around the corner. You are dismissed."

I didn't mean to be rude. I was up and out of my seat in a second, my book bag over my shoulder and rushing toward the exit, running into students on my way out.

I was outside and rushing across the parking lot in no time. The weather today was perfect. The sun was perched high above the earth in the nearly cloudless sky. Small, white cotton-like balls of puff scattered the skies, beautifully displaying shapes against the blue blanket of space.

My veins pulsed with excitement but the excitement started to evaporate from my veins, leaving me just as dry as the air. I only saw Emma and Claire as I neared closer to them though I could clearly see both the crimson red Camaro and jet black Range Rover present.

Emma started to approach me, her magnificently long, curly, icy blonde hair pinned up and what hung flipped over her left shoulder and swayed in the lightness of the wind. She was wearing a white sundress with yellow flower petals dancing all over it. Over her right ear sat a white artificial flower but her beauty made the flower seem as real as any other flower that blossomed from the soil of the earth. A flawless beauty.

Her perfect lips parted and her voice chimed like a cupid playing a harp. "Hi Kayden." She greeted me with a smile.

"Hi." An automatic response.

"Uhmm," her perfect face fell slightly, a hint of sadness present. "There has been a change in plans." she turned her head, looking at Claire over her shoulder and then looked back at me. "Brycin and Jakob have gone after Balavon and the others. Try and thwart his plans. They don't want him to get that close to you again."

My mood seemed to be constantly shifting. I wanted to spend the day with all four of them. Not just two of them. Especially not just me and the girls. "So what now?" I asked folding my arms and placing all of weight on my legs.

"I was thinking about taking you to Crater Lake."

"I?"

"Claire is going to be joining them while I stay behind and keep you safe."

My eyes narrowed. I felt confused, angry, worried. No offense to Emma, but I didn't feel safe with her. So what if she was a half-breed? She was too beautiful, too fragile looking for me to take her serious.

I would rather be left alone here with Claire. At least Claire looked a bit more intimidating. Not to mention Claire saved me from Ester's attempt to destroy me once before.

Of all the people I could have gotten left with, it had to be Emma, the angel I was most uncomfortable around. The one whose beauty intimidated me and altered my behavior at times, forcing me to stare or stammer over my words whenever I spoke to her. What if I said something stupid, something so lame that would make her laugh in my face?

The wind lightly blew again, playing with Emma's hair and sending her fragrance flying in my direction. Her scent was heavenly, invigorating, causing my heart to accelerate a fraction. Absolutely beautiful, absolutely perfect. I could tell this was going to be hard.

The fragrance was enough to distract my thoughts. "Okay." I nodded, agreeing to go to Crater Lake with her. Plus, it would be nice to go there again.

"Perfect." She stated curtly, twirling gracefully on one leg and walking over to Claire.

After several seconds of speaking with Claire, Claire was hopping inside of the Range Rover and pulling out. Emma walked back over to me and wrapped her arm in mine. "Let's go."

The drive to Crater Lake took forever. Maybe it wouldn't have taken so long if it wasn't for the uncomfortable feeling I had in the pit of my stomach, the one that Emma always gave me whenever I was within two feet of her. The car was silent the entire trip. Not so much as a cough or a sniff disturbed the silence or the awkwardness in the car.

I wanted to say something but I didn't know what to say. My mind was with Brycin and the others, wondering if they had gotten any luck in finding Balavon. It was hard for me not to worry when the sake of my safety had potential to kill my friends. And if Brycin fails in battle, I would suffer the same fate.

Indeed, it was impossible not to worry.

We pulled in beside the lake. It was exceptionally green today with all the sunlight. The large cedars, ferns and springtime floral all combined their scents together, creating a fragrance that could never be replicated and sold in a bottle.

The wind here was brisk, cooler than the one at the school as it traveled over the surface of the lake. The surface of the water glistened from the sun's rays, displaying an array of blues, greens and whites.

Emma shut the car off and stepped out.

I sat in the car and watched her as she walked over to a large boulder and sat on top of it. She gazed over the lake. At this very moment, she was more beautiful than any mystical creature. Though, in a way, she was one. No mermaid or siren could come close to her beauty.

Few more seconds had gone by. I just watched. She seemed trapped in thoughts, her face perfectly and flawlessly sculpted but there was essence of disturbance. I was curious but I didn't want to pry. What had enough power to sadden such a creature?

I opened the door to the car, stepped out and began to walk toward her after shutting the door. I shoved my hands into my pocket, nervous as I approached the angel.

I stood on the edge of the lake as she sat motionless on top of the rock, staring at the tiny waves skate across the surface of the water. The sight was indeed calming. I could see how she was easily drawn into thought. The scent of the water and the rustling of its waves were pretty hypnotizing.

"What's it like?" Her mesmerizing voice punctured the silence that had been with us since the university parking lot. "To be human I mean?"

I turned to her, meeting her childlike stare. She was genuinely curious. My eyes and face were just as curious, wondering why such a perfect creature would want to know what it was like to be imperfect.

I pondered on the question for a while longer, looking up toward the sky as I constructed the perfect answer for her. But I failed miserably, answering, "Uhmm…heavy." I chuckled, looking back at the angel's face. "But I'm sure it varies from human to human. Some probably enjoy it I'm sure but…" I paused. The malevolence of my sea was getting violent and full of rage, ready to pound me mercilessly.

Brycin and Rachel were the only two people who I've ever spoken to when it came to my emotions. I gazed over the water, embracing its scent and the cool breeze shooting across the waves. I allowed the combination to calm my raging seas before they could destroy me and I ruin this trip.

"Well you see, I never, truly ever, felt human. I felt like being a human was never what I was meant for, that I had a purpose but not as a human. I always felt I was something more, something better. Though it was just a thought at the time, I held dear to it.

"Pretending was so easy. It's easy to make everyone around you happy and discarding your own happiness to benefit the rest. Faking a smile, laughing when it was only necessary, answering and replying back to people with a close enough perfect answer but never to the point where it would start a prolonging conversation. But still, even after all of the effort and faking, you still feel out of place, you still don't belong. I never belonged. Never."

"And you think that becoming an angel half-breed will fix all of that?" I turned to face her. Her expression was heart throbbing, full of sorrow and pain and hurt and anger. She seemed very concerned. "We are different. This isn't some lifestyle that if you aren't satisfied with it, you could easily choose to be something else. This is forever, Kayden."

"But it's what I am and what I want."

Her head hung and her eyes closed. "I wish there could be a choice. I wish I could have chosen."

I still couldn't fathom with her unnecessary obsession and interest. I didn't understand any of it, how something of such caliber was willing to give it all up. "Why?"

She took a deep breath. She looked back up, eyes glistening as the water reflected in them yet still full of sadness. Her stunning face was full of so much sorrow. Why? Was it possible for a creature so perfect to suffer? "I received my wings when I was sixteen." She paused and looked at me. "Twenty-seven years ago. I am the youngest of my half-breed family."

Twenty-seven? Years? Ago? Realistically she was…forty-three years old.

"Twenty-seven years ago, I had everything I could ever want. A loving mother, father and Cedric, the love of my life who promised me since the day we started dating that he would marry me as soon as I graduated. He was two years older than me. He was the most beautiful man I'd ever seen." Her face gave her away. She wasn't in the present at this moment. She was in the past.

"It was the Winter Bash at our school. The most anticipated dance of the year. More so than prom. Every girl imaginable had their eyes set on becoming the White Queen. But many didn't run because it was said that only a senior girl could receive the title White Queen.

"That year, I would make history at my high school. I was only a sophomore and I had beaten every senior girl who ran. The guys of my school would have thrown themselves in front of a speeding bus if it meant saving me and the girls envied me for that." She spoke with a smile, proud of the powers her beauty had over men and women. "But Cedric was the only one for me and he knew that.

"On the day of the dance, my mom went all out — flawless make-up, my hair was elegantly pinned up with several curled strands draping over my shoulder. I wore the most stunning, silver dress. It submitted to my curves, hugging them and baring my shoulders. My mom had given me the most perfect shoes for the occasion. My grandmother's wedding shoes. My mom wore them to hers and I would wear them that night and for my own wedding someday. They were perfect. Silver with a bow in the front and a beautifully carved diamond stone in the center. I was perfect.

"My father cursed beneath his breath, saying intelligible things. If it were up to him, I would have attended a private all girl school.

"I had never been so excited in my life. I couldn't wait to see my Ceddy.

"When Cedric arrived, he was dashing in his light gray suit. I could see my dad's eyes and face flush with anger. I think on that day I saw steam project from his ears." She stated with laughter.

"When we made it to the dance, it was unimaginably breathtaking. A long, silky blue carpet rushed through the entrance of the gymnasium. There were five, large arches created out of several blue, silver and white balloons. Hundreds of other individual balloons floated all over the gym. The floor was covered in some cotton-like material that was meant to give of the impression of snow. Fifteen rows of tables with six tables in each row had a velvety silver cloth on top of it, white rose petals scattered across the tables with a single lit candle stationed in the center of the table beaming bright with romance.

"Cedric and I danced most of the night. I didn't want to be away from him for a single second. I was forever in love with him. He was sweet and kind, a real gentleman but he was always misjudged because of his appearance. He was large and muscular. His copper eyes were breathtaking. His face was beautifully structured, high cheek bones, full lips covering a full set of perfect, straight, pearly white teeth. And his perfectly cropped sandy brown hair made him all the more beautiful.

"We danced some more. But I suddenly felt a sharp pain in my back." I watched as her expression fell, her tone was turning icy and her face turned whiter, ghostly. I sensed that this was where the story turned for the worst. "I grabbed my right shoulder. The pain was high on my back, about three inches from my shoulder. I had never felt a pain like it. It felt like someone was stabbing me over and over again with prefect precision and accuracy. I then felt the exact same pain on the left side.

"Cedric was immediately worried after catching me as I stumbled forward. I explained to him the sudden shock of pain. He suggested he take me home but I was too stubborn to go. I hadn't even received the title of White Queen yet. Besides, there was a girl named Connie Mitchell who always wanted to outdo me in everything and I couldn't wait to see her face when she witnessed the sparkling silver and blue crown get place on my head.

"I pardoned myself from Cedric and went to the ladies room. I stared in the mirror and couldn't believe what I was seeing. My right eye. It was once a dazzling and vibrant blue. But now it was white, completely colorless.

"Then the sharp pains returned and another sensation joined the two pains in my back. The combinations in pains were enough to bring me down to my knees. It was my entire spine. Oh, it hurt so bad. I tried my best to suppress a scream but it was difficult.

"I couldn't help but give meaning to what was happening to me. Was I dying only moments away from making history at my high school?

"Then, a pain more devastating, more agonizing than anything else shuttered through my torso, spreading and forcing me to feel the pain everywhere else in my body. I heard a sickening snap in my back and I couldn't help but let out a howl cry of pain. The music must've been too loud because no one came for me.

"It felt as though my entire spine shifted, twisting around inside of me and ripping from my ribs. It all burned and I cried in agony.

"Just when I thought the pain couldn't get any worse, my lungs felt like they were set ablaze, burning horridly in my chest. I was barely able to breath and when I did, it felt like I swallowed fire. My heart raced and pounded against my broken ribs.

"Then, I started to feel them grow. I could hear them slicing through my muscles and flesh and tearing my dress. I felt the warm liquid seep down my back, to my dress and cooling it, staining it.

"In on rushing and painful second, the bones rushed out of my back, gushing blood all over the bathroom walls and floor, all over my dress and skin and my grandmother's wedding shoes. Two, large bloodstained wings full of gorgeous feathers became part of me that night."

The process of getting my wings was going to be morbid, grueling, and unbearable. It was going to be a pain I'd never witnessed before. For a split second, I almost didn't want them.

"It was a tiring thing to go through." She continued. "I felt weak, frozen by the pain. There was a strange noise that invaded the painful silence I was trapped in. It was funny hearing everything heal for the first time. The gashes my wings created on my back sealed up without a trace of a scar and I could feel my torso reconstructing itself, my ribs becoming one with my spine again and the pain slowly dissipated.

"With the little energy I had left, I lifted myself up. My eyes pulled up and I stared at my reflection. It was the first time in my life I ever felt hideous. I was covered in blood, my makeup ran down my face because of all of my crying and my dress was completely demolished. Both of my eyes were now white and the reddish pink wings behind me made me break out into a fierce sob. My fairytale dream had become a haunting nightmare.

"The agony of what I was continued to rip through me but I had to pull myself together. I straightened up, released my hair from all the pins, kicked off my grandmother's shoes, my feet soaking in the thick, red liquid beneath me and I opened my wings for the first time. I must admit, they were hard to deny. They were beautiful. I flapped them down, launching myself straight up through the ceiling, breaking plaster, pipes, wires, and wood boards.

"It was an amazing feeling, hovering in the dark sky adjusting to this new me. My sight was ridiculous. I could give you the exact description of a person from over a hundred yards away. I could hear just about every conversation going on and the sound of the music raining from out of the gym seemed amplified a hundred folds. It felt like my ears were going to bleed at any moment. It was all so very overwhelming, something I was sure I would have to eventually adjust to.

"I looked on either sides of me, watching the pinkish wings flap, bending and creasing, reopening in the center repeatedly, preventing me from plummeting into the ground. They were gorgeous and strong but they had taken away everything from me in minutes.

"I floated down to the roof of the gym and sat with my wings bare, my eyes white and my knees up against my chest.

"It was easy to find his voice, frantic it was. He was asking everyone in the gym of my whereabouts and his voice was getting more and more frantic with each passing person. I heard his voice for the last time that night as he asked a girl who saw me wander into the bathroom."

"Yeah, I saw her go into the bathroom not too long ago." The girl stated

"Oh, thank goodness." Cedric breathed. *"Do you mind going in there and making sure she is okay. She was having a little back trouble earlier and I wanna make sure she is okay. Please."*

"Sure thing."

"He followed behind her to the back of the gym where the restrooms were, past the thundering music and to the bathrooms. Their footsteps stopped."

"I'll be back."

"The girl entered the bathroom. I could hear her heartbeat flutter. I heard her suck in a great lungful of air and with it, released a shrieking cry but with the music as loud as it was the only people who would be capable of hearing her scream would have been anyone inside the bathroom or anyone right outside the door. Cedric rushed through the door, analyzing the scene of horror. Blood all over the place, my shoes and a large hole in the bathroom ceiling. I couldn't even imagine the pain that must've been on his face and I don't want to.

"I heard his footsteps dash across the gymnasium floor and outside. He screamed my name over and over again. I wanted, more than anything, to fly down to him and tell him "Here I am. I'm alright. I'm ok. We're ok." But we weren't and we wouldn't.

"After a while, it got too unbearable and I shot off the roof and into the brisk nighttime sky, no intentions of ever seeing my high school again or the love of my life." Her voice was serene and she wiped away the tears that had escaped as she told me her story. She remained silent for a while longer. I would have said something but her story seemed unfinished.

After taking another deep breath, she began again. "Both of my parents carried the bloodline. But there human blood was more dominant than their angelic blood. When the two came together, it was enough to make me a half-breed. It was enough to give me wings.

"I was presumed dead that night and when the news got to my parents, my mom fainted and for the first time, I seen my father cry.

"He took it harder than my mom. Both the men in my life did. Cedric…" she'd lost her words. Her expression looked too painful to speak. Her eyes were quickly filling up with tears and her perfect frame almost seemed to tremble. "He uhmm…he…killed himself. He hung himself from the balcony of his house and my father died in a car crash. One too many drinks, ha." She tried to make a joke out of it, laughing halfheartedly.

"The hole in my heart grew larger and larger and I didn't want to be consumed by it. I had to protect my heart from anymore pain. I had to protect my mom from insanity and despair.

"Once I realized I had the ability to manipulate the minds, emotions, and moods of others, I immediately went to work on mending my mother's broken heart.

"I led her to Ronald. Handsome, well educated, a real gentleman.

"Eventually they married.

"Nine years later, after my disappearance and my father's tragic end, James was born. Beautiful and delicate baby James. I prayed it would be enough, him and Ronald, to keep my mom's heart beating.

"Fate apparently was against me. It was an era that gave birth to gangs and violence. James had been left with the sitter one night as Ronald treated my mother to a dinner and a picture show. Upon their return, a few members of a gang approached the two of them walking to Ronald's car, harassing them for money. I tried to invert their hostile behavior but my powers weren't working. I hadn't slept in months — watching over my family and my baby brother had become my only priority. My restlessness weakened me, lowering the efficiency of my abilities, preventing me from saving them.

"It was at that very moment that I hated everything I was. The *thought* of my death killed everyone I loved. Had I not received these damn wings, I would've married. My father and mother would be alive *and* together." She spat the words icily. She was breathing heavy and her jaw was tight.

She ran her hand through her hair, composing herself. She took a deep breath. She looked at me, eyes glistening more so with the assisting of the glittering lake. "But James would not have been born. And I love him more than anything now.

"I vowed that I would not be so reckless with James. Angel or not, I was going to be a physical part of his life. I took him that night, away from his home and I raised him.

"I invested my entire existence into that kid. Best home, best lifestyle, keeping up with the trends of society. Though I got money by the means of my abilities, I did all of it for him.

"On one particular night, he was about ten, he rushed into my room because he had a nightmare. He said there was lots of screaming in it, that planes were crashing into two high buildings and they fell to ground, burning and everyone was scared. I told him that it was just a dream and that he shouldn't obsess over them. The next morning, I watched wide eyed as the media broadcasted terrorists launching planes into the Twin Towers.

"That's when I knew. I knew he was just like me and that someday, he would have wings too. I was afraid for him, remembering the pain I had endured as if it had happened to me the day before. With what I knew, I would remain at his side through it all, until he had his own wings.

"Fourteen years, fifteen, sixteen, seventeen, still no wings but he continued to have dreams predicting events in the future." Her voice was breaking and she appeared to be shaken with heartache.

"James is only an In-Between." She turned to me, a tear falling over her creamy cheeks and resting under her chin. I've never seen her so vulnerable, so…human.

"James is my life now!" She was sobbing now. "And one day, I have to watch someone else I love die! My heart can't bear it!

"You don't understand Kayden! I hate being an angel! I would give it all up than to face eternity without my brother! I would give anything to be human with him! To die with *him*! He is more than my brother! In a way, he's my son!"

My heart felt like it was in just as much pain as hers. Before I knew it, she rushed into my arms. I was taken by surprise by her touch, her scent. It was all mind-boggling.

She sobbed into my chest. I slowly wrapped my arms around her and rested my chin on top of her head — closing my eyes and allowing the combination of her sweet fragrance and touch and the light breeze of the wind and the scent of nature which rode on the breeze to drift me into thoughts.

She'd faced a lot in the past twenty-seven years. And though she hoped for the best, she knew what the future held for her and her brother. As she remained ageless, James was dying every day.

Hard to believe that I was willing to face that exact same pain with Rachel.

We stood on the edge of the lake for moments more, my arms still consoling her.

She gently pulled away, wiping her tears from her eyes. "I'm sorry. I didn't mean to get frantic and I didn't mean to make this outing about my demons."

"No, it's fine." It was fine to me. Emma was very compassionate and able to feel. She really loved the people in her life. Especially James. My first impressions about her were entirely wrong.

She straightened up her dress and her hair and laughed away the tears. She then turned to the dusk that settled over the lake. I turned to face the sunset with her. The sun was settling within the trees across the lake from where we stood, painting the sky in bright reds, dark pinks and purples. The wind continued to sway through the air, cool and light.

"Kayden?"

She didn't turn to me as she said my name and I didn't turn to her as I replied. "Yeah."

"Brycin never wanted to get us involved." That caused me to turn and look at her.

"So you can read minds to?" I asked almost irritated that she invaded my mind without my permission.

"No, I manipulate thoughts and moods. I can't read minds. Claire can but even she wouldn't invade someone's mind without permission or feeling as if it was truly necessary. Brycin told us." I calmed a little, my frustration targeted to Brycin who wasn't here. "You see Kayden, you're not normal."

I laughed. "Really? I had no idea." I spoke sarcastically.

"Not in the world of half-breeds either." Her voice was serious. "In theory, I'm still sixteen. Jakob's twenty one, and Brycin and Claire are eighteen. We raise our human year by one every century we've lived."

I frowned with confusion.

"Fourteen, fifteen, and sixteen are the primary years when one is supposed to receive their wings. A year before or a year after the primes is relatively normal, acceptable. But you're nineteen with no wings, yet your blood flourishes with angelic blood, potent with it. You have more angel blood in you than I do and I *barely* made it. That's not normal."

I stared blankly at the lake. *Fourteen, fifteen and sixteen?* I questioned in my head. *Three years late?* Even in a world where I belonged, I wasn't normal.

"Brycin's afraid that the delay is suppressing a lot of power and when you finally get them, you may be a loose cannon, detached from reasoning and incapable of controlling yourself. That's why he brought us into your life. So we could do all we can to help you if it comes to that.

"Everyone is still bewildered how more than sixty percent of your blood is angelic yet you are wingless."

I felt more useless now than ever before. I felt completely empty. I was speechless though I tried extremely hard to think of something to say.

"Aris believes that because you have so much angel blood in you that it could be the key to why you haven't received your wings yet and why Balavon is so interested in seeing you dead. You may have potential to destroy him. He doesn't like feeling that his life is in danger."

"Aris?" I questioned with a dead tone.

"You can somewhat say he is the father of our family. He found me and James five years ago and brought us here. Neatholytes are very sociable creatures and rarely live alone, always in groups or a family. Some stray away and try to live as normal lives as possible but it gets hard because we aren't normal. You'll meet him soon. He's very eager to meet you."

My eyes were still locked on the waves of the lake. I could feel my eyebrows furrow, my eyes squint and my lips pursed. I was annoyed. I just couldn't a get break. Not as a human and not as an angel.

I could see Emma from the corner of my eye looking at me. She pulled my face so that I was looking at her. Her hands were soft, silky and warm. I gazed into the depths of her sapphire blue eyes. She gazed back into mine and I wondered what did she see in them. Perhaps a boy who was suffering, wanting to feel normal in some way, even in an abnormal way. Or maybe the pain everything seemed to inflict on my already shredded soul. Or maybe I had no soul. Perhaps she saw that. A boy who was utterly empty, vacant and soulless. Perhaps.

"Kayden, you are a Neatholyte. It's just a matter of time." She smiled and her smile was assuring. I smiled back. "Now com'on before it gets too late."

The ride back to Corvallis was easier than the drive to Crater Lake. It was much easier to hold a conversation with her now. I was still somewhat baffled that speaking to her or being around her for such a long period of time that I remained composed.

We talked mostly about the others. Apparently, there were three more half-breeds I haven't met yet. Aris, Elaina, and Matt. Aris is over seven hundred years old. Elaina is almost eight hundred years old and she and Aris are best of friends. Matt was born a little over a century ago and Aris his protector. I wanted to know more but Emma told me that I would be meeting them soon enough.

I looked forward to meeting the rest of them. I looked forward to joining this family of angels. I especially looked forward to the day when I would receive my own wings.

Chapter 10: The Family

SATURDAY WAS HERE.

The sounds on the opposite side of my room walls forced my eyes to jolt open. The sounds were heart-wrenching, a bearer of bad news.

Ferocious, never-ending taps launched against the window of my room and a dull gray light escaped through it, replacing the creepy shadows I had gone to bed with last night and turning all the objects my room contained darker than what they actually were.

The annoying taps that catapulted themselves against my window were being produced by the million aquatic bullets shooting rapidly against it like a machine gun. It was as though they were trying to penetrate the glass shield that protected my room from their onslaught, but miserably running down the glassy surface in streams of failure.

I continued to listen to the atrocity occurring outside my room walls, wide eyed. The winds sounded violent and lethal. I could hear objects skid across the pavements, overwhelmed by the strength of the wind. The thunder had such a grizzly growl to it and in an instant cracked fiercer than any manmade whip.

Suddenly, a bright flash entered my room, making me jump a little, illuminating the objects in my room but as quickly as the brightness came, it disappeared and the grayness returned and so did the darker toned objects in my room.

I leaped out of bed, half wrapped in my blanket still and tripping over the black thermal shirt and black jeans I had worn out with

Emma yesterday, and sped to the window. Everything was blanketed by a shroud of dark, moist clouds. I could barely make out anything. Everything was deformed, disfigured by the many streams of water that ran down my window. The shapes of cars, trees and houses were all inconsistent, as if they were drawn with squiggly lines on the glassy canvas. From what I could see, the pavement and road was just as dark as the sky, paved by the stains of the infinite water droplets.

How could this be? I'd watched the forecast earlier this week. There was to be slight cloud coverage this weekend and yet I was witnessing something terribly different from what was predicted.

My body trembled with anger. I could see my face tense and flush red in my reflection. Today, Emma and I were supposed to go on another trip to Crater Lake but with this weather, I would be trapped in this house all day like a rat in a cage begging for freedom.

This week without Brycin, Claire, and Jakob was surprisingly pleasant. Emma had almost become my new best friend in the week I've spent with her. We'd gone to Crater Lake every single day and I never got tired of going nor did I get weary of her presence.

Yesterday, I mustered up enough courage to actually tell Emma the unforgettable history Rachel and I shared with Crater Lake. How it became a phantom to Rachel, stripping her of her happiness effortlessly. Though I was absolutely sure Brycin already mentioned it to them, it was more personal coming from me, a better understanding. I even showed her our rock.

We spent hours at the lake until the sun bathed in the trees across from us and painted the horizon in beautiful shades of reds, pinks, oranges, purples and yellows.

We would even spend an endless amount of time on the phone talking about useless, insignificant human stuff.

Thursday, she joined Rachel and me for dinner. Rachel immediately noticed our constant hanging out, instantaneously jumping to absurd conclusions. She cracked jokes about possibly seeing Emma more often for dinner and around the house. She even went as far as asking us was there some sort of future brewing between us. Emma blushed while I rolled my eyes. Emma was still the most beautiful girl alive, perhaps the most gorgeous creature on the face of the planet, but even with this newfound understanding and likeness for Emma, the thought of me ever being hers intimately remained unchanged.

But I still enjoyed every minute with her.

She explained to me over and over again that her constant presence was a form of supervision, a request of Brycin's. Still, I couldn't help but prefer her level of security over Brycin's. Sure it was a constant one but it was tolerable. She didn't suffocate me with her presence forcefully. She always wanted my permission before she made any plans. Indeed, I preferred her supervision over his.

I huffed out a powerful sigh of disappointment. It took everything within me to suppress the child that wanted to emerge and force me to pout and stomp.

I strolled over to the closet, still angry at the storm for trapping me inside, and shuffled through the collection of clothes. I pulled a white v-neck shirt off its hanger and a pair of gray denim jeans. The attire screamed indoors to me.

My ears fluttered with the faintness of voices as soon as I opened my room door. They trailed from downstairs. Rachel's voice was easy to identify but the others, two I think, were somewhat unfamiliar to me. My main thought was why would someone be here when there was a monster of a storm outside that would keep them trapped here.

I quickened my pace in getting ready and rushed into the bathroom. I showered, brushed my teeth, got dressed and fixed my hair.

When I emerged from the bathroom, refreshed and fully awake, as I guessed, the voices were still here.

I slowly walked down the steps of the stairs. There were two other voices, a male and a female's. There was no point in trying to be sly and sneaky as I walked down the steps. Both the storm's activity and their obnoxious laughter drowned out any evidence of my approach.

I followed the voices into the kitchen.

"Kayden!" Emma called out my name cheerfully, teeth blazing bright and face utterly flawless. She wore a tight, black, long-sleeve shirt, fitting her body perfectly and molding to the curves of her chest. Her hair was flat, some of it tossed over her right shoulder. The center bar cut off the rest of her body but even as half a creature, nothing could subtract her unique beauty.

Sitting next to her, equal in uniqueness and beauty was her brother, James. He wore a purple, black and white flannel button up. His sleeves were rolled up and two buttons remained unbutton, baring his ivory skin beneath the shirt. The corner of his mouth pulled up into an awkward smile and he waved at me.

To be nearly three decades apart from each other, they were almost identical. High cheek bones, icy blonde hair, glittering eyes, perfect smiles, incomparable beauty; they were practically twins.

I remained beneath the archway entrance to the kitchen, confused at their presence.

Rachel, who sat across from these two creatures of indescribable magnificence, twisted her torso around in the stool to face me. "Morning." She greeted me with a smile. "Emma and James *had* come to pick you up to go out but then this storm came out of nowhere."

I couldn't help but eye both Emma and James as Rachel spoke. Something was definitely wrong. This storm and their presence was no coincidence. They both seemed a bit…tense. Their eyes gave them away each time they looked at me because the smile on their faces slightly faded.

Were they…afraid? Of what? I couldn't control the thoughts of possibilities as they swarmed through my brain.

It had to have been the others. Someone had to have been hurt… or worse. What if it was Brycin? What if he never returned? Would I be able to replace his friendship, to fill the void in my chest that his death would leave? *Could* I even replace his friendship?

His death…

Had he died, then I wouldn't be standing here right now breathing perfectly and fully alive. No matter the magnitude of the damage, I would feel it and if his heart stops so does mine.

That left Jakob or Claire.

"I invited them to stay 'til the storm passes." Rachel stated, bringing my ravaging thoughts to an immediate halt. My thoughts must not have shown too much on my face because Rachel didn't appear to be the least bit worried.

"You don't mind do you?" Emma asked with apologetic eyes.

"No!" I almost shouted the word. I was glad for them to be here. Just their reasons *for* being here is what gave me a sense of anxiety. "I mean, it's fine."

"Well what are you kids going to do in the mean time?"

"Where are you going?" I asked, noticing that she excluded herself from any agenda created.

"To bed. The week has been ruthless to me. I have never felt so deprived of sleep before." There did appear to be black and purple bruise-like circles beneath her eyes.

"Okay. I'm sure we'll come up with something." I smiled halfheartedly.

She smiled and nodded and excused herself from the center bar. Before passing me underneath the archway, she kissed me softly on the cheek. I managed a smile. The lavender scent brushed past me as she began her way up the stairs.

I mentally watched her walk up the stairs, the sound of her footsteps guiding my mental image. I heard the floor directly above me creak and finally...her door closed.

"What's wrong?" I asked in almost a whisper, looking back at them with worried eyes.

The both of them looked at each other with troubled eyes and then back at me. They both hesitated to speak. Was it that bad?

Emma's lips parted. "Everything." She stated. "Everything is wrong. Nothing is making any sense anymore. We thought you were his main concern. Killing you and initiating this war. Brycin and the others went after him, to destroy him and prevent this from happening. But..." she looked at her brother and then back at me. "He's killed others."

I was more than positive that everyone reacted the same way when realizing Balavon's new agenda. A sense of absence, nothingness and numbness consuming everything. Complete confusion.

"They, Brycin and the others who have been trying to track him for days now, came to the conclusion that he is eliminating any Neatholyte who would prove to be a threat to his plans but his actions don't match our assumptions."

"He isn't just killing Neatholytes." James spoke. "He killed two Neatholytes in Houston, Texas before killing a flock of humans in Brazil. Then he went on to kill a couple of In-Betweens in Russia. But here is where everything gets all the more confusing. Four Demilytes in London. His own kind. There were a few more killings in South America, Northern Europe and now he's back in the states. He's hit New York, Florida, Nebraska, Nevada, and Wisconsin."

I shook my head, incapable of making any sense of all of this information coming to me at once. I was receiving a headache from it all. Just when everything seemed to be making sense, Balavon deals with a new deck of cards.

"The tricky part is trying to track him." James continued. "He is hitting all these places simultaneously and there isn't much we can do to follow him. So, we think he's organized. Meaning, that he has access to Demilytes other than the ones you or they've encountered."

"Well what does it mean?" I asked approaching the bar where they sat. "I thought he was after me? Now you're telling me he isn't?"

There was that look again that they gave to each other. Emma looked at me first and began. "I'll get there. They thought it was some sort of backup plan. He saw your line of defense and noticed that it wasn't as easy to get to you as he had hoped.

"These "occurrences" will be broadcasted I'm sure and other half-breeds will be watching and anything could happen. They may mistake these disappearances as a gesture, an attempt in starting a fight. That's why we thought he killed the Demilytes, to make it look like they are being targeted and blamed for the disappearances.

"If this war erupts, it could potentially expose us. A life of secrecy is the code in which we live by. It's what's kept us alive for this long. Any attempts of exposure, and The Three Houses of Amos, an ancient legion of powerful Neatholytes who maintain the secrecy of our world will find the threat and eradicate it."

"But," James leaned forward in his seat and braided his fingers together. "Apparently, none of the Houses have made any moves yet."

"But that is something we are going to have to worry about another time." Emma intruded. "Right now, this storm is our concern. It was supposed to be partly-cloudy today. Clearly it isn't. That's because this system isn't a natural one. They think Balavon created it somehow. They have another theory now. They think that his reign of terror across the globe is not an alternate way in starting the war. They believe that everything that Balavon was doing was a diversion, a wild goose chase. They now think that it was a method to thin out your defenses."

"So he *is* still after me?" All of this was really taking a blow towards my sanity. I felt like my breaking point was near. Countless lives were being lost and it is all because some lunatic wants to see me dead.

"How do you know all of this?" I asked trying not to make my question come off disrespectful.

"Claire has been informing us." Emma answered.

"She has the ability to read minds and send messages telepathically using brainwaves no matter the distance." James began, completing Emma explanation. "The more familiar she is with your mind, the easier it is to send messages to you."

"And it wasn't until earlier today that they actually questioned the consistency in the disappearances. That's when they figured that maybe Balavon is leading them as far away from you as possible. The fewer angels protecting you, the easier it will be to take you out."

My head dropped. My thoughts swirled out of control incoherently. Everything was getting heavier and heavier, harder to bear, harder to endure. My fist slammed against marble counter, alarming only James. Emma was perfectly still, like a statue, no signs of startle from my surfaced anger. "I don't get it! He had the chance to kill me! Why send me through all this torment and emotional distress when he had the chance?!"

"What do you mean?" Emma questioned, her head tilting and her eyes narrowing.

I had to take a few breathers to calm myself. "At Portman's mansion — or whatever it was. I was there all alone. Just me and him. Why didn't he just kill me then?"

"You were alone with him before?"

I forgot I had never informed Brycin on my visit to Portman's estate. "Yeah." I answered flatly, ashamed.

"That must've been the day when Brycin came to us frantic. He couldn't sense you. It was almost like you fell off the face of the earth. Claire couldn't even get a read on your mind. It was almost as if you never existed."

"So what, he's playing some kind of game with my head now?"

"I don't think…"

I looked at Emma she never finished. "What? You don't think what?"

"Uhh, nothing. Just a silly thought."

She was lying to me. For the first time, Emma lied to me. It had to be for good reasons.

"Well as we were saying," James started. "That's why we think this storm is the way it is. No half-breed would dare fly in it. He, on the other, may be able to fly through it because he created. That's why we rushed over here so early. To make sure Balavon hadn't gotten to you yet."

My head was killing me. Couldn't I just become a Neatholyte in peace? Why must there be some asshole out there making everything so difficult. "So what does that mean? What happens now?"

"Well, Brycin, Claire, and Jakob now have to find other means in getting here. It's much too dangerous for them to fly. Secondly, we are bringing in the others earlier than expected." Emma rose from the bar revealing the lower portion of herself that the bar amputated from my sight and walked out of the kitchen and into the living room.

I followed behind her. She was staring out the window facing the front lawn. She looked scared. I stood about seven feet away from her. "The original plan was to wait for them to attack you again to bring in the other, when we felt that your life was very much in danger. But it looks like with the way things are going," she turned to me. "We are going to need as much help as possible." I felt James pull up beside me as she finished her last statement.

She appeared very apprehensive. She positioned one of her hands on her hip and with her other hand, ran it through her icy blonde hair. She gazed back out the window with that same apprehensive expression. She was absorbed in thought, worried about how they were going to succeed with any of this. It wasn't just me who need their protection. They needed to keep an eye out for each other, especially the ones closest to me every day.

My death *will* lead to the apocalypse. It will lead to a retaliation that will break a sacred promise made thousands of years ago, a promise that kept Demilytes from being exterminated by Neatholytes and allowed every half-breed to live in a harmonic world. Peacefully somewhat.

I hadn't thought about it before but the sense of belonging…it was always there. I was just too stubborn to realize it. I wanted my old life back, the life where there were fewer complications in it. The life where everything seemed perfect in its own little way. Frankie and Jakob quarreling over the girls. Laughter and careless young adults talking about anything and everything. Where did *that* life go so fast?

"Don't." I murmured in a lifeless tone. Balavon wants to see the world plunge. We can't give it to him. I am destined to die. In-Betweens have foreseen it and I'm sure James has seen it if he is able to have dreams about future events.

I let my head hang shamefully for the thought that was pressing itself against my lips wanting to rush out. I walked over toward the window and faced it with my eyes closed. I was sure that the both of them were looking at me with curious eyes. I lifted my head and my eyelids and stared out the window. I couldn't face the reaction in their faces after they heard what I had to say. "Don't retaliate." I muttered. The suggestion would require them to accept the death of both me and Brycin.

"Don't…retal…don't retali…" Emma couldn't even finish the sentence. The pain in her tone was far worse than I could have imagined.

Her silence gave me an unsettling feeling in the pit of my stomach, as if someone had kicked me there and the pain was permanent.

"Then what?" she hissed venomously. "Huh?! Then what?! What if we do stand still and he goes after another family who isn't as disciplined as we are?! Huh?! What then?!"

I finally broke my attentive stare away from outside and to Emma. It felt like two knives were shoved through my chest and stomach simultaneously, twisting and wrenching to inflict more pain.

Guilt streamed through my veins. I didn't mean to intentionally hurt her but I had to spare her feelings if this could save everyone. I couldn't help but speculate what if her prediction didn't come true. What if by showing some restraint burns all of Balavon's hope? "I don't know what'll happen then."

"That's what I thought."

"But neither do you. I am looking at all of our options. Especially the ones that don't send us into World War III. Besides if you retaliate, does that make you any better than him? Are you willing to kill millions because of a few? And who says the Houses won't come after you guys?"

"Standing still is a sign of weakness. Something that I am not. Fighting for someone you love and honor and justice is an act of nobility. Even if I have to face him alone, I will do so and I'll die with dignity." She left it at that, my mouth open and ready to respond. She left the words trapped in my throat. Her shoulder nudged me and her sweet scent passed with her. The roar of the wind and its freezing touch infiltrated the house, chiming the chandelier's glassy fragments in the entryway. The frosty air sent a chilling shudder up my spine and then the door slammed, giving the chandelier one last rattle.

I wasn't a stranger to feeling horrible or feeling lower than dirt but this time was different. Worse. There had to be some ultimate punishment for hurting an angel. Especially one of magnificent splendor such as Emma. Something worse than being beaten with a whip with sharp teeth at the end of it or being burned alive a stake.

"Let her calm down." James's voice echoed through the solitary of the house and disturbed the silence of despair Emma left me to dwell in.

"Will she be okay? Out there?" I looked up at him as he continued to approach me.

"Ha, it'll take more than some ravage storm to take out Emma. She's a lot stronger than you give her credit for."

"Yeah I know." I said shamefully.

"I never thought of it before 'til now but I may have an alternative that doesn't require you dead and them surrendering to the fact. I have dreamt it. I've seen it for myself. You die and they retaliate and the war begins. But in my dream you were wingless and only Brycin was with you. One of his wings had been removed cutting his powers in half. Death was inevitable for the both of you.

"But the thing I am trying to get at is that you had *no* powers whatsoever. I have never had a dream be proven wrong." That left no room for any kind of hope. "But we have never tried to fight one of them from coming to pass." He must have thought he implanted a glimpse of hope in me with that thought because he smiled crookedly. There actually was a fire of hope rising in me. "If we could keep you safe long enough for you to receive your wings and inherit whatever abilities that may come with them, then we might stand a chance and the fate of the world is immediately altered."

He was making sense. But there was a side of me that doubted it. A side that took heed to the fact that he said he had never had a dream be proven wrong before. What if it was all pointless?

He sighed heavily. "Look, it's worth a try. It's not that easy for them to just sit still and do nothing about the death of someone they love. Our powers, especially half-breeds, are heavily linked to our moods and our emotions. When we are calm and content, our powers function properly and they are under control. But when we are under any type of heavy emotion, rage, stress...sadness..." I noticed his hesitation before he got to the word sadness. His head had fallen and his eyes were closed.

I knew that face. I remembered it so well. It was the exact same pain I had seen on his sister's face several days ago at the lake. It was when she told me how she had to watch this boy in front of me...

My heart felt heavier as I almost thought the word. I couldn't even imagine the tear it would cause for his sister when the time came. "Are you afraid?"

His head lifted at the question and when his eyes opened, they had no life in them. They were deep and dark like a void. They were empty. "To die? No. I'm not afraid to die at all. But I am afraid for Emma. When heavy emotions consume a half-breed, they can become lethal and dangerous, virtually unstoppable. Their powers become stronger and more damaging. That's why the promise was made long ago. Because so many families had been established. Had any half-breed lost a loved one and suffered a heavy and powerful emotional blow, the world may have ended centuries ago.

"Emma is very special. She can alter thoughts and moods. Along with those special abilities, she is virtually indestructible and she can wield electricity. Control it, create it. With her enhanced human instincts she would become lethal. If anyone tried to stop her, she could easily alter their thoughts and she would become of no concern to them.

"Now you see why it'll be hard for them. Some might become consumed in their emotions. It's enough, Kayden. If you and Brycin die, it will be enough to resurrect the war that was never really finished. When you have six different half-breeds, six different minds caught under a heavy emotion like emotional pain and sadness, the results can be catastrophic. You can't imagine the scale of destruction they can inflict on this planet. Especially Aris."

"Why especially Aris?" I asked with a suffering and shaky tone. I didn't realize that his story was scaring me. My legs were just as shaky as my trembling voice. I immediately regretted making Emma think about surrendering.

James let out a deep sigh. He placed his hand on my shoulder. "She'll forgive you. I know she will. Just don't mention submitting to them anymore. If he succeeds, he will become their only concern." Why was he trying to comfort me? It was easy to read that he was just as shaken up by it. Probably more than me. And why did he evade my question?

His hand fell from my shoulder and he headed toward the kitchen. "James." I called to him. He never turned around.

My heart felt like it was in my belly, burning in the acids. I'd just inflicted a lot of grievance on the both of them, both unintentionally.

There was moisture filling up behind my eyelids as I turned back to look out the window. Was it going to happen? Would today finally be the day where I drowned in my tears? I waited.

Nothing.

Expected.

The storm continued to rage on. I hadn't seen Balavon use his abilities during our last encounter. Everyone else fought for him. If he was able to construct a storm as malevolent and vicious as this one, what else could he possibly do?

The clouds were thick, dark, shadowing the world beneath in darkness. They looked to be growing fuller and heavier with moisture. The lightning licked the skies with a bright venom and the thunder was deafening, rattling the walls and windows of this fortress. Amazing how Rachel was sleeping through this. The wind ripped the limbs of trees off, catapulting them through the sky. Along with them blew cardboard signs, pieces of shredded rooftops, and debris.

This storm. I had seen it before. It was just like the storm I had drove with on my way to see Portman at his manor. Balavon had to have done it. Even if Brycin and the others knew where I was, they wouldn't have been able to get to me in time to stop anything from happening.

It was all so frustrating. Nothing fit anywhere anymore. Balavon wants me dead but had the chance before so why didn't he take it? Was he taunting us? Toying with us? Trying to break us down little by little so that it weakened us? Could he have been trying to weaken my defenses from the inside rather than the outside?

For the first time in my life I wished I were human. A human without a protector. Normal. Everything would be normal. I wouldn't be stalked by demons in both my conscious and my unconscious state of being. I wouldn't be the key to some war that was rising on the horizon. But most importantly, I wouldn't have to face a near eternity without Rachel.

I struggled to pull my eyelids open, the weight of tiredness still lingering on them. I couldn't even recall falling asleep or how I even got on the sofa for that matter. And someone had placed a cerulean and almond brown decorated blanket on top of me.

It was quiet now. On both the outside and the inside.

I bolted up remembering that Emma and James were here. Did they leave?

I hurried into the one other room where they could have been. The kitchen.

As I turned the corner, I was greeted by two overly attractive faces.

Emma's attire was different now. She now wore a white turtle neck sweater with blue denim jeans.

"You guys stayed." I stated with a hint of enthusiasm.

"Well of course we did." Emma answered, the venom and the hiss that she once had in her tone toward me completely absent. She approached me and gently tossed her arms over my shoulders. That surprised me. For a brief second, my mind was blank, numb, incapable of responding back to her hug. I was almost paralyzed by her touch. It was the second time I had been this close to her.

Finally, after a few more passing seconds, I lightly wrapped my arms around her, responding to her hug.

She slowly pulled away from me. "I'm sorry, Kayden. There is no excuse for my behavior earlier. You were only trying to help." It was the softest I'd ever heard her voice.

I gently pulled her face up by her chin with the use of the side of my finger. "You have nothing to be sorry for. I understand now. James explained it all to me. I was wrong."

"That's sweet of you. Thank you." She took my hand that lifted her head up into her hands. For a split second, I felt a pull toward her in an unconceivable way. Was I falling for her? I continued to stare in her eyes as she stared back in mine.

It was peculiar to me, being attracted to someone who I *thought* I had no intents on being attracted to. But, the reality is, the more time I spend with her, the more I…care for her.

She broke the connection between our eyes, looking over at James. They exchanged smiles. And then she turned back to me. "Up for a ride?"

My eyes were squint, looking back and forth between the two, accusing them with my eyes. There was something in the way she asked me, something that forced me to question them. It was as though they were being underhanded about something. I took my hand back. "What's going on?"

As soon as I asked the question, James snickered and dropped his head. *What are they up to?* I thought to myself.

"Well, the others are back now." She stated with a glowing smile.

There was a joyous light in my eyes and a softening of my expression. I knew they could see my excitement.

"They are waiting for us at the park. Along with Aris, Elaina, and Matt." And just like that, my expression was vacant.

They both seemed to laugh and I grimaced at their laughter. I was sure Emma was listening to my heart rate accelerate. And I was absolutely positive that Brycin felt this nervousness and was probably broadcasting it to the others. I didn't find any of it humorous.

"Ready?" Emma pressured.

I was frozen. I was not ready. In fact, I didn't want to go. How about I go upstairs and I could meet them tomorrow? That sounds less stressful. Besides, I am too ill-prepared to meet them. I don't even know what I would say or how I would act for that matter. Hell, I don't even have a mental image of what each of them looks like.

"Yeah?" she continued to press.

Sweat stood out on my forehead. I had never felt so stumped before, so unsure. I want to go, I really do and finally put some faces to these names and become accustomed to their faces (which I'm sure are utterly gorgeous). But I also don't want to go. It's like the first day of school. Full of anxiety and wishing you knew what everyone thought of you upon first impressions.

Ugh.

Go with them. It'll be alright. The loud voice in my head told me. But I couldn't help but notice that there was a faint voice yelling too. All I could make out was "no" and "don't" but never any complete sentences.

It'll be fine. Don't worry.

The voice was annoying but I couldn't help but listen to it. "Okay?" I responded lackadaisically.

Emma smiled. "Great! Grab your coat, okay? It's going to be slightly cold."

"Okay."

"Splendid!" she shouted with enthusiasm. "We'll be in the car! Com'on, James!" Emma grabbed James by his wrist and darted out of the house with him.

They left the door open and the brisk air swam up my arm and ventilated throughout my shirt, raising possibly every single hair on my body. I walked over to the coat rack beside the open door and removed the black leather jacket from the hook.

As I removed my coat from its hook, the small voice in my head was trying to get louder and louder saying "stop" and "why aren't you listening to me?" But the louder voice overpowered effortlessly countering with "just go" and "you are family; you are one of them." They were both starting to annoy me.

I felt so disconnected from my body. It was functioning on its own. Like…autopilot but for the human body. Before I knew it, I was locking the door to my house and walking the paved pathway that led from the sidewalk to my front doorsteps, shoving my arms through the sleeves of my coat.

On the side of the road, glistening under the street light from remaining condensation was the fiery red Camaro. The passenger side door was open. Though my body had a mind of its own, my stomach was still turning with anxiety.

I let the seat back and got in.

I didn't even get my seatbelt on good enough or close the door before Emma took off.

Swiftly, I closed the open door and threw the seatbelt over my shoulder and waited to hear the…*click.*

"Are you insane?! You could have killed me! And Brycin and I would have haunted you for the rest of your life!"

She laughed. "Ha, that'll be a long time to haunt me. I'm sure your souls would eventually find something better to do than to bother little ol' me."

"Oh, trust, we'll make it fun."

The car went silent but as soon as it did, that soft voice was screaming at me and the loud voice was completely absent, silent along with the car. *You IDIOT! Tell them to take you back! Convince them in to taking you tomorrow!*

I looked at James in the back seat. He stared out the window, his hand covering up a smile. I then looked at Emma and she was smiling too. Not just any smile. The kind of smile that would give someone away whenever they played a prank or a joke on someone. There was almost a hint a triumph in her eyes.

My mouth plopped open. I couldn't believe it. I couldn't believe she used her powers on me.

She started laughing. Then James started laughing.

"That's not funny."

"Oh, Kayden lighten up." James spoke from the back seat, his hand on my shoulder. "She does it to me all the time to get me to do dishes."

"This isn't dishes!"

"Ha ha, you know what I was afraid of? I was afraid that it wasn't going to work on you. That you would have figured it out as soon as I starting playing with your thoughts." She looked at me and she caught the irritation radiating off of me. "Oh, com'on Kayden. You were scared. You heart was about to jump out of your chest." No argument there. "There was no need to be scared. I had to get you to come someway and trying to convince you with words would have been futile." No argument their either but I was still pissed.

With every passing second, my anger calmed. It was impossible to stay mad at her for an extended period of time. Another ability she possessed that I resented.

Or *was* she using her powers to silence me, to keep me from ripping her limb from limb (though as a human I wouldn't do much damage).

No, this was me. The duality for dominance that was once occurring in my mind was not present. I didn't hear a voice telling me to let Emma off the hook and another countering, telling me to annihilate her where she sits.

I sighed heavily in defeat. I sat far back into the seat. "Well, can you talk to me at least? Ease the anxiety?" I asked with my eyes closed, trying exceedingly hard not to think of what awaited me beyond the labyrinth of trees in the large moonlit field.

"What do you want to talk about?"

"I dunno. Something. How about…" I trailed off and opened my eyes. Deliberating through thoughts as they passed through my head. "How many of you can do that? Capable of altering the thought processes of others?"

"Well, I can only do it externally I guess you can say. Meaning I can't actually get into your mind, read what's going on and then change your thoughts and decisions. I can only make assumptions by getting a read on your emotions and external things such as body language or heart rate.

"There are also our default abilities. The ones we are granted with once we get our wings. Dexterity, enhancement of our five human senses, speed and super strength and my favorite, the ability to manipulate, create, and wield electricity. But only Neatholytes can manipulate and create electricity. Demilytes on the other hand can control and generate fire.

"But those are in normal cases. Like I told you, you're not really normal. And I don't think it's in a bad way. I think you are special, Kayden. Unique." I rolled my eyes. The car fell silent after that.

It was strange. Not being normal amongst something that was already ruled as abnormal.

"You know, I heard you and James talking when I left and I think what he was saying is a great idea. I couldn't help but play the match out in my head. Seven Neatholytes versus four Demilytes. The advantage is ours."

I glanced at her. Her eyes never left the road. She was really something else. She was really willing to do this. To die for Brycin and for me. She was a pretty, exceptional blonde warrior.

I sat back in silence, watching the streetlights trail over the red exterior of the car and up the windshield, making way for the next streetlight reflection to do the same thing.

"There is a reason why I thought my abilities wouldn't work on you."

I looked up at her. "And why is that?"

"Well, my powers aren't that affective on half-breeds."

"But I'm not one. At least not yet."

"Yeah, but because you have so much angelic blood in you, it made me question whether or not my ability would work on you."

"Oh." I stated thoughtfully.

My anxiety was wholly absent. There was really no more need for talk but I still had one last question to ask her regarding the very characteristic that separated them from humans. "Hey, Emma? Where do your wings go? I mean aren't they apart of your body?"

"Uhmm…" She bit her lip. I came to the conclusion that she really didn't know the answer to that. "Well, the only way anyone can see our wings physically is if we change our eyes. It is almost as though our human eyes completely cloak our divine characteristics, making our wings invisible, like they're not even there. Though as I speak to you right now and you can't see them, I can feel them."

I nodded thoughtfully, soaking in everything, preparing myself for my upcoming day. That is if I make it there.

After she was done explaining, I noticed we were pulling into the park. Off in the distance stood a figure. As we pulled closer toward the figure, I was happy to see that it was Brycin.

She parked the car and Brycin walked toward my side. I exited the car and closed the gap between us. We exchanged a friendly hug. He seemed happier than me that he was back.

Emma and James were shutting the door to the car and approaching.

As soon as they were close to us, the air started to roar and the wind picked up a little. The others didn't seem frightened at all though they studied this spontaneous change in the atmosphere. There was a thickness forming around us. It was cold. Really cold. It was a fog.

"Don't be alarmed. It's just Aris. He's protecting Emma's car from being towed away." I looked at Emma and she nodded.

"Well, let's go." Brycin said in a bright tone.

I watched as one by one they disappeared into the thickness. I hurried behind them so I wouldn't get lost. I felt the terrain change. We must have been in the forest. It was already hard for me the last time I tried walking through these trees due to the darkness but at least with the darkness I was able to see the outlining of tree trunks and the hanging branches and the canopies of moss that hung from them. But with the combination of fog and darkness, I could barely see anything. I might as well have been walking blindfolded or with my eyes glued shut. Branches smacked me in the face and I had lost count to how many times my knee rammed into a tree trunk or I tripped over a raised tree root.

I suddenly felt a change in the air. It was cooler here. We must have made out of the trees. Little by little, I saw the three in front of me become more and more visible. The fog was parting and making a clearing. I could finally see again. The fog continued to move toward the perimeters of the large field and remained there.

That's when I saw them. Probably a hundred meters or so away. I was nervous again and Brycin chuckled beneath his breath. Brycin started to approach the center of the field. James and Emma trailed directly behind him. I never took my eyes off of them for a second.

Their features started to come into focus. There was a man and a woman. The man had mocha colored skin and deep, set in almond brown eyes. He was tall and athletic in physique. He was very mature in the face though he seemed virtually ageless. The woman had long, curly, flowing honey brown hair. Her eyes shimmered in an elegant bronze color. She too was mature in features and just like the male beside her, she too looked ageless.

As I suspected, they too were beautiful.

But there were only two of them. Where was the third?

Brycin's voice reached across to the others. "Aris, Elaina. I would like to formally introduce you to Kayden." I felt like the new stray dog a kid brings home to mommy and daddy, begging them to keep it.

"Hi." I stated nervously and my eyes flashing between both faces.

"Hello." Aris bowed his head as he spoke in a deep, velvety tone.

"It's really a pleasure to finally meet you." Elaina greeted me. Her voice was poetic. I almost wanted to go to sleep to it because of how soothing it was. Angels no doubt.

Brycin was looking around. "Where is Matt?"

Something suddenly hit me hard from the left side, spinning and swirling me around, turning everything into a bright blue blur. There was a flapping sound along with the spinning and swirling. I couldn't scream. I couldn't speak. I couldn't even breathe.

"Finally, Brycin takes you out of hiding!" The unfamiliar voice rang out. The spinning stopped but everything still seemed to be moving. I was on my feet and waiting for the dizzy spell to wear off. "Ouch, what was that for?"

"He isn't one of us yet, stupid!" Brycin yelled. "He isn't used to that!" There were two hands on my shoulders. "Kayden, you okay?"

"Yeah, just let my stomach stop moving."

"Kayden, this obnoxious little monster here is Matt."

"You are going to let him talk about me like that?" Matt questioned. He then sucked air in through his teeth. "Some protector. Sorry about that. It's nice to meet you." He extended out his hand.

My focus was back to standards. Matt looked a lot like my age. His wings were gone. He had curly bronze colored hair, bright skinned and he had deep gray eyes. He was slender but I will never underestimate his strength. "Kayden." I shook his extended hand.

"Brycin, what did you find out?" Aris asked. Regarding to their long trip away I suppose.

"Nothing. We're back to square one." He answered in defeat.

"Well don't beat yourself up." Elaina chimed in with her soft, soothing voice. It was so easy to tell she was the mother of the family, the comforter. She walked over to me and braided her arm with mine. "Kayden has much protection now and little to worry about."

"Yeah, I wish those bat bastards would come and strike. I've been dying for a real fight. Not some petty little spar match."

"Matt, calm down." Aris muttered in a voice that could only belong to an angel.

There was some rustling coming from behind me. Claire and Jakob emerged from the fog both baring their wings. She punched him in the arm. "Dammit, Jakob! Because of you, I missed his first meeting with Aris."

"Sorry, ha."

"Ugh, don't talk to me!"

"Ha! What did I do?"

"Ugh, whatever!"

They continued to bicker back and forth, their wings slowly faded into invisibility and their eyes returning to normal until they were finally beside the rest of us. Elaina left my arm and stood beside Aris.

I looked at all of them and I wasn't as nervous as I thought I would be. I was, for the most part, used to all of it. This was it. This was my new home. My new family.

Chapter 11: Family Origins

THERE WASN'T MUCH THAT COULD BE SAID. MY LIFE finally possessed some type of meaning, regardless if the meaning turned out to be a good one or a bad one. It didn't matter much to me at this very moment. Whether that meaning required my blood to spill, which would inevitably kill my protector who also so happens to be my best friend, and force the hands of my new family to retaliate against those responsible for our deaths and potentially plunge the world into its final days or if the meaning was to allow me to evade my foreseen death, embrace the half-breed within me and alter the future on a global scale. Either way, my life held significance.

It was all so amazing, a breath of fresh air. It was invigorating to know that my life was no longer a routine. A month ago, the events within my day would go as so: wake up with the weight of my emotions crushing and pulverizing my already aching heart, greet the warmhearted being who bared the scent of lavenders and feel much worse about myself and the life in which I didn't appreciate enough, go to school, complain some more about my life to my best friend, after blowing off hanging out with my friends with some lame excuse (which worked most of the time but now I know that Brycin was actually being courteous because he knew my true feelings due to his protector abilities allowing him to sense my shift in moods) go home, attempt to complete my homework but be too distracted by my uncontrollable emotions and thoughts that

I give up on everything, go to sleep and begin the process all over again. Now, tomorrow is such a mystery. It is also, almost, unnerving.

We were all congregated in the center of the field. Claire and Brycin stood closest to me. Aris and Elaina stood across from us. Completing the circle on the right side of me was Emma and James and completing the left side was Matt and Jakob.

"I believe," Aris began in a deep, silky voice. "That in order for you to be one of us, you must know each of our stories; you need to know who we are and how our family is what it is today."

His eyes paled and the ground shook. I was nowhere near as balanced as the others. They were perfectly still as the ground quaked beneath them while I stumbled a little for balance. The ground then lifted about three feet, traveling around the exterior of the family circle. After the rumbling seized, I heard a large snapping of some kind coming from beyond the barrier of the fog. A tree that was snapped completely in half at the center of its trunk floated over toward our circle. It hovered directly above us. A bright surge of light suddenly ripped through the trunk of the tree, shattering it into an assortment of smaller pieces of wood. The broken limbs and logs floated down to the center of the circle, Aris completely in control over the entire phenomenon.

"Jakob?" he prompted.

I turned to Jakob. There was something his eyes were doing that I had never seen anyone else's do. It was as if the irises in his eyes were completely made up of a blazing, purple flame. He then held out his fist downward over the pile of logs. He flipped his hand over and opened it. Burning bright and unique with its color was a purple flame. It was breathtaking. The flame breathed in dark purples, soft pinks and bright whites. The flame floated down on to the pile of logs and roared deeply with life. I couldn't take my eyes off of it. The flame was completely of the unnatural and if it was possible to replicate this purple flame, I'm not so sure if the duplicate would come close in comparison to the one Jakob created.

In synchronization, they all sat on the risen earth. After converting the disbelief of the purple flame into belief, I did so as well and sat in between Brycin and Claire.

"I believe it'll be best," Aris began, disrupting the burning roar of the purple pyre. "If I begin since this family somewhat began with me." The majesty in his voice as he began couldn't have been anything short of royal. He spoke almost as if he were a king. "Seven hundred and fifty-two years ago, I was born. I was born to a very prestigious family. Well, at least to those who actually *knew* our family, we were quite renowned.

"Long before my birth, my great ancestors lived in the age of the colossal war between Sapharius and Azer. Nations were falling left and right and it seemed that the worst was inevitable. They were merely peasants to a village in the lower parts of Southern Europe. With scarce natural resources, they needed some sort of assertion, a guarantee of their survival.

"When they gained knowledge of this pro-human organization, this cult that promised to rid the world of these creatures and reclaim their human pride, my family declared their allegiance.

"They helped the cult destroy some of our kind and earned prominence and respect in favor of the cult.

"When our kind hid themselves from the dangerous cult targeting them, it brought fear to my family. The cult had given them everything they wanted and then some all due to their loyalty to the cult and without any half-breeds to slay, they feared they would be of little use to the cult and would go back to living a life of survival. But leaders of the pro-human organization never believed wholly for a second that our kind had just gone away. They knew we were hiding and they were going to wait for our next slip up.

"Centuries passed and my family became a very valuable asset to this cult. My great-grandfather had become one of the six councilmen to the head, underground organization in Rome known as the Order. Powerful men belonged to this organization. And the generations to come would continue to pass on the belief. My great-grandfather passed it on to my grandfather, he passed it down to my father and my father presented me with the legends and stories and the reasons why we must exist.

"My father wasn't prideful of being a part of this cult as were my grandfather and great-grandfather. He was very medium-hearted about belonging to such a family. He tried to shield me away from it as much as possible but when you had strong believers such as my grandfather and great-grandfather who honored being a part of the Order so strenuously, it was pretty much futile to even try. My father believed it to be a waste of breath and life. There hadn't been any sightings of them in centuries. It was a ridiculous obligation to him. An obligation he had no choice but to submit to.

"I would soon find out the deeper reasons for why he kept himself so distant from the Order.

"I was seventeen years old and outside our home, in the streets of Rome, a ruckus had manifested. Someone reported seeing a human girl with wings, bird-like wings. The Order wasted no time. They interrogated the man who claimed he had seen this creature. How did she look? Approximate height? Skin complexion, length of hair, color of eyes, any question imaginable they asked. It wasn't long 'til the figured out who it was."

The majesty in his voice was fading and it was rapidly filling with sorrow and grief.

"All six councilmen burst into our home, restraining me and my father and went after my mother with a sword."

"WHAT IS THIS?!" My grandfather bellowed. "OUTRAGED! YOU DARE BRING SHAME TO OUR FAMILY NAME?!"

"My father shouted, pleading with them to have mercy, grant exemption. But they didn't listen."

"Father please," My father pleaded. "You don't know what you're doing! You're wrong!"

"I am never wrong!" My grandfather roared with the blade to my mother's chest. "Such a creature shouldn't exist! We humans inherited this planet from beasts and I refuse to just give it away."

"It isn't yours to have, Father!"

"I will not refuse this world for the likes of these wretched fiends! There is only one way to discard of you, wench!"

"He dragged my mother out of our home and into the streets. To be an angel was far worse than being a gypsy or a murderer. I watched it all unfold. There was nothing I could do. My father was mortified, defeated because he couldn't do anything to save his lover."

"Show them! SHOW THEM!" My grandfather lashed out.

"And if I don't?" She hissed through her teeth.

"He walked over to me, pushing two other members of the Order off of me and sticking the blade to my throat."

"Or watch your son parish!"

"Her weakness. Me. I was her prized possession. She would do anything even if that meant saving me."

"No!" My father yelled from the crowd. "You would kill your own grandson for the sake of your own ridiculous beliefs!"

"My ancestor's belief is what kept us here! It's what kept all of us her. Yes, I would kill my own grandson for the sake of mankind."

"You're a barbarian!"

"I'm your father! I know what's right for us!"

He pressed the blade closer to my throat.

"Okay," She spoke, crying. "Alright. I'll show them."

"It was the first time I'd ever seen such beauty. How could something so beautiful be wretched and a fiend? The councilmen and other members of the Order seized her at once. Her cries rang out into the streets of Rome as they chopped her wings off. The callous crowd wasn't in such an uproar like they were several minutes ago.

"I watched in horror as they set her up to die a fiery death. I couldn't hide the pain. I sobbed as I watched the ruby liquid gush from her back.

"In minutes, the fire was lit and her screams would forever haunt those who heard it. I fought my hardest to free myself from the clutches of the Order. My heart ached. I felt betrayed by my own family and I would have my revenge.

"That's when it began happening to me. My legs went weak, my head was pounding ferociously, and my chest hurt with every single breath I took. I fell to my hands and knees. My spine twisted once and hard. The pain was excruciating, too much. It completely disconnected from my ribs. My lungs were expanding in my chest and every single muscle in my body contracted and relaxed, growing at an exponential rate.

"Everyone gazed as I transformed into the very thing they had just killed.

"I felt them, pushing and slicing through muscle and flesh to reach the surface. It was an insufferable pain. The pain seemed to amplify my anger and rage, turning me into a lethal and dangerous weapon. In one fast, sharp move, they rushed out of my back, showering a portion of the crowd in red fluids.

"It was over. I felt the bones grow heavier and heavier. The muscles were wrapping themselves around the hollow bones, then the flesh over the muscles and finally my feathers. Everything in my body was constructing back to as it was before the gruesome transformation."

"SEIZE HIM!"

"I looked up and my powers immediately kicked in, fueled by rage and hate. I was unstoppable. This beam of light shot from my hand and catapulted the rampaging members of the Order over the crowd. I remember staring at my hand, amazed at what I was capable of. I felt the flow of energy pass through me and consume me. I would feed my revenge until it no longer hungered. I launched myself into the skies where I would conduct my symphony of destruction. I wrecked buildings, destroyed homes, claimed countless lives. I was a monster.

"The skies blackened with a coat of dark, stormy clouds. The earth quaked and bellowed, roaring as it split streets in half. My powers were rising. Dark pillars extended from the abyss of clouds and reached to the earth, ripping up everything and destroying anything in their paths. The winds were just as destructive and the lightning struck the earth like meteorites.

"I couldn't control myself. My thirst was too strong to ignore.

"After showcasing what I was capable of, I descended back to the earth. Six councilmen in my sight, six with the same fate."

"You kill us, you only prove us right! There will be more of us! Trust me! Someone will come looking for you!"

"I didn't care. Revenge was mine. In one bright flash of light, all of Rome perished.

"The blast did nothing to me. I was untouched. When the dust settled, Rome was now a wasteland. Nothing but dirt, dust and debris and the base of some structures composed the scenery. I couldn't believe it. I was a god. I had wiped out an entire city in a matter of minutes. But I would only lather in triumph for only a second. I fell to me knees and sobbed, realizing that I had accidently killed my father as well.

"I felt empty, betrayed. Because of them, I had no family now. I was abandoned and alone and I wanted nothing more than to die myself.

"That's when I heard them land behind me. Seven others. A family of angels who were there to destroy me for exposing our world and obliterating an entire city."

"I…I…" A male voice stammered. "Never in the four hundred years have I seen something so atrocious! As followers of the laws of Amos, it is our duty to destroy the accused!"

"I didn't care. I wanted it. I wanted to perish with the city I had destroyed.

"He kicked me to the floor and pressed his foot to my back but before he could terminate me—"

"I stepped in." Elaina's voice chanted, continuing with the flow of the story. "I was part of the family who stumbled upon Aris and the destruction he had descended upon Rome. I sensed that his heart was heavy but it wasn't because we were there to kill him. He felt bad for what he had done.

"I stopped my brother, Elijah, before he could kill Aris. I knelt beside him as he lay beneath my brother's foot. Motionless he was. If it wasn't for my acute hearing, I would have presumed him already dead. I requested permission from him to touch his head so I could witness what he had seen. He didn't answer me but I did so.

"As if I were living it, I had witnessed everything that had happened. From the raging citizen who caused the ruckus to the point of where my hand lay on his head.

"I removed my brother's foot from his back and spoke with him in private, requesting that Aris's life be spared. He immediately objected, reciting the laws of Amos to me. I explained everything to him. I explained how Aris had no teachings and didn't know our laws. I also told my brother of his deepest desire. To belong to a family again and that his heart was innately good. If that wasn't enough to persuade him, telling him that Aris had eliminated all remains of the Order would surely grant him exoneration.

"I offered to teach him and look after him. My brother was very skeptical at first but, he spared Aris's life. But it came with a price. Since I was to look after Aris, if he experienced another disastrous episode again, the *both* of us would be held accountable."

My mind was jumping from present to past, back and forth, placing understanding in areas where it belonged. I had finally realized what James meant by *especially Aris*. Aris had potential to destroy a city as a young angel. If he goes through that same type of grief due to losing his family he has today or just a portion of it, the results could be monstrous. If before he was able to destroy a city, today it could be a nation. If not a continent, possibly, Earth itself.

"My brother has the ability to renew things, make things as they were. Though he could bring cities back to life, he could never bring an actual human or half-breed back from the dead. He could only reverse physical damage done to inanimate objects.

"In seconds, Rome had been revived. But it wasn't really acceptable to have an empty city. Rome had become a new dwelling place for us half-breeds. And travelers were sure to come, mingling and mixing humans with us half-breeds."

"After saving me," Aris began. "We became best of friends. She trained me, taught me how to control my overwhelming emotions, told me of our kind and where we came from. And she promised me a new family. But I wouldn't have it for centuries to come.

"Over the centuries my powers began to grow. At one point, I kept receiving these images in the form of a dream of two children in trouble. A boy and a little girl. They were always running, running to safety but from what I had no clue. Every dream ended the same thought. Both of them would lay lifeless and scorched. The dream would resurface every night. Their screams haunted me every day. I was so uneasy, on edge, and the smallest things would frighten me. I couldn't function with such thoughts. So, I stopped sleeping for a while but that didn't help at all. It was still all so easy to remember and so hard to ignore. I couldn't ignore them anymore.

"After concentrating hard enough on the dream, I was able to identify where they were. In London."

Aris had stopped speaking. The pause allowed the crackling of the purple fire to amplify in sound. My attention was now on the blaze. Being so easily drawn into the stories being told around me, I had forgotten how much the color of the blaze appealed to me.

"I was born to a very unfortunate family," my head snapped in Jakob's direction upon the sound of his voice as it overrode the cackling of the fire. "In a time full of plagues, despair, and disasters of all sorts. London had just recovered from the fire of 1633 and everything seemed to be looking up for London.

"In 1654, I was born. Though my parents loved me dearly, they were very careless with outside things. My mother and father weren't the best with keeping up with paying taxes and in the end we suffered miserably. If that wasn't enough, adding an additional member to the family was going to be a lot harder to assess to.

"My mother had become pregnant in 1661 with my younger sister, Juliet. Though they were very excited about the coming of our new family member, they both knew the predicament it would place them in. With that knowledge came stress and with the stress, a virus that would kill my father and render my mother brokenhearted. After his death, she valued everything he was able to give her, especially this golden locket which she had offered to sell on numerous occasions to save us from our life of poverty but he always refused her to do so. She had become very dysfunctional and I wasn't up to the task to provide her with everything she required. I was only seven.

"But when my sister was finally born, everything seemed to slowly return to normal. However, it would only last for so long.

"Five years later, September 2, 1666, the Great Fire of London was upon us. I was awakened by the roaring sound of flames and black smoke. Our house was falling quickly. Parts of the house were collapsing and it seemed that we only had minutes to get out before it all fell.

"I quickly rushed to my mother's room where she and my sister slept. My mother jolted up and immediately took heed to the roaring flames. She scooped Juliet, who was still half asleep, tight into her bosom and rushed for the exit.

"But, then she stops." A sob was forming in his throat. He gulped hard, trying to swallow the sob and stared into the violet flames. "She gave me my sister."

"Hurry out, sweetie!" she yelled over the flames. "I will be back!"

"But—"

"Take your sister and go!"

"I safely got me and my sister out of the house and we waited for our mother. But she never came. The house was weak from the scorching flames and it began its collapse — my mother still inside.

"She'd forgotten that stupid locket and went back for it. Cost us our mother.

"I didn't know what to do. All I knew was that I had to protect my little sister. I resisted every urge to cry. I had to be a big boy, strong — for the sake of both of us.

"We ran what seemed like forever, trying to find an outlet to the city but everything seemed like a big, burning maze, a puzzle with no way out. We tried following others but parts of buildings would collapse in front of us, leaving us with no way to pass through so we had to find other ways.

"We were rushing through an alley way and my sister had tripped. The tugged forced me to fall. As I was hurrying to my feet, part of a building..." he stopped. I could see why. None of them had a perfect history so far. There was always some major loss. Well, in that case, I fit right on in. "Part of a building collapsed on one of her legs. I tried so hard to pull her from underneath the pile of burning wood, but, I couldn't. I wasn't physically strong enough.

"I wasn't just going to give up though. I had to do whatever I could to save her. I ran to where the flaming wood pinned her leg down and I grabbed the hot, burning portion of wood with bare hands. It hurt like hell. But my efforts were still useless. It wasn't budging the slightest. She cried for me to help her, but—" his voice was breaking. The sob in his throat was expanding. I couldn't imagine the pain he was enduring as he forced himself to tell the story. "The building beside me was falling and I wasn't aware of it. As it fell, I felt something tug me really hard and take me into the air. I watched with horrific eyes as the building crushed my baby sister."

There was a moment of silence. I dropped my head, almost exhausted with the tales. The only thing speaking was the crackling fire.

Everyone had a story. Everyone. The entire time, for as long as I'd known them, I assumed all of them to have had a perfect life — nowhere near as painful as my life. In reality, pain orbited them as well.

"I was saved by Aris that day." My head was up and Jakob was looking over in Aris's direction. "And I couldn't thank him enough for saving me." He then turned and looked at Claire with a devious smirk. "Plus if he hadn't, I wouldn't have received the privilege of looking at you every day." He said biting his lip.

She pushed him away and laughed. Jakob was always the one to crack jokes at the wrong time but this time was acceptable.

"Ha, no. I'm only kidding. Even though I miss her terribly and feel like a failure to her in some way, I know she is in a better place and I will do all that is for the greater good in the name of my little sister."

"And Jakob has been a fine addition to our family." Elaina complimented.

"Thank you." He acknowledged

"Even though many find it barbaric for us to live in a cooperative family, we manage just fine."

"Though in the beginning," Aris interjected. "When he first received his wings, he was a bit of a handful. It's a Demilytes instinct to be bad and do evil deeds, just like it's ours to do good things. But eventually he came around." I glanced over at Jakob who was smiling with a smile of accomplishment. "The next addition to our family was Claire."

I turned to the right of me, studying Claire, her dark red hair shimmering lightly with the gentle touch of the moonlight and swaying softly in the wind. She was hunched forward, the purple flame resting in the reflection of her eyes. She was fidgeting with her hands, flipping them over and over again as if examining them, as if she were unfamiliar with her own hands. She'd must've been dreading the moment when time would introduce her.

She sat up straight and placed her hair behind her ear. "Pain and suffering both seem to be inevitable occurrences in the life of a half-breed. We are the strongest species on this planet yet at times," she looked at me with eyes I weren't familiar with. Sorrowful eyes. "I feel like we are more fragile than humans." She turned back to face the flame. "I wish I could have been given the privilege of learning the faces of my parents, distinguishing between their touch and adapting to their voices. But wishes are nothing more than a deep desire conjured up by our subconscious. The reality is and forever will be that I will never know them." She looked away from the fire and back at me. "So if anyone feels the void that you have in your heart by never knowing your real parents, I do."

I'd lost all awareness to where I was. For a second, the moon blackened along with the specs of lights surrounding it, turning it into a void of despair. The fire faded along with the light breeze of the wind and all of the faces in the circle disappeared. All of them except for Claire's. It had almost become a forgotten fact to me, that I never knew my actual parents, and with a slight reminder from Claire, that neglected truth in my life had returned. I had seen my entire life's pain project through the face and eyes of this angel and with that came the discomfort of my destructive sea. My sea had paralyzed me. I didn't know how to react, how to breathe, how to blink. I just stared blankly at her.

"Samius and Eliza," Elaina's voice brought with it the light of the moon and the tiny freckles around it, the roar and the brightness of the purple flame, the icy yet soft touch of the wind and the faces of the circle. "Were dear friends to us, members to this family long ago. They had joined our family a little after Jakob received his wings. They were best friends to one another. Lovers."

"We had decided to remove ourselves from having any social life," Aris's voice followed after Elaina's. "Because Jakob was having difficulty suppressing his demonic side. It was his instincts to destroy but in order to be part of this family, it had to be controlled. Jakob was suffering from power lashes. Power lashes are dangerous. When you deny too much of your power, suppress too much of it or experience a severe blow to your emotions, your power builds and builds until it reaches a point where it just erupts and you become a walking vessel of pure power."

"And that's what you are afraid of is happening to me. That because I have not received my wings yet, it is suppressing a lot of power and if I *do* receive them, then I would experience a power lash."

They were silent but their silence was confirming.

"Power lashes can be very dangerous. They are the very things that nearly get us exposed and there is only one way to handle one experiencing a power lash if they are incapable of retracting or satisfying the outburst. They must be destroyed.

"So we found refuge in a forest in London at the time. There, he would have access to control his inner instincts and when he did experience power lashes, there would be no one there for him to hurt and we would try our best to detain him and calm him."

"We had seen progress in him." Elaina stated looking at Jakob. "It had been two years and he had not experienced a single power lash. So we felt that maybe it was under control. That maybe he was ready to mingle with people other than us. We took him into the city with us one day. It had been a while since he had seen any faces other than Aris's and mine. He was very excited."

"But I think the excitement was making me relapse." Jakob stated. "It had been over half an hour and I felt a twist in the pit of my stomach.

It was always the first thing I felt when I was about to experience a power lash. I tried to control it. I felt my eyes changing.

"I then fell to my knees and when I looked up, *they* were watching me, waiting. Aris and Elaina came and pulled me off my knees and fled with me back into the forests. Once hidden in the trees and out of the city, Elaina and Aris accelerated their paces and raced with me through the trees.

"They were following us. They were just as fast. I heard them as they sped past branches and leaves.

"Once Aris and Elaina had me in an open field in the depths of the forest, they laid me on the ground and awaited their approach."

"Samius's appearance was the very definition of a gladiator." Aris started once Jakob was finished. "Large and built. His hair was a reddish brown and his eyes were a sea green. His wings were enormous, especially compared to his partner's, Eliza. She was small and petite. Long, flowing red hair rushed down her back and her eyes were a bedazzling blue."

"*I hope you brought him in here to dispose of him.*" *Samius's deep voice echoed throughout the forest.*

"*No.*" *I had answered.*

"*No?*" *Eliza questioned.*

"*He is our family and we won't kill our family. At least here, he can reign as much destruction and no one would get hurt.*" *Jakob was twisting and turning on the floor, fighting the lashing, grunting from the pain. He pounded the floor with his fist and it nearly caused an earthquake.*

"*He is…fighting it.*" *Samius witnessed in amazement.*

"*He's strong. This isn't the first time he's encountered a power lash.*" *Jakob's breathing was calming and his vigorous shaking was turning into a lethargic tremor.*

"*But he is a Demilyte.*" *Samius pointed out.*

"*He is more a part of this family than he is a Demilyte.*" *I acknowledged. Jakob pulled to his feet victorious.*

"We had explained how Jakob had become a part of our family, how he was fighting his inner demonic side and that's what's been causing him to experience power lashes. They were intrigued. After, they had apologized and introduced themselves.

"They were married and deeply in love with one another. It was that very moment Elaina presented them with the invitation of joining our family. They accepted."

I couldn't help but be mindful of Claire sitting beside me. How uneasy it must've been to listen to stories about your parents and not have been a part of those stories.

"Years had passed and Eliza had become pregnant. We were all so excited but not as much as Samius. We all pitched in to help Eliza have an easy birth.

"The day had come for little Claire's arrival but it wasn't going well. Eliza wasn't surviving it. She was fading swiftly. We did everything we could to try and keep her alive but..." He stopped. I got the gist. I didn't want him to say it, not in front of Claire. My head dropped and I shook my head. Hopefully he understood that I didn't want him to say that she *died*.

"Samius," he continued without finishing his previous sentence. "Took it very hard and though he had a new baby girl, he couldn't celebrate her birth. A severe blow to his emotions. He experienced a power lash. Elaina looked after the new baby while Jakob and I tried our best to detain him but he was stronger than the both of us. Restraining him was out of the question." He bit his lip and dropped his head. "We had to take care of him." He stated lifting his head.

I thought that this entire time, my sense of neglect of my parents, the unanswered questions, my human mother who I didn't appreciate enough, and not being able to fit in anywhere was the greatest pain anyone could ever experience. Clearly I was wrong. They had lost just as much as me or more.

Breathing was starting to become difficult. Not due to exertion but because of the lump that was forming in my throat. My heart felt for all of them.

"Brycin was next," Aris drew everyone back to the circle with his voice. "But he'll tell you his story."

Oh. I hadn't thought about it 'til now. The story he had told me before was a watered down version of what truly happened, a believable story for a human mind to grasp.

"Matt came next. It was strange, the pull, the fusion of our souls upon the day of his birth. It was like the effect of magnetism. I had to close the gap between us."

"I was born in Salem, Massachusetts in 1901." Matt finally spoke after a long time of being silent. "I'd lived with my biological parents up until my transformation, when Aris showed up. I was out in the family barn when it happened.

"I had fallen to the barn floor screaming for help but it was useless. No one could hear me."

"You're fine." Aris's voice came from a corner. "What is happening to you is normal. Let it happen."

"Aris was right there, telling me that everything was going to be all right, coaching me through the transformation, making sure I was taking in as much air as possible.

"I remember grunting and Aris's face would twist and tense up when I did. Every time I grunted or cringed, so would he. It was annoying. I thought he was taking it as a joke at first. But the agonizing transformation left no room for me to remain angry.

"I disregarded the fact that he was mimicking me and braced myself as they sliced through my skin.

"We both fell to our hands and knees, both of our breathings almost identical. He stood first and I watched him walk away. Seeping through his white shirt was blood. Directly where my wings had sprouted from on me.

"He pressed his hands up against the wall and calmed his breathing. He then turned to me and began to explain to me what had just happened and who he was.

"It was hard for me to consider it though the evidence was overwhelming. But I didn't have time to sit and speculate. He told me I had a choice to make. Either I could stay and live with my parents but be forced to watch them age and die because I would effortlessly surpass their age or I could go with him and join a new family of people like me. I couldn't live knowing that as they grew older and sicker, I would be frozen at this age for quite some time. To endure that would have been more painful. I left with Aris that day with no intentions of ever returning back home."

Silence. And with that, came the conclusion of everyone's story. Everyone except for Brycin. Emma and James's story was already familiar to me.

I felt the weight of all the stories crush my chest from the inside. I'd gone so long thinking that they all were perfect, privileged to have lived lives with no regrets, no remorse, no faults but none of them had it easy.

"You're feeling sorry?" Brycin asked with surprise.

Aris chuckled. "Don't feel sorry for us. We've lost much but I feel we've gained more. We all believe that." I looked around the entire circle and everyone seemed to nod in agreement. "If none of those events occurred in our lives, this family you see before you wouldn't be here."

He was right but…I feared that I may not get a chance to be a part of this extraordinary family.

"Now you're sad?" he asked with a light chuckle this time.

"Okay, that's getting really annoying." I indicated in a slightly harsh tone.

"Sorry. I'm still getting use to having two sets of emotions."

I sighed. There was no reason to be mad at him. After all, it wasn't his fault he could feel my every emotion. "Yeah. I just fear, even though you all believe undoubtedly that I will, that I *won't* see the day I become a member of this family."

"You already are." Brycin added.

"Officially." I corrected. "Wings and all. I want to know what powers will I inherit, how big will my wings be? I want to experience that first day when I take off for my first flight—"

"You will." My head snapped over in Emma's direction. I forgot she hated me mentioning failure.

"Trust us." Elaina chimed in but my eyes were still trapped in Emma's stare, raging with affirmativeness. "We'll die first before we allow you and Brycin to fall."

That wasn't something I wanted to hear. That wasn't something I wanted to imagine. I didn't want that to be an option.

"It's an option we're willing to follow through with." Claire stated, running her hand through her silky, dark red hair and her eyes staring at the purple blaze. I probably would have been mad at her for invading my mind if I didn't feel so crappy right now. She turned to me. She smiled nervously, or shamefully.

"Well, we haven't got all night." Brycin muttered. I turned to him as he fixed himself to begin his story. His *true* story.

Chapter 12: The Fall of a Family

BRYCIN STOOD AND PACED AROUND THE VIOLET FLAME.
"In order for you to completely understand what is happening to you now, what happened to me, and to prevent anything from happening to you," he began with the same majesty I recognized in all of the others voices when they began the tale of themselves. "I need to back track a little." I simply nodded. "When the Order fell, news traveled swiftly. Just about every half-breed, every In-Between grew aware that a major threat against our existence had been eliminated. You would think the time would have called for celebration but when one evil dies it only makes room for another one to rise.

"An underground gathering of Demilytes began. The vilest, most treacherous, most dangerous of Demilytes capable of unimaginable evil were sought out to give rise to this new evil that threatened Earth. The leader of this new evil was the most malevolent of them all. A heartless and foul creature. His name was and is Balavon."

The power that name seemed to possess as it rolled off of Brycin's tongue was overpowering, rendering me vacant and breathless. I was frozen into a stare and every limb in my body went stiff. I was more than positive that my reaction towards his name was becoming more and more of a realization that my life was endangered, threatened by this foul monster. I was, in fact, really scared of what the future held for me.

Brycin was walking toward me but I was frozen by the name. I couldn't respond. I was completely isolated from the outside world, trapped by my thoughts and my fear. He squatted down in front of me, my focus still looking pass him and at nothing. His hand touched my shoulder and the touch was enough to bring my focus to him. His eyes were white and full of worry.

I shook my head in disappointment, amazed at how easily this villainous name could make me so uneasy. I was also hoping that by shaking my head, it would remove all of my thoughts and hopefully my fear. "I'm sorry." I murmured, realizing he had felt everything I had just now. This was going to be a lot harder to get used to than I thought. Him being able to feel every time I am uneasy.

"No need to be. But there is also no need in being afraid of him." Easy for him to say. He could easily defend himself, fly away to safety. I have no way to defend myself yet and my human speed is no match for any of them. They will easily take me down.

His hand fell, his eyes returned to normal, and he rose to a stand. He walked back toward the flame and stared into it, as if he saw the story he was telling play out within the dancing purple flames. "Balavon had reached his limit of tolerance. To him, it was already bad enough that Demilytes were forced to live a life as righteous as possible. Then to let the human race, a race that in his eyes he believed possessed far more evil capability than any demon on Earth, make the decisions for every life on the planet was degrading.

"Balavon knew that in a world without humans, there would be no fear, no one to pass judgment on our kind and we could walk as freely as ever. But no matter how right he was, this is their planet. Not to mention the sons of Sapharius passed the law that no human or any other half-breed should be killed by the hands of another half-breed. That was also during a time when it was okay for us to walk with our wings bare.

"But the decades would pass, the decades when the ancestors of the Order began slaughtering our kind, and a new law would have to be made. A life of secrecy in the midst of humans is the only option a half-breed has. Any kind of exposure to our kind will and must be eradicated.

"These laws were the source of his gatherings. He knew that no Neatholyte would ever back him up on this plan, that they would quickly remind of him of the laws. But a Demilyte would and why not find the ones with the most devastating of abilities. He would need their help to eliminate us, to completely fulfill this desire.

"So this notorious group of demons had gone from city to city. In every city, Neatholytes were sought out and killed. Mysteriously, they would vanish and at the time, no one knew who or what this threat was."

I couldn't have been any more attentive as he told the tale of the demon that haunted me. But as attentive as I was, I was simultaneously prepping myself for the fall of this story, when it reached his part, because with each of their stories came a tragic end.

"I was born two and a half centuries ago in a small village in South Africa made up of nothing but Neatholytes. But this village had to stay small in numbers due to the fact that if we become too congregated, we may steal the world of its good so we kept our numbers as low as possible. Everyone in the village knew each other. We were all one big family.

"My mother, my father, and my younger brother made up my household along with myself."

I didn't want to sit through this again. I didn't want to hear this devastating story all over again even if the last one lacked detail or wasn't as precise as this one was going to be. I knew how this story began and ended. Adolescent brother, juvenile group of friends, gang, death, revenge, more death. I had had enough of all of the sad stories but I'd made it this far. Just one left.

"I loved my mother and father equally but it was my little brother who I lived for. Ha," There was a smile on his face. "I remember whenever my parents used to tuck us into bed and we would misbehave they would always tell us that if we didn't go to bed, the vicious gang of demons would come and steal us from them and they would never see us again. Ha, it worked every time." He let out a deep sigh. The memory must've been a joyous one, yet painful to reminisce on. "But the older

I got, the more absurd the scary story sounded to me. Kinda like the Boogeyman is to humans. But I would soon regret that assumption.

"When I inherited my wings at sixteen, my parents were ecstatic. It was like my first step into adulthood to them. The entire village knew within minutes. The transformation as you know was exhausting and if you ask me, there was nothing to celebrate about. The crap was painful.

"All of the attention I received from getting my wings made my brother want his just as bad. He had only a few more years to go before he had his own.

"My father wasted no time in getting me use to them. Our first spar was intense and I more than impressed my father. He bragged about our match to the neighbors and to the family at the dinner table. I had never seen him so proud of me in my life. And after hearing the story of the match my dad and I had, my brother really couldn't wait.

"Three years later, he received his. He was fifteen when he got his. My parents were just as excited for him getting his wings as they were for me. We all had our wings. Our family you could say was finally complete.

"Weeks had passed and my brother had adopted some new friends, all of which who had their wings slightly longer than him. One day he'd come home passed his curfew and I had been more worried than my parents. They said that they knew he was fine but I still didn't feel comfortable with it. That night when he came home, I questioned his late coming in."

"Where were you?" I'd asked.

"Out with my friends. Why? Is mom and dad mad?" He asked with a shocked expression.

"No and as far as I'm concerned they don't really care."

"Oh, well, then neither should you." He indicated.

"Well I do. You can't honestly think that there is nothing wrong with coming in at six in the morning."

"Nope."

"You left yesterday at noon, Josh."

"Why do you even care, Avin? Damn, ever since you got those wings you've become a tight ass."

"I'm looking out for you because your delinquent friends apparently aren't."

"You don't even know anything about them. You are always cooped up in this house like a pigeon. You need to get out." He brushed passed me and headed toward his room and I followed.

"Maybe I would if someone learns to be more responsible."

"Look, Avin, you aren't Dad and you never will be. If I want to go out with my friends, I will and you can't stop me. You don't even know what we do. It's not like we are going out there and exposing ourselves. You have told me this over and over again and every time I have come back in one piece. Leave me alone." He turned and left it at that.

"Fine, do whatever the hell it is you want. I can care less."

"That day, I would regret those words.

"Days had gone by and no one in the village had seen my brother or their children who were in this clique. The entire village went looking for them and when we found all ten of them, they had no more life in them. Their wings were torn. You could tell that they tried to fight back, but in the end, they failed.

"The entire village was grieving and every one of them wanted their revenge on "whoever" did this.

"They had pieced it all together. Apparently there had been news fluttering around that Neatholytes in other areas of the world had gone missing. With the disappearances of other Neatholytes and now the death of their children, they knew who did it. It was the iniquitous gang of Demilytes.

"I was asked to stay home. I didn't want to. I was just as angry. I felt guilty. I let him go. I stopped caring. Had I cared, I would have gone looking for him the moment it had passed twelve hours. I thought about it but I never acted on it. I needed to go. But they feared I was too young and my powers were still under developed. I had to stay.

"I didn't know how they were going to be able to find the demons responsible but they were determined. The entire village left and I stayed behind. I waited.

"A day had passed. Then two. And finally three. I hadn't stepped foot outside those doors since my parents asked me to stay home. When I finally left the comfort of my home, the village was completely abandoned, barren. I was the only one left.

"I rushed to the place where I had seen my brother, the place that now became the grave site of my family. My village family and my immediate family. They were all dead. I was devastated. I could hardly bare to look at them. Bruised corpses, shredded wings, a river of blood seeping through the land of bodies that lay scattered all over.

"I had never cried so hard in my life. I had failed them all. My brother, my mother, my father, my village. All of them were dead and here I was alive. It didn't seem fair."

I didn't need to feel his emotions like he was able to feel mine to know how much pain he was feeling. His face gave away the immense pain and grief he was feeling at this very moment. That determination I had seen in his eyes was no longer there and though the purple pyre continued to burn bright in beauty, it reflected dully in his eyes.

"But my grieving would come to an end real soon. I realized that none of their bodies had ascended."

"Ascended?" I asked.

"When half-breeds die," Aris answered. "We aren't left with a body. We, Neatholytes, turn into, I guess you can say light — prismatic patterns of light and we rise into the air, ascending, coming one with Earth. Demilytes ascend in a bright and fiery ash-like mineral. Even nature cannot afford to expose us. Little is known what happens afterwards. Many believe that you are reborn as a human and you get to start life all over but with no recollection of your previous life."

I nodded thoughtfully.

"I knew someone had to have been keeping their bodies from ascending. Just like they had with my brother and his friends.

"That's when I heard them approach."

"Awww, look at this," Balavon began. "A poor, defenseless child mourning over the death of his village family."

"Ha, yeah, what a baby!" A demon on the side of him with a greasy voice spoke.

"Why?" I asked.

"Why? Because I don't need any Neatholytes getting in my way. If you aren't with me then you must be against me. And clearly no Neatholyte is with me. A world of demons sounds sufficient enough to me.

"For centuries we've lingered in the shadow of the human race! I for one will not be led by the weak! Survival of the fittest they say. Well, that's us.

"I will get what I want. Even if I have to start a war to do so."

"You killed my parents." I spoke with resentment, the words traveling through my teeth. *"You killed my brother! You killed my entire village family! AHHHH!!!"*

"I launched countless amounts of lightning projectiles at them and they dodged them effortlessly. They never fought back. They were toying with me but I wasn't going to give up. The pain, the anger, the loneliness, it was all fueling me, making me stronger by the second.

"I remember the clouds turning a dark gray and roaring over the land like a beast. But what I mostly remember was hundreds of lightning bolts crashing down to the earth, piercing it like bullets and ripping the ground in half until the earth bellowed and quaked. And it was all of my doing.

"I'd injured a quarter of his gang with the attack. Feeling threatened now, he wove in and out of the rampaging lightning bolts like an agile cat, effortlessly, and knocked me unconscious with a single attack.

"I awakened in the care of Elaina. To this day, I don't know why he let me live. He could have easily killed me but he didn't.

"Aris and Elaina told me they found me lying on some deserted plain alone. They didn't see any bodies of other angels. They saw no blood, no broken wings, just me. My village wasn't even there anymore. They had taken it all. They'd taken everything from me."

"And in no kind of way," Elaina began. "Did we want to replace that family you once had." He turned and looked at her over his shoulder. "You see," she looked over the blaze and at me. "I can feel anyone's emotions, no matter who they are, whenever I choose. Sometimes I have had cases where I felt too much of their emotions and acted out as they were or as they were wishing to.

"That day I felt his loneliness and offered him refuge."

"Though he didn't take our offer right then and there," Aris chimed in. "He soon came to join this beloved family you see here today."

Finally. I had learned the origins of all of them, the reasons for why they are what they are today. The thick cloud of mysteries I once had in my head was becoming thinner and thinner. These were now the most important people in my life. They had all been through a lot and even though it seems that this very moment is the most perfect moment, there is still something that needs to be taken care of.

Both Brycin's and my life were still threatened and until I get my wings it will always remain that way.

It was easier now to identify why it would be so hard for them not to retaliate if the time ever came. The time where my life would be claimed and Brycin's life would inevitably seize as well. This family, though smiles and contentment was always expressed on their surfaces, was very unstable deep down within them. Aris had destroyed Rome at one point, which had been renewed, Brycin was capable of massive lightning storms which no man had ever witnessed, and everyone here seemed that if they suffered one more painful experience, their volcanoes of emotions, which they tried their hardest to control, would erupt and the world would fall into dark days.

He who seeks vengeance must dig two graves; one for his enemy and one for himself. I remember one of my high school teachers would always recite that saying whenever a student thought it was okay to get revenge on someone who had done something to them. I had never given it much thought before but in a sense, that saying made sense.

I looked around at the circle. They were all talking to each other now that the story telling was over. I would have joined them but I was worried. If Brycin and I die, not only will we be the cause of chaos returning to Earth but also the death of this family.

Matt scurried over to the open seat beside me. "So what do you think of this bizarre family of ours?"

"I honestly don't find it that bizarre."

"Oh sure you don't." the sarcasm in his voice burned brighter than the flame in front of me. "Eight half-breeds all brought together by pain and devastation. Right, very normal."

I watched almost the entire circle roll their eyes simultaneously. "Well when you put it that way—"

"Kayden, you don't have to explain yourself to him." Brycin interjected.

"Sometimes I think you guys don't like me." He arranged his face into a pout. "Naw, I'm just teasing but it has been a real pleasure. Though you don't talk much, you're pretty cool."

"Well this was more of a listening type of gathering — well, for me at least. There wasn't much room to speak." I responded.

"Oh, that reminds me." Emma's melting voice, which had been silenced for a while, reached over the flames, seizing any other conversations. "Kayden revealed to me that he had gone to Portman's home once before." Everyone's eyes were now on me. "They were there alone. They had opportunity to take care of Kayden then."

"Was that the day when I couldn't sense him?" Brycin asked Emma who was nodding before he even finished his question. He turned to me with eyes of rage though the rage wasn't targeted toward me. I felt an unnerving sensation invading me. "What happened?"

I swallowed the nervousness. I didn't want to replay that day. Just thinking about it makes me angry. "I had gone to Portman's house once before, to learn more about that legend which apparently I now know I didn't really wanna know much of. He invited me in but as soon as I acknowledged his invitation, he kicked me out. But he left me with a few words to think about. He told me that my angel would tell me soon. I didn't know what it meant then but that's when I started questioning things even more.

"When you all left me at school one day, I had gone back to see him, to get answers to his bizarre behavior. When I got there, there was no house, no street — nothing. Just grass. That's when something attacked me. I still don't even know how I got out of there."

That seemed to take everyone for a loop. No one was expecting that. "I rushed to where you were as soon as I felt your panic. I had never felt you so full of fright before. I had an idea though on what had you so afraid. You had to have come into contact with something of our world.

"When I reached you, I was severely weak. Seth and Ester nearly finished you off but I gathered all of my last remaining strength and saved you. *I* saved you that day."

That last image, me flying over the clouds, it was real and the soft object I was leaning against was Brycin.

"So you knew the entire time that I was attacked, well of course you knew. You made me feel like such an ass that day."

"That time I knew, but what about the time you were in his house. I didn't know then."

"And why would Balavon allow Ester and Seth to attack you so freely uncloaked but not Portman?" Aris questioned.

"Wait, wait what?"

"When Seth and Ester attacked you, you weren't cloaked from our abilities to sense you but when you were with Portman, when we couldn't sense you, they didn't make a move. Why?"

The entire circle was trapped in thought. Brycin paced back in forth and it was more and more unnerving.

"I was thinking," Emma began, "That what if they don't want to kill Kayden, that killing Kayden was never their initiative strategy? What if James's vision is a false one, implanted by Portman or someone or something like that? I think he is trying to destroy us from the inside out, making us more and more uneasy, so that when Kayden does receive his wings, they can dispose of us."

"Leaving Kayden emotionally unstable." Brycin said in awe.

"And Balavon just might be aware of the percentage of angel blood he has." Aris pointed out. "If Kayden somehow looses it—"

"Like you had—" Elaina entered with realization.

"He can expose the entire divine world." Emma finished.

I was lost and my head hurt from all of the discovering and unraveling. First he wanted me dead, now he doesn't?

"But my visions are never wrong and I had never met this Portman. So manipulating my abilities would have been impossible for them to do." James explained.

"Yeah but I'm positive he knows this family inside and out." Aris murmured.

"I'm not so sure," Jakob objected. "He seemed surprised during our first encounter when he noticed that a Demilyte was protecting Kayden."

"Probably in an indirect sensing. Without seeing you physically, they may have read our numbers in family members and sensed your goodness, thus presuming you to be angel."

"So you're saying that James's vision might not be accurate?" I asked. "That it was somehow "planted" in his brain by Portman or someone?"

"But that's-ahhhh!" Everyone turned to James. He was holding his head.

"James, are you okay?" Emma questioned.

"Yeah, I'm fine." He didn't sound fine at all. His breathing was heavy and his eyes were shut tight evidently due to the pain in his head. I could see the veins in his forehead press against the surface of his flesh. "Go on. Continue."

I was worried about him. He was starting to sweat and though the flames were warm, it wasn't enough to make one sweat like that. His other hand was on his lap and clutched into a tight fist and the only ones who seemed to acknowledge his outburst was Emma and myself.

"So what happens now?" Brycin initiated the conversation again.

"AAARRGGHHH!!!" James yelled boomingly over the fire. He was shaking and breathing really hard. What was the matter with him?

Chapter 13: The Vision

JAMES WAS COMPLETELY DISCONNECTED FROM THE rest of the circle. He'd fallen to his knees, compressing his skull in between his hands, grunting wildly. We all surrounded him, concerned for him. But Emma shoved everyone away, giving him room to breathe. She was nearly frantic.

"James?! James, listen to my voice! Please, try and talk to me!" He didn't respond, continuing with this brutish behavior. "Please, talk to me! Elaina," she turned to her. "What can you sense?"

"Nothing." She stood tall and erect with an awed expression. "I can't sense anything. It's like he's not even there."

She stared at Elaina for a brief moment, the same awed expression spreading across her goddess-like face. She then turned back to James, attending to his needs.

His shakes were becoming more and more untamable, his breathing unstable and harsh and growl-like. He was slipping further and further into insanity. I was beginning to doubt his ability to recover from this.

His head snapped up and his eyes were luminous, bright and white. There was no evidence of blue in his eyes anymore. *"Abandoned!"* he hissed through his teeth.

Before any of us had the chance to question it, we were all soaring through the air, away from the gathering area. The bedazzling purple blaze was now extinguished. I hit the ground with a loud thud. It took me a while to recover from the attack but when I looked up from the ground, everyone had their wings exposed except for Brycin. James stood opposing them with glowing white eyes.

The wind had become vicious, swirling the leaves and other small particles throughout the meadow. The fogs were dissolving into nothing.

Was James doing this?

Jakob, without question, charged James.

"NO!" Emma shrieked. She flung a bolt of lightning at him, hurtling him through the air.

"Emma, we must stop him!" Elaina yelled.

A horrific cry suddenly ripped through Emma's throat and echoed throughout the meadow. James had shot Emma in the back with a lightning bolt and the blast catapulted her through the air. But how? He was only an In-Between. Those were Neatholyte abilities.

Elaina jumped in the path of Emma's soaring body. The impact echoed through the meadow, sounding like two boulders crashing into each other.

The rest of the circle charged him, attempting to detain him. All except for Brycin. He must've been aware that an attack to him would hurt me.

I stood to my feet, groggy, mind-boggled by what I was witnessing.

None of them could get their hands on him. He was just as fast as them, just as strong. He fought back with his new Neatholyte abilities. But he fought differently than them. He fought with such malevolence. He fought ruthlessly, out for more than just a fight. His eyes were coated in rage and his agenda was simple. To terminate everyone in his path.

He flung a bolt of lightning in Claire's direction as if he was throwing a javelin. She flew into the air, dodging it easily. He continuously rained surges of electricity in her direction. Preoccupied with Claire, Aris flew close to the ground in his direction. His wings sliced him through the air mutely and swiftly. He must not have heard Aris's approach because his attention remained locked on Claire.

In one swift motion, James turned, snapping his arm toward Aris, and struck him with a ray of lightning, sending him flying into the trees of one of the several forests surrounding us. His senses were just as acute as theirs too.

"Aris!" Claire shouted but as soon as her concentration was distracted, James disposed of her.

After eliminating Aris and Claire, he headed toward Matt. "Abandon!" He cried sorrowfully.

"You're stupid!" Matt yelled. He shot a lightning at Matt. Matt threw his arms up in front of his face. Aris was in front of Matt in a second and some sort of barrier of light deflected the attack. Aris was amazingly swift.

I searched the field for him. My eyes had only left James for a second but he was no longer in the spot where he original cast his attack. He was nowhere in sight.

I heard some heavy breathing coming from the side of me. Standing about ten yards away, hunched over and breathing monstrously was James. His eyes were full of hate though they were a pure, glowing white just like…just like the one eye the demon in my nightmare possessed.

"Abandoned!" he hissed at me. I felt myself begin to hyperventilate.

Both of his hands met in front of him, releasing a venomous looking surge of lightning in my direction. I was immobilized by horror. My knees were growing weaker and weaker and I couldn't breathe.

Brycin was in front of my instantly, intercepting the attack and taking it as his own. The attack crashed into his chest and he fell over, clutching his chest.

My chest burned rampantly. The pain was so unreal, something I've never felt before physically. It felt like someone had torched my chest and threw a ten ton bowling ball into it all at the same time. The force catapulted me through the air. I felt my back hit something and my body hit other objects as it fell before slamming into the tarnished floor. The pain throbbed. I couldn't help but allow the waves of darkness to consume me.

I didn't feel the muckiness of the earth anymore. I was lying on something soft, wrapped in something warm and thick.

My body was aching tremendously. My chest was burning, my ribs were hurt, my head pounded louder than an orchestra of drums, and I couldn't feel the lower half of my body.

I struggled intensely to open my eyes. I was losing the fight but I wasn't going to give up until I knew where I was. It was dark wherever I was but there was a dim light glowing to the right of me in the distance. My vision was so blurry. I could barely see a thing.

I felt fear the instant I saw it. A shadow passed in front of the dim light. I tried to widen my eyes but it didn't really improve much. They were coming toward me. One on the right of me and two on the left. The three dark figures were now hovering directly above me. I shut my eyes really tight, hoping they would go away.

"Hey." That was Brycin's voice.

When I reopened my eyes, Brycin, Claire, and Jakob were standing above me. "Brycin?" My voice was scratchy and horrible. My chest hurt from trying to speak.

"Are you okay?" he asked coming down to my eye level. "I am so sorry."

For what?

"We are so sorry, Kayden." Claire spoke, breaking into a sob on my name.

For what?! What was everyone sorry for and why was I in so… much…pain?

The instant I questioned the pain, the instant the event replayed in my head from start to finish. James had attacked all of us. He'd gone berserk. He even attacked his own sister.

Brycin's head was down in defeat, Claire was off in a corner silently sobbing and Jakob seemed to be the only one with some composure. "What happened to James?" I asked, my chest hurting from speaking.

Jakob approached me and sat down on the mattress. Mattress? I was in my room? The dim light was coming from the small lamp on my computer desk. I *was* in my room. "We don't know what happened to him. He's never done that before." He answered in a surprised tone.

"Did you at least stop him?"

"Aris hit him a little too hard. Though he had the power of a Neatholyte, he wasn't as durable as one. He's in the hospital right now. Everyone else is with him right now."

"I want to see them."

"No." Brycin objected as his head shot up, spitting the word out. "No more half-breed gatherings with you until you are one of us."

"That's not fair. I am here and alive and-"

"Yeah this time. What about the next time? Do you realize had I not taken that hit for you, you wouldn't be here right now? Neither of us would. Your human body could not have withstood an attack of that magnitude."

"But—"

"No. We'll see each other at school. As far as hanging out goes, you're gunna have to wait."

I could feel my blood begin to boil. How could he make such a decision for me? "And what if that takes another year, huh?" My throat throbbed and burned in pain as I attempted to force the words out as harsh as possible.

He stood and walked towards the room door. "Then you'll have to wait a year. It seems we are no less a threat to your life than Balavon. I'm sorry." He opened the door and exited.

"Sorry, kid." Jakob pulled himself off the bed and pulled Claire by the waist as he left. They shut the door to my room and left me there. Alone.

I rose from my bed, the pain still slightly intense and a little disoriented. I sat there for a moment, reminiscing on the night I had had. It was still a little foggy to me. I still couldn't believe any of it happened. What began as an innocent getting-to-know-each-other gathering turned into a night that caused my protector to consider himself a danger to my life.

He was probably right though. Maybe they *were* a threat to my life but did it require this? Did it require him to remove some of the most important people out of my life for a long period of time? Who knew how long it would be until I received my wings.

Ugh it was all so frustrating.

Not to mention they believe there to be a new agenda. Now they believe that Balavon doesn't want to kill me but rather use me and my unstable emotions to expose the divine world.

I inhaled deeply, filling myself with composure. I looked over at my alarm clock. Six o'clock in the morning. There was no way I had slept only for a couple of hours after that night. It had have been Monday. I had to have slept through all of Sunday.

I stood to my feet and sheepishly limped to the door. I sniffed the air. Lavenders. It felt like it had been so long since I'd smelled the scent of my own home. Well, I guess I was back into routine.

After getting ready, which took longer than usual considering I had a huge red mark in the center of my chest which made showering very difficult, I headed downstairs to meet Rachel but she wasn't there. I was hoping I would see her. I hadn't seen her since Saturday morning. Felt like she was slowly slipping to the bottom of my list of priorities.

Great. I was definitely back into routine. Here I go feeling horrible about myself and how I don't deserve someone like Rachel. Ugh. I need her right now. She is usually my boost of energy for the morning. Now I was forced to head off to school a wreck, disoriented and in pain.

I limped to the key rack and pulled my car keys off of the hook. I was completely out of it today. I wanted nothing more than to go back upstairs, skip a day of school, and go back to sleep. But I couldn't. School was now my only option to seeing any of them. Plus, I wanted to know the status on James.

I made it to school late. Like I even cared. I was prepared to hear Professor Yates and his redundant remarks to my tardiness. I would care as less as possible. All I wanted was to take advantage of the only time I had to spend with my friends. My family.

I entered Professor Yates class, showered by his annoying comments to my tardiness. But *two* empty seats resting in the middle of the class, I didn't expect. Brycin wasn't here. Again.

My feeling was indescribable. I didn't feel angry. I didn't feel sad. I felt nothing.

I walked up to my seat, hiding my expression of disappointment. Afraid that the students would relate it to Professor Yates and his comment.

I sat in my seat, again, staring at the empty seat beside me. It was too hard to concentrate on class with this empty seat beside me raising so many questions.

How could he tell me that this would be my only access to being around them and not be here to acknowledge that promise? My world *did* revolve around them. I am one of them for crying out loud.

I sat blankly through the rest of class, completely disengaged with the activities of the class and incoherent with the second abrupt absence of my best friend.

I continued the day like a zombie, mindlessly. My body was on autopilot but my mind was fixed on one thing. Brycin's absence. I was about ninety nine point nine percent sure that if Brycin was not here, the others weren't going to be here either.

I entered my Theology class, no thought to who was teaching. But when I registered that the characteristics were not of Portman, I was almost skeptical to *who* was really my professor for the day. Was it really Mrs. Hay, round in shape, curly, blazing red locks, and tiny, circular spectacles resting on the tip of her nose? Or was it someone else disguising themselves as her?

I don't know why, but I proceeded to my seat cautiously, making sure that I was able to see Mrs. Hay in my peripheral no matter the angle of my head. Maybe I thought that in some way it could have been one of them disguising themselves as my old professor.

But when I saw the two empty seats sitting next to each other, the thought of one of them being my professor in disguise was no longer my concern. Having to sit through another class without my best friend was all I was thinking about.

I couldn't help the direction my mind was going in. I was now hoping that one of them was disguising themselves as Mrs. Hay. I wanted it to be on their conscious that something happened to me and they weren't here to do anything about it. I hoped that as I'd be taking notes, an orange and yellow luminous ball of fire is hurled my way and that wherever Brycin is, he feels my excruciating pain. My lips pulled up into a devious smirk as I thought the scenario through.

Class dragged on and when it was over, anger had seeped its way into my blood stream. The day was a "normal" day but not my type of "normal." It was a normal day for a...human. I had never had a day that was this normal, this humanlike. It was frustrating. No best friend to talk to about visions or half-breeds, no enemies trying to come after me. Nothing. Normal.

I stepped out into the beating heat of the sun and rushed to my car. I pulled out my phone and searched the contacts for Brycin's name. After finding it, I pressed the "send" button.

It rang six times. No answer.

I quickened my pace, angrier now than before. I entered my car, brought the car to life and allowed the rush of cool air to fly out of the vents. The A/C calmed me somewhat. I pulled out of the parking lot and headed for home.

If being mad at Brycin for not being at school today wasn't enough, the ridiculous drivers were going to send me into a frenzy of shouts and profanity. I wasn't the type who gave in to road rage so easily but today was a "normal," human day for me. Why not indulge?

When I made it home, I slammed the door hard enough to shake the picture frames hanging on the walls crooked. After fixing them, I pulled out my cell phone and called Brycin again.

No answer. Again.

I'd almost thrown the phone into a wall.

I give up. I could care less at this point. I headed up to my room and proceeded to do my homework. Mrs. Hay wasted no time in slapping us with more than enough assignments. She'd assigned all of chapter ten for us to read and answer all section reviews.

I laid down at the foot of my bed and pulled out my work. I was in no mood for doing homework but hopefully during the activity, I would become slightly calmer.

But the work was too boring. I felt myself slipping away into a dream.

A ring startled me, waking me. I was nearly drenched in sweat. My breathing was fast, short, and heavy.

I searched for the ringing beneath the scattered papers on my bed. I grabbed the phone and flipped it open. "Hello?" I answered out of breath.

"Are you okay?" Brycin asked.

"Yeah," I replied. "I'm fine. Uhmm," I rose to a sit and rubbed my face with my free hand. "Where were you guys today?" I was still slightly out of breath and he was more concerned with that than the question I'd just asked.

"Why are you breathing so hard?"

"I just woke up. But never mind that." I breathed, wanting to get to the point of discussion.

There was a moment of silence on the phone. "We were all down at the hospital."

My concern for James and the fact that I was still shaken up by my dream left no room for any anger toward Brycin and the others. "How is he?"

"He's stable but he hasn't awakened yet."

I let out a heavy sigh.

"It's been two days. Emma's becoming more and more aware of her brother's condition and is becoming quite frantic with every passing second he remains asleep. We would have come to school today but Emma really needs us right now. We can't afford for her to have a power lash right now."

I guess that was understandable. The sake of hundreds was more important than me right now. "Well I guess no one knows what he saw then."

"Claire has been trying to get a read on his mind and see what he saw but his mind is too active for her to hold on to anything for too long."

"Well how long will it be?"

"We aren't sure but we will keep you as updated as possible."

"Will you guys be at school tomorrow?"

There was that silence again. "I don't know. Hopefully."

Though he said hopefully, I wasn't going to get my hopes high and have them crushed. "Okay."

"Talk to you later."

"See ya."

I close the phone and buried my face into my hands. I felt so useless. I wanted to help as much as possible but as long as I remained in any type of danger, I would be restricted, sheltered from everything like a caged animal. Little do they know, it's more dangerous being trapped than being free. Being caged results in aggression and fear. This may result in me slipping into madness.

It was hard identifying how I felt. I felt…abandoned.

James had been saying that word over and over again and everyone is saying he was overtaken by his vision. Could he have been playing out a vision of…No, that was not likely.

It had to have been someone who was already a half-breed. But who?

Thoughts of James and is belligerent behavioral outburst immediately reminded me of my dream.

I had dreamt of that night, detail by detail chronologically. It was so unexpected. No one had seen it coming. No one was prepared for it. No one knew how to fight back against him.

I lifted from the edge of the bed and walked to my room door. I placed my hand on the cold steel knob and turned it, the door creaking slightly as I opened my room door. The air was cooler in the hall than it was in my room. Probably due to the fact that I hadn't stopped sweating yet.

I saw a light on downstairs. I headed down the stairs casually. I knew it could only be one person. A face that I had almost forgotten. A face that I needed to see right now. A face that I felt I was neglecting.

Sitting at the counter in her bathrobe was Rachel. Her hair was damp and loose, draping over her shoulders. She was reading a magazine and drinking a bottle of water.

I smiled instantly once I saw her. I leant up against the side wall beneath the archway. It was so easy. This life with Rachel. She made it obvious that she loved me. The more my life became enveloped with being a half-breed and becoming part of this new family, the more I felt like what I always wanted, needed, was sitting right in front of me.

I felt so torn, obligated to both my new family and Rachel. I wish I could just tell her. But I can't. It's against our laws to commit any type of exposure. Even something as little as telling your adoptive mother could result in exposure.

"You're up a little late." She indicated, her head never leaving the magazine.

"Couldn't sleep." I answered, folding my arms. "Besides, Brycin's call woke me up." She looked up and smiled. I smiled back. "Why are you up so late?" I asked pulling myself off the wall. I pulled a water bottle from the fridge and sat across from her. "Shouldn't you be getting as much rest as possible?" I asked twisting the cap and taking a drink of the icy water. The freezing liquid gushing down my throat and settling in my stomach cooled me entirely.

"Ha, no. I called off the entire week. I have invested a lot of time into my work. I need a break."

"Yeah," I breathed. "We both do."

"Yeah, you have been bit too busy for me lately."

So she realized it too. Even though she said it jokingly, I knew it was true. "Yeah. Brycin and the others have been doing their best to keep me as preoccupied as possible."

"Ha, mission accomplished." She rose her bottle of water as if it was a cheer.

I bit my lip. I had never asked the question before but with all of the overwhelming evidence pointing to what I truly was, I needed to ask it before I became anything. "Mom?" Her head shot up at the word and I completely had her undivided attention. "Do you *know* anything about my *real* parents? I know you've told me that no one came looking for me but, well, you are a district attorney. Have you ever wondered or looked into it out of curiosity? Or at least for my own knowledge?"

The question caught her off guard. She seemed to be a bit choked up by the question. I'd offended her in some way. I knew I had. "Uhmm," she flipped the magazine closed. "I did at one point look for your biological parents. It was about three years after Michael had passed. I had the birth files of every hospital within a hundred miles of where I found you according to the approximate date of your initial birth. But," she released a heavy sigh. "I came up empty handed."

My expression fell slightly. Just disappointed.

"I wanted to find out for you. I really did but it was like looking for a needle in a haystack."

I think my reaction surprised her. I smiled. I may not know their names or what they look like but I know what they are. I was happy to know that she cared enough about me to look into. "Thank you." I pulled the bottle up to my lips, allowing another river of water to flow down my throat. When I brought the bottle down, Rachel was staring at me. "What?" I asked, forced into a smile.

"Nothing. Just ever since Emma's been coming around, you have been very busy." I rolled my eyes. I knew exactly where she was going with this. "You two make such a cute couple and she is not a bad girl. You two seem to have a lot in common."

Ha, if only she knew how true that was. "Mom, we are just friends. Yeah, maybe one of the most beautiful girls I will ever meet but she is family to me in a sense."

"Sure. Whatever you say." Her lips pulled over her teeth and into a wide, brilliant smile.

"What about you? When are you going to get back on the dating horse?"

"Ha, I think at a certain age, people should just be happy with what they got if they don't have anyone in their life. I have you and that's all I want."

"You are too independent." I chuckled.

"No I'm not!" she laughed. "I do depend on someone." I stared awaiting her answer. She reached across the bar and pressed her palm to my cheek. "I depend on you. My life revolves around you. I now know that that's why I found you. Because if Michael passed and I had no one else around me to live for, I might be lying beside him at this very moment."

I closed my eyes and embraced the warmth of her touch. It felt so serene. There was a wave of comfort washing over me by the simple touch of her hand.

Her hand fell and my eyes opened. "I love you, Kayden. Michael would be proud of the both of us. Proud of me 'cause I didn't give up and proud of you because of how much you've grown. You are a spitting image of him."

I felt my cheeks flush red. "I wouldn't say that."

"Ha, but you are. Kind of scares me how much you remind me of him." It probably wasn't her fault why she compared Michael and I to one another so much. It could have been a coping mechanism her mind created just to get her through life, get her through every second, every minute, every hour of every day. She probably dissected my entire appearance and personality and became more accustomed to the ones closest to his.

But maybe, just maybe, she was right and I was too stubborn to agree because of how pure and genuine he was.

He had this sureness and outlook on life in which I lacked. Until I gained that quality, I would forever object to the comparison.

"Well, we need to go to sleep. You have school in the morning and I am getting tired."

I nodded and took one last swig of the icy water. After cleaning up the condensation that flowed down the side of the bottle and onto the bar with a nearby rag and tossing what remained within the bottle into the refrigerator, I kissed Rachel goodnight and headed to my room, into the shadows, into deep thoughts.

I pulled into bed and underneath the blanket. I placed my hands behind my head and drifted into the thoughts that were gnawing at my brain all the while I was downstairs.

I didn't think I had a choice before. I didn't think that there was much to think about, that when the time came, when I received my wings, my *new* family would be the only reasonable route to take.

But I see now, more than ever before, that there *is* a choice I have to make. But if I choose Rachel, I have to let her know what I am. I mean, if I look nineteen at the age of forty, it is going to raise questions.

But I couldn't. It was *our* law. And I couldn't break that.

But If I told her, who would know? Well, perhaps Claire but what are the odds that it would remain on my mind when I am around her. Besides, clearly it would classify as some type of intrusion if she did read my mind without permission.

Well, for the time being, I belonged here. I have to see her through the end. She lives for me. And I will live for her until her time comes.

Chapter 14: The Strangers

I'VE TRIED TO UNDERSTAND THEM ALL WEEK, TRIED making up excuses for them. I'd considered that their consistent absence was linked to some reasonable excuse. I tried telling myself that they will be here the next day, answers in hand and everything would go back to the way they were...somewhat.

But I soon realized that all I was doing was lying to myself, preventing myself from facing the truth.

I accepted their absences on Monday. Brycin called me and informed me about everything that was going on. Fearing that under the powers of so many heavy emotions, Emma could experience a power lash. Therefore she required serious supervision. Understandable. I accepted that.

But that was Monday's excuse. What were the reasonable justifications for Tuesday and Wednesday? Thursday?

I was more than absolute that Emma had calmed down by now and I was willing to bet my life that James had made a full recovery. So what was it? What could possibly be an adequate enough excuse for not being here for three days, for not being here when I too was just as concerned about everyone, just as shaken up from the event that nearly ended my life?

Tuesday I was positive that they were going to be here, all of them. Even Emma. But when school let out and I'd gone to where they usually parked, right across from me but a bit further down, neither the Camaro nor the Range Rover were where they should have been. I tried calling Brycin on his cell phone. He didn't answer. I then tried calling the other and they too did not answer.

Officially annoyed at this point, I decided to take matters into my own hands. I ran back to my car infuriated, opened the door with frustration, slid in with such intensity, listened to the car as it came to life with thoughts of killing all of them at first sight and sped out of the parking lot.

I'd probably broken many traffic violations and disobeyed the speed limit as I rushed to the hospital but I didn't care. I was too disturbed by it all to care.

The day before, according to Brycin, there were no signs of James making an immediate recovery. His condition had not changed much so I figured chances were he was still hospitalized. And if this was true, then the others should be there as well, waiting for him to come to, waiting for answers as soon as he awakes.

I entered the hospital and the nurse at the front desk, the same nurse I had seen working the front desk when I came to visit Frankie, notified me that James Brackbill had checked out earlier that day.

At first, I was trapped in awe. I stood in disbelief, consumed by it. I felt lied to. Cheated would probably have been a better word.

James had recovered? I thought in amazement. *And they didn't even care to tell me? Why?*

I was well aware of the possible dangers that came with hanging out with half-breeds and I was willing to commit to not being around them as much. I had accepted school being the only opportunity optional for me to see them. But was it wholly acceptable for them to steal that only option from me so secretively just because of these possible dangers?

After swallowing and accepting the disbelief, I couldn't help myself from being mad. I could feel my blood turn hot. I could feel my skin turn just as hot. The anger was feeding me momentum. I didn't care how long it took. I was going to search all of Corvallis until I found them.

I sped to Willamette Park. It was a near guarantee that they would be there and if so, I wasn't going hold back. I was going to let them have it and disregard the possibility of hurting their feelings.

I pulled up directly in front of the edge of the variety of plants and cedars covered in thick moss. I entered the boundless maze of the forest life and headed straight toward the enormous meadow.

When I reached the opening that granted access to the massive field, yards and yards of rich, green grass surrounded by the several, now familiar, forests was all I could see. I was there all by myself. I yelled all of their names, mainly Brycin's. I yelled and yelled and yelled until my voice went raspy and hoarse.

I fell to my knees in defeat. I remained there, debating. It had been a while since I'd gone to my treacherous and torturous seas for comfort. It would be the easy way out. Though crying was completely out of the question, I would allow my seas to destroy me, cleanse me of these uncompromising emotions and let them sink to the depths of it, the place that I had no access to.

But I didn't. I picked myself up and went home.

It was difficult finding some alternative thing to do knowing that they were keeping things from me again. I felt like I was back at square one, back to wondering what was the point in doing things in secrecy. I knew just about everything about them. There wasn't much to hide.

Luckily for me, the next day I didn't have to find anything to preoccupy myself with. Frankie was back. His right arm was wrapped up in bandages and his left leg was cocooned in a cast. He was walking with the assistance of two crutches but with his size, I feared that he would break them and inflict further injuries to himself.

He, Jennifer and Amber all wanted to hang out since it had been so long. Brycin, Claire, Emma, and Jakob were invited too but they were a no show still.

It was different hanging out with humans. The conversations were so bland and normal. We talked about school, careers, relationships, television shows, Frankie's time spent in the hospital. No angels, no demons, no fights, nobody out for world domination. It was normal. It was *too* normal. Too human.

I couldn't even completely enjoy myself. I felt out of place, an outcast.

We had gone to some local restaurant. The others seemed to be the subject of choice for both Amber and Jennifer. They interrogated me mostly on their consistent absence.

I didn't know. If I did, I wouldn't be sitting at a table with only humans. Either they'd be here or I would be with them.

Amber and Jennifer didn't believe me when I stated I didn't know where they were. But Frankie intervened, defended me by pointing out to the girls that if I didn't know then I didn't know.

It was scary, this new relationship I shared with Frankie. Before, he was the thick-skulled, cocky, overly masculine guy who I tried to keep my distance from as much as possible. Now, he was one of the most understanding individuals in my life. He was surely going to be one of the human friends to follow me into my next life.

After the somewhat uneventful, uninteresting evening ended, I rushed home. Rachel was already out cold when I came home so I went to bed myself.

As I laid in bed, I had time to think things over.

Surely James was awake now. And if he was awake, then that meant that everyone knew what his vision had to have been about. His vision had to have had something to do with me because clearly I am the one reaping the repercussions of this vision. Whatever he saw placed me in danger. Placed me at a risk that none of them were willing to take.

But why not tell me? Why not give me the heads up? Sure, I would've been pissed for about two seconds but I would have gotten over it. I would have came to my senses eventually.

That was yesterday.

Today continued this uninterrupted absence of theirs and my irritation towards them. School only annoyed me further. It was supposed to be the only place I had access to keep in touch with Brycin and the others but they'd snatched that rug from beneath me without me knowing.

It was also the eeriest day I'd seen all year. A thick fog took residence here in Corvallis. The air bit icily. Most of my clothes were dirty and I was forced to wear a white, v-neck thermal which was thinner than most of my shirts like it and a pair of black jeans. For once, I appreciated my collection of shoes because I was able to find the thickest ones to keep my feet as warm as possible.

I had thoughts of cutting class today because of the weather but two things kept me from doing so. First, I feared that maybe today would be the day they showed up. Wrong. Despite the thick fog, I didn't see the overly conspicuous red Camaro or the Range Rover on my way in this morning.

The other thing that prevented me from cutting class today was the lavender scented angel who protested against me about staying home just because of the weather. She assured me that it would dissipate later on in the evening.

It wasn't until I actually arrived at school today that another feeling washed over me, another reason to why I should have cut class today. Something always went wrong when the weather was very abnormal. Something involving *him*.

Class dragged on as usual. I eyed the clock as always, feeling no need to be here.

When professor LaBurn released the class, I was in no type of hurry. Besides, I had to wait for Frankie to get out of class anyways. He text me in the middle of class, asking me if I could help him to his car today. With the blinding whether tool the rested on top of Corvallis, what type of friend would I be if I said no. Especially with his condition. I wasn't the type of friend to abandon the needs of my other friends. I wasn't *them*.

I remembered how much of an obstacle it was for me to get here, desperately squinting as I drove to make out everything in front of me. I was afraid to even let him drive home. I felt very protective of him now. I concluded that my behavior was linked to the fact that I felt like I owed him, considering my actions nearly killed him. It was my way of redeeming myself, easing my conscience of the heavy guilt that seem to be crushing it.

I walked the hallways as I waited for Frankie's class to release. I found myself acknowledging useless bulletins posted throughout the halls. Students searching for trustworthy roommates, posted pricings of used books, invitations to club meetings around campus. It was strange reading the bulletins. Before, I would always rush out the halls, to either my car or to Brycin and the others, and never think twice about looking at what hung from the walls. I was never the type to join clubs but now, looking at them and seeing my current situation, had I joined something, I wouldn't be so desperate in finding something to occupy all my free time with.

Through my peripheral, I saw several classes being released. The students flowed out one after another, after another, some in twos and in my direction. None of them of which was Frankie.

I eased my way carefully through the oncoming traffic of students and toward Frankie's class. Half way through the crowd, a girl with long, ginger brown hair and the most dazzling blue eyes stood at the door with one arm weighed down with books and the other holding open a door. She wore a gray long-sleeved shirt with jet black denim jeans. She was somewhat petite and delicate looking but beautiful nonetheless. She was fair-skinned with an appealing figure. Her heart-shaped face, her full lips left me bedazzled and breathless, a feeling I usually only felt around Emma.

A crutch appeared, and soon, all of Frankie.

It was weird, this feeling in the pit of my stomach. It was like a horde of butterflies fluttered relentlessly in my stomach, drunkenly ramming themselves into the walls of it. I was nervous just by the look of her and *blushing*. How embarrassing! I was more embarrassed when she caught me gazing at her, forcing me to blush even more. The crowd thinned out, Frankie hopped toward me, and the girl too approached with him.

"What's up, dude." Frankie greeted me.

I acknowledged by nodding. I was afraid that if I'd spoke, my voice would crack, amplifying my embarrassment and forcing me to flush redder. I tried my best not look directly at the beautiful girl beside him.

"Thanks for waiting for me. I hope it wasn't a burden."

"Naw, it's fine."

"That's really sweet of you." She commended me, her voice chiming like a masterpiece symphony lost through time, never allowing the world to hear and listen to its splendor.

"Thank you." I blushed, her complement forcing me to smile. The silence was very discomforting but in a good way.

"Oh, Kayden, this is Elizabeth. Elizabeth, this is Kayden."

"Elli. And the pleasure's mine." She responded.

Hadn't I been tongue tied I would have replied back. But smiling would be sufficient enough for now.

I looked at the books in her hand and noticed that she had a book bag on her back and Frankie didn't. "Are those your books?" I asked Frankie. He nodded mortified. I could tell that he hated being so dependent on others. "Here," I requested, reaching for the books. My fingers slightly brushed against hers as I reached for the books. The touch was a simple one, yet I made it mean a lot more to me than I should have. I couldn't help my eyes from wandering up to hers. I smiled awkwardly. The corners of her mouth were pulling back into a smile. I cleared my throat before the level of the awkwardness could intensify. "I'll take those from you."

"Thank you."

"I've never seen you before." I pointed out.

"Well, I've seen you." she laughed. "You were just always in hurry. You must really hate school or something." She chuckled lightly.

Only when I didn't want to be here. Like today. "Ha, no." I fibbed.

She smiled. Her smile left me warm inside. It was perfect.

She turned to Frankie, breaking the lock both our eyes seemed to be connected by. "Well, I will see you next week then Frankie."

"Sure thing."

"It was nice meeting you Kayden."

"Likewise." I replied.

She parted and as soon as she hit the corner, Frankie nudged my arm *oohing*.

"What?" I asked with a wide smile.

"I saw how you were looking at Elli. You like her." he spoke childishly.

"Ha, I do not. I don't even know her."

"So. I know the look, dude. It was how I looked at Emma when I first saw her." he laughed.

"Sure, whatever. I am not interested in her." I lied. We headed toward the exit. "So, why haven't you ever invited her to one of our outings?" I asked, breaking my concentration on the pattern of his crutches.

"I thought you weren't interested?"

"I'm…I…I'm not," I stuttered. "I was just curious."

"Elli and I have known each other for a while now, since we were young. She is one of my really good friends who I can wholly trust with anything. She is a very smart and intelligent girl. But she has an issue with meeting groups of people at one time. Not to mention, I don't want her to see the way I act around Emma." He chuckled. "She would just make me more embarrassed about it all."

She seemed like the perfect girl. "She's nice."

"Yeah." he agreed almost out of breath. The crutches were more of a workout tool than a walking assister.

We'd reached the exit glass doors. Rachel was wrong. The fog appeared to have gotten worse and the temperature seemed to have dropped since earlier. It was hard to even find the handicap ramp in it but I did my best to guide him to it.

After finding the handicap ramp and guiding him down it, I led him through the parking lot, which was very empty now.

We found the truck with no problem. He hopped over to the driver's side and tossed his crutches into the bed of his truck. I was right behind him, helping when he needed. Once he was in his truck, I handed him his books.

"Be safe, all right?"

"Ha, yeah, sure thing, Kay." I shut his door and proceeded to my car…if I could find it. I heard Frankie's truck roar from behind me. It'd been a while since I heard the roar of that white monster. "Hey!" His call stopped me and I turned around. "If it's any consolation, I can tell she likes you." He assured me

I smiled gleefully with hope. I turned, heading to my car with her in my mind.

I never thought I would see *this* day. When someone would appeal to me. I was beginning to take Rachel a bit serious when she spoke of Emma, that maybe I was somewhat falling for her. But I didn't feel this way for Emma.

It was almost like in her presence, time wasn't a factor. I was frozen in space, spending an eternity in that one moment. Was it love at first site? I wholly disbelieved in such things. But…here I was, feeling like even a simple separation like this one is draining me of something internally.

My face suddenly frowned in disgust. My veins pumped with irritation upon my late realization. Every emotion I had been feeling toward Elli wasn't as private as I wished they could have been. Wherever he was, Brycin was sure to be feeling exactly what I was feeling. In that case, I hope he felt the hate I felt toward them all, the magnitude of my anger and the loneliness they've forced me to feel yet again.

The parking lot seemed entirely empty and it sent a chill up my spine, forcing my entire body to quiver. It was possibly due to the emptiness of the parking lot but I could feel all of my senses heighten. The incredibly light breeze I hadn't noticed before was chilling as it ventilated throughout my white, v-neck thermal. My ears were alert, listening closely to everything around me. All I could hear were the faint conversations of those who lingered in the parking lot, hidden by the fog and the light whistle of the wind. I kept my eyes locked on my car in front of me but completely aware of the slightest movements in my peripheral.

I reached into my pockets, my attention slightly falling to see what I was doing, and freed my keys. I brought my head back up and the fog revealed a second car to me, surrounded by four body figures.

The car was across from mine but a bit further down. As I approached, I was capable of applying detail to the figures and the car they surrounded. It was two boys and two girls. All four of them unfortunately very familiar to me as they stood beside the Camaro.

My eyes narrowed and every muscle in my face tensed up. It was almost painful. I wouldn't be surprised if every muscle in my face remained contorted, leaving me with this angry expression for the rest of my life.

Some nerves they had! They can all drop dead for all I care! They were strangers to me for all I know.

Brycin seemed shocked when he noticed that I wasn't walking in their direction. Did he really expect me to be joyous about their sudden presence? Did he really expect me to run to them with open arms and acceptance after leaving me as long as they did? They took the only form of seeing them away from me. I would not forgive them for this for a long time.

His face fell. It was full of shame but cared nothing of it. I wish I could feel it, feel the intensity of the shame he felt, feel the magnitude of his remorse for his abandonment to me. It warmed me slightly inside.

It all happened so suddenly. It was exactly like the scene within a movie. The scene when a character is suddenly overwhelmed with a powerful emotion and time slows down dramatically. I was able to see and hear everything perceptively better than before. I saw Brycin's posture slowly shift from shameful to alert. I could see the wrinkles in his forehead relax for a fraction of second and reappear but in an entirely different expression this time. His expression emitted defeat, then worry, and then terror. His eyes were wide with fright, as if he'd seen a ghost or something. I then noticed Claire, Emma, and Jakob's posture stiffen, their facial expression overwhelmed with terror as well.

Something boomed over and over behind me rhythmically, forcing my ears to ring. The sound had left me immobilized. I'd heard sounds like it before but it'd been a while since then. I could feel the fear start at my toes, work its way up my legs, hit my gut excruciatingly hard and continue its way through my body until every portion of it ran icy with terror.

Chapter 15: Pursuit

WHEN I TURNED TO ACKNOWLEDGE THE SOURCE OF the booming, I was rammed by an unbelievable force, shooting directly into my chest and gripping me at the waste. The impact forced any remaining air resting in my lungs out. I felt my feet drag against the pavement until...I felt nothing.

Time seemed to speed back up and whatever had me in its clutches was moving at intense speeds. Everything was coated in darkness. I couldn't see a thing. That sudden sensation one would receive as a rollercoaster takes its first dip, the dip that gives the coaster its momentum and speed was forever present in the pit of my stomach.

I clutched tight on to whatever had me, the blackness shrouding my vision, fearing for my life. I couldn't feel the ground anymore, the light wind that I once felt was raging violently, swirling my hair all around and the sound of the constant booming was close, too close, leaving my ears ringing mercilessly.

The fear was no longer icy. It ravaged through me like a raging wildfire now. My hands, my face, my blood, it was all hot and rampant with fright. My heart was racing in my chest, hammering ruthlessly against my rib cage. My lungs seemed to be moving too fast, never allowing enough air to sit in them before releasing it all.

I suddenly felt a softer thud hitting against my chest. It was steady, relaxed.

A heartbeat...

A person…

I opened my eyes, fighting the shroud of darkness that demanded my vision and focused. All I was able to make out were…

Two, large black objects moving repetitively up and down connected to what looked like a human back. My body suddenly trembled violently in more fright than before. It was a…Demilyte. And one I didn't know.

"KAYDEN!"

I heard Brycin's voice rage over the gushing winds and the constant booming sound being emitted by the wings.

My vision was returning to normal. Brycin and Claire flew behind whoever had me, white wings bright and flapping. Their eyes flared white with terror. With them was Jakob, wings flapping just as fast but his eyes took on the characteristic of an abyss, infinitely dark and empty.

"Hope you aren't afraid of heights." the voice whispered in my ear with malice.

I knew that voice.

Portman.

Before I could confirm my assumptions, my body was launched through the air at a faster speed than we were flying. I no longer had a hold of Portman. He shoved me away, forcing my body to hurtle ragingly through the air.

I couldn't help but flex my stomach tighter, grunting and biting my teeth firmly together to endure this rushing speed and the unbearable sensation it left in my stomach. As soon as he released me, he shot straight up like a rocket.

My body continued to catapult in one direction until something grabbed my ankle and yanked me down. I couldn't yell. I couldn't stop myself from making grunting noises. Flexing the muscles in my stomach and keeping them tight seemed to be the only way to withstand the rushing speed.

The winds whipped my clothes and my hair viciously. No air had been allowed into my lungs since Portman threw me and now something else had me. Someone else.

I felt our direction shift and we were no longer going down, but forward again. My body fell up and down with the motion of whoever had me. My bag slipped from over my shoulder and fell into the endless grayness below. It hadn't even crossed my mind how high we were until I saw my bag free fall and disappear into the fog.

I turned my head up, afraid, yet curious to who had me by my ankle. This Demilyte was new. He was somewhat scrawny. His skin was a soft ivory. His black hair was short and cropped and his eyes were dark, fueled with malevolence and enthusiasm. He was enjoying it.

His grip on my ankle tightened, smirking when he saw my face grimace from the pain, and he shot us faster through the air like a bullet.

No matter how hard I tried, I was incapable of opening my lungs and allowing air in them at this speed.

I was completely unprepared when we shot up abruptly, leaving my neck aching somewhat from the whiplash.

I was able to allow some air in my lungs, but again, not a sufficient amount to completely inflate them. My head ached from the intense speed and the whiplash I'd received when we shot upward.

I felt my eyelids become heavy. I didn't know if I was because my body was tremendously weak and exhausted from it all, the high altitudes, the rushing speeds, my aching head and my airless lungs or if death was slowly creeping up on me.

I was suddenly hit by a wave of hope. Bursting through a thick gray cloud below me was Brycin, Claire, and Jakob. All of them were determined to get me in their custody. Brycin's wings flapped the fiercest. He was most determined to get me safe again and, regardless of the feelings I've felt toward him all week, I yearned for it.

My eyes were locked on them, my hand reaching for them as they flapped their wings relentless and exhaustingly to get me. Brycin arm extended to me.

I suddenly felt my body swing back slightly. For a minute, I thought I had been released, but I still felt his grip.

In an instant, my body whipped upward, flipping like some flimsy object uncontrollably. My breath was trapped in my lungs, suffocating me. It felt like everything in my body was being tossed around, mixed and mingled and disorganized. The harsh speed battered against my skin. It felt like there were millions of invisible, microscopic bullets shooting against it all at once.

Something yanked me aggressively at the wrist and I was flying forward again. Every part of my body tingled in the most uncomfortable way. My heart pulverized my chest as it raced out of control and the air that slammed into my chest made the pain that much more intense.

I looked up and gazed into the eyes of Seth as he laughed evilly with me in his hand.

I didn't know where the sudden rage came from, but my fear was being replaced by anger and annoyance. I was sick of this constant game of hot potato. I swung my body back once. "Let me go!" I flung my body forward and my foot crashed into his face. It felt like kicking a stone. I wasn't sure that I'd hurt him in any way but his grip failed and I plummeted through the atmosphere.

Free falling gave me a worse feeling in the pit of my stomach than flying at mach speeds in the custody of a demon because all I did was fall. I had no assurance of living. Even if I was in the hands of a demon, at least I knew death was at a distance. Here, as I was falling, it was like staring death in the face.

I rushed toward the earth like a meteor. I continued to fall for several more seconds. Where the hell was Brycin and the others? I was sure that at any moment, one of them would rush after me and catch me, removing death from in front of me. But…I was still falling and I began a mental descent into hopelessness and my only company was the unsettling sensation slamming against the walls of my stomach.

I closed my eyes and gave into the hopelessness. The sound of the gushing wind in my ears and the piercing feeling in the pit of my stomach were my only company as I fell. You would think, even now, as close as I am to death, my last departing gift would be the satisfaction of producing a single tear, the gift to cry. I was seconds away from death, seconds away from my remains being splattered across the pavements below or dismantled as I crash through some building, seconds away from my death ending the life of my best friend, seconds away from leaving Rachel all alone in this world, and I couldn't produce a single tear.

It was heart-wrenching. I know it was. I felt my heart ache from it as I fell. But not even the void my death would create in Rachel's heart or the fact that my death *will* kill my best friend wasn't enough to make me cry.

Then I deserved death. I didn't deserve to live if I wasn't allowed to feel the entire effects of my final moments. If I couldn't cry for the one's I was going to kill then surely, someone as hollow as me deserved to die.

I opened my eyes and I was greeted by the face of an angel. His eyes white, full of resolve as he reached for me. He grabbed me and placed me in safe arms and we darted parallel to Earth's floor.

Brycin saved me from my death and my remorse. Perhaps, the determination I had seen in his eyes before was the assurance I needed to know that he wasn't going to let me die today.

"Hold on!" He shouted. His wings flapped faster and they sliced us through the air.

I cringed tighter to Brycin when I saw a ball of fire hurtle over his head, nearly missing his wings and scorching the air around us. I peeked over Brycin's shoulder. Flying at full throttle right behind us were all three Demilytes. The unknown Demilyte, Seth, and Portman.

"Hold on tight!"

We started a descent and they were right behind us, projecting balls of flames at us. He weaved us in and out of the falling flames as they came raining down. He was agile and accurate, never making a single mistake. Amazing how he was in total control of himself, his breathing, his wings and his concentration. He was completely calm but I think it was only to keep me from freaking out. I clutched to him tight as he propelled us toward the ground.

I suddenly noticed a flame glowing with light pinks, shades of purple and a pure whiteness rain down alongside the other flames made up of oranges and yellows. Then, a lightning bolt mixed in with the raining pyres. I looked over Brycin's shoulder once more and flying directly behind the three Demilytes were Claire and Jakob.

I suddenly heard lots of pounding coming from below. Must've been the many projectiles crashing into the earth. We were getting closer to the ground. I knew he didn't want me up here. It wasn't safe for me. Even in his custody, I was still at risk of getting hurt. At least on the ground, there was one less thing that had potential to kill me.

Our direction in flight suddenly shifted one last time and we were flying parallel to the ground again but this time I was able to see it.

My attention stayed locked on the ones flying behind us. Especially the Demilytes who were trying desperately to accomplish what they've been waiting so long to accomplish.

This proved previous assumptions correct. They did want to kill me. They were just toying with us the entire time.

A loud roar, followed by an earsplitting thud shook us. Brycin yelled in pain, we shook and his flying pattern became imbalanced. My back was hot and it burned. I felt us as we spun ragingly out of control and finally slam with an impressive force into the ground. I bounced across the ground before finally skidding to a stop, face in the dirt.

The pain was excruciating, unbearable. I was feeling both my pains and Brycin's pain simultaneously. My back was still burning from the ball of fire that slammed into his back.

I lay face down on the moist terrain, face possibly covered in muck, trying to find the strength to get up. My arms were weak, damaged and inoperative. My muscles were not cooperating with my mind. I wanted to get up, aware that my life remained in danger, and run to safety, behind one of my divine friends where I would be somewhat safe. But my body ached all over.

I felt something scoop me up off the ground and a loud explosion followed after. The force of the blast sent me and whoever had me hurtling through the air, flipping and bouncing on the mucky soil again and again skidding to a stop.

My pains had multiplied. "Com'on, Kayden! Get up!" the male voice yelled. It was Jakob. "Com'on, kid!" He rolled me over. I felt him tug on me and pull me up. I gazed at him weakly, his face overtaken with worry.

I helped him by using any energy I had left to pull myself up to a stand though he was more than capable of managing without my help. I was on my feet, groggy and disoriented, my arm wrapped over Jakob's shoulder.

He walked with me backwards. I had to force the muscles in my neck to work. I pulled my head up and Brycin was up on his feet, fighting the three Demilytes with Claire by his side. They were an unstoppable force. They were barely capable of landing any hits on Brycin or Claire but they, however, even with the odds two to three, were winning the fight.

"They're…amazing." I breathed.

"Save your energy." Jakob muttered with intensity. "The stronger you are, the stronger he will be."

I was bruised and all beat up. I was surprised that I was capable of standing this long but I came to the conclusion that my legs gave out a long time ago and Jakob was just holding me up with brute strength.

"Why…aren't…you…helping them?" Breathing the words out was the only way to get them out. I was exhausted. My lungs weren't familiar with air being in them now considering how long they went without it. My body was weak. It hurt to even use the muscles in my throat to speak.

"Neatholytes fight better against Demilytes and vice versa. It's like putting water on fire. It puts it out and if you deliver too much heat to water, it evaporates. They are each other's weakness. I could fight against them, and I could kill them, but it would take more effort. But now, considering being around Neatholytes for so long and I no longer possess an orange flame but a purple one, it may not take as much effort."

I continued to breathe heavily, my head down and weak soaking in this knowledge.

I suddenly felt my body get tugged and jerk to the side and a loud bang followed immediately after the pull.

I looked up. My arm was still around Jakob. So what was with the unnecessary tug that took more breath out of me?

I noticed that we weren't facing Brycin and Claire's fight anymore. We were facing the opposite direction and Jakob's eyes were locked on something with rage.

I followed the line of his sight. My jaw instantly fell to the floor. Fear ran potent through my veins. Three more Demilytes were approaching fast. Two familiar. Balavon and Ester. One a complete stranger. He possessed a russet skin complexion. His hair was a dark brown and spiked in and every which direction. His eyes burned with the same blackness. He was medium built, ripped and toned, evidence due to his short sleeve, skin tight black shirt.

Balavon flew in the middle, wearing a black trench and his eyes on me as he descended. I could see a small grin sweep across his face.

Jakob pulled my arm from around his head and gently pushed me behind him. It was challenging for me to support my own weight.

"Kayden, listen to me. I need you to be strong right now. You have to run. Far. I know you are tired but I really need for you to do that for me. I will try my best to hold them off 'til Emma returns with the others." I stared blankly at him. Was all this really happening? Was today the day they succeeded in killing me? I wanted to fall in defeat.

It was hopeless for him. He was weaker against his own kind. So what if he had an infinitesimal advantage over them? It wasn't enough to guarantee him his life. The odds were still against him because it still would require more effort to beat his own kind. Plus it was three of them fighting against one of him. They wouldn't have to work as hard to dispose of him. Things weren't looking up for him at all.

His dark wings stretched out as wide as they could reach and they darted him up. "GO!" he yelled from the sky.

Still disoriented, I had to do my part in helping them succeed no matter how weak I felt. I ignored the agonizing pain in my legs and the rest of my body and ran across the field. I had to do this. For my family.

My entire body ached and running only made matters worse. But I couldn't give up on them. My legs burned with agony as I forced them to dash across the soft soil, my lungs inflated and deflated with no noticeable rhythm, completely out of control. Even the sweat that came from running felt too heavy for my skin to hold.

I continued to force my body forward, my legs running their fastest. I wanted to move them faster but they wouldn't concede.

I continued to run forward, refusing to look back. Looking back would only slow me down at this point. I didn't know where I was running. There was nothing in sight. Just more and more rich green terrain. No trees, no shrubs, nothing. Just a vast open field.

I stopped, exhausted and breathing hysterically.

I turned to see what I had missed while I was running away. Claire and Brycin continued their fight with Portman, Seth and the unknown Demilyte. Flames and lightning bolts were being showered throughout the air and to the grounds below. Their movements were agile. From where I stood, they seemed faster than I'd noticed before. I couldn't catch any of their attacks from here.

I then turned to Jakob's fight. The fight was mostly a dodging game. Attack, dodge, attack, dodge. He fought a lot like Brycin had the first time they had come after me.

Suddenly, Jakob slipped up, attacked when he should have dodged. He was launched to the ground like a missile from an attack by Ester. He hit the ground with a force that shook the earth and traveled to where I was, shaking the ground beneath me, knocking me slightly off balance.

They all appeared to have turned to me in unison. My heart raced as they peered over in my direction. I was probably about a half a mile away from them.

Ester and the second unknown Demilyte flew into the fight with Claire and Brycin and Balavon charged for me, wings flapping ferociously. Had this been my first time encountering such a monster charging toward me, I probably would have allowed the iciness of fear to freeze up my legs and prevent me from running. I would have stared vacantly as he approached, overwhelmed in terror.

Luckily for me, this wasn't my first encounter. I turned and raced across the grassy plains. There was nothing in sight, nowhere to go but hopefully it would buy me enough time to grant one of the three behind me some reaction time.

My feet moved swiftly beneath me, faster than before, fueled with determination. My lungs felt like they were about to explode in my chest. I felt more threatened by my own body failing than the creature that was flying after me.

I looked back. All hope seemed loss. I was trapped in a nightmare, the helpless, defenseless human being haunted by a vicious monster. The clock corresponding to my life turned inevitably to the end of everything. The end of my life, the end of Brycin's life, the end of my family, and the end of possibly mankind.

Claire and Brycin were overwhelmed in the fight with the five Demilytes and Jakob remained motionless on the ground. Balavon was gaining on me and my legs seemed to be moving all on their own. I had already given up hope but they still moved fast across the field, my heart still pounding relentlessly against my chest and my lungs continued their climb toward explosion.

I could see the predator in his eyes as he closed the gap between. I could see that I was only prey to him. I could see that I was just a prize, seconds away from being claimed.

Chapter 16: Face to Face

I RAN, FUELED AND CONSUMED BY MY OWN FEAR. MY HEART PUMPED THE fear throughout my entire body, spreading it like a virus. My feet felt like they were bleeding and my skin ran hot from the panic like a fever despite the freezing temperature surrounding me.

I looked around, searching for somewhere to hide. But nothing offered me refuge.

I felt my lungs grow weak and now my legs were given out on me too. I would have no choice but to give up soon.

I felt the gust that his wings produced get stronger and stronger with every passing second. My end had come.

A loud bang startled me, stopping me in my tracks and forcing me to turn around. Aris came out of nowhere and catapulted himself into Balavon. The collision sounded like two eighteen wheelers slamming into each other at full throttle. I didn't know how that sounded like or how loud of a bang would it produce but I had a pretty vivid idea.

Aris mounted Balavon. He pulled his arm back to strike but Balavon struck him with a vicious, unseen force that catapulted him yards away. Aris bounced once and flipped to his feet, wings stretched and crouching in defense.

I stared at Aris's wings. His were…different. His wings were a purer white than the others and a lot larger. But what made them even more unique were the golden threads that lay here and there in his expanded wings.

He didn't appear to me as a fighter before but today was the day he'd prove that thought wrong. He wore an all white ensemble. A white sleeve-less shirt that molded perfectly against his angelic physique with white pants that shined exuberantly with his wings against the gloomy sky. His arms were cut and they appeared larger than the first time I met him.

Yes, when I first met Aris, he appeared as the peacemaker of the family, the one who was never willing to fight but I should have known that when time would require it of him, he would fight.

My head turned to Balavon as he rose off the floor, his arms stretch out wide. They never assisted him in getting up. His arms dropped to his sides, his posture erect and his body calm.

He stared into Aris's eyes. The darkness and the evil that resided in them were most haunting. The corner of his mouth pulled up into a demented smirk. His long and dark flowing hair swayed gently in the wind.

"Kayden!" Aris yelled my name. My head snapped in his direction, my breathing still hard.

I turned my head back in Balavon's direction. I slowly headed to Aris's side, my sight never leaving Balavon. When I was close enough to Aris, he pulled himself in front of me.

Elaina, Matt and Emma suddenly dropped out of the sky.

Balavon didn't look the slightest bit worried that he facing four Neatholytes.

An object in the corner of my eye caught my attention. Ester was flying our way. He landed into this little meeting, standing to the right of Balavon.

It was then that the two was coming together now. Members of Balavon's family were joining his side as were the ones of this family.

We were all here, face to face for the first time.

"It's over Balavon." Aris's voice echoed with power. "Your attempts stop here."

"Aris." Balavon called out his name with astonishment. "Your reputation perceives you. What an honor it is to finally come face to face with you."

"This is madness!" Though I didn't turn to see who it was, I knew it was Claire he was yelling. "Don't you know that what you are doing puts us all in danger? You can kill us all!"

"Why should that be of my concerns?" he responded.

"You're a monster!" Claire gasped.

"A monster? I think the real monster rests within that very family. Aris, the angel with the infamous reputation. The angel who could destroy cities. The very angel who wiped out an entire nation. Now, who is the real monster?

"I'm no monster. I aim to give Kayden here a true family. One that won't desert him."

"We've never deserted him!" Brycin lashed out, jumping in front of all of us in a tense crouch and with expanded wings.

"No?" he inquired. "That's not how he feels right now." Brycin's tensed posture relaxed. He stood and his wings folded. His head fell and he looked over his shoulder at me. "I know you've felt his loneliness." Balavon's tone was growing. "I know you've felt the emptiness you forced him to feel while you were playing protector with everyone else!"

"SHUT UP!" Brycin's wings shot open but before they could launch him forward, Jakob and Matt restrained him. "You don't know anything!" he barked.

"Let Kayden choose then. Let him choose which family is the best for him. Someone with *that* kind of blood should be with a more understanding family." Brycin pushed forward again but Jakob and Matt both had him locked in their grips.

I didn't mean to do it, but my mind was reevaluating everything post this encountering. I did feel lonely. I did feel empty from their abandonment. Maybe he was right. Maybe I was with the wrong family. Maybe they didn't care as much for me as they said they did. Maybe, just maybe, they were more concerned with saving the world from its end days than me.

I must be destined to be something truly extraordinary if evil wanted me on its side. How different life would be if I chose to leave the side of good and join this evil covenant. How would destiny for me change?

But…

Brycin was my protector. I couldn't abandon our bond, our friendship…our soul.

"Kayden," Balavon called me. "Take heed the decision you make now. For one will have dire consequences. A sacrifice that I believe not even you would be willing to make."

"You really think he will choose to go with you?!" Brycin hissed, tugging on both Jakob and Matt's hold on him. "How mistaken you are! You wish to kill not only us but all of mankind! He's not a killer! He's not a monster! You're the monsters here! You are the ones out to destroy us!"

"We are aware of what the future holds if they die." Aris began again in a much calmer voice this time. "We know the magnitude of grief that will come from the loss and we all will be coming after you for revenge.

"Fueled by rage, hate, and sorrow, millions will die, nations will fall, mankind will seize to exist. A war will arise and with it, the death of mankind."

"And what's so wrong with that?" the scrawny new Demilyte questioned. "Since the dawn of our existence, they've had a problem with us. We are merely out to destroy the true monsters in this episodic tale."

"We drew first blood. They had every right to react in which they did." Elaina spit through her teeth.

"But to continue to hunt us like animals? The wars had ended and we showed our peace to the human race! And they hunted us!" His voice roared.

"But you're talking about exposure. The beginning of another war. And this one will result in more bloodshed than the last."

"The weak shouldn't run a planet." Balavon spoke again. "We are the evolution of man. We're stronger, faster, more intelligent. We are better than them. Yes, I am aware that some of my blood is human," his last sentence he spoke with such disgust. Clearly it was a trait in which he found distasteful. "But we are not them. I've seen them do more evil than any Demilyte could have imagined possible. *They* are the true evil in this."

Rachel was in that category. Rachel was a lot of things. Kind, compassionate, loving, empathetic but she was not evil.

Millions will die. Millions whose personality matches Rachel's. I will not make that decision. I will not be one of them.

Balavon chuckled. "I guess you've decided. I wish I didn't have to do this." He walked the line of his family. He stopped in front of Seth. He raised his arm straight up into the air. He turned to us and smiled mischievously. His arm bolted down, Seth's head in the line of his attack. Clearly no one expected to see what happened next. At least no one from our side of the field.

Balavon's strike passed through Seth's body and it dematerialized, turning into a black smoke-like substance.

Did he just kill Seth?

"Aryes here," he looked at the scrawny Demilyte who had flew with me by my ankle earlier. "Can make duplicate copies of anyone, fully capable of its counter part's reasoning skills, physical capabilities, and any other extraordinary abilities the original self may possess. And Isaac," the other new member. "Can target someone's specific ability and negate it, leaving no room for suspicion."

"Where is Seth?!" Brycin yelled, ready to breach the hold he was in.

"He is taking care of some…*human* business." Balavon answered.

Human business? I thought I was their main…

Human business! I turned to Aris. "Rachel!"

"Claire, get him out of here." Aris demanded. "Get him to Rachel now!"

Before I knew it, Claire had my arm and flipped me over her back and we catapulted into the air away from the fight.

"Portman after them!" I heard lots of grunting and pounding coming from below but my mind wasn't concerned with the fight that broke loose below. I was more concerned with the monster who was at my home, threatening the life of the one who meant the most to me.

We flew high over the earth, the wind rushing through my hair. My hands were shaking with fear as I gripped onto Claire's shoulders.

Good thing the fog was dissipating now. It made flying for Claire easier and it made me more aware of where we were. There wasn't much below but acres of green pastures, scattered trees and isolated homes here and there.

A ball of fire flew over our heads, knocking Claire's flying patterns a little off. We both looked behind us simultaneously and Portman was right behind us and right behind him was Jakob, flying relentlessly to catch Portman.

"Hang on, Kayden!" she screamed.

She spun over on her back, my back now facing the earth's ground and we dove into a descent. That overwhelming sensation I had forgotten returned. Portman followed our descent with devilish enthusiasm. I held on to Claire as tight as I could. I was almost positive that I might have been hurting her but she barely reacted to my grip.

He continually threw hordes of flames at the two of us as we dove. Claire's movements were more graceful as she wove in and out of the raining flames. They were much smoother than Brycin's movements and less thought put into them. I realized that before Portman could even launch an attack at us, Claire had already seen it played out in his head, making dodging his attacks easy for her. That's probably why Aris sent her instead of Brycin. She would know of any surprises the chase may inherit.

She continued to weave us in and out of the fiery meteors that surrounded us as we unrelentingly descended. I felt a spray of water as we sustained the dive. We were heading straight into a bluish gray wall that was full of motion. In seconds, we would crash into it and I didn't have this down to a science, but I was almost absolute that wings and water didn't mix all that great.

With much abruptness and sharpness, our direction changed, flying parallel to the dancing waves below us. Her speed forced the water to part, forming two walls on both sides of us. The icy touch of the water as it sprayed against my face forced a shiver through my body. Both my hair and my clothes were becoming soaked.

I looked behind us. Portman was still on our tail and Jakob was right behind him still.

"I need you to hold on as tight as possible this time and take a deep breath." Claire requested. I turned my head back around. I pressed my head tightly to her back, inhaled deeply and gripped her shoulders much tighter than before. She still didn't react to the strength of my grip even though it nearly hurt me to put so much strength into it. Felt like my hands would lock up in any minute.

Without warning, we propelled upward in a diagonal faster than a bullet being released from the barrel of a gun, faster than the world's fastest aircraft possibly.

I couldn't breathe as we shot up even with the trapped away air stored in my lungs. The vigor of the pull forced me to grunt unintentionally. I wrapped my legs tightly around her, praying that I wasn't interfering with the way she flew. It was the only way I could endure this speed.

My eye lids were pressed tightly shut. My wet hair slapped unremittingly like tiny whips against my forehead. These types of speeds were not made for the human body clearly.

A wave of air forced itself down my throat, punching my lungs as it entered and pushing my chest out. I panted hysterically. We were flying straight and our speed decreased slightly but only to the point where I could breathe through it. If I wasn't so out of breath, I probably would have yelled at her for what just happened.

We proceeded into a congregation of thick gray clouds. The air here was icier than the freezing touch of the waters below. And with this cold air ventilating through my nearly soaking wet clothes, my torso was beginning to numb.

I looked behind us to see where they were. I could barely see two feet ahead of me with these thick clouds.

"Where are they?" I yelled over the harsh winds.

"They're there but they just can't see us." she answered elegantly and calmly. "He will have to rely on other senses now if he intends to—" she broke off mid sentence. She gasped and I felt the terror tremble through her body.

"What's the matter?"

"His mind." she gasped. "I can't sense it anymore."

"Is he still there?"

"I'm not sure. I can't even get a read on Jakob's mind."

"Isaac." I accused through me teeth.

"We have no time to waste now." she spoke urgently. "We have to—" she shrieked. Something delivering a devastating blow knocked me off her back and I plummeted toward the earth's floor for the second time today.

I flexed my stomach tight, again, trying my hardest to withstand the mixture of unbearable elements occurring all at once. The rushing speeds, the fright that came from the possibility of not being saved this time, and the insufferable sensation forever present at my body's core was proving to be a bit much for my human body to handle.

My body flipped over so that I was falling facing the earth's floor. I couldn't see, still engulfed by the thickness of the clouds.

The clouds were beginning to thin…

I could see the ground now and everything that rested on it. Clearly. It was ridiculous how high I was and how swiftly the gap was closing between the floor and myself.

I grunted and groaned as I continued to fall rapidly toward the earth. I had to stay positive, remain hopeful. I needed to know that no matter the circumstance presented, they would always come through for me, even when things looked this bad. I just had to wait for one of them to…

Before I could even finish the thought, someone swooped in and caught me. It was Jakob this time and he had me clutched tight against his chest as we flew downward.

His wings vanished. In one fluid move, he tossed me over his shoulder and onto his back. He fell into a grove of trees, grabbing on to branch after branch, swinging and swaying himself until finally he hit the forest floor with a loud thud.

I hopped off his back. "Kayden run as fast as you can and don't stop!" He demanded. "I need to go and help Claire! Don't stop! Just go!" His wings reappeared and he shot through the branches above him.

I turned and dashed through the forest of trees as fast as I could. My lungs were overused and exhausted from the constant abuse they'd been receiving. I was sure they would detonate in my chest after this was all over.

My speed was nothing compared to theirs, nothing compared to what I'd been introduced to all day today. I was so slow, barely making any progress. The muscles in my legs burned feverishly and throbbed achingly, proof that I was moving fast but in actuality, I wasn't.

But my speed isn't the most important thing at this moment.

I was running to save a life. A life in which didn't deserve to be lost. I had to get to Rachel. I had no idea where I was or where I was running but running forward seemed to be the best way to go. I needed to get some distance covered through these woods so when whoever returned for me, there would be less distance for us to cover.

This was my fault. My actions, my decisions had placed Rachel in danger. If I was capable of placing her in this much danger as a human, how much more danger could I possibly put her in as a half-breed?

As I ran, I evaluated my stay with Rachel.

I could leave but stay in close contact. Move out and say I am ready to be on my own. It would break her heart but it would be a sacrifice worth taking to save her life.

My feet patted against the floor inexorably. The blackness, the dark browns, and the dull greens were blurred, mixed and inadequate in detail. My attention was straight ahead of me, looking out for any canopies of moss that may slow me down or any branches that may be hanging low enough to smack me.

My panting was annoying me. It was raspy and uneven. My lungs felt like they were going to give out at any moment but no matter my pain, no matter my suffering I had to keep going.

I heard a snap behind me. My head turned and analyzed the dark woods behind me. But I saw nothing.

"Whoa!" The ground suddenly disappeared, turning into a steep slope. I tripped and rolled uncontrollably down the hill. A sharp, sudden fierce blow to the face nearly knocked me unconscious. Must've been a tree I hit. A warm liquid oozed from my nose directly after. I continued my violent roll down the hill after the first blow to the face but not without encountering many more devastating attacks from the forest's natural makeup. My clothes snagged on roots, scratching the bare skin beneath, my shoulder hit a small boulder in the ground and I hit many more trees before finally, rolling to a stop on a leveled plain.

I pressed my hands against the mucky floor, dreadfully trying to force my body off of the floor but falling miserably in failure.

I lay there defeated, panting, every body part aching tremendously, throbbing uncontrollably. My forehead throbbed more than anything and I could feel the thick liquid flow down my face. My clumsiness was sure to have affected Brycin in battle.

There was no way we were going to get to Rachel in time. Here I was, lying on the ground debilitated with no hope of anyone finding me. Even if Claire and Jakob finished off Portman in time and came searching for me, I may not even have an active mind for her to even get a read on.

What if it was the other way around? What if Portman proved to be too strong for either of them and came after me? Before death could kill me off first?

I didn't know what was more heart-wrenching. Portman reaching me before Claire or Jakob did or failing at saving the life I felt was irrevocably more precious and worth more than my own.

"I can't." I murmured aloud into the ground, the sound of defeat scorching my tone. "I can't do it." I inhaled the earthy scent of the floor and exhaled out any dust or mud that may have escaped through my nostrils. "I failed."

My tormenting sea had come for me, taking one last beating at my emotions before I died.

I felt the shroud of death coming over me. It started low at my toes and worked itself up, numbing me. My ankles seemed to have locked themselves permanently. I felt the numbness travel up my legs, locking my knees, and continued its path up my spine.

My mind drifted for the last few moments I remained alive. I was no longer on this floor giving into death. I was at Grandma Muriel's house in Eureka, California. It was my first birthday with my new family.

Grandma Muriel had just placed a warm, delicately crafted birthday cake in front of me. She'd baked it herself. It was a chocolate cake, smothered with her homemade peanut buttery frosting and sprinkles of nuts over the top. On top of the brown cake, written in a beautiful handwriting were the words: Happy Birthday to Our Loving Grandson, Kayden.

She pressed her prune-like lips to my forehead and began placing six candles on top of the cake.

"Seems like yesterday he was brought into our lives."

That voice. I hadn't heard it in almost six years. I knew it well and surprisingly my memory remembered it well.

"I know. Before you know it, he will be on his way to college."

I looked for the voices.

"Rachel, you deserve nothing but the best. Your heart was molded and crafted by genuine angels. Your love is unconditional and I will fight for that love perpetually."

That was Michael's voice.

"Kayden?"

I saw both of their faces together again, young and full of life and love. Not only for each other…but for me. I turned to Grandma Muriel and now standing next to her was Papa Irving. They too smiled at me. Their love for each other and the unconditional love toward me was evident.

The warmth of all of their smiles surrounding me and the love that radiated from them, was somehow eliminating the numbness death was bestowing upon me. I felt my spine relax, my knees loosened and I was able to move my toes.

I would see to it that Rachel lives to see tomorrow. I will do all I can.

I felt the determination building up inside me like a flame and spreading like a wildfire. I pressed my arms against the floor again, my mind fixed on getting the hell out of this godforsaken forest.

I didn't know where Jakob and Claire were right now but I really wished they'd hurry up.

I forced myself off the floor. I found a nearby stick to assist me. The muscles in my legs were still in pain from all the running and the fall added to my insufferable soreness. After struggling to my feet I limped the rest of the way through the unknown forest.

I staggered feebly further into the forest, hoping to see a familiar, friendly face soon.

I twisted my ankle on some softer soil. I sucked air in through my teeth. This forest would surely be the one to kill me first.

I didn't know how much time had passed. Time ticked towards the end and I couldn't find my way out. I wasn't making any progress. I swear I'd seen this tree before. All of it was covered in a rich, green moss except for a tiny, dark spec located directly in the center of the tree bark.

I abruptly stopped. I felt the wind begin to funnel its way through the forest. I looked up and the trees swayed ferociously beneath the gray cotton-like sky.

I limped away to escape this forest, fearing whatever lurked in it. This wind was not natural. Fear was soaking every previous emotion out of me, intensifying the pains in my aching body. I couldn't run fast enough with two injured legs and this stupid stick.

I heard another snap. I stopped and turned around. I hadn't noticed it before, but I hadn't seen a single wild animal since I entered this forest. So whatever made that snap was not an animal.

I walked backwards slowly and weakly, the stick no longer assisting me to walk but rather gripped in both of my hands tight like a weapon. I was ready to make a swing at the first thing I see.

I looked through the dark woods for the slightest movements but everything was in motion because of the wind.

I continued to back away.

Something grabbed my shoulders. My heart jolted forward, ramming into my already aching chest. I stumbled away in fear and fell to the floor. I rolled over.

My heart continued to pound away at my chest but the fear had disappeared and relief replaced it.

It was Claire, eyes white and wings exposed.

"Boy, am I glad to see you." I panted, reaching up for her assistance in helping me. She pulled me up and stared at me.

"What happened to you?" she asked but her face corrected itself, from worry to aware. She read my mind. Good. It was embarrassing to talk about it.

"I leave you for two seconds and you nearly kill yourself!"

I chuckled once. I looked behind her. I reached the end of the forest—a small stream running fierce and blue behind her. The water gushed over the rocks near the riverbed, staining them. The smell that radiated from the stream of water was invigorating.

With a loud thud, Jakob landed a few meters away to the right of me. He folded his wings and approached us.

"Ha, well will you look at that." Jakob said with a smile, looking in my direction.

A strange sensation overpowered one area of my forehead. It was where the blood flowed from the gash. It was tingling, almost burning but not hot really. Then I felt the skin pull together and I heard it seal.

"I healed myself?" I asked with a jaw dropped expression.

"Seems you're getting closer to your transformation." Jakob stated.

"Fate might be changing for us after all." Claire stated. It was something about the way she said it. It was downing. It was as if she didn't want me to inherit what belonged to me.

Before I could question her on it, I remembered that fate tried to kill me more than once today and if they were here, what happened to one of the threats fate had sent after me, the one Jakob and Claire were preoccupied with. "What happened to Portman?" My tone serious again.

They both looked at each other with a blank look. Sighing, Claire spoke, "He won't be coming after you anymore."

"What does that mean? That he's—" I broke off in mid sentence refusing to say it.

She nodded.

"We had no choice." Jakob announced. "It was either him or let him kill you."

I was trapped in awe. My head hung low as I figured out Portman's whereabouts. I didn't want anyone to die. Why did it have to be *this* way?

"Jakob." Claire turned to him. He looked down at her. "Go and help the others. They need you. I will get him to Rachel. Time is still ticking for her."

He nodded. He ran in the direction in which he made his entrance, unfolding his wings, extended every noticeable feather in them and launched himself into the air.

I walked over to the stream and gazed at myself in my reflection. I looked hideous. I knelt beside the stream and placed my hands in the freezing water, splashing the water into my face and rubbing it clean, shuttering from the temperature. I washed all the dirt and mud from hair, pulling it out in clumps.

After fixing myself up in the stream, I reanalyzed my reflection. It wasn't my best look but it will do for now.

"You set?" Claire asked.

I nodded.

"Come on." She turned around and extended her wings. "We still have an agenda." I approached her, feeling completely refreshed and rejuvenated. My legs were even feeling good as new. My *body* completely free of pain. My forehead must not have been the only thing that healed. My entire body must've healed itself. I felt better now than I ever had all day.

I mounted her back, my mind now focused on Rachel and getting to her in time. There was no room for mistakes now. Her life was on the line and every second that passed was crucial.

Her wings pushed us up and she launched us through the sky and to our final destination.

Chapter 17: Tragedy

TIME WAS NOT OUR FRIEND AT THIS VERY MOMENT.

Every second that passed ticked away more hope. Claire was going as fast as my body would allow, a speed that would allow to me to breathe comfortably but I was willing to risk that, push my limits, but she wasn't.

As we rushed to my home, a thought invaded my mind, a thought and a fact that left me alone all week this week — question that required an answer. "Why did you guys leave me this week without telling me?"

Though we flew in silence for the most part, the awkwardness this silence possessed was sharper than knives. "I don't think this is the best time."

"Now is as good as any other time. It might be the best time. We don't know how this day will end."

"Your negativity is really bringing me down."

I chuckled once because of the irony that statement possessed. She seemed to notice it too because she chuckled lightly. "I'm not being negative. I am being optimistic. You don't know if I am going to make it out of this alive or not. James's dreams are never wrong and that doesn't leave much room for hope."

I noticed her body cringed when I mention James and his dreams never being wrong. "For our sake, I hope that some are." I knew she meant to say it low enough for me not to hear, hoping that the whooshing winds surrounding me would drown out her voice. But I heard her.

I knew she was in my mind at this point. I felt her. So I knew that she was aware of the question that statement implanted in my thoughts.

She sighed. "I would love to tell you Kayden, but…" she broke off mid sentence. Possibly trying to find a way to let me down easy. "Ha, am I that easy to read?" she chuckled.

"Ha, ha will you stay out of my head?" I laughed.

She laughed once. "It's hard these days. Not being in someone's thoughts. I usually have much self-restraint, respecting boundaries and the privacy of other minds. But…things are getting difficult. I do it more now as a safety precaution. With the chances of an uncompromising future, I cannot afford for *us* to be two steps behind. It's unnerving these days when people don't speak their minds fast enough for me or when I feel as though they are lying to me."

"But I'm not doing either."

"I know." She sighed deeper and heavier this time. "There is a reason why I am in your head…" she hesitated. "It was…more of a request."

That took me off guard. I was not expecting that type of answer at all. I was expecting one thing, one truth. To find out the real reasons behind their four day absence. Not find out a whole separate truth.

"Kayden please don't make me tell you more." She calmly requested. "I'd rather we all be in one room and discuss everything."

Still in awe, I lowered my head closer to her back until, finally, I rested it there — my ear against her back. I concentrated on everything else around me to distract me from thoughts regarding their betrayal.

I listened to her breathe, even, slow, and relaxed. No signs of fatigue or exhaustion. Her wings made two different, distinct sounds. A loud booming-like sound whenever they went down and an airy, weightless sound when they went up.

The air blew over me with an icy touch that should have made me quiver but instead, it felt like it was only cool to relax me. The air bestowed as much serenity in me as it could but my own sense of feeling betrayed barricaded some of the calmness from entering my body, something in which I was in desperate need for.

And just like that, I was thinking about it again.

I wasn't sure if Claire was in my head this very instant, reading my every thought, my every emotion like an open book.

A drop of anger invaded my bloodstream when I analyzed the truth. It wasn't because Claire had a better chance at fighting the others because she could read their moves in their mind before they ever launched anything at her. That was only a plus. It was because she was the only one who could read *my* mind. Brycin could only read my emotions and that wasn't enough for him.

What type of accusations were they going for? I hadn't done anything and yet my privacy was being invaded by people I *thought* I trust.

She sighed heavily again.

"In my mind again?" I hissed with sarcasm, my head still down and on her back. "Hope you find everything you're looking for."

"I only entered at the last minute." she defended with an edge to her tone. Though my head was down, I knew she was rolling her eyes. "You still can trust us. We just need to discuss things a little further with you and probably before you become a Neatholyte."

My head bolted up. "What am I, in trouble or something?"

"Indirectly." she breathed.

"What does that—" I lifted my head and my eyes were locked on something implausible, hoping that it was some type of illusion. It hadn't crossed my attention whether or not we were over the city yet, but we were. There was a black pillar of smoke rising into the air, the base of the pillar burning bright and orange.

If I wasn't mistaken…that was…my house. "Claire?" I asked frightfully. I gulped. "Is that…my house?"

I felt her body shutter with fear, confirming *my* fear.

"Claire! Hurry!"

She kicked forward, her wings propelling her at a speed I found most unbearable but it was something I was willing to endure to get to Rachel in time. We were diving low, in sight of human eyes. Hopefully against the dark gray sky, they would mistake us for a large bird.

We sped closer to the street I lived on. It *was* my house burning ferociously. There was a crowd perched in front of it watching the blaze eat away my home. The house was lit up in bright oranges and yellows, a thick cloud of blackness hovering above it and swirling upward.

She landed us across the street in the neighbor's backyard. I wasted no time in getting off her back. Before I knew it, I was already unlatching the side gate to the house, dashing across the front lawn and disregarding the awed look on the owners' faces as they watched me run from out their backyard, pushing my way pass the callous crowd relentlessly, and sprinting into the burning fortress.

"RACHEL!" The heat roared with intensity as I entered, my forehead immediately breaking into a raging sweat. I couldn't believe my eyes. Everything. Everything I loved was on fire at this very moment — swallowed up in the vicious inferno.

I stood in the front of the house debating on where to search first. But what if I wasting my time in here? What if Rachel wasn't in here, safe somewhere outside? She was smart. I don't think she'd linger in this house.

But Seth was here. Knowing him, he probably tied her up somewhere — as theatrical as they all seemed, I wouldn't have been surprised if it was a stake they tied her to. I had to be certain that she was not here. That she was undeniably safe.

I took a step forward and the house suddenly began to shake as if it were in the midst of an earthquake. I searched for my balance in all of it. The staircase rail tilted at an angle, some of the wooden parallel pillars to the rail were shaken loose and spiked outward.

Something then hit me on the top of my head with a soft thud and bounced to the floor. It was a shard of glass. I looked up and the chandelier rattled ferociously, scattering shards of glass everywhere and jingling like a symphony of bells during holiday season. In that instant, the screws hoisting the chandelier up were knocked loose and it began its line of descent with my head marked as it landing platform. I dove out of the way toward the living room, listening to the shards of glass break and ricochet across the room.

I hurried to my feet, breathing hysterically at this moment. A combination of it being impossible to breathe in this house with all the oxygen it lacked and nearly being pummeled by the chandelier.

I then turned and stared at the living room as it seared into nothingness. The flames licked every inch, every object with its burning venom. The curtains were all smoky, the television was melting and the sofas were scorched. For a moment I wanted to save *it* from the flames.

This place meant a lot to me too. Not as much as Rachel, but a lot nonetheless.

What should I do? I wanted to save this fortress, this asylum where I grew up, the memories that I knew would never be triggered if I lived elsewhere. But there was a reason that towered above all these reason. It was Michael's home. It was truly the only thing that she kept of his.

But I needed to save her. I had to. I have to sacrifice the fortress for her, this heaven where I grew up, the precious memories forever. I had to…for her.

She wasn't in here. "RACHEL!" I yelled her name as I hit the corner, rushing to the kitchen. I was coughing uncontrollably now. Smoke had made its home in my lungs, torturing me from the inside.

The kitchen was just as smoldering as the living room. Maybe even worse. The ceiling was on fire here. I was afraid. Afraid that if I take a step forward, the burning ceiling would fall on me. *That* had potential to kill me. The chandelier not so much.

It was as if I could read what the house was going to do next. The burning ceiling suddenly collapsed on to the kitchen. Burning plaster, wood and pipes now decorated the kitchen in a vile way.

There was only one last place to search now. I darted around the corner and up the ragged stairs, careful not to put too much pressure on each step. I would have turned to the left and gone to my room, just to see it one last time, but I was on a mission right now.

I ran to her room, carefully maneuvering my way around the large hole in the floor. The door was stuck. I rammed my shoulder into it continuously until the hinges broke and I stumbled inside.

I was left standing in awe, watching the fiery lake lick its way up the walls of Rachel's room, across her canopy bed, across everything she held dear. But I didn't have time to gawk over the treachery.

I rushed to her closet, ablaze. Her bathroom, scorched. Beneath her burning bed, nothing. She was nowhere to be found.

I was darting out of the burning room when something had caught my eye on her nightstand and stopped me dead in my tracks. I walked over to the cherry oak nightstand and grabbed the photo that sat in the stainless steel picture frame.

The picture was of me, Rachel, and Michael. I was twelve. We were at Crater Lake, the year before the attack. We were wrapping the day up early because Michael had no luck in catching any fish and had gotten frustrated with it. Rachel had laughed at his childish behavior. He kept telling her that it wasn't funny but she kept laughing hysterically. Before I knew it I was laughing with her and in the same hysterical manner. After a while, he couldn't fight it and he started laughing along with us.

He'd caught a fisherman leaving and Michael kindly asked him if he could take a picture of him and his family...

"KAYDEN!" Someone yelled my name from downstairs disrupting the memory. A female voice.

"Rachel?" I whispered.

I slammed the picture frame into the edge of the nightstand, removing all the broken glass, cutting myself once but I didn't worry much on that because I knew that it would heal, folded the picture and slid it in my back pocket.

I rushed out the room.

When I hit the staircase, it wasn't Rachel at all. It was just Claire.

I carefully darted down the stairs. A small explosion had erupted in the kitchen, startling me and forcing me to stumble a bit.

Claire reached for me.

"Kayden we have to get out of here!" She protested as I grabbed her hand.

"I have to find her!"

"Kayden! We have to leave now!"

I let go of her hand and rushed back into the living room, making certain I'd checked every portion of the room.

"Kayden," I turned to her. Her expression had fallen and was overpowered with sadness. "I'm not sensing her anywhere. Not even her mind."

I forced a swallow. *No.* An indescribable feeling washed over me, leaving me vacant, burning internally like this abandoned fortress. The worst was all could think about. Dead, burned, scorched, her beauty forever seared by flames.

In that instant, I felt my tormented sea yank me to fathoms below, where I dreaded and longed to be at all at the same time. The pain was like none I'd ever felt. It was like someone had a hold of my heart and their grip on it got tighter and tighter, destroying it inside my chest — squeezing it dry and loveless.

My eyes were quickly filling with moisture. In that moment, like a waterfall, the tears began to spill over for their first time ever. *I'm... crying?* I questioned in my head. But I'd hoped that when the time came, I would enjoy giving in to my sorrow. I couldn't enjoy this. This hurt. The pain that came from giving into my emotions was unbearable. Nineteen years worth of damage spilling over all at once. My knees felt weak and I pressed my body against the wall for some support, my head hanging in defeat.

"Kayden," her arm pressed lightly against my shoulder. "You need to calm down! Com'on."

Calm down? I questioned with acid in my mind. *How could I calm down when everything I know, everything I lived for is gone?*

"That's not true Kayden! You have us!"

Is it always all about you? Always about you and those damn angels who are supposedly fighting for me?*!* I hissed, my anger building to a place of no return. My head lifted. I glared at her, terror swept across her face. My teeth gritted. ***"HUH?!"***

I slammed my fist into the wall that was once supporting my weight, bits of plaster shooting against my face.

I was feeling too many emotions at once. It was tiresome. I felt my knees buckle, too weak to fight against my heavy emotions, too weak to fight against my plundering seas. They were destroying me. My heart continued to ache severely in my chest. I fell to my knees and I pressed my hands against the floor.

Panting and crying, the pain was like nothing I'd ever felt or ever wanted to feel. The tear drops raced across the surface of my cheeks, cooling them for a fraction of a second, then turning hot because of the heat around me and finally falling to the floor. I couldn't handle the force of my own emotions erupting out of me at one time.

Suddenly, a strange shutter ripped through my body, tingling my spine, vibrating through my arms and to my hands. The surge emitted a force through my hands, causing a crack to rip through the ground. The entire fortress shook from the quack. The crack traveled outside and I could hear the shrieks of terror begin to rain.

The screams were almost like music to my ears, hearing someone else's terror other than mine. A grand symphony it was.

Another shutter ripped through my body, harder and a bit more unbearable than the last. It traveled as it had before, creating the same force as it had before.

The earth bellowed with anger and shook violently this time. The screams intensified.

I listened as a storm rushed in, the thunder cracked deafeningly in a second, lightning bolts lit up the outside and the wind howled monstrously, making any Alpha male wolf feel like a pup.

I wanted to see the terror being caused. But I couldn't. I was stuck to the ground with someone constantly in my ear telling me to calm down.

I felt a cooling sensation overtake my eyes and my hands started to burn feverishly. I lifted off my hands and turned them over. They were burning painfully, like there was an invisible flame resting on them and blistering them. I couldn't contain the scream. I yelled as they burned, extending my throat, looking up so that the scream's power was amplified.

I looked back down at them, biting my teeth powerfully together. My hands were glowing a bright, dazzling blue.

I stood to my feet, my teeth still locked tight from the excruciating pain, breathing and grunting horridly as I stared at my glowing hands. There were sparks jumping from them now and the small surges of electricity wrapped themselves around my entire forearms.

Wanting to get rid of the pain, I snapped my right arm, extending it in the direction of the burnt sofas, and in that instant, a lightning bolt launched from my hand — the intensity of the burn now decreased.

Now realizing how to minimize the burning, I flicked my left arm forward. It was on a collision course with the girl who was in the house. She dodged it.

It was a frenzy of lightning bolts as I flung my hands in every which direction, trying to free myself of this pain.

Crunch! A powerful, undeniably sharp pain shot through my back. I fell to my knees again. No word could describe how agonizingly painful it was. I felt like a tear…or a break of some bone.

SNAP! I howled in pain, biting my teeth as hard as I could together. I'd lied. *This* pain was none like I'd felt before. A bone had snapped inside me with no external cause.

The rips, the snaps, the tearing all continued, and with each rip, each snap, each tear, I screamed horrifically.

I crawled to the center of the room, the snapping and the cracking and the crunching continuing. The fire was now of no concern to me. Whatever was attacking me from the inside was.

With much abruptness, one, sharp, agonizing twist of my spine ripped my insides apart, tearing away from my ribs, forcing a scream to rip out of my throat like none before. I gritted my teeth to the pain, fighting it but it was becoming harder to bear by the second. I moaned and groaned, defeated by whatever was killing me.

A nauseating feeling came over me.

I suddenly felt a sharp object poking against my upper left shoulder. I grabbed my shoulder with my right hand and turned my head up. No one was there. Just fiery walls. Nothing external had produced that pain either.

I suddenly wondered what would kill me first. The wood and plaster and ceiling parts that fell all around me or the monstrous entity inside me?

The sharp poke was still there. But it was joined by a second one only this one was on the opposite side.

"Kayden!"

That girl. The one who was telling me to calm down. She called me Kayden. She was at my side, her hand pressing against my agonizing shoulder. She was pulling me by my arm.

You're annoying. I hissed at her in my mind. She seemed surprised after I thought it. I pressed my hand up to her, emitting a force through my hand that launched her through the air, slamming her into the wall beside the entrance to this house.

The sharp pains returned, pressing harder and harder against my flesh. I tried to fight these invaders inside of me, trying to withstand everything that they could dish out.

But they attacked back. Two more sharp pains were now present. They were directly below the first two sharp pains.

I gritted my teeth…

They originated in the middle of my back.

I locked my jaws tight….

Something was pressing against the flesh, waiting to…

I grunted, every muscle in my body was flexed, attempting to force the excruciating pain out of my body.

A piercing shriek escaped my lungs again as something sharp extended from out the left side of my back directly below my shoulder. I could hear the fluid gush from out my back and all over the walls and everything else around me.

The pain forced me to my feet. I couldn't even look at what it was because when I went to look, directly below the first pain, another occurred. Another sharp object sliced its way through the muscle, then flesh and extended outward.

I was panting, screaming, crying from this unbearable pain.

I quickly clutched my chest, knocking over burning objects. My chest was suddenly burning from the inside. The muscles in my torso seemed to all be on fire.

I ripped open the white shirt I had on. It was like they had life. The muscles in my stomach were moving, becoming tighter and tighter, growing and pressing harder against the ivory but fiery lit skin. The muscles in my chest were displaying the same behavior. Everything, all of it was twisting and burning, adding to my symphony of torture.

Another tug from the middle-right side of my back forced me to scream yet again. I fell to my hands and knees.

I could hear my heart beat frantically, clearly as if someone was holding it directly up to my ear. I could hear my lungs expand and contract inside me. It was all so clear to me.

I could hear another invader begin to rip itself through the flesh in the upper right corner of my back. I braced myself for it. I shut my eyes tight and bit down hard…

It shot out of me like a speeding train, no mercy at all for me.

My breathing suddenly relaxed. The burning, the twisting, the aching, the snapping, the tearing…it was all gone.

Chapter 18: The Imperfect

EVERYTHING SEEMED TO RISE IN VOLUME. THE SOUND OF THE ROARING flames, my panting, the quickness of my heart.

"Kayden?"

My head snapped up to the sound of the voice. It was a girl whose hair was darker than blood and she towered over me.

I was on my hands and knees breathing hard and heavy. Why? *Did she do this to me? Did she attack me or something?*

"What do you mean attacked you?" she questioned.

She could read my thoughts? Who is she?

I looked around at this burning asylum. Everything was destroyed and burning to ashes quickly and *I* was on my hands and knees—breathing as if I'd just got through fighting for my life. Not to mention I was in somewhat of pain.

But…this house. I couldn't escape the thought. It…looked familiar to me. But I couldn't…

That wasn't my biggest concern right now. This girl who bared wings and towered over me was.

"What's the matter with you?" she questioned me.

I rose slowly to my feet and she flinched away. I could feel it. It was in her eyes, it was on her breath. Even with the thick smoke infiltrating the room, I could smell the fear that radiated from it. She was afraid of me. As she should be.

I could feel the power I possessed flow through me ragingly, begging for me to free it.

She stood with an enthralled expression on her face, fearing me like I was the predator that stalked her in the wild, cornering her so she had nowhere to go.

I felt them stretch, not fully, but wide enough for them to lift me off the ground. They produced a powerful gust of wind that scattered the fires around me.

I turned to examine these things. They were dazzling, truly amazing. Four beautiful, youthful wings hoisted me into the air, bending and reopening over and over again to keep me from falling. They were large, too big to fully extended themselves in the puny room. I could feel that they were the source of all this power I possessed.

But they all weren't the same. Three shared the same features. Beautiful and white with threads of silver scattered in the flock of feathers. They were large and full of life. Breathtaking and elegant.

But the one located in the upper-right corner of my back however, was black, threads of indigo and dark blues hidden within its flock of feathers. It too was gorgeous.

After becoming acquainted with my wings, I turned to look at the girl and compared me to her. She only had two white wings. Apparently, we were not comrades. Enemies? Must be. It seems as though she was opposing me.

"I am not opposing you! I am trying to help you!"

Help me? I questioned in my head. *I don't see anything wrong with me.*

"Snap out of it Kayden!"

"Claire! Kayden!"

Two boys entered the doorway to the house, screaming names—one of them of which this girl called me.

They know her? Comrade of theirs no doubt which makes them my enemy as well!

I pulled my right arm back. A warming sensation started from all four regions of my back and worked its way to my arm. The surge of heat as it passed through my body made my bones tingle, it sent ripples through the blood and as it traveled down my arm to my palm — my hand was consumed by the heat. A gush of force projected out of my hand, forcing the flames to consume this entire house, engulfing everything in arrays of oranges and yellows, tossing the boys back out the door and hurtling the girl through a window.

The house was no match for the combining powers of the flames and the force I produced. Everything began its collapse.

The entire first floor of the house exploded. My wings shot me up into the air, through the floors and plasters and out the roof — the flames trailing my wings as I shot up into the air, into the darkness above. I watched as the house below me was swallowed up by the flames — a breathtaking sight.

It was a glorious sight from up here. All of my senses were free up here. The smell of the storm's scent and the burning pyre of rubble below, the frosty touch of the wind, the sight of the destroyed streets, pillars of rock spiking out of the ground, in the middle of the streets, in the middle of yards. The road was in complete ruins — it was all so spectacular.

The fury of the storm was immaculate, taunting and vile. The clouds were pitch black and they stretched down toward the earth as if it wanted to merge with the ground.

This storm and I were one and the same. We both were a force to be reckoned with, bringers of destruction. I would destroy anyone who deemed it necessary to stop me.

I felt so free, so alive. It felt like I'd been trapped away and rotting in some depressive confinement forever.

I didn't know who those people were down there but at least they see I am no force to be taunted with.

My ears vibrated — the origin of the sound was coming from the west. I could see more of them approaching in the distance. Four of them to be exact. A man, boy, and two women.

The man flew with much aggression — his wings enormous compared to the other three beside him. The boy with bronze hair looked frightened. The women, both breathtaking, one blonde and one with honey brownish hair, flew with compassionate eyes. They didn't appear as frightened as the boy or as aggressive as the man. They looked…worried.

So the real fun begins. I thought viciously.

This would be fun. I could tell.

The screams from below, the rolling of the thunder and the ripples of lightning fueled me—feeding me more power.

I darted toward them, pushing myself at a speed at which they didn't possess. I'd covered half their distance in less than five seconds.

The man in the middle launched an attack first. A ray of light of some sort. I dodged it, flew over it, then under it. He seemed to me to be the better fighter of the four. I pressed myself forward and with an unbelievable strength, I catapulted myself into him. The earsplitting impact produced a gush of wind that blew the others away like rag dolls.

I charged through the air with him still in my arms. He pressed his hands against my arms, gripping them tight and swung me around. I no longer had a grip on him and was hurtling through the air.

My wings stopped me from hurtling out of control any further and I relaxed myself, my wings the only things in motion. I was right. He was the strong one. He gazed piercingly at me with bewildered eyes. Though beneath those bewildering eyes, I could read his hate and disgust for me. I could tell he wasn't going to take this battle lightly. I smirked devilishly at the true meaning in his eyes.

It all took about three seconds to accomplish. Someone was charging me from every angle. The boy from the back. I could tell by how light his wings flapped. He had the smallest of them all. The blonde from the left. Her fragrance radiated from that direction. This left the dark haired woman charging me from the right.

I somersaulted backwards, snagging the boy by his wing when he passed under me. He released a shrilling cry. In that instant the man grabbed his right shoulder.

The dark haired woman was inches away from me now. She attempted to punch me. She was quick but not faster than me. I dodged, rolling over—the boy's wing still tightly clutched in my hands. I grabbed her by her wrist, rolling her with me and the boy now. After completing a whole three hundred and sixty degrees, I flung the boy down toward the ground, his body a hundred feet in descent within a single second. I completed one more full circle and released the dark haired woman and she hurled toward the earth's floor like a meteor as well.

The man was still weak for some odd reason. I pressed a force through my hand again, pushing him away from me at mach speeds. He flipped uncontrollably — he couldn't stop his body from hurtling out of control.

The blonde.

I grabbed her by her throat and hoisted her up. Snarling at her as she squirmed in my hands. She was…beautiful. I almost felt like I knew her.

"Kayden! Kayden, stop!"

There's that name again.

"It's me! Emma!" she stated chokingly.

Emma?

Kayden?

Emma?

I continued to go back and forth between the names. They were familiar to me. But…

"You rushed here, afraid that Seth killed Rachel! Remember?!"

My eyes widened.

I remembered.

Rachel…

A sharp pain to the back of my head forced everything to turn black. I could hear the wind gush violently as I fell for the earth's floor. The blackness was getting darker and darker until…

This dream was completely black. Though my sight was overwhelmed in darkness, I could hear…everything.

Breathing, all so different and unique in their own way. Some lungs were larger than others and required more oxygen to fill them, some were smaller and they breathed quickly yet calmly. Some weren't so calm. Some seemed frightened.

Alongside the breathing was a many heart beats. All, too, distinct and unique. Some fluttered out of control and others remained steady but still fast. And one was a bit slower, not as fast as the others but faster than your average human heart beat. I counted the distinct heart beats.

One…two, three, four. Five. Six. Seven…eight. Nine. Ten.

Eleven. There were eleven people congregated…downstairs? Yes. The sounds were coming from below me rather next to me. How was I able to hear this acutely?

"I want to thank you for coming at once, brother." The lyrical voice spoke. Elaina.

"This is absurd, Elaina!" a voice roared in a condescending way. I did not know this voice at all. It was strong and dominant—full of power. "I agreed to let *him* live because it promised us freedom from the Order. Not to mention *he* is a Neatholyte. That *thing* up there is *not* a Neatholyte!"

"That *thing* up there is a part of our family." a voice snarled back. A voice I knew all too well. Brycin. A pair of footsteps began walking, each step forcing the carpet beneath their foot to produce a crunch-like sound. "And we will not just stand by and watch you and your House destroy him." Brycin's voice had moved.

"There is no need to fight against one another." Another unfamiliar voice chimed in, softly and youthful. It sounded like a little boy. "We didn't come here to fight one another but merely discuss the ramifications for that individual's actions. There will be no personal vendettas involved today."

"He's right, Elijah." A deep, brooding voice vibrated the walls.

"I know he is!" the voice, I now knew as Elijah, snapped. Elijah filled his lungs, allowing the air to calm him, his eyelids dropping as he did this. He released the air slowly and his eyelids fluttered back open. "Yesterday's event nearly exposed us all. And we can't afford risking the chances of another outburst like that. Especially with someone's whose blood is so unstable."

"It was the results of his transformation." Claire had spoken on my behalf. "We all know that when too much power is stored away, well, trapped I guess you can say is a better word, your blood, your body, your mind, your emotions, all of you becomes imbalanced and once that power is finally released, it's going to pour out until balance is found."

"And are you willing to bet your life that his balance has been found?" A male voice with an accent asked. British I believe.

"Maybe not completely but at least some of its been restored." Jakob assured.

"How are we certain that if we leave you, he won't have another outburst?" a feminine voice asked. Her voice was poetic, soothing. "What happened yesterday was far worse than some episodic power lash. He nearly killed humans."

Were they…talking about me? I was so trapped in wanting to know who was who that I didn't take it into consideration who they were talking about. I nearly killed humans yesterday? But how?

So…everything they've been talking about…referred to me? I'm that thing Brycin spoke of protecting.

I transformed yesterday. I nearly exposed our world yesterday. Human lives came close to being lost because of me. I wasn't…a Neatholyte.

What am I then? A…a…Demilyte?

NO!

NO!

Everyone had been telling me I was a Neatholyte! How could they *all* be wrong?! I tried getting up, tried defeating the darkness that shrouded my eyes, but I was completely paralyzed. Who was doing this to me? Someone down there had to have been doing this!

"No humans saw anything." Aris's velvety voice halted my raging thoughts. "There was too much smoke and the skies were too dark for anyone to see us. So you have nothing to charge us with."

"Can you control him?" Elijah hissed through his teeth poisonously.

There was a period of silence. The sounds of their heartbeats and breathing mixing and mingling in the room. I was so annoyed I couldn't separate them. I didn't know who was who. It sounded like a marching band performing during a vicious wind storm.

I was more than capable of controlling myself. I don't need any supervision.

Kayden, keep quiet.

Claire? Claire! What's going on? Why can't I get up? And what's going on downstairs.

You're fine. Don't panic. We'll explain everything when they leave. But first, let us get rid of them, okay.

'Kay.

I went silent, listening to their conversations again.

"You can assure us that you will not be hearing from us again." Aris stated but in an incredulous manner. Though he was being optimistic, I sort of allowed it to get to me.

He should have a lot more faith in me. At least I knew I would always have the faith and support of my protector.

I could slowly feel mobility returning to my body. I curled my fingers into a fist and then released them. I could hear my breathing and my heartbeat again. But…they were different. Not in a bad way but in a good way. When I breathed in, it was much calmer, relaxing, graceful. The oxygen quickly began its duty of restoration throughout my body.

My heart beat was quick and sharp. Two-hundred and fifty beats per minute to be exact. But I felt no type of fatigue, under any stress. I was calm. Okay. Better than okay.

The darkness was thinning out. My eyelids slowly lifted, burning from the brightness that greeted them.

It took some effort but I was able to lift my body up. I didn't know where I was so I waited for the blurriness to leave my eyes, assisting them by rubbing it away.

When the images of the room came into focus, it wasn't what I was expecting. *I* don't even know what *I* was expecting but I wasn't expecting to see my room, my disgustingly, disorganized closet of clothes, my computer desk.

With that, came to realization of where they were. My house.

I pulled my legs over the side of my bed and stood but I was instantly brought back down from a pain in my side. I looked down and my waist was wrapped in bandages. I thought I could heal. Why was I in pain? As soon as I realized that pain, another pain arose, but this one throbbed in the back of my skull. I cringed. Shouldn't I have healed by now?

I placed my hand on my waist where the pain originated and stood again, wincing at the tiny yet overwhelming tingle.

My legs were weak as I shuffled them across the carpet. I felt heavier. I instantly understood what Emma had once told me. Though they were hidden, my back felt slightly heavy, invisible objects adding weight to it.

I reached for the doorknob but before I grabbed it, I stopped as I heard the voice of Elijah speak again. "Looks as though he came to quicker than I'd expected. I guess we'd be leaving now. But mark our words, as leader of the First House of Amos, the next time something like this happens, we will have no choice but to dispose of him—no matter how much he may mean to you. And not even you, my little sister, will come in between me and world order."

I heard as they all, the four unknown individuals downstairs and Elijah, left one by one. Feathers fluttered from the opposite side of the door and each of them launched into the sky one after another, flying into the distance until the booming of their wings was nothing more than a muted memory.

I grabbed the icy doorknob and I winced from it. It should not have been that cold. Had my sense of touch been enhanced as well? Wow.

I twisted the knob. I could hear almost everyone hold their breath.

As I walked along the hall, turned the corner and began my descent down the stairs, I tried my best not to think about the faces that awaited me at the bottom. I tried occupying my mind with other thoughts. Like where was Rachel in all of this? Why was everyone in my home but not the one person who belonged in it? They would not talk that recklessly about what I was and what we are in front of her. Unless she was secretly one too.

Naw, I would've been warned beforehand. Not to mention I counted only eleven heart beats, all fast. Hers, I am presuming since she was human, would have been slower than the others.

I hit the base of the stairs and just like that, the thoughts of those around the corner invaded my mind again. The invasion brought along with it the presence of butterflies in the pit of my stomach, thrashing around callously.

"Kayden." Brycin's voice as he called my name beneath his breath caused the butterflies' ruckus to intensify, possibly scaring them from the inside of my stomach. "You can calm down. There is no need for the apprehensiveness."

I sucked in a lungful of air, more than necessary actually and turned the corner.

I don't know what surprised me more. The fact that everyone seemed down or the fact that even though they appeared defeated, they were all undeniable, incomparably beautiful. Especially Emma. Her beauty was much more radiant with these eyes. Her scent was more invigorating. A mixture of honeysuckle and lilacs. All of their scents were beautiful. I guess everything about me had enhanced.

Elaina sat closest to me, on the arm of the recliner. Brycin, who was on the edge of his seat, Emma, who ran her hands through her golden locks over and over again, and James, who seemed nervous for some odd reason all sat on the sofa. Claire sat gracefully on the floor. Jakob and Matt stood against the far wall next to the windows and the curtains. Aris stood in the center of the room, eyes locked on mine as I entered. He was the only one who actually looked at me directly.

"Am I in trouble?" I questioned, alarmed at the sound of my voice. Yep. Everything had enhanced. My voice was softer, silkier, more confident, a voice of an angel…or whatever I was. That would be one thing that would take some time getting use to.

"No." Brycin answered. He was trapped in a deep thought.

"He's thinking about you." Claire announced.

"Claire!" he hissed.

"What? One word answers aren't going to cut it this time." She defended in which I agreed.

"Thank you, Kayden."

"Do you do that regularly?" I asked, walking a tad bit further into the room.

"Not until recently." Brycin scoffed.

"I only do it, like I said before, when people don't speak their minds fast enough for me. Plus, once my power is on, it isn't targeted to one person, but everyone who is in the room. I can't help it how my powers work."

They all sounded so different, too. Yes, before I said they all sounded like angels, but I had no idea. They really *did* sound like angels.

"So…is anyone going to fill me in?" I asked, walking further into the room, next to Elaina.

Everyone all seemed to sigh at once. Freaky.

"Things have gotten a tad bit more complicated." Brycin answered.

I walked in front of Elaina and sat down in the recliner. I knew this was going to be long.

"The Houses of Amos are involved now."

I rose one eyebrow, a perplexed expression on my face.

"The Houses of Amos," Elaina began, voice beautiful and elegant. "Is made up of three sub-houses. The First House of Amos just left."

"Yeah, I am aware of those who left but *who* are they." I asked.

"Amos was the oldest Neatholyte alive. Six thousand, four-hundred and ninety years old. He was one of the direct descendants of Kasi— one of the three sons of Ishta. He possessed the greatest of abilities and tried his best to keep order. One of his abilities consisted of him being able to summon the presence of other Neatholytes. Once summoned, it was virtually impossible to resist. You somewhat came bound to him, a puppet almost, doing whatever it was he pleased. He usually used his abilities when a half-breed broke laws, whenever a potential threat of exposure arose."

"But when he grew aware that his death was near," Aris continued the story. "He summoned fifteen angels to carry out his visions of world order. The most powerful of Neatholytes. I was one of them, but I already had Elaina, Jakob and Claire as a family. I wasn't going to just abandon them. So, of course I was replaced.

"He created three houses. One in charge of more intimate affairs, face to face encounters. They are the escorts. Either you come with them willingly to die or they kill you by force. That House just left. Elaina's brother Elijah is in that one. The second House are known as the watchers; they pay close attention to world events and make sure that nothing supernatural is causing any harm. And the last House are the council. They keep track of those who are severely capable of exposing us." His head fell and he took a deep breath. "Today your name was added their list."

"But," I gasped. "I don't remember anything. I don't even know what happened! Aren't I exempt from persecution in some way?"

"Sorry, I wish it worked like that."

"So I am on a list that has Balavon's name on it?" I hissed rhetorically.

"Actually," What did he mean "actually?" The word actually was a word that was meant for objections. Why was he using it? "Balavon's name has yet to hit that list. The Houses of Amos know nothing about Balavon other than that it's a name. They hadn't heard it in centuries until today when we explained everything to them but they didn't buy any of it. They were more concerned with you than him. They can't really charge a ghost for anything."

I ran my hands through my hair, overwhelmed by what I was hearing. It was like I was America's most wanted but little did they know the real villain orchestrating the symphony of disaster was Balavon.

"Everything we do from here-on-out has to keep us under the radar of the Houses. But I promise we *will* get rid of Balavon."

I was too caught up into the idea of my name being on a most wanted list and how Balavon's was not. Everything he put me through, his attempts to kill me, his plans to rid the world of humans, all of it was being overlooked because of what I was.

Now that I think of it, "What am I? Why was I classified as a *thing* earlier?"

Everyone hesitated to answer, reading each other's faces but I read something deeper than their faces. Their eyes. All of them asked the same thing. *How should we tell him?* Was it really that bad?

It *was* that bad.

All of their eyes said so. Matt, who was leaning up against the far wall next to Jakob, leaned forward to speak. "Kayden you really don't remember anything?"

I shook my head. "No. The last thing I remember was…" I broke off into thought mid sentence, reflecting over events that possibly could have led to this moment. "Walking Frankie to his truck…at school— then I saw Brycin," After I stated his name, my eyes narrowed. I instantly remembered them leaving me for the entire week without any explanations or warnings. "Standing next to the Camaro with Emma, Claire and Jakob." I spoke their names with that same glare. I instantly wanted to turn the interrogation around and get some answers to their absence but I shoved it to the back of my mind. I would not forget.

"And after that?" Aris compelled.

"Then…" It took me only but a second to remember being snatched into the air by Portman, tossed from demon to demon like it was some type of game. Everyone knew I remembered when my eyes went wide with shock from the memory. "They came for me." I gasped.

"Then what?" Brycin pressed.

"I uhh," The memories were making me feel uneasy now. They were so vivid. I could feel every emotion and feeling running through my body now as if it were happening this very moment. I noticed Brycin fidget on the edge of the sofa as I remembered. I didn't try to cause him discomfort but this was too much — even for this new me to handle. "Brycin saved me." I breathed looking in his direction. A sentence like that would have made anyone else prideful and arrogant but not him.

"Then someone else saved me…Jakob?"

He smiled shyly with a hint of pride.

"After that?" Aris pushed.

All this remembering was making my head hurt. I didn't like it. But I continued with it. "We were all face to face. Both families and… they offered me allegiance with them." My mouth flew open with a pop sound. "And I considered!" I spoke the last sentence disgustingly. "But…I refused. And they said—" I pressed my hands against my head, squeezing the memories to the front of my skull.

It was like getting hit by a ton of bricks once I realized it. I jumped up. "Rachel?!"

Aris was at my side in a second, his hand pressed firmly on my shoulder. Had it been my human body, it probably would have hurt. "She's fine but we will get to that story next. What else do you remember?"

I sat back down. "Flying to save Rachel, Portman followed us." I winced, realizing that he no longer existed anymore. He may have put me through hell but it was all due to Balavon's brainwashing. "After…" I swallowed. "Portman was dealt with, we headed back to the house—" I stopped again. "This house!" I spoke in awe. "It was burning!" Horror getting the best of me again, forcing me to jump up as if someone had placed a tack underneath me. "But everything looks the same."

"My brother has the ability to renew, remember?" Elaina reminded me. "He fixed everything back to the way it was."

"Shouldn't that classify as exposure in some type of way, I mean people witnessed the house burn."

"The small boy, Aaric, has the ability to lock memories away inside one's mind. Not erase them per se but make it nearly impossible for the individual to remember the event."

"Ah." I said pensively.

"And what do you remember after that?" Aris asked, intrigued somewhat with my reflective journey. I must've been getting to the part that he *wanted* me to remember. The part that placed us in this predicament.

"Rushing in and failing at finding Rachel. Claire came in and said we have to go but I refused. Then she told me that she couldn't sense Rachel—" I stopped mid sentence. My memory was getting thinner and thinner, blurrier. It wasn't coming to me as clearly as the others had. "I remembered…" I searched for the memory. When I discovered the next memory, I couldn't believe it. I didn't believe it. It had to be some sort of fulfillment I wanted to happen. It couldn't have happened. "I cried?"

Aris nodded. "What else?" he asked, noticing that I lingered on that memory. But I had good reason to. I'd never cried a day in my life. I thought nothing would ever push me to experience sorrow to its fullest extent. But I shook the memory away for the time being. I would have nearly an eternity to reflect on that unforgettable memory.

"Pain. Lots and lots of pain and then…" Everything went black. I couldn't remember anything after that. It wasn't there. I don't remember it. The transformation, how I made it out alive, none of it. "I don't remember."

My voice was serene, pure and full of truth and everyone noticed it at once. It was almost a disappointment to them. Not that I couldn't remember it for myself but that they'd rather I remembered than them tell me.

Aris backed away from me. "You became something completely unexpected." He took in a deep wave of air and turned to me with intense eyes. "You aren't what we thought you were. We all thought you were going to be Neatholyte like us but you aren't."

"So I'm a Demilyte?"

He shook his head. "You are neither. You are a Nexusyte."

That word sounded familiar. Where had I heard it though?

Oh. I thought, remembering where I'd heard it. I asked Portman what was the name of an angel/demon half-breed—

"I'm one of those?" I asked. "I'm a Neatholyte and a Demilyte."

"No, you are neither. You share and angelic and demonic bloodline. You are a Nexusyte."

"Which is mind-boggling." Jakob said under his breath, looking away off into the corner.

"Why is that?"

A heavy sigh erupted out of Brycin. His eyes were shut tight and his fingers were pressed against his head as though it was hurting in some way. "Nexusytes aren't supposed to exist. Nature is *supposed* to keep them from being born. They are tormented, evil, vile creatures. If a mother so happens to be carrying a child bearing both bloods, the baby dies in her womb. *It* isn't supposed to survive. But somehow you managed. And we knew you were becoming this and soon.

"James saw you as it in his vision. It was the reason for our absence."

I stared pass Brycin, pass Emma and at James. He refused to look at me. "James had a vision of you becoming this thing, this Nexusyte," he looked at me now but it was almost in a shameful way. "And the vision was so powerful, it fused your future mind, powers, and body with his present mind and body. He portrayed you that day—coming after us...to kill us."

I couldn't believe what I was hearing. "What...what? Are you kidding me?! I would never! There has to be some sort of mistake!" I protested.

Claire's head fell to the floor. She let out just as deep a sigh as Brycin had earlier. "Kayden you attacked us after your wings grew." I stared at her, my eyebrows pulled together and low. It hurt me to know that I attacked them, that I was the reason for their absence. I drove them away. Because of my stupid blood! I knew she heard my thoughts but she disregarded them. "You are strong." She looked up at me now, running her hands through her deep red hair. "I've never seen someone capable of what you did seconds after their transformation. It was scary, I give you that. But it was still amazing." She suddenly sighed...remorsefully.

"But..." she paused and looked around at everyone in the room, taking another deep breath. "I thought that it would be best if I brought it up after the House left."

Suddenly everyone's attention wasn't on me. It was on Claire. She stood and was on the other side of me in a fraction of a second, my hair the only thing submitting to small wind she produced, the smell of ginger and vanilla following her, and she pressed her hand lightly against my shoulder.

"The event I read in James's mind, though his human mind wasn't capable of holding on to everything he saw, I know, that without a doubt, wasn't what happened yesterday. James's vision was not fulfilled yesterday."

I should have been relieved but I wasn't. Yeah, I was off the hook for now but my future still threatens the lives of everyone. James's dreams, and now I guess visions, always came true.

"Not necessarily." Claire corrected my thoughts. "Kayden was considering the possibilities of James's visions coming true and how they always come true." She announced my thoughts to the room. "But if that's so true, then you shouldn't be sitting in front of us now. The vision where you die and our hearts burn with a vengeance and we bring about the apocalypse should be occurring right now. But it's not. You're alive and the world is, for the most part, safe. We can work just as hard to prevent this vision from coming true as well."

I slouched back into the recliner, rocking Elaina with me but the abrupt rock of the chair did not falter her balance. I shut my eyes and rubbed my fingertips across my forehead.

"What are you thinking about?" When I opened my eyes, Brycin was knelt down in front of me, eyes full of worry.

I placed my hand down at my side and stared him in the eyes. There was something else in them. Something he never would have admitted to. He was afraid of me. "You're afraid of me?!" I whispered harshly with disbelief.

His head tilted, surprised.

"I can see it, pass the worry, pass the care, you're afraid of me."

He was taken by surprise at my new ability. I was too sort of. I was able to read the true feelings of others by looking deep into their eyes. It wasn't mind reading but it was close enough. It was a cool ability and I liked it.

"Not afraid *of* you. Afraid *for* you." He corrected. "Afraid for us. You would think it would be easy now. But things just got a whole lot crazier." he flashed a bright smile at me. Hadn't it been a halfhearted smile, it probably would have comforted me.

I smile back with the same efforts. I stood and walked over to the window, gazing at the day's magnificence. It all looked so normal, like the end of a fairytale. The happily ever after. The birds chirped lively. The sun radiated its warmth across the streets of Corvallis, patches of clouds here and there. The exuberant shades of green that scattered all across the neighborhood were breathtaking. It felt like the end. But it wasn't. This was only the genesis.

Epilogue: The Genesis

THE NIGHTMARE RETURNED LAST NIGHT.

But it was very different this time—haunting nonetheless. It sickens me to my stomach to even think of it.

Usually, I always saw my demon as its own person, but not in this nightmare. In this one, I was it. I stood on a vast ocean of corpses, scattered all about the plains of this world. They weren't just any types of corpses. They were all half-breeds—dismembered wings and limbs. And I was their executioner.

In the distant, I could see someone approaching me, walking across the field of the dead.

When he was inches away from me, I tilted my head. He mirrored me. In fact, he *was* me. The old me. Small and tenuous looking compared to how I now knew me. Dazzling sea blue eyes, dark scattered hair, soft skin complexion. Yeah, it was the old me alright. I could even see a dimness of depression in his eyes

He lifted his head and I mirrored him this time. I was no longer in control of me...or the demon me. He looked down and I looked with him. I would have freaked out had I been in complete control of everything but he was controlling me now. I was standing on Brycin's body. I wanted to hurl from the sight. Next to him was my family. All of them dead, breathless, lifeless.

My head lifted back up and he stared at me. The scenery began to change and we were no longer in the field of the dead but in my bathroom. I couldn't tell if I was standing in the bathroom gazing into the mirror or if it was the other way around but one of us was real and the other was the reflection.

It wasn't until we remained trapped in each other gaze, breathing in unison, that I placed it together. I now knew what my demon symbolized. The red eye represented my demonic blood and the white eye represented the angelic half of my blood. It was a subconscious representation of who I really was.

But if that held representation, what did everything else mean?

I woke up with no meanings tied to the rest of the dream, only a portion.

I'd beat the sun up another morning. I lingered in bed before getting up, reflecting what the future had in stored for me. Balavon was still out there somewhere and considering we thwarted his plans, he was going to return with a new plan. I knew that without a doubt he was not finished.

They told me how the fight went down between them and Balavon. The beating I received from the forest effected Brycin dramatically. Though he was doing well on the fight scene externally, internally he was feeling the beating I'd received. He told me it was the hardest thing he ever had to do. He compared it to someone being torched on the inside and keeping a straight face through it all.

He also admitted enjoying it, that it was the best fight he'd had in centuries.

When Jakob returned, Portman now eliminated from the equation, the "real fight," as Jakob put it, began. It was a match none of them had ever been involved in but with neither side giving in, there was no room for error.

That is, until, Brycin felt the degree in my panic, when I saw my house ablaze. Aris told him to go and he wasted no time rushing to my aid. Jakob went with as backup.

Surprisingly, Emma, Aris, Elaina, and Matt were more than capable of handling Balavon, Ester, Aryes, and Isaac.

Aris explained how he grew concerned because their defense was dissolving and he feared losing someone. After fast thinking, he emitted a bright light, a light that the eyes of Demilytes cannot handle. And with that, came their window of escape.

But the story brought with it an uneasy feeling when I was told of the destruction I caused. Apparently, I parted the earth floor and created pillars with a simple touch to the ground. I destroyed the entire house with Jakob, Claire and Brycin in it and when Aris and the others flew to the scene, I wasted no time in giving them a fight. Aris mentioned never being afraid of a fight until that day. One because he was fighting me and hurting me would hurt Brycin and he of all people knew how that relationship worked. And two, he was well aware of the power I possessed.

I was glad he was able to stop me from injuring anyone else. I didn't like being looked at as a monster.

I was then relieved when I found out that Rachel was actually in Eureka, California visiting her parents. She left me a note but the burning house had seared the note to ashes so I never knew. When she came in yesterday evening, after everyone else left, I was ecstatic to see her. I rushed to her and hugged her viciously but it was a bit too tight. I forgot I wasn't the same Kayden I was the day before. I was going to have to be a lot more careful with her considering how frail she was compared to me.

I wasn't sure how long we talked but I knew I enjoyed every second of it. Even everything about her was a tune up with these heightened senses. The lavender smell she possessed was implausibly sensational. Her voice was like a soft, melodic hymn.

Yeah. Everything seemed peaceful and normal. Why couldn't things stay this way? As long as Balavon wanted me dead, this would not be over but with these new powers of mine, it was going to be most difficult for him to succeed.

I was out of my bed, out the room door and into the bathroom all in the same second. I moved so elegantly and fluidly, that I wasn't the least bit worried about disrupting Rachel. What usually took me fifteen to thirty minutes to get ready, now took me two to five minutes. Ha, this was so fun.

I dashed down the stairs, into the kitchen. The only sound I made was with the flip of the switch. I searched the entire kitchen in seconds but found nothing interesting to eat. I wasn't really hungry though, just needed something preoccupy my time with until they got here.

Today was going to be my first official day of training with the others. Easy stuff though. Like how to summon my wings at will, how to use them, when is it okay and when is it not okay to fly. The basics.

I sped into the living room and settled myself into the recliner. Soundless.

There was one other thing that still bothered me—the entire downstairs triggering the thought. All the different scents that my ultra sensitive nose was capable detecting were still here. The First House of Amos. They were here to destroy me yesterday but luckily, even under the hypnotism of my powers, I didn't kill or injure and humans. That's what really saved me.

They informed me of all the members of each House. The First House of Amos, the escort, consisted of Elaina's older brother, Elijah, Sora, Aaric, Maxius, and Remus. The Second House of Amos, the watchers, involved Marcus, Victor, Azriel, Saul, and Cain. And the members of the last House, the council, were Sameal, Hamon, Lior, Morrigan and Lylidus. All with unspeakable abilities. All who will be looking forward to taking me down as soon as I slipped up. All because I was a Nexusyte.

So what? I didn't ask to be this. If I ever intentionally hurt someone though, then I deserved to die, even at the expense of Brycin's life.

Kayden, we're on our way. Claire spoke to me with the use of her mind.

Okay. I answered. I dashed up the stairs, into my room, and found something to wear in two seconds and with another second, my clothes were on.

An all black ensemble. I can dig it.

Three soft thuds landing on my front lawn. I darted out my room door, back down the stairs, and I was out the front door, closing it gently so I didn't wake Rachel.

I turned with a childish smile. All three of them bestowing exuberant beauty, fragrances more invigorating as they mixed with one another.

"So are we flying there?" I asked.

He chuckled once. "No. We still have to keep up with appearances and you have a human mother so we have to be a hundred percent thorough with everything we do." He pointed to the driveway, in the direction of my silver car.

I groaned, dashing back into the house, retrieving my keys, and coming back out the door this time all within half a second. I was getting good at this super speed.

Brycin gestured with his arms for me to proceed before him. "Newbies first."

I glared at him with narrow eyes and walked at a human pace and unlocked the car doors. When I slid in, Brycin was in the front seat already and Jakob and Claire were in the back, putting their seatbelts on. "Yeah you guys really don't mess around with keeping up with appearances. Seatbelts?"

"What?" Jakob asked.

"You guys could withstand getting hit by a diesel truck outside of the car and walk away with no scratches." I spoke to them through the rearview mirror.

"Do you want the ticket?" he protested.

I laughed and started the car. To my old ears, the car roared quietly. With these ears, it was like having my ear pressed up against the engine of a muscle car. I knew that with time though, I would become very accustomed to everything around me and its enhanced definition.

The sun was peeking over the horizon when we made it Willamette Park.

When I stepped out of the car, I could smell every single individual fragrance, sandalwood, birch, juniper, rosewood, the scent of the river—I could smell the entire park as they fused to create an overpowering, thrilling fragrance. But as I took in a deeper, lungful of air, they were scents that weren't so…attractive. The scent of animal droppings and some rotting carcasses were just as powerful.

I wrinkled my nose. Brycin, Jakob, and Claire laughed as they dashed into the woods all at once.

I laughed once and darted through the woods, surprised at how fast I made it through the forest and into the meadow. Even with the head start, I'd beat Brycin and the others to the meadow.

When Jakob breached the forest edge he complimented my agility. "Man, your fast!"

Brycin and Claire followed up behind him. Brycin was impressed. "How did you do that?"

"I guess that's the benefit of being a Nexusyte." I muttered with a prideful smirk.

The trees from the north swayed. I turned and saw Aris, Elaina, Matt and Emma rushed through the forest edge. I smiled wide, excited to get the day started.

I waited impatiently, bouncing up and down on the tips of my toes, ready to start my training.

"Well you're super excited." Emma murmured as she approached.

"Why shouldn't I be? I made it. Not how or what everyone intended but I made it. This is my first flight with my family. It's special."

"Good attitude, Kayden." Aris acknowledged. "At first it's hard to summon your wings. The more of a positive attitude you have, the easier it will be for you to summon them. Once you get the hang of it, it won't require a specific att—" he stopped and was looking to the east.

We all were.

It wasn't an animal—the scent was different. It was flesh. I was able to see clear across the field, the detail in the tree barks and the leaves and the insects scattered all over them. I could see that. Why couldn't I see the intruder?

My head snapped up. He wasn't on the floor. He was in the trees, swinging gracefully through them, barely ruffling the leaves. He landed gracefully on his toes, barely even making a sound.

I snarled, an immediate reaction to seeing *him* here. I was in the mood for flying, careless and free with my new family for the first time. But I was willing to set that on the back burner and bring revenge forward.

Ester.

I took a step forward. Claire moved in front me, her hands pushing against my chest. I looked down at her perplexed. Why was she stopping me? "He's not here to attack us."

"Then why is he here." I spit.

She turned, dropping one hand and the other still pressed against my chest. "To talk."

Claire fell back to the side and we waited for Ester to close the vast field that gapped us.

He was careful not to get to close. Smart. "Why are you here?" I spit.

"Oh, I didn't know that with your transformation ranks had changed." Ester sarcastic tone nearly pushed me to attack him but I restrained myself from ripping his head off his shoulders.

"What are your reasons for being here?" Aris questioned with seriousness.

His antagonizing glare left me and his attention shifted to Aris, his face relaxing instantaneously. "I'm here to warn you."

Was my mouth the only one that dropped? Just as quick as it popped open, I closed it, trying to show some self control.

"Balavon isn't done with you. Somehow, you all are still an essential tool to his plans."

"What are his plans?" Brycin asked.

"I don't know. I just know the *he* is involved." he shot at piercing glare at me when he said "he."

"What are you saying?" Elaina stepped forward.

He hesitated. Gulped, breathed, and replied, "Balavon never had any intentions on killing him. It was all a game. He was pushing him to his transformation because he knew *what* he was. I don't know what his direct intentions are. With Isaac by his side, neither will you guys."

"How do you *not* know?" Brycin's voice was aggravated. Finally, someone who showed some aggression to all of this.

"He never told us directly what his plans were. He gave us orders, we followed them. When someone as powerful as Balavon tells you to do something, you do it. No questions asked."

"But you're here. Is that part of his plans?"

He didn't answer. His head fell and for a split second, I felt sympathy for him. "No. I believe in a lot of Balavon's visions. A race as vile and disgusting as the humans should not be our superior. But," he paused and looked at me. I didn't expect to see *that* in his eyes. Compassion. "It was bewildering. You all were willing to sacrifice yourselves for him and his human mother. You are truly a family. And I envy that."

This guy, who had once came after me with haunting eyes, had my *sympathy?!* I didn't mean to feel sorry for him, but I did. He was just a slave to Balavon. "Why don't you stay with us?" I offered, just as surprised as everyone else. "As you can see, this family has one from every bloodline."

He snorted. "No thank you." He turned and extended his dark wings, stretching them as far as they would go. "Besides, I'm already dead." And with that last statement, he shot into the air, leaving us mind-boggled and awestruck.

"Are we just going to let him leave?" I asked, turning to my family.

"We have no choice right now." Aris muttered. "Even I want to save him from whatever it is he is about to face. But *you* need to learn the essentials to being a half-breed because the essentials could save you in the harshest circumstances faster than special abilities."

I turned back around, gazing into the sky as the sun began to rise, trying to find Ester. He was long gone.

"Com'on." Emma tugged me. I was reluctant at first but it wasn't like I could go after him.

I walked with Emma by my side. The rest of the clan was in the center of the field.

"Now don't be afraid. Relax. Breathe." I obeyed, breathing deeply and fully inflating my lungs. She then stopped me. "Focus all of your attention on your wings. Closing you eyes makes it easier." She was right. I was more aware of them with my eyes closed than with my eyes open. "Feel your eyes cool and once they cool, they'll change." Before she even started her sentence about my eyes cooling, they were already behaving in the manner.

I opened my eyes and her reaction spoke for itself. She smiled widely and with accomplishment. But it slowly faded as she examined me. "What?"

"When I first saw you as a Neath...Nexusyte, your eyes were black." She continued to analyze me. "Now there white. But there is a sapphire rim circling your eyes. It's glowing."

It was kind of cool—being different.

I examined each side of me. It was instantly hard to believe they were mine. They were beautiful. I immediately took a fancy to the black one. Though it proved that demonic blood ran deep in veins, it was too gorgeous to deny.

"Rules," Brycin stated, his wings bare and eyes flushed white. "Avoid airplanes at all cost and never fly recklessly in urban areas. Never land unless you are absolutely sure no one can see you." I nodded after every rule. "Hope you are fast in the skies as you are on land."

He shot into the air, forcing me to feel the gust of wind his wings made. One after another, their wings exposed and they shot up into the air.

"Whoo hoo!" Jakob wailed as he shot himself upward.

I took a deep breath. I stretched my wings, fully in control of them. It was like having another pair of arms or legs. Well, two more pairs.

I lifted them and then I dropped them. I didn't expect that to lift me off the ground but it did. I dropped back to the ground, catching my balance instantly. It was exhilarating.

I was ready now. I lifted my wings high and forced them down and I shot into the air. My veins ran hot with adrenaline. Automatically, I flew like I had been flying for years, like this wasn't my first time flying.

Everything up here was beautiful. The sun, the birds which joined us in our flight, the scent of the city from up here, it was all so delightfully calming. I needed this. It took my mind off of Ester's warning, it took my mind off of Balavon, it took my mind off of the Houses. It was just me, my half-breed family, and the skies.